BUNNICULA
THE GRAPHIC NOVEL

BY
JAMES HOWE
AND
ANDREW DONKIN

ILLUSTRATED BY
STEPHEN GILPIN

BASED ON THE NOVEL BY
DEBORAH & JAMES HOWE

Atheneum Books for Young Readers
atheneum NEW YORK LONDON TORONTO SYDNEY NEW DELHI

In memory of Deborah Howe, my collaborator on the
original book—and with gratitude to my collaborators
on this graphic novel version: Andrew Donkin,
Stephen Gilpin, Justin Chanda, Michael McCartney,
Julia McCarthy, and the unsung Jeannie Ng
—J. H.

For my mum, Jean Florence Donkin 1929–2021.
The best support a writer could have. She was a
first-time Bunnicula reader at the age of ninety, and read
James & Deborah's book twice because "I love it so much!"
—A. D.

For Mike Blake.
Thanks for all the encouragement.
—S. G.

ATHENEUM BOOKS FOR YOUNG READERS • An imprint of Simon & Schuster Children's Publishing
Division • 1230 Avenue of the Americas, New York, New York 10020 • This book is a work of fiction. Any refer-
ences to historical events, real people, or real places are used fictitiously. Other names, characters, places, and events
are products of the author's imagination, and any resemblance to actual events or places or persons, living or dead, is
entirely coincidental. • Text © 1979, 2022 by James Howe • Illustration © 2022 by James Howe • Cover design ©
2022 by Simon & Schuster, Inc. • All rights reserved, including the right of reproduction in whole or in part in any
form. • ATHENEUM BOOKS FOR YOUNG READERS is a registered trademark of Simon & Schuster, Inc. Atheneum logo
is a trademark of Simon & Schuster, Inc. • For information about special discounts for bulk purchases, please contact
Simon & Schuster Special Sales at 1-866-506-1949 or business@simonandschuster.com. • The Simon & Schuster
Speakers Bureau can bring authors to your live event. For more information or to book an event, contact the Simon
& Schuster Speakers Bureau at 1-866-248-3049 or visit our website at www.simonspeakers.com. • The text for this
book was set in Colleen Doran. • The illustrations for this book were rendered digitally. • Manufactured in China •
0422 SCP • First Edition • 10 9 8 7 6 5 4 3 2 1 • Library of Congress Cataloging-in-Publication Data •
Names: Howe, James, author. | Donkin, Andrew, author. | Howe, Deborah, 1946–1978. Bunnicula. • Title: Bunnicula
/ James Howe [and] Andrew Donkin. • Description: First edition. | New York: Atheneum Books for Young Readers,
[2021] | Audience: Ages 8–12. | Audience: Grades 4–6. | Summary: Though scoffed at by Harold the dog, Chester
the cat tries to warn his human family that their foundling baby bunny must be a vampire. Presented in comic book
format. • Identifiers: LCCN 2020036999 (print) | LCCN 2020037000 (ebook) | ISBN 9781534421615 (hardcover) | ISBN
9781534421622 (paperback) | ISBN 9781534421639 (ebook) • Subjects: LCSH: Graphic novels. | CYAC: Graphic novels. |
Rabbits—Fiction. | Vampires—Fiction. | Mystery and detective stories. | Howe, Deborah, 1946–1978. Bunnicula—
Adaptations. • Classification: LCC PZ7.7.H8 Bu 2021 (print) | LCC PZ7.7.H8 (ebook) | DDC 741.5/973—dc23 • LC
record available at https://lccn.loc.gov/2020036999 • LC ebook record available at https://lccn.loc.gov/2020037000

A NOTE FROM THE EDITOR

THE BOOK YOU ARE ABOUT TO READ WAS BROUGHT TO MY ATTENTION IN A MOST UNUSUAL WAY. ONE FRIDAY AFTERNOON, JUST BEFORE CLOSING TIME, I HEARD A SCRATCHING SOUND AT THE FRONT DOOR OF MY OFFICE. WHEN I OPENED THE DOOR, THERE BEFORE ME STOOD A SAD-EYED, DROOPY-EARED DOG CARRYING A LARGE, PLAIN ENVELOPE IN HIS MOUTH. HE DROPPED IT AT MY FEET, GAVE ME A SOULFUL GLANCE, AND WITH GREAT, QUIET DIGNITY SAUNTERED AWAY. INSIDE THE ENVELOPE WERE THE PAGES OF THE STORY YOU NOW HOLD IN YOUR HAND, TOGETHER WITH THIS LETTER:

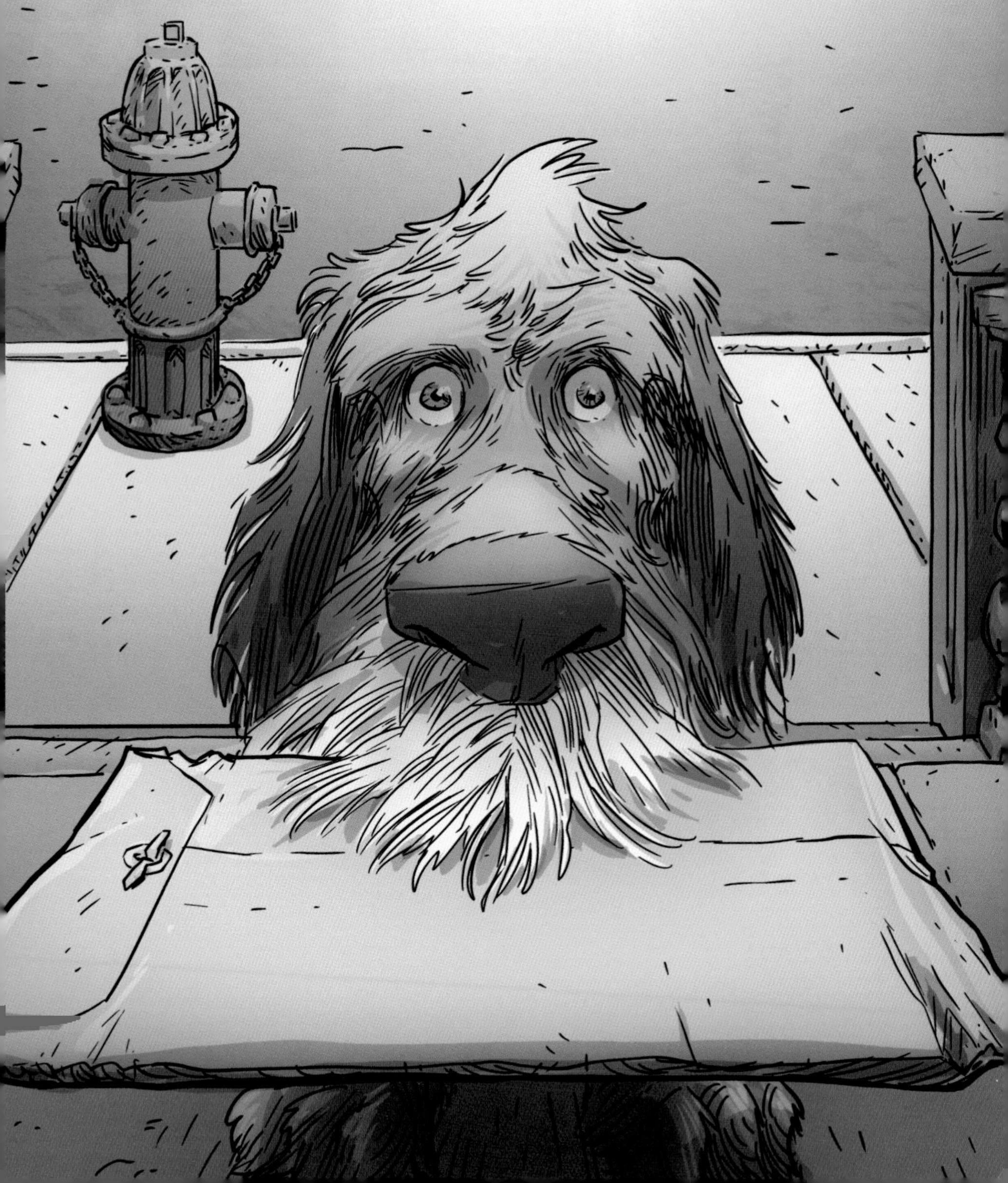

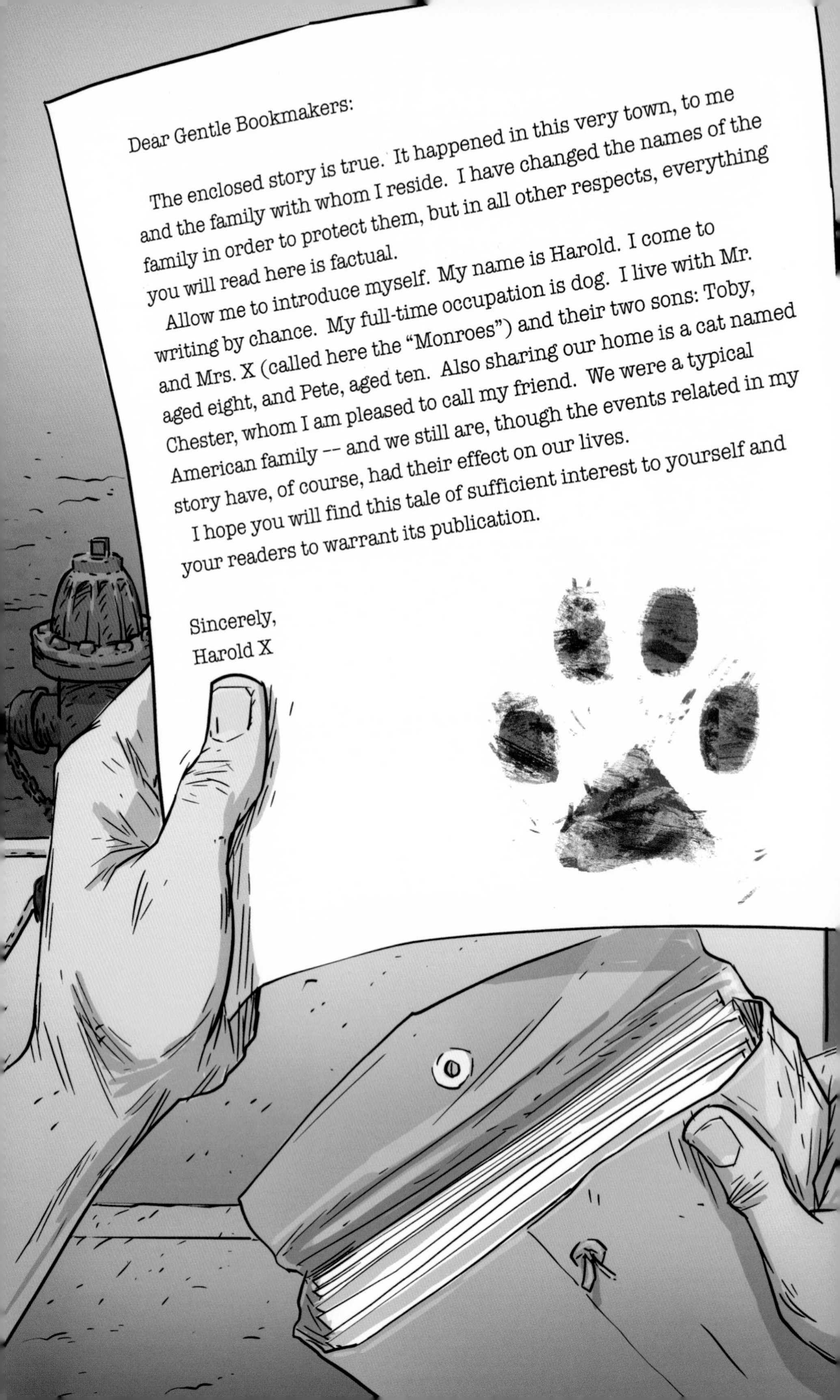
Dear Gentle Bookmakers:

The enclosed story is true. It happened in this very town, to me and the family with whom I reside. I have changed the names of the family in order to protect them, but in all other respects, everything you will read here is factual.

Allow me to introduce myself. My name is Harold. I come to writing by chance. My full-time occupation is dog. I live with Mr. and Mrs. X (called here the "Monroes") and their two sons: Toby, aged eight, and Pete, aged ten. Also sharing our home is a cat named Chester, whom I am pleased to call my friend. We were a typical American family -- and we still are, though the events related in my story have, of course, had their effect on our lives.

I hope you will find this tale of sufficient interest to yourself and your readers to warrant its publication.

Sincerely,
Harold X

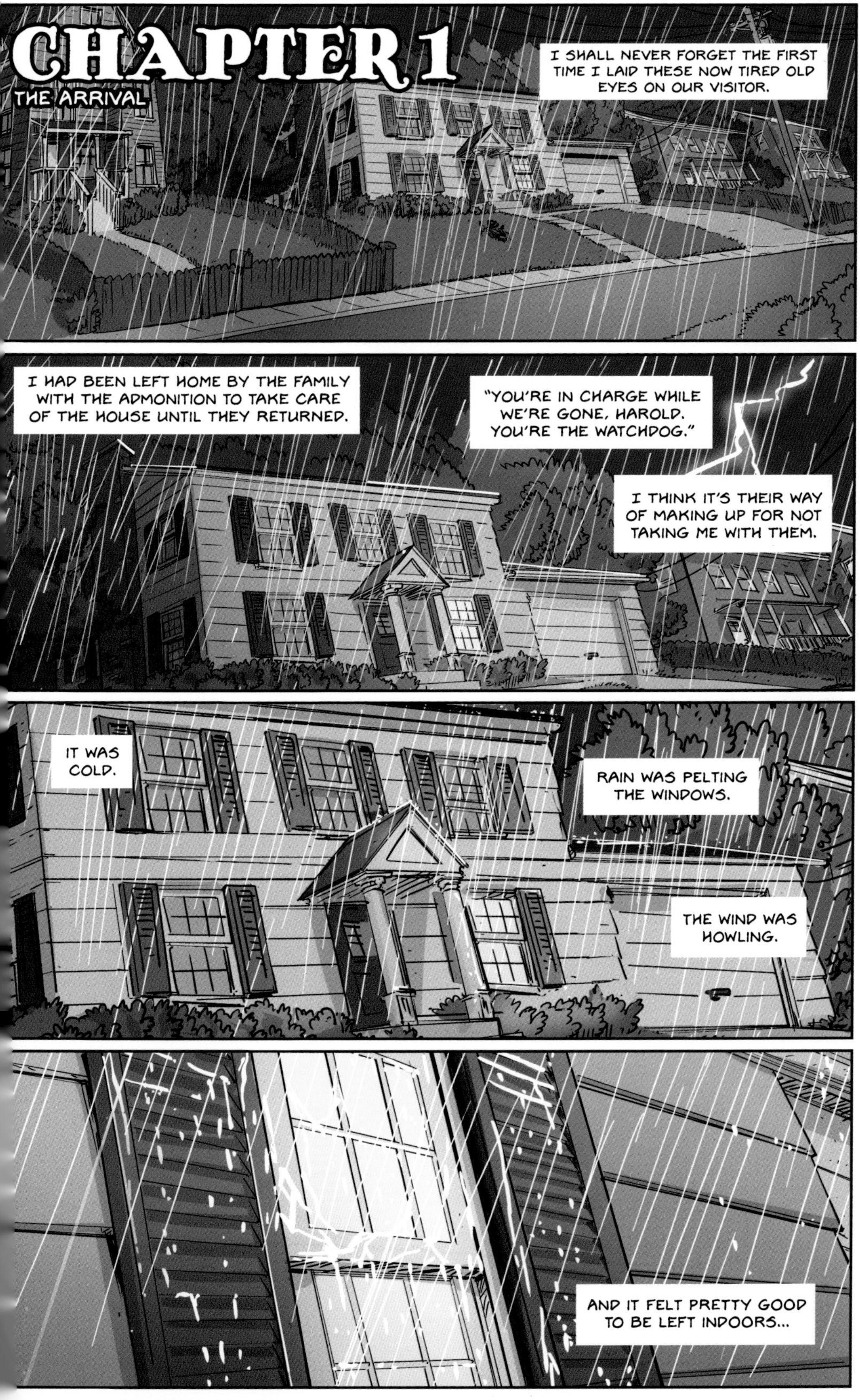
CHAPTER 1
THE ARRIVAL
I SHALL NEVER FORGET THE FIRST TIME I LAID THESE NOW TIRED OLD EYES ON OUR VISITOR.
I HAD BEEN LEFT HOME BY THE FAMILY WITH THE ADMONITION TO TAKE CARE OF THE HOUSE UNTIL THEY RETURNED.
"YOU'RE IN CHARGE WHILE WE'RE GONE, HAROLD. YOU'RE THE WATCHDOG."
I THINK IT'S THEIR WAY OF MAKING UP FOR NOT TAKING ME WITH THEM.
IT WAS COLD.
RAIN WAS PELTING THE WINDOWS.
THE WIND WAS HOWLING.
AND IT FELT PRETTY GOOD TO BE LEFT INDOORS...

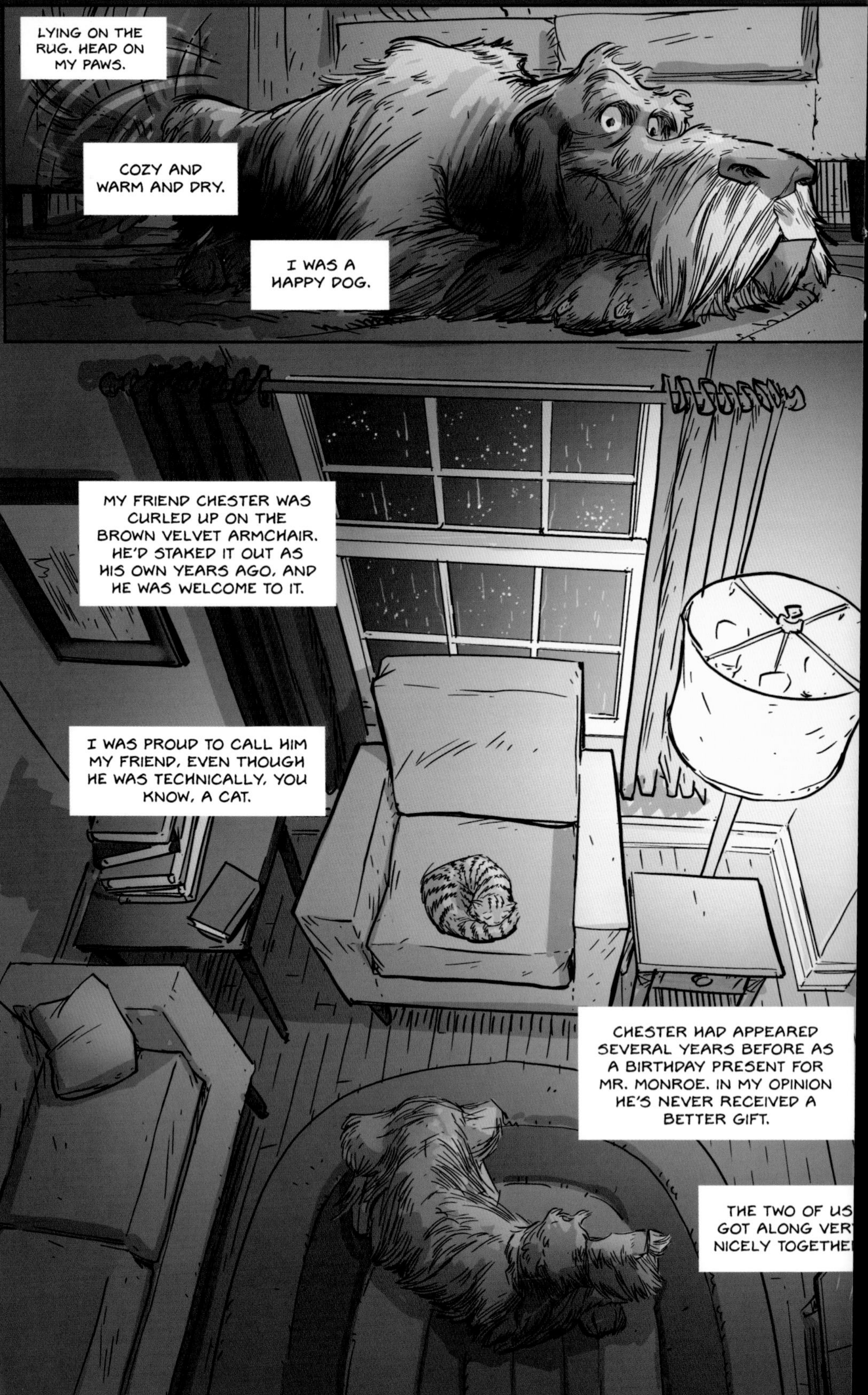
LYING ON THE RUG. HEAD ON MY PAWS.
COZY AND WARM AND DRY.
I WAS A HAPPY DOG.
MY FRIEND CHESTER WAS CURLED UP ON THE BROWN VELVET ARMCHAIR. HE'D STAKED IT OUT AS HIS OWN YEARS AGO, AND HE WAS WELCOME TO IT.
I WAS PROUD TO CALL HIM MY FRIEND, EVEN THOUGH HE WAS TECHNICALLY, YOU KNOW, A CAT.
CHESTER HAD APPEARED SEVERAL YEARS BEFORE AS A BIRTHDAY PRESENT FOR MR. MONROE. IN MY OPINION HE'S NEVER RECEIVED A BETTER GIFT.
THE TWO OF US GOT ALONG VER NICELY TOGETHE

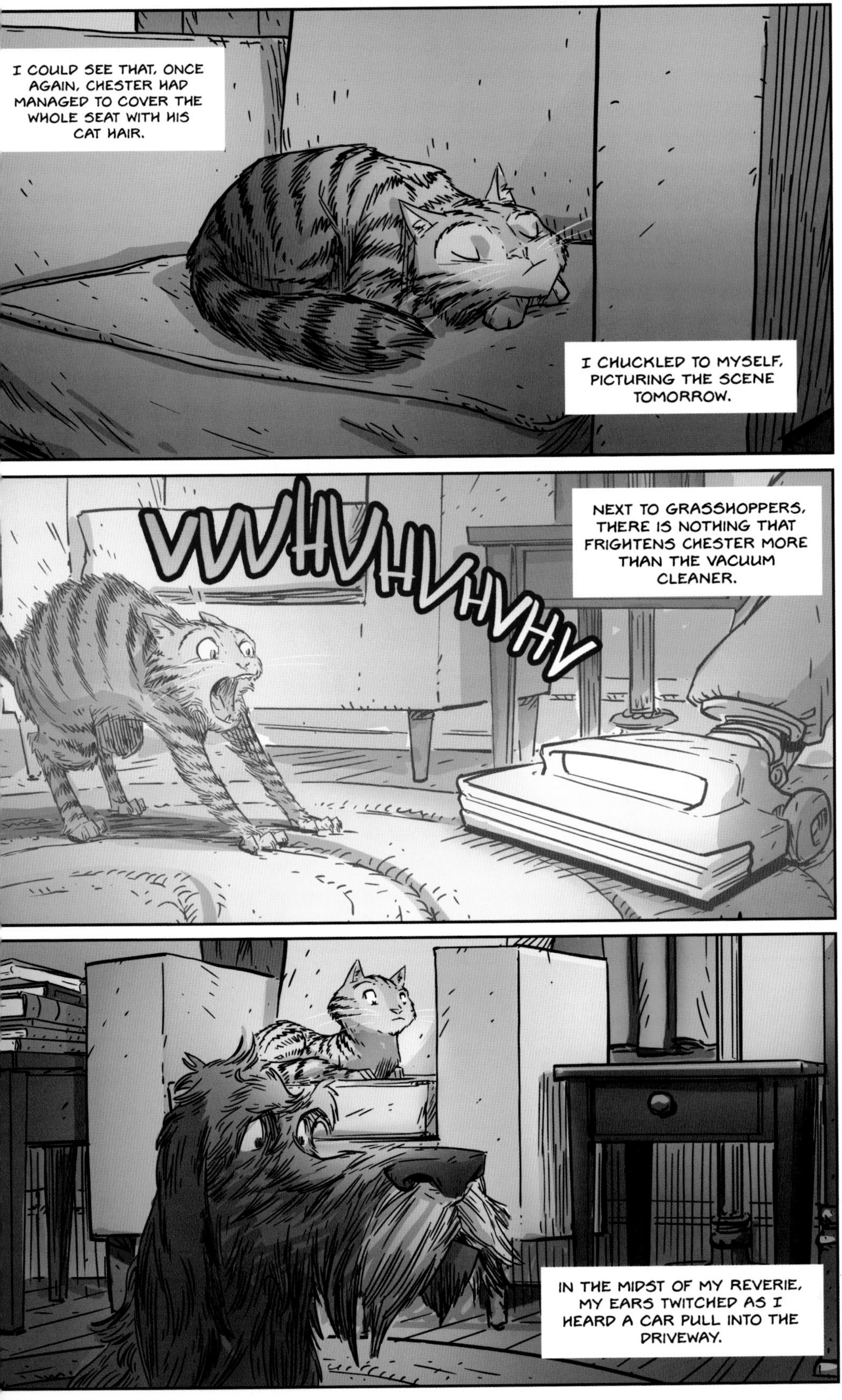
I COULD SEE THAT, ONCE AGAIN, CHESTER HAD MANAGED TO COVER THE WHOLE SEAT WITH HIS CAT HAIR.
I CHUCKLED TO MYSELF, PICTURING THE SCENE TOMORROW.
NEXT TO GRASSHOPPERS, THERE IS NOTHING THAT FRIGHTENS CHESTER MORE THAN THE VACUUM CLEANER.
VVVHVHVHVHV
IN THE MIDST OF MY REVERIE, MY EARS TWITCHED AS I HEARD A CAR PULL INTO THE DRIVEWAY.

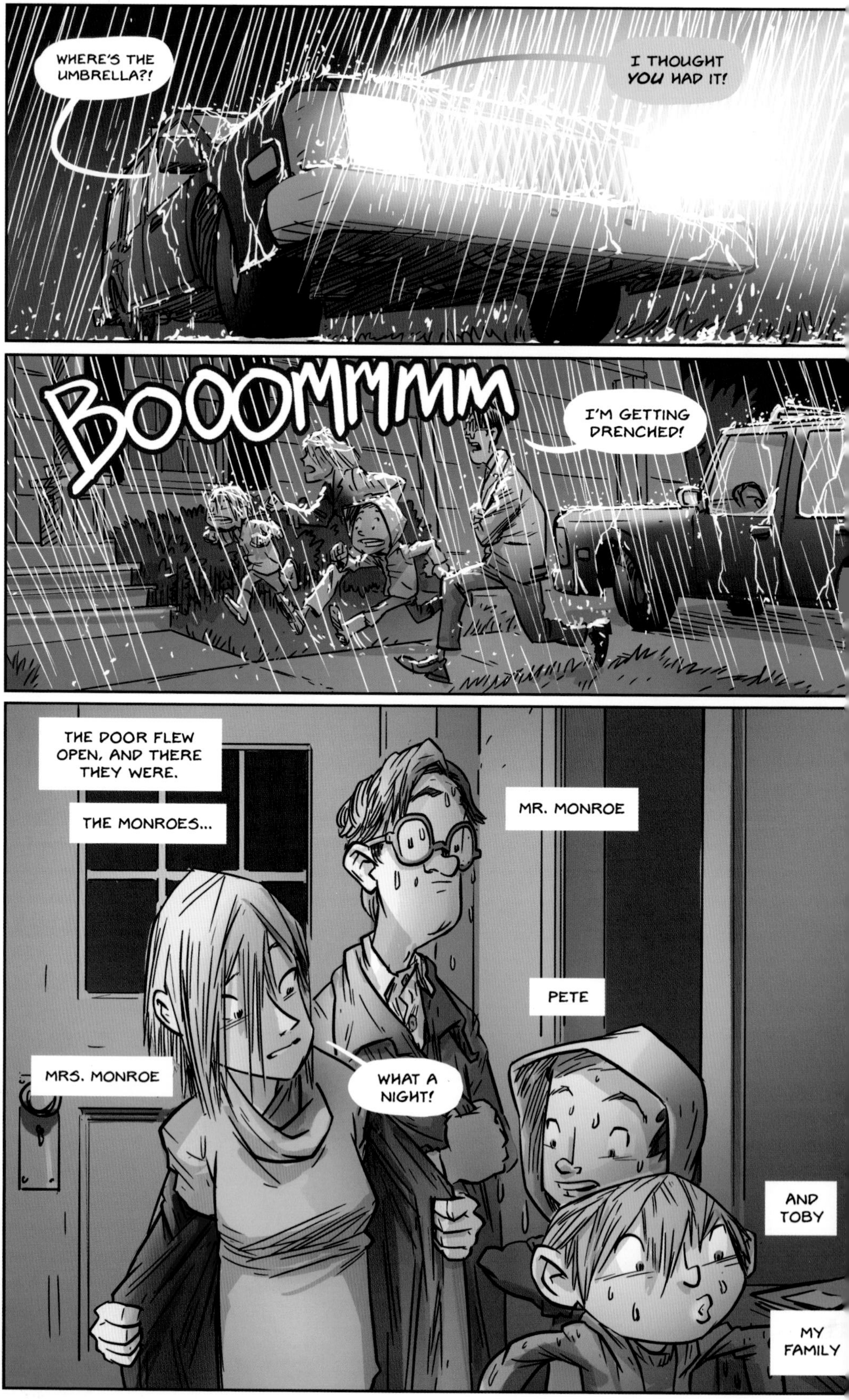
WHERE'S THE UMBRELLA?!
I THOUGHT YOU HAD IT!
BOOOMMMM
I'M GETTING DRENCHED!
THE DOOR FLEW OPEN, AND THERE THEY WERE.
THE MONROES...
MR. MONROE
PETE
MRS. MONROE
WHAT A NIGHT!
AND TOBY
MY FAMILY

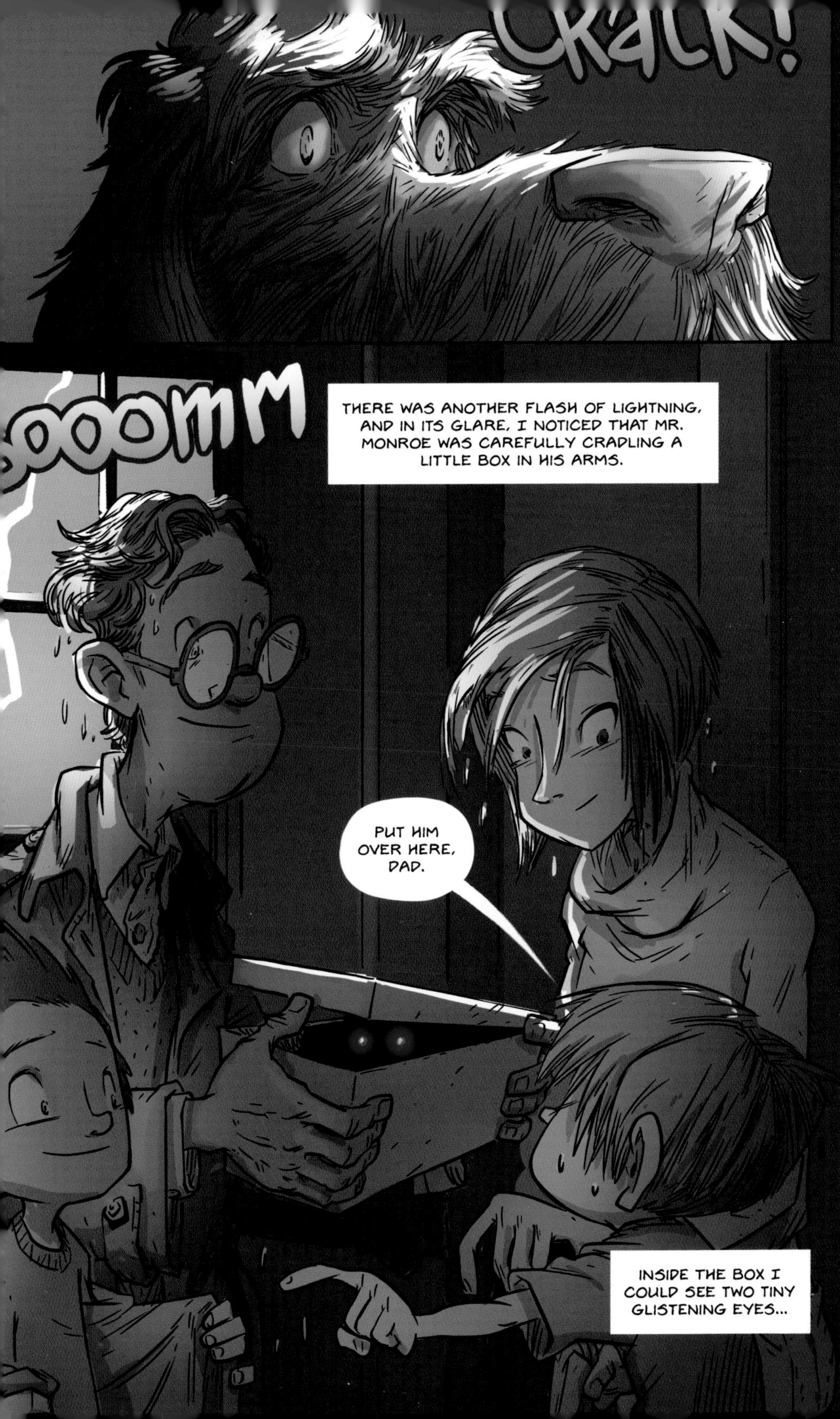
CRACK!
BOOOOMM
THERE WAS ANOTHER FLASH OF LIGHTNING, AND IN ITS GLARE, I NOTICED THAT MR. MONROE WAS CAREFULLY CRADLING A LITTLE BOX IN HIS ARMS.
PUT HIM OVER HERE, DAD.
INSIDE THE BOX I COULD SEE TWO TINY GLISTENING EYES...

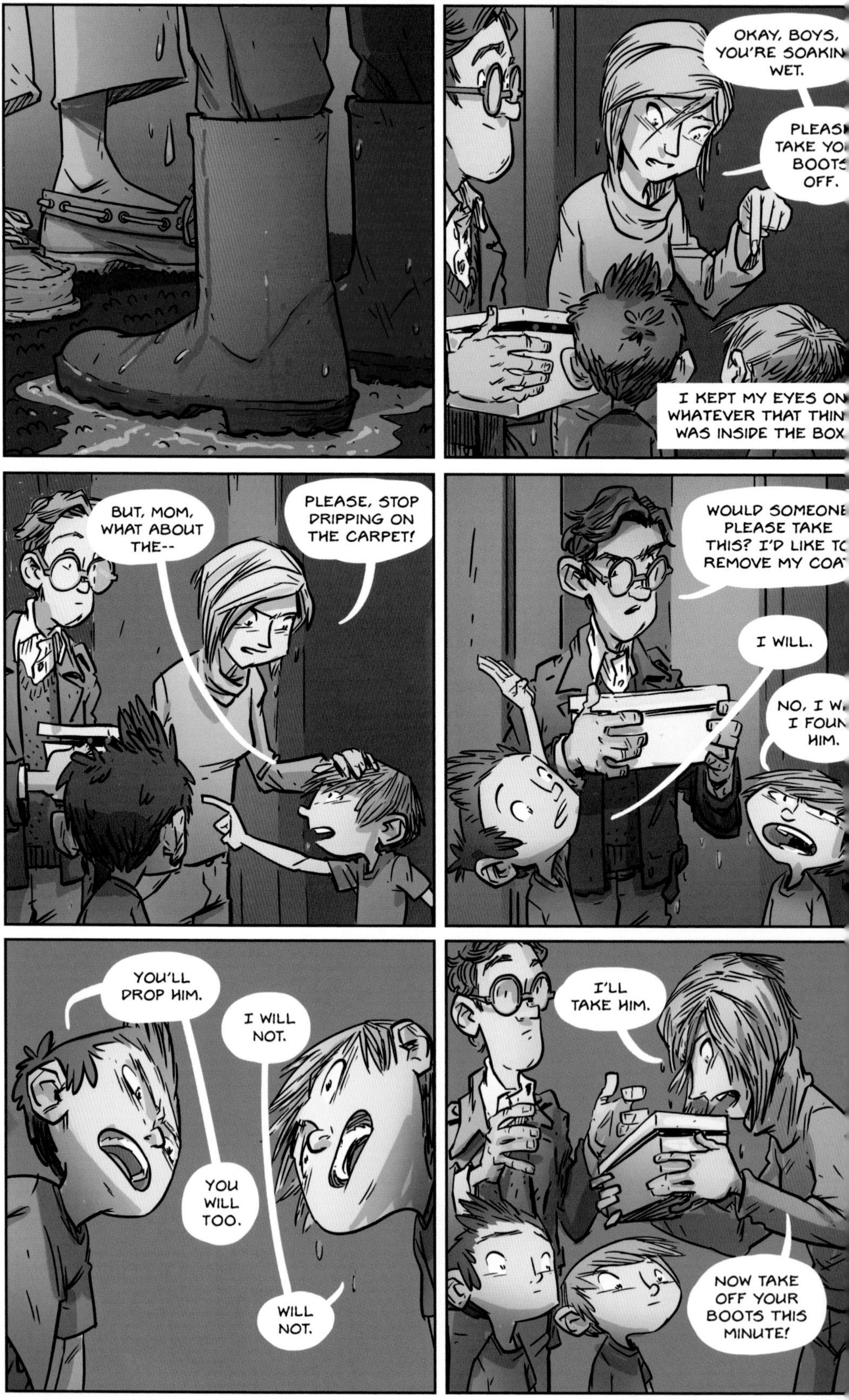

OKAY, BOYS, YOU'RE SOAKIN WET.
PLEAS TAKE YO BOOTS OFF.
I KEPT MY EYES ON WHATEVER THAT THIN WAS INSIDE THE BOX
BUT, MOM, WHAT ABOUT THE--
PLEASE, STOP DRIPPING ON THE CARPET!
WOULD SOMEONE PLEASE TAKE THIS? I'D LIKE TO REMOVE MY COA
I WILL.
NO, I W I FOUN HIM.
YOU'LL DROP HIM.
I WILL NOT.
YOU WILL TOO.
WILL NOT.
I'LL TAKE HIM.
NOW TAKE OFF YOUR BOOTS THIS MINUTE!

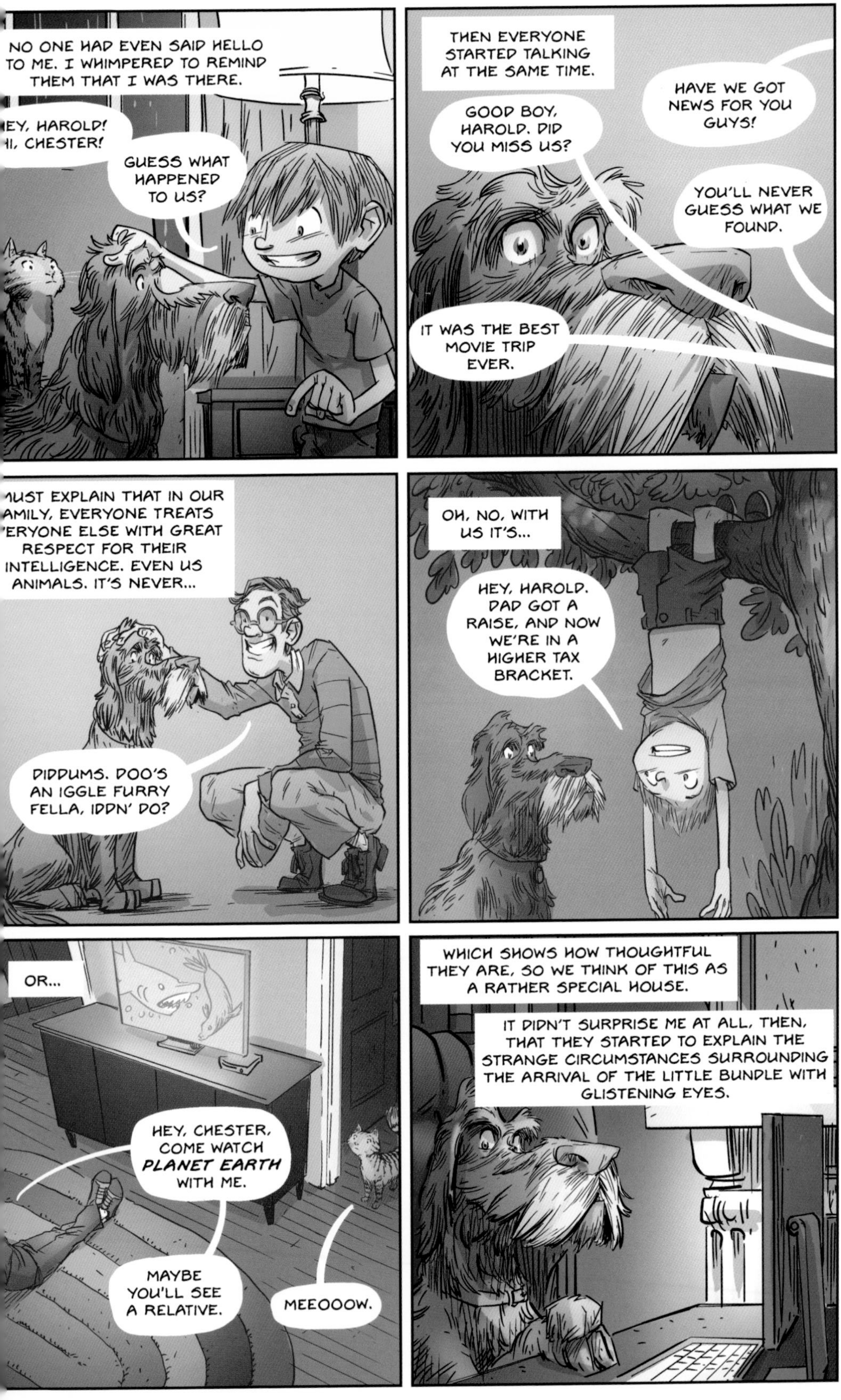
NO ONE HAD EVEN SAID HELLO TO ME. I WHIMPERED TO REMIND THEM THAT I WAS THERE.
EY, HAROLD!
I, CHESTER!
GUESS WHAT HAPPENED TO US?
THEN EVERYONE STARTED TALKING AT THE SAME TIME.
GOOD BOY, HAROLD. DID YOU MISS US?
HAVE WE GOT NEWS FOR YOU GUYS!
YOU'LL NEVER GUESS WHAT WE FOUND.
IT WAS THE BEST MOVIE TRIP EVER.
UST EXPLAIN THAT IN OUR AMILY, EVERYONE TREATS ERYONE ELSE WITH GREAT RESPECT FOR THEIR INTELLIGENCE. EVEN US ANIMALS. IT'S NEVER...
DIDDUMS. DOO'S AN IGGLE FURRY FELLA, IDDN' DO?
OH, NO, WITH US IT'S...
HEY, HAROLD. DAD GOT A RAISE, AND NOW WE'RE IN A HIGHER TAX BRACKET.
OR...
HEY, CHESTER, COME WATCH ***PLANET EARTH*** WITH ME.
MAYBE YOU'LL SEE A RELATIVE.
MEEOOOW.
WHICH SHOWS HOW THOUGHTFUL THEY ARE, SO WE THINK OF THIS AS A RATHER SPECIAL HOUSE.
IT DIDN'T SURPRISE ME AT ALL, THEN, THAT THEY STARTED TO EXPLAIN THE STRANGE CIRCUMSTANCES SURROUNDING THE ARRIVAL OF THE LITTLE BUNDLE WITH GLISTENING EYES.

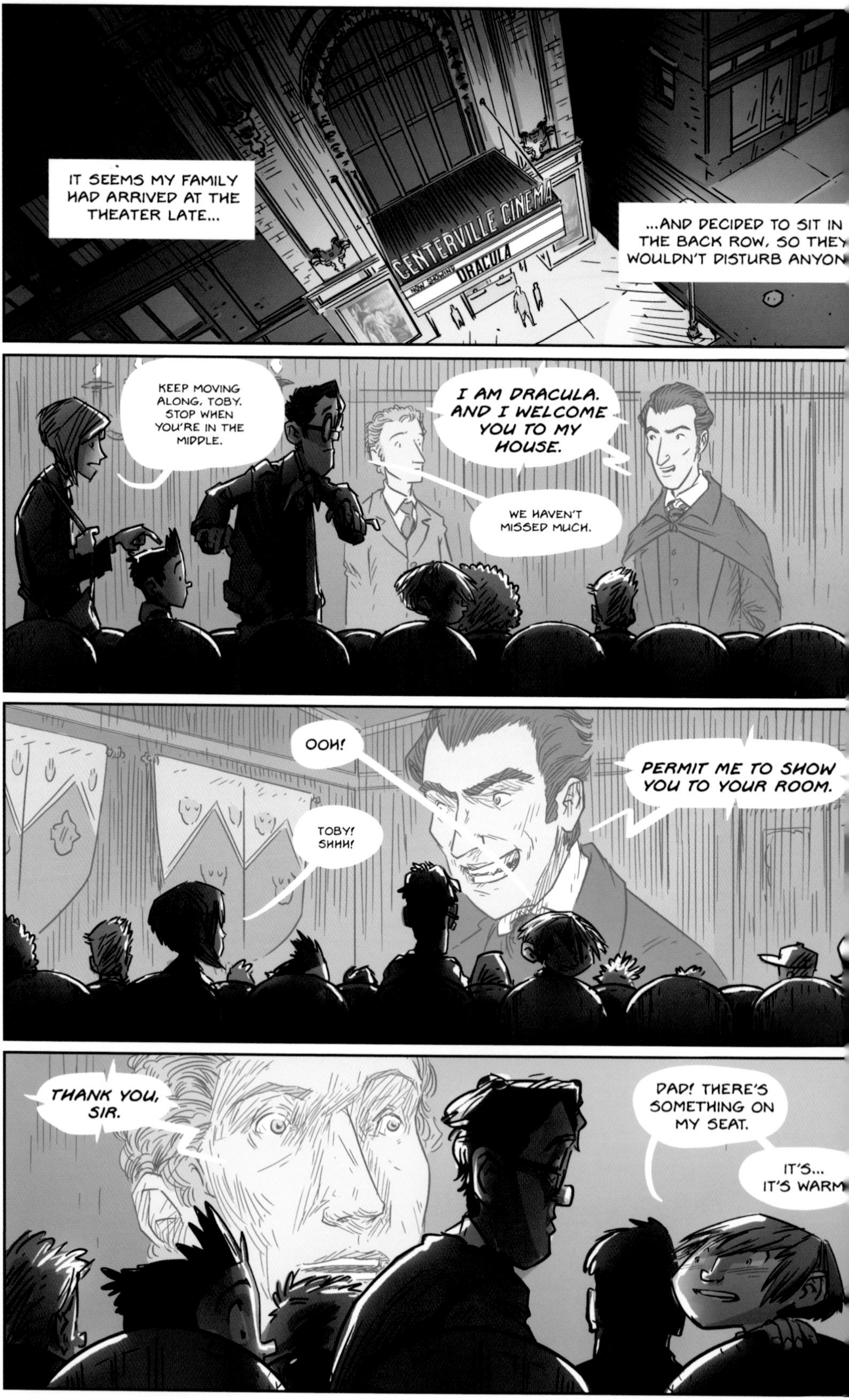
IT SEEMS MY FAMILY HAD ARRIVED AT THE THEATER LATE...
CENTERVILLE CINEMA
NOW SHOWING DRACULA
...AND DECIDED TO SIT IN THE BACK ROW, SO THEY WOULDN'T DISTURB ANYON
KEEP MOVING ALONG, TOBY. STOP WHEN YOU'RE IN THE MIDDLE.
I AM DRACULA. AND I WELCOME YOU TO MY HOUSE.
WE HAVEN'T MISSED MUCH.
OOH!
PERMIT ME TO SHOW YOU TO YOUR ROOM.
TOBY! SHHH!
THANK YOU, SIR.
DAD! THERE'S SOMETHING ON MY SEAT.
IT'S... IT'S WARM

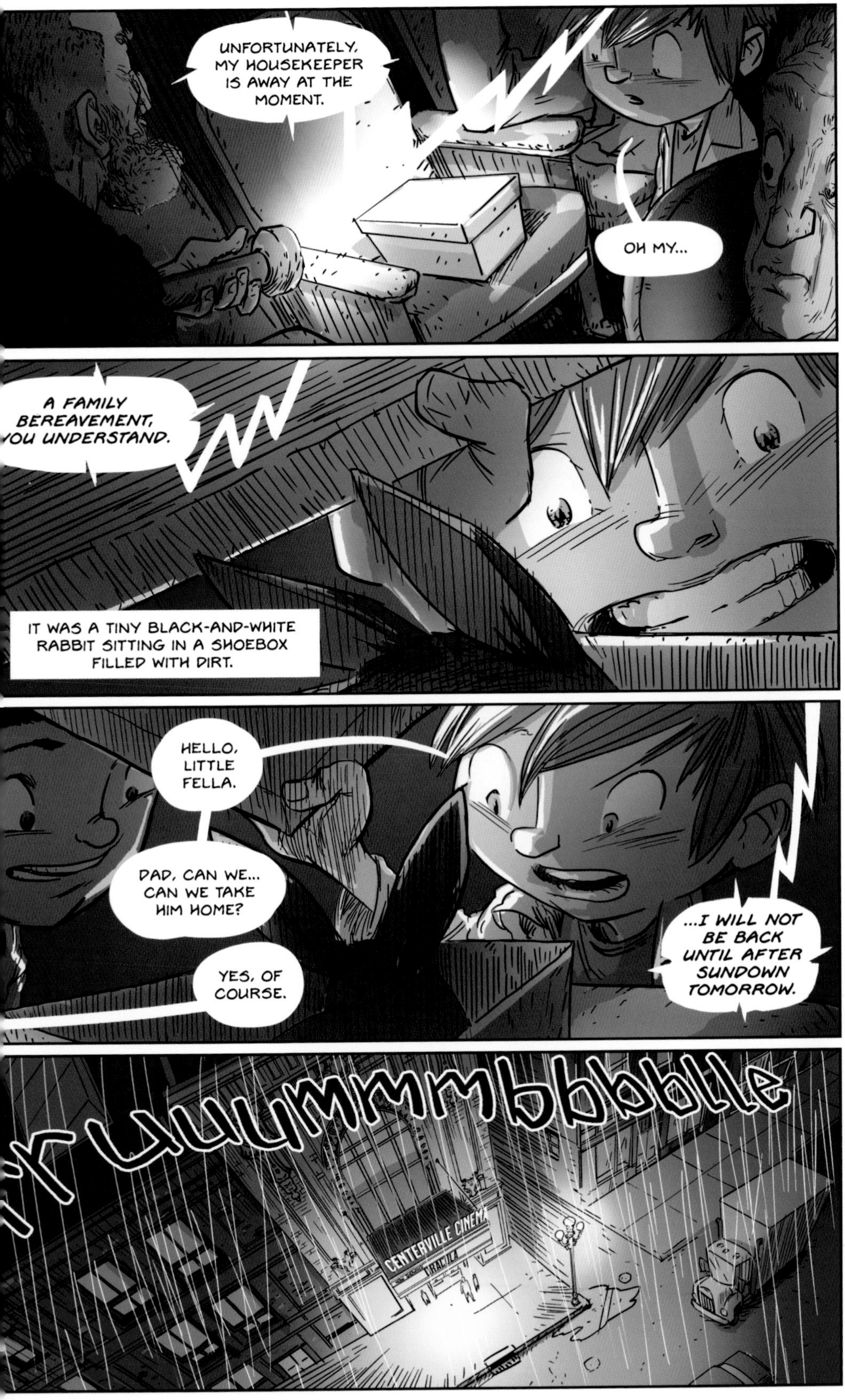
UNFORTUNATELY, MY HOUSEKEEPER IS AWAY AT THE MOMENT.
OH MY...
A FAMILY BEREAVEMENT, YOU UNDERSTAND.
IT WAS A TINY BLACK-AND-WHITE RABBIT SITTING IN A SHOEBOX FILLED WITH DIRT.
HELLO, LITTLE FELLA.
DAD, CAN WE... CAN WE TAKE HIM HOME?
YES, OF COURSE.
...I WILL NOT BE BACK UNTIL AFTER SUNDOWN TOMORROW.
rUUUMMMbbbble
CENTERVILLE CINEMA
DRACULA

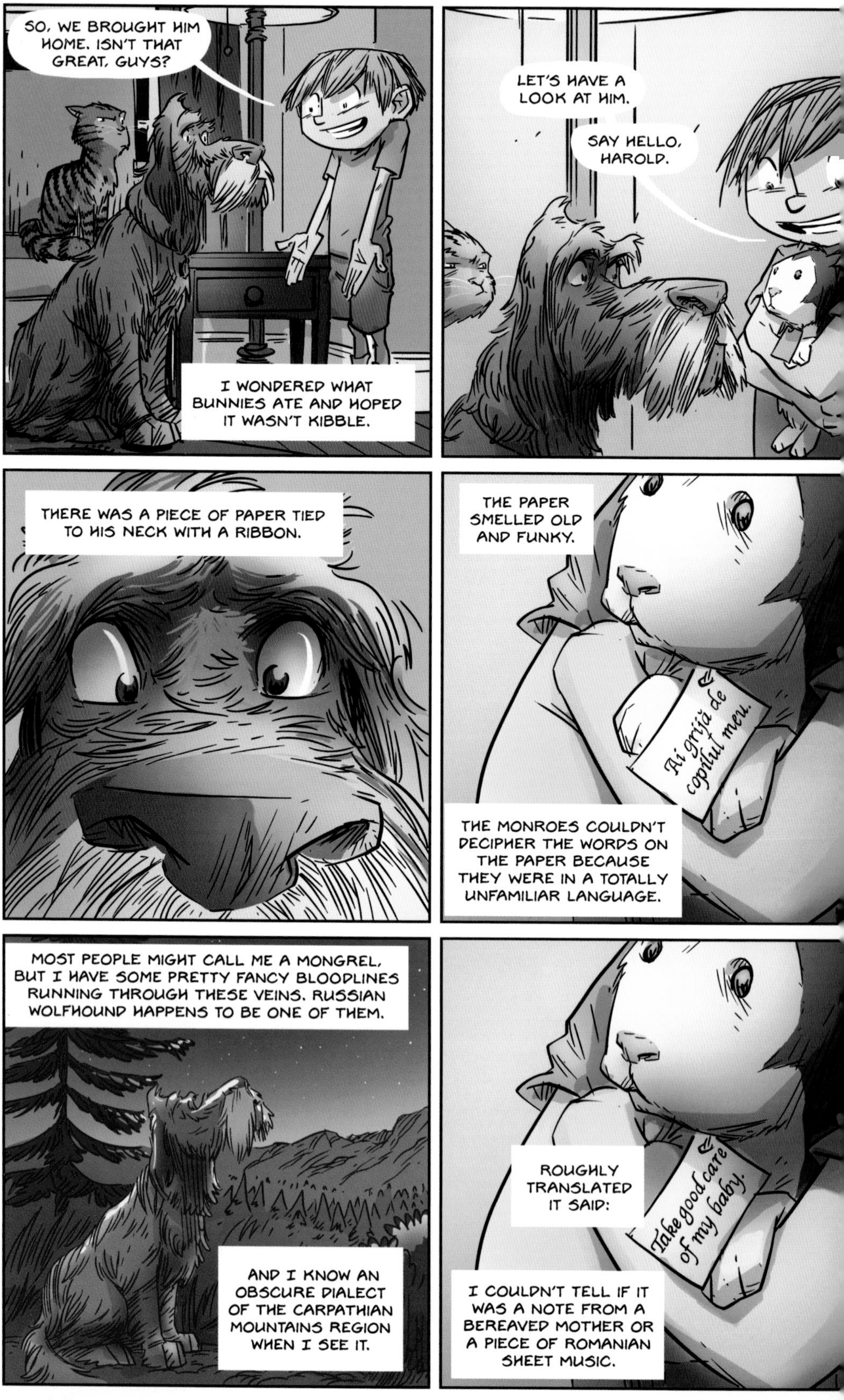
SO, WE BROUGHT HIM HOME. ISN'T THAT GREAT, GUYS?
I WONDERED WHAT BUNNIES ATE AND HOPED IT WASN'T KIBBLE.
LET'S HAVE A LOOK AT HIM.
SAY HELLO, HAROLD.
THERE WAS A PIECE OF PAPER TIED TO HIS NECK WITH A RIBBON.
THE PAPER SMELLED OLD AND FUNKY.
Ai grijă de copilul meu.
THE MONROES COULDN'T DECIPHER THE WORDS ON THE PAPER BECAUSE THEY WERE IN A TOTALLY UNFAMILIAR LANGUAGE.
MOST PEOPLE MIGHT CALL ME A MONGREL, BUT I HAVE SOME PRETTY FANCY BLOODLINES RUNNING THROUGH THESE VEINS. RUSSIAN WOLFHOUND HAPPENS TO BE ONE OF THEM.
AND I KNOW AN OBSCURE DIALECT OF THE CARPATHIAN MOUNTAINS REGION WHEN I SEE IT.
ROUGHLY TRANSLATED IT SAID:
Take good care of my baby.
I COULDN'T TELL IF IT WAS A NOTE FROM A BEREAVED MOTHER OR A PIECE OF ROMANIAN SHEET MUSIC.

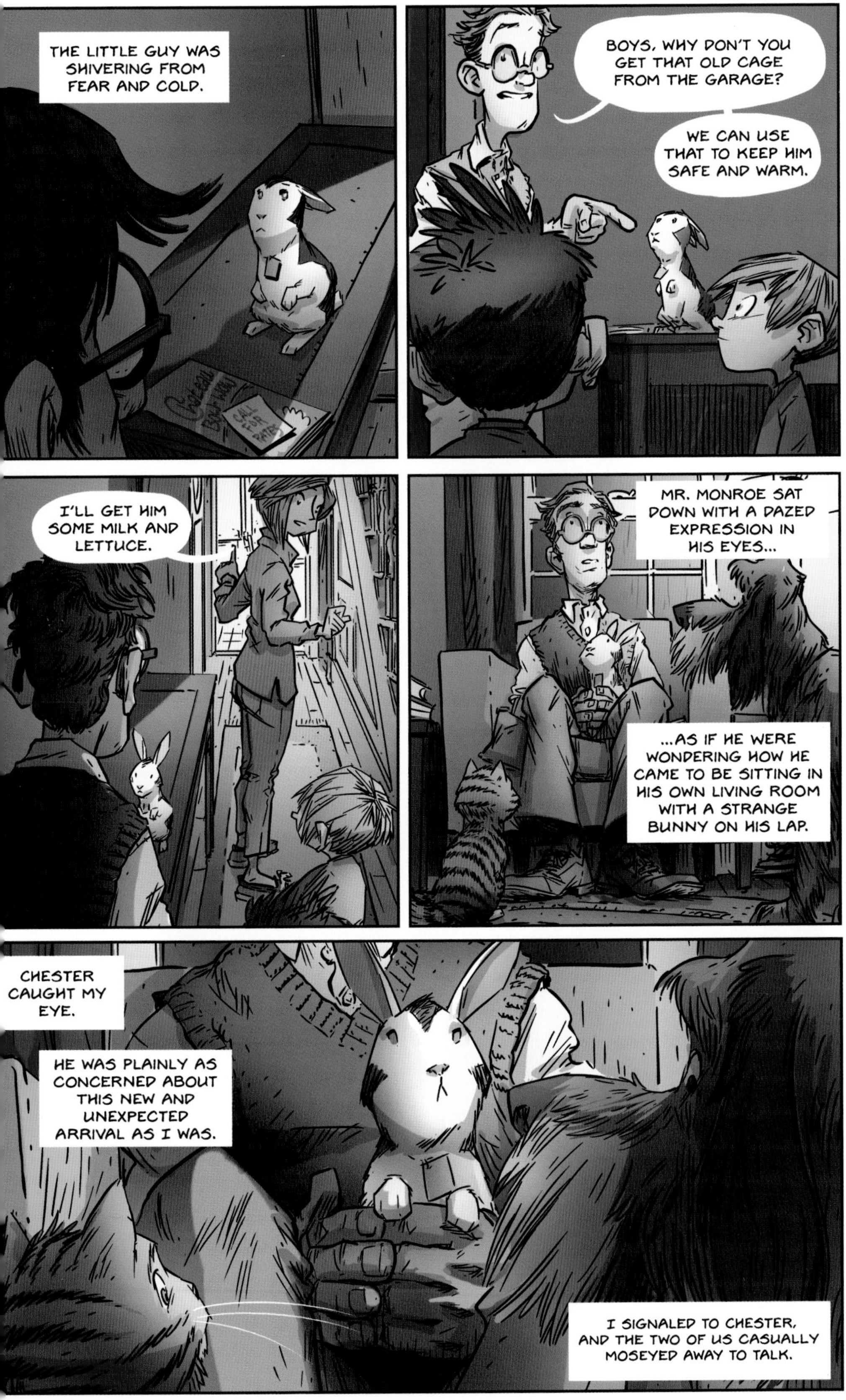
THE LITTLE GUY WAS SHIVERING FROM FEAR AND COLD.
CHOCOLATE BON-BONS
CALL FOR RATES
BOYS, WHY DON'T YOU GET THAT OLD CAGE FROM THE GARAGE?
WE CAN USE THAT TO KEEP HIM SAFE AND WARM.
I'LL GET HIM SOME MILK AND LETTUCE.
MR. MONROE SAT DOWN WITH A DAZED EXPRESSION IN HIS EYES...
...AS IF HE WERE WONDERING HOW HE CAME TO BE SITTING IN HIS OWN LIVING ROOM WITH A STRANGE BUNNY ON HIS LAP.
CHESTER CAUGHT MY EYE.
HE WAS PLAINLY AS CONCERNED ABOUT THIS NEW AND UNEXPECTED ARRIVAL AS I WAS.
I SIGNALED TO CHESTER, AND THE TWO OF US CASUALLY MOSEYED AWAY TO TALK.

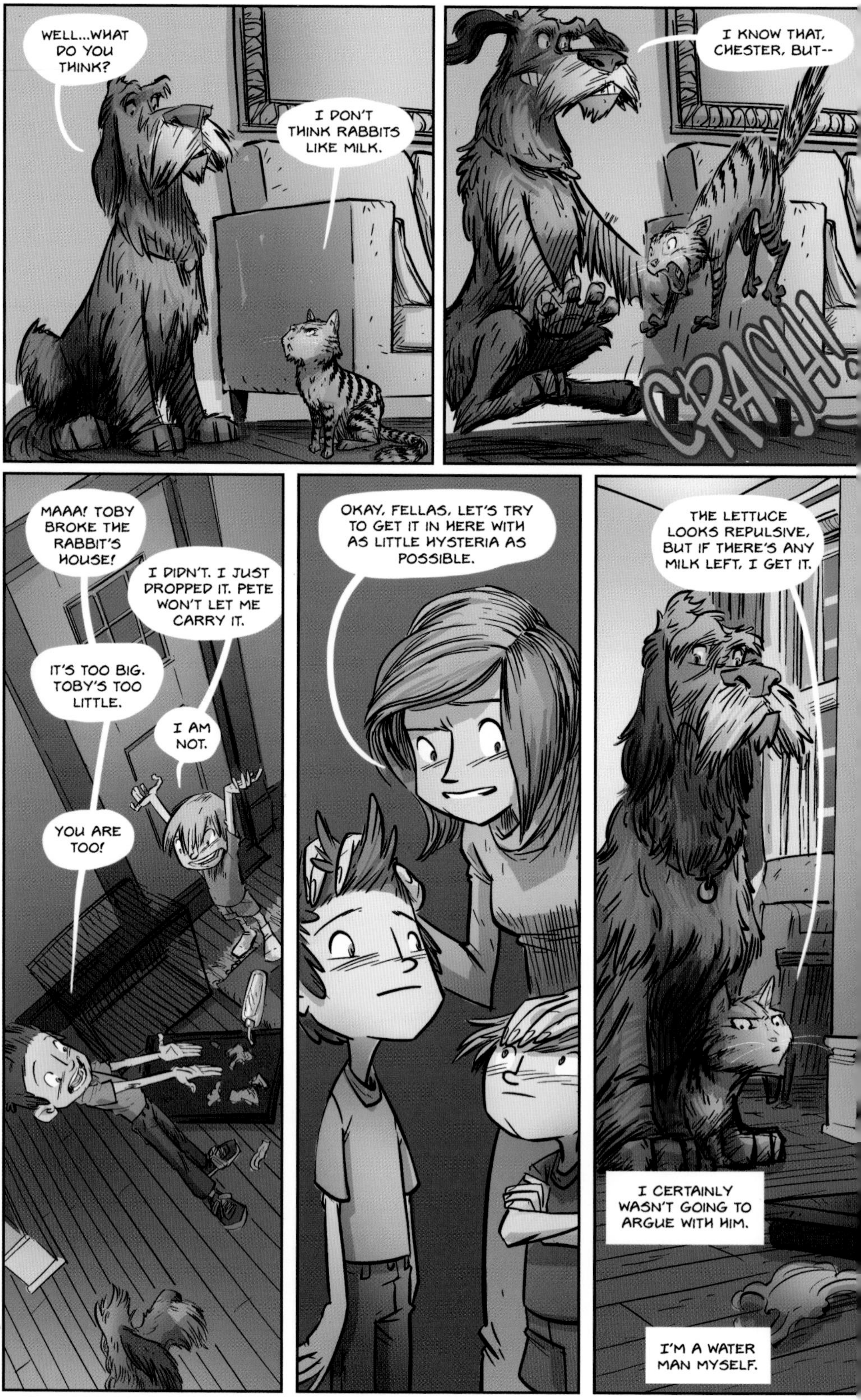
WELL...WHAT DO YOU THINK?
I DON'T THINK RABBITS LIKE MILK.
I KNOW THAT, CHESTER, BUT--
CRASH!
MAAA! TOBY BROKE THE RABBIT'S HOUSE!
I DIDN'T. I JUST DROPPED IT. PETE WON'T LET ME CARRY IT.
IT'S TOO BIG. TOBY'S TOO LITTLE.
I AM NOT.
YOU ARE TOO!
OKAY, FELLAS, LET'S TRY TO GET IT IN HERE WITH AS LITTLE HYSTERIA AS POSSIBLE.
THE LETTUCE LOOKS REPULSIVE, BUT IF THERE'S ANY MILK LEFT, I GET IT.
I CERTAINLY WASN'T GOING TO ARGUE WITH HIM.
I'M A WATER MAN MYSELF.

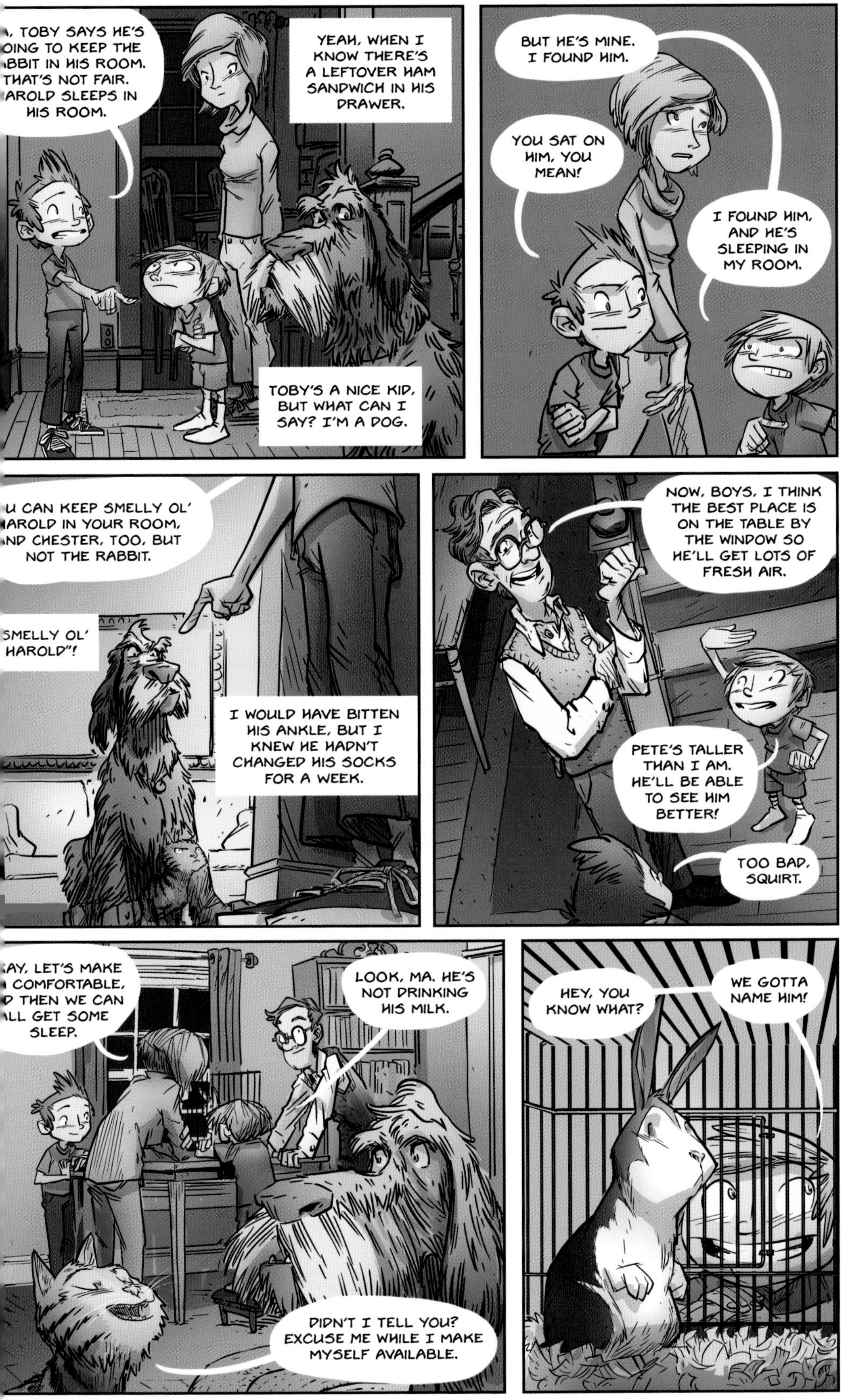

, TOBY SAYS HE'S OING TO KEEP THE BBIT IN HIS ROOM. THAT'S NOT FAIR. AROLD SLEEPS IN HIS ROOM.
YEAH, WHEN I KNOW THERE'S A LEFTOVER HAM SANDWICH IN HIS DRAWER.
TOBY'S A NICE KID, BUT WHAT CAN I SAY? I'M A DOG.
BUT HE'S MINE. I FOUND HIM.
YOU SAT ON HIM, YOU MEAN!
I FOUND HIM, AND HE'S SLEEPING IN MY ROOM.
U CAN KEEP SMELLY OL' AROLD IN YOUR ROOM, ND CHESTER, TOO, BUT NOT THE RABBIT.
SMELLY OL' HAROLD"!
I WOULD HAVE BITTEN HIS ANKLE, BUT I KNEW HE HADN'T CHANGED HIS SOCKS FOR A WEEK.
NOW, BOYS, I THINK THE BEST PLACE IS ON THE TABLE BY THE WINDOW SO HE'LL GET LOTS OF FRESH AIR.
PETE'S TALLER THAN I AM. HE'LL BE ABLE TO SEE HIM BETTER!
TOO BAD, SQUIRT.
AY, LET'S MAKE COMFORTABLE, D THEN WE CAN LL GET SOME SLEEP.
LOOK, MA. HE'S NOT DRINKING HIS MILK.
DIDN'T I TELL YOU? EXCUSE ME WHILE I MAKE MYSELF AVAILABLE.
HEY, YOU KNOW WHAT?
WE GOTTA NAME HIM!

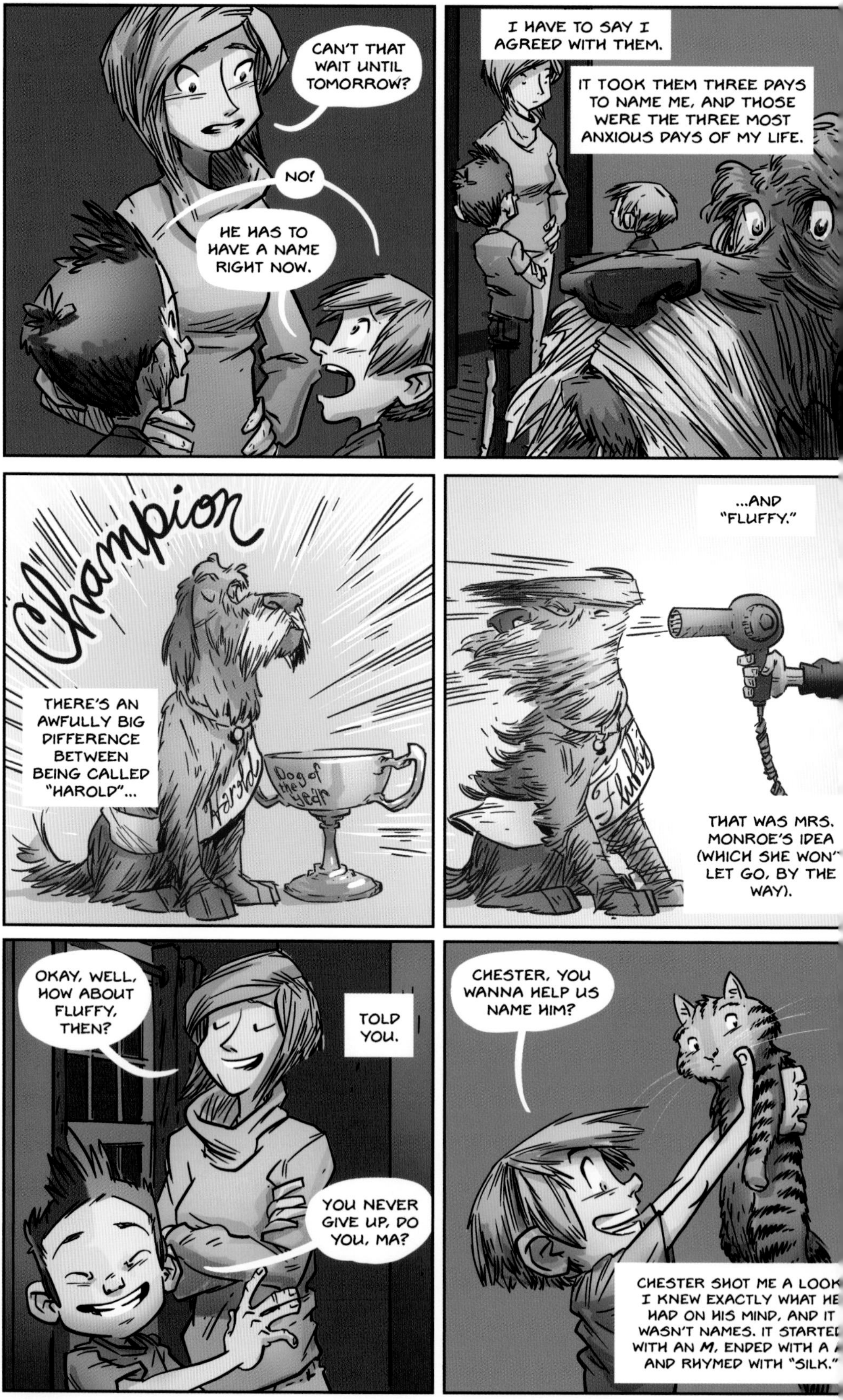
CAN'T THAT WAIT UNTIL TOMORROW?
NO!
HE HAS TO HAVE A NAME RIGHT NOW.
I HAVE TO SAY I AGREED WITH THEM.
IT TOOK THEM THREE DAYS TO NAME ME, AND THOSE WERE THE THREE MOST ANXIOUS DAYS OF MY LIFE.
Champion
THERE'S AN AWFULLY BIG DIFFERENCE BETWEEN BEING CALLED "HAROLD"...
Harold
Dog of the year
...AND "FLUFFY."
Fluffy
THAT WAS MRS. MONROE'S IDEA (WHICH SHE WON'T LET GO, BY THE WAY).
OKAY, WELL, HOW ABOUT FLUFFY, THEN?
TOLD YOU.
YOU NEVER GIVE UP, DO YOU, MA?
CHESTER, YOU WANNA HELP US NAME HIM?
CHESTER SHOT ME A LOOK. I KNEW EXACTLY WHAT HE HAD ON HIS MIND, AND IT WASN'T NAMES. IT STARTED WITH AN *M*, ENDED WITH A *K*, AND RHYMED WITH "SILK."

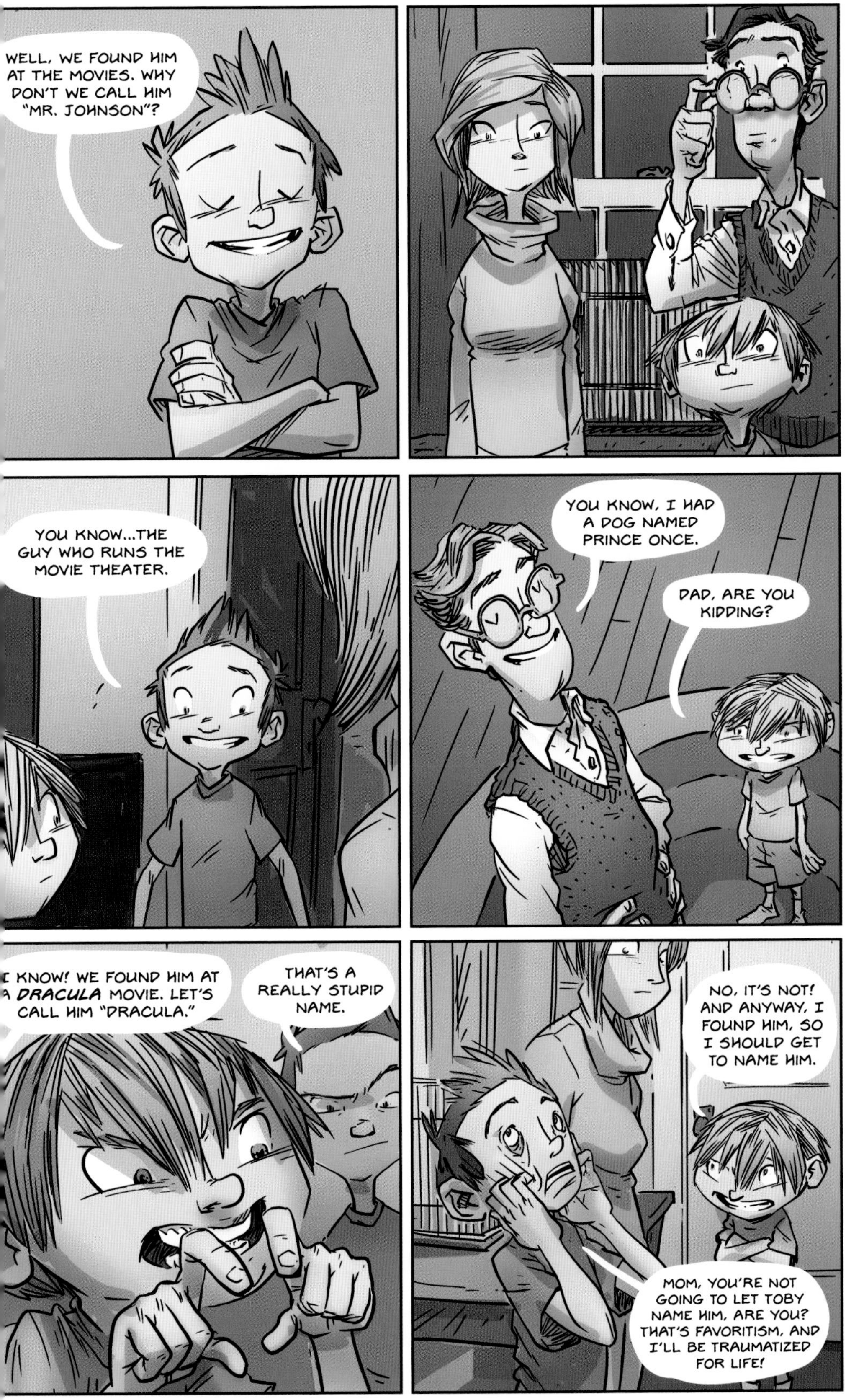

WELL, WE FOUND HIM AT THE MOVIES. WHY DON'T WE CALL HIM "MR. JOHNSON"?
YOU KNOW...THE GUY WHO RUNS THE MOVIE THEATER.
YOU KNOW, I HAD A DOG NAMED PRINCE ONCE.
DAD, ARE YOU KIDDING?
I KNOW! WE FOUND HIM AT A *DRACULA* MOVIE. LET'S CALL HIM "DRACULA."
THAT'S A REALLY STUPID NAME.
NO, IT'S NOT! AND ANYWAY, I FOUND HIM, SO I SHOULD GET TO NAME HIM.
MOM, YOU'RE NOT GOING TO LET TOBY NAME HIM, ARE YOU? THAT'S FAVORITISM, AND I'LL BE TRAUMATIZED FOR LIFE!

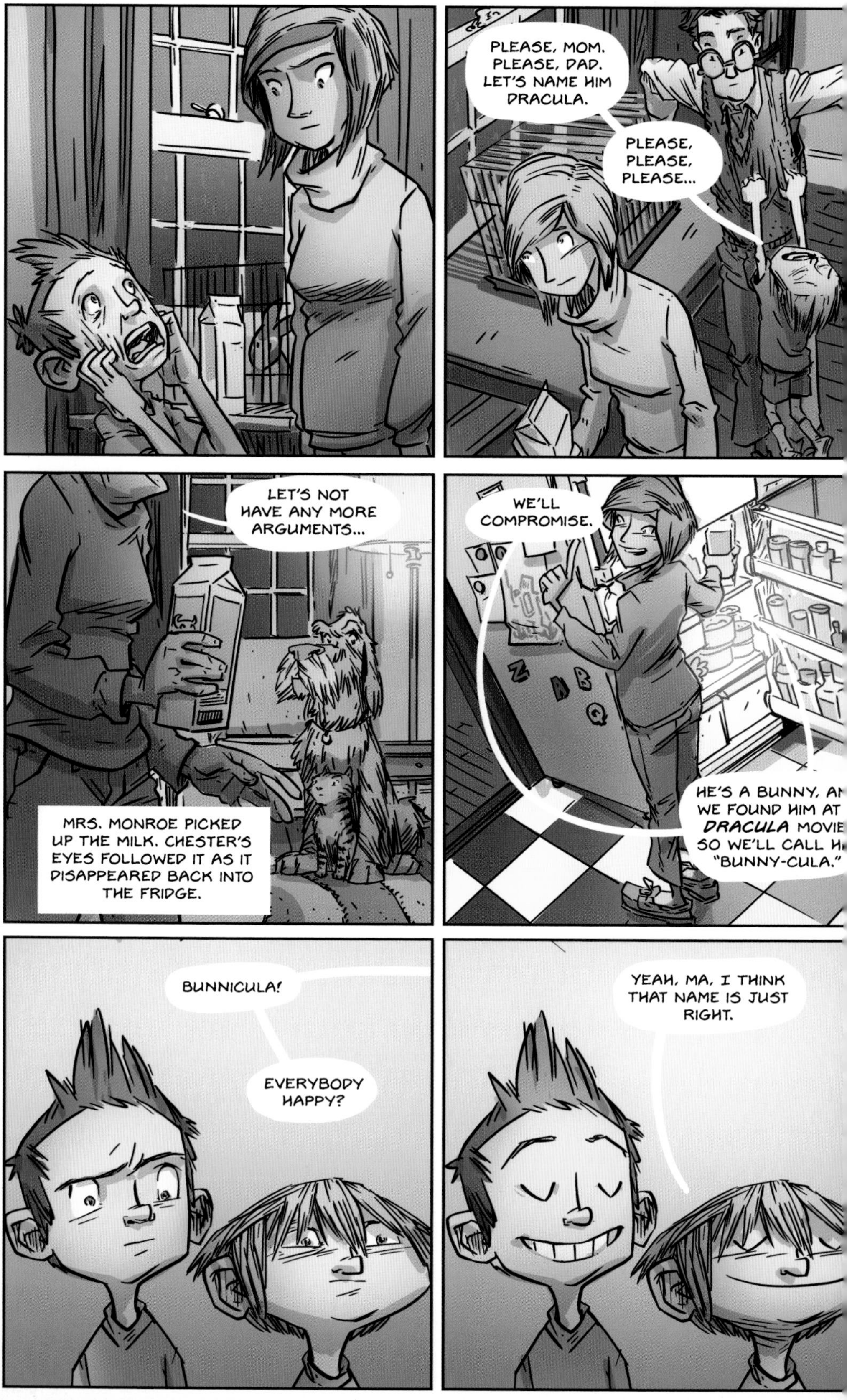
PLEASE, MOM. PLEASE, DAD. LET'S NAME HIM DRACULA.
PLEASE, PLEASE, PLEASE...
LET'S NOT HAVE ANY MORE ARGUMENTS...
MRS. MONROE PICKED UP THE MILK. CHESTER'S EYES FOLLOWED IT AS IT DISAPPEARED BACK INTO THE FRIDGE.
WE'LL COMPROMISE.
HE'S A BUNNY, AN
WE FOUND HIM AT
DRACULA MOVIE
SO WE'LL CALL H
"BUNNY-CULA."
BUNNICULA!
EVERYBODY HAPPY?
YEAH, MA, I THINK THAT NAME IS JUST RIGHT.

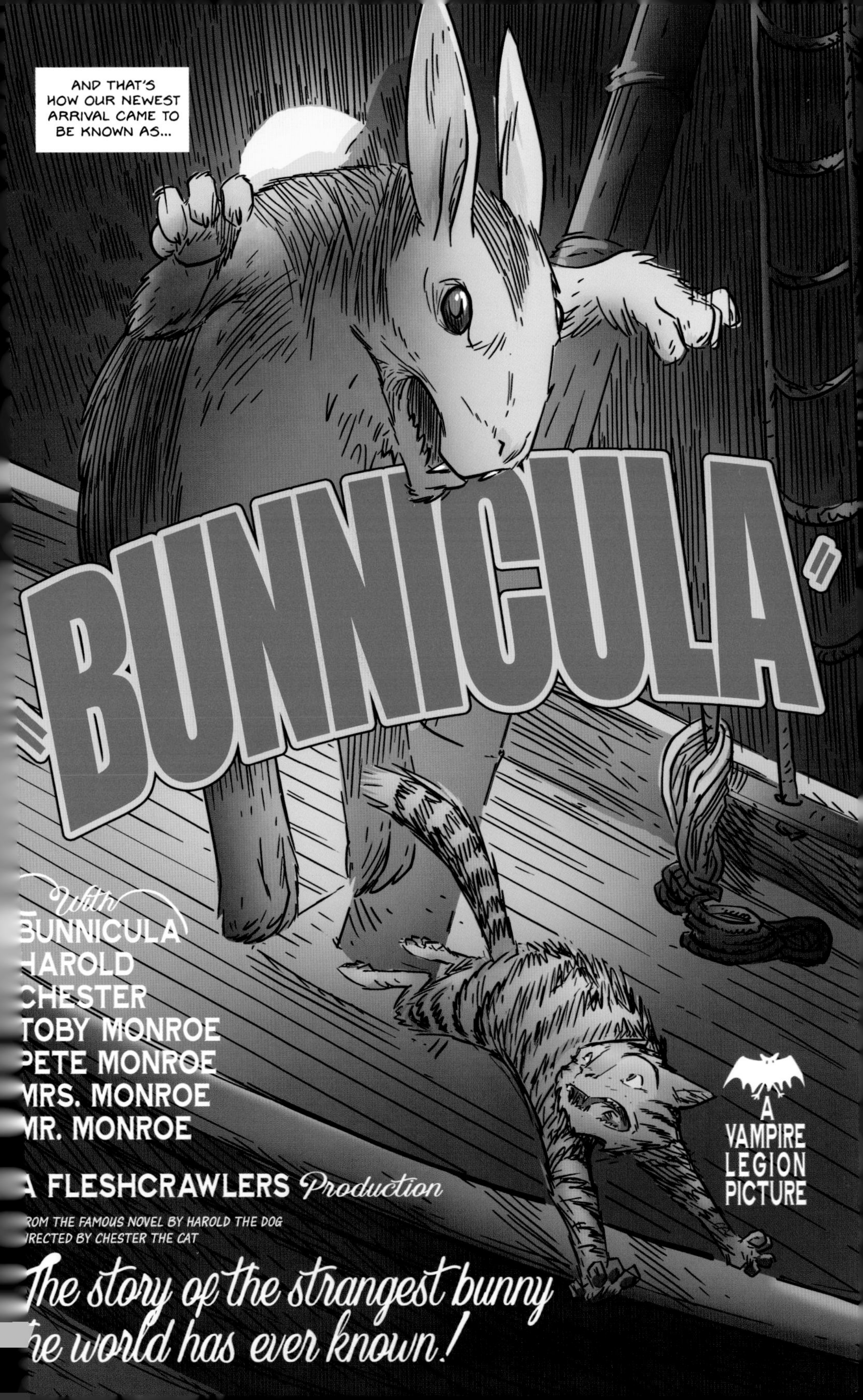

AND THAT'S HOW OUR NEWEST ARRIVAL CAME TO BE KNOWN AS...
"BUNNICULA"
With
BUNNICULA
HAROLD
CHESTER
TOBY MONROE
PETE MONROE
MRS. MONROE
MR. MONROE
A FLESHCRAWLERS Production
ROM THE FAMOUS NOVEL BY HAROLD THE DOG
RECTED BY CHESTER THE CAT
The story of the strangest bunny
he world has ever known!
A VAMPIRE LEGION PICTURE

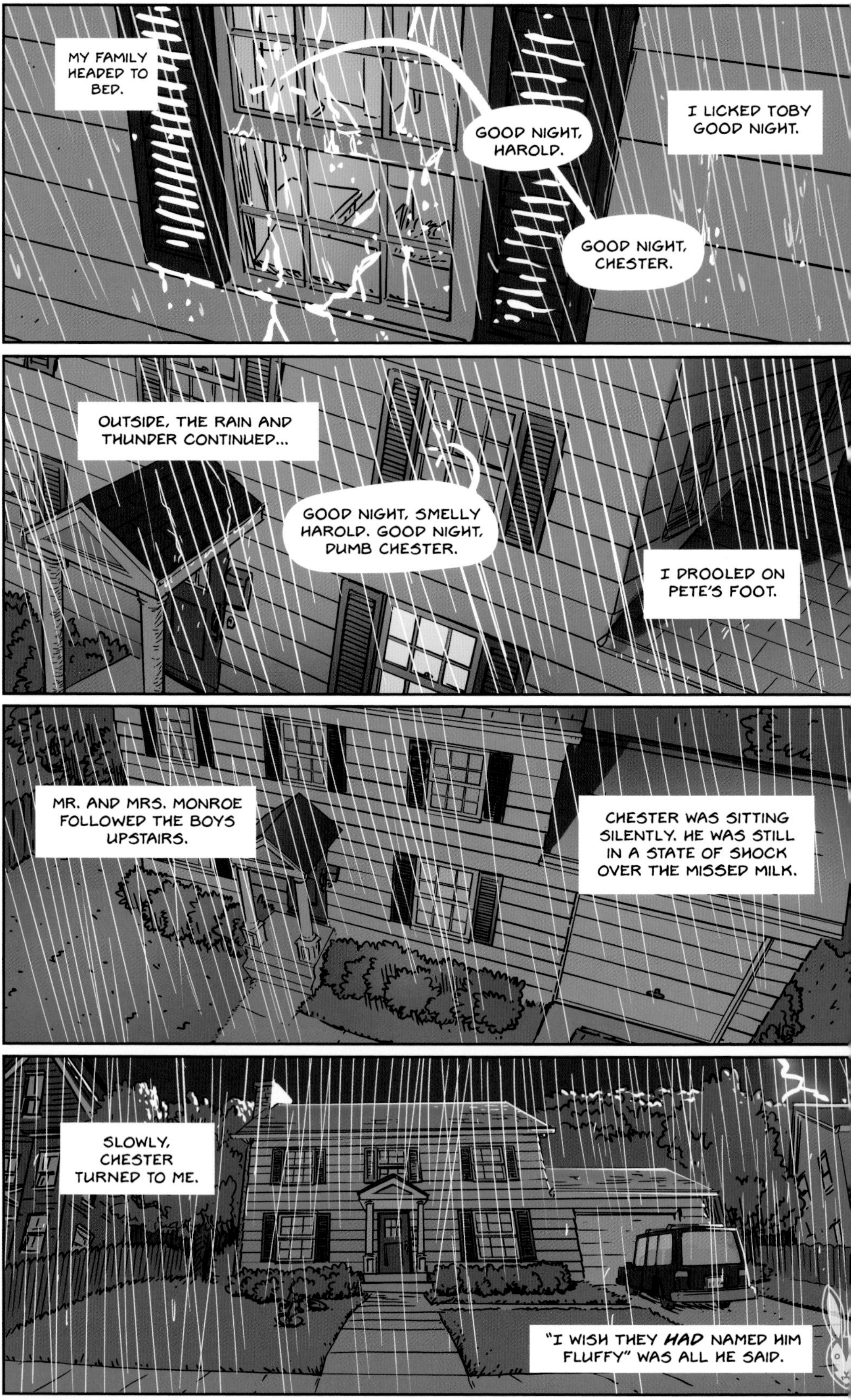
MY FAMILY HEADED TO BED.
GOOD NIGHT, HAROLD.
GOOD NIGHT, CHESTER.
I LICKED TOBY GOOD NIGHT.
OUTSIDE, THE RAIN AND THUNDER CONTINUED...
GOOD NIGHT, SMELLY HAROLD. GOOD NIGHT, DUMB CHESTER.
I DROOLED ON PETE'S FOOT.
MR. AND MRS. MONROE FOLLOWED THE BOYS UPSTAIRS.
CHESTER WAS SITTING SILENTLY. HE WAS STILL IN A STATE OF SHOCK OVER THE MISSED MILK.
SLOWLY, CHESTER TURNED TO ME.
"I WISH THEY *HAD* NAMED HIM FLUFFY" WAS ALL HE SAID.

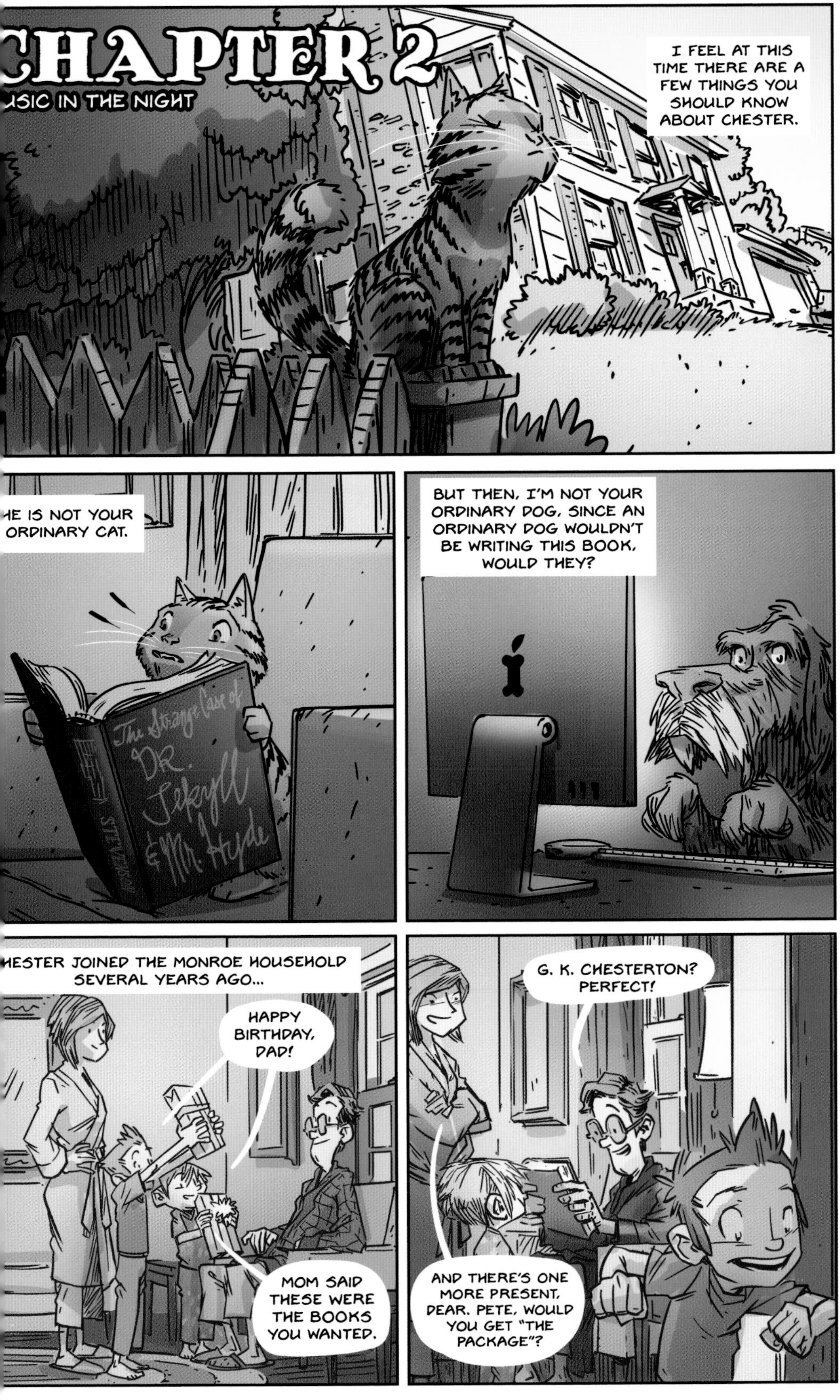
CHAPTER 2
USIC IN THE NIGHT
I FEEL AT THIS TIME THERE ARE A FEW THINGS YOU SHOULD KNOW ABOUT CHESTER.
HE IS NOT YOUR ORDINARY CAT.
The Strange Case of Dr. Jekyll & Mr. Hyde
STEVENSON
BUT THEN, I'M NOT YOUR ORDINARY DOG, SINCE AN ORDINARY DOG WOULDN'T BE WRITING THIS BOOK, WOULD THEY?
HESTER JOINED THE MONROE HOUSEHOLD SEVERAL YEARS AGO...
HAPPY BIRTHDAY, DAD!
MOM SAID THESE WERE THE BOOKS YOU WANTED.
G. K. CHESTERTON? PERFECT!
AND THERE'S ONE MORE PRESENT, DEAR. PETE, WOULD YOU GET "THE PACKAGE"?

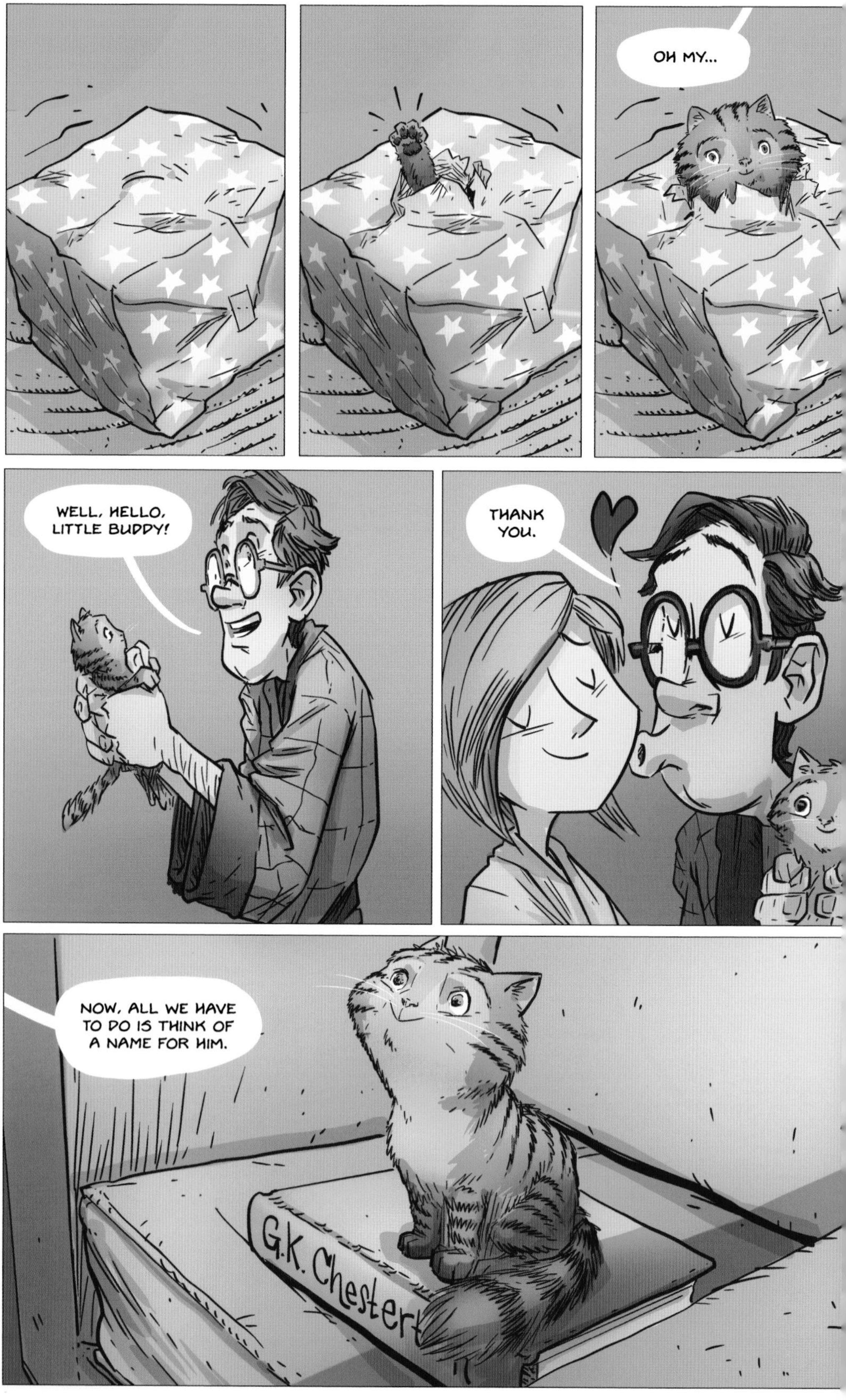
OH MY...
WELL, HELLO, LITTLE BUDDY!
THANK YOU.
NOW, ALL WE HAVE TO DO IS THINK OF A NAME FOR HIM.
G.K. Chestert

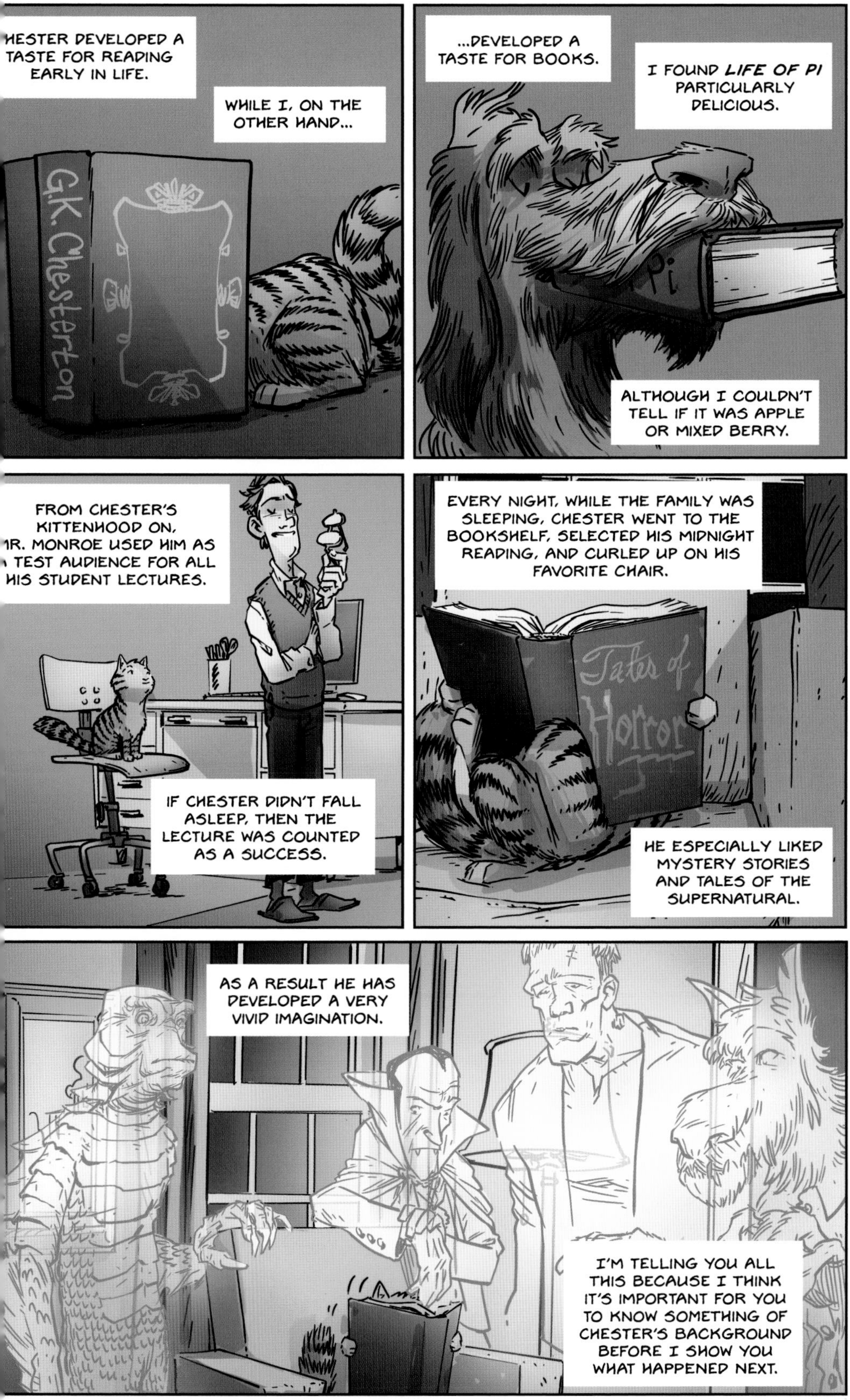
HESTER DEVELOPED A TASTE FOR READING EARLY IN LIFE.
WHILE I, ON THE OTHER HAND...
G.K. Chesterton
...DEVELOPED A TASTE FOR BOOKS.
I FOUND *LIFE OF PI* PARTICULARLY DELICIOUS.
Pi
ALTHOUGH I COULDN'T TELL IF IT WAS APPLE OR MIXED BERRY.
FROM CHESTER'S KITTENHOOD ON, 1R. MONROE USED HIM AS TEST AUDIENCE FOR ALL HIS STUDENT LECTURES.
IF CHESTER DIDN'T FALL ASLEEP, THEN THE LECTURE WAS COUNTED AS A SUCCESS.
EVERY NIGHT, WHILE THE FAMILY WAS SLEEPING, CHESTER WENT TO THE BOOKSHELF, SELECTED HIS MIDNIGHT READING, AND CURLED UP ON HIS FAVORITE CHAIR.
Tales of Horror
HE ESPECIALLY LIKED MYSTERY STORIES AND TALES OF THE SUPERNATURAL.
AS A RESULT HE HAS DEVELOPED A VERY VIVID IMAGINATION.
I'M TELLING YOU ALL THIS BECAUSE I THINK IT'S IMPORTANT FOR YOU TO KNOW SOMETHING OF CHESTER'S BACKGROUND BEFORE I SHOW YOU WHAT HAPPENED NEXT.

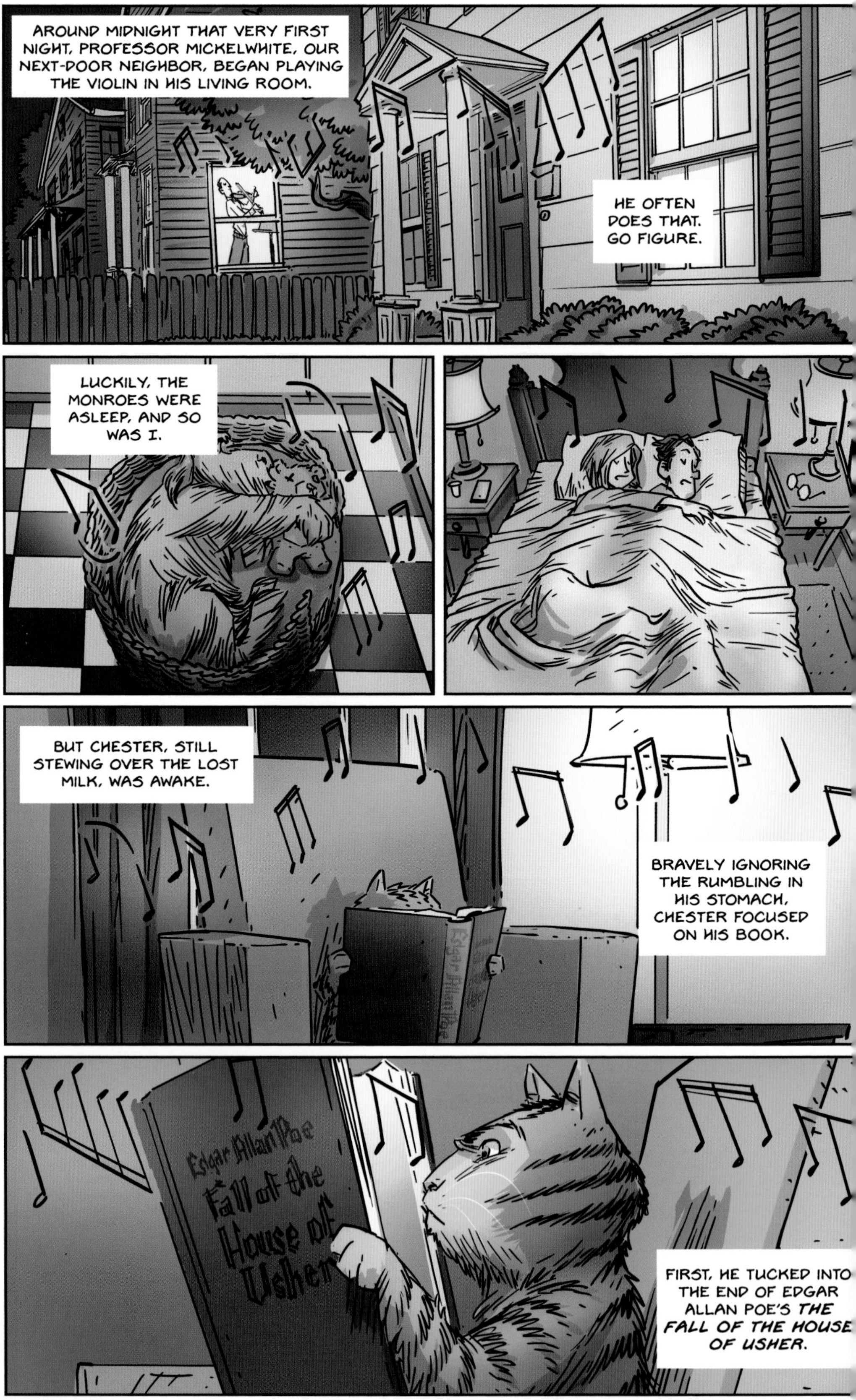
AROUND MIDNIGHT THAT VERY FIRST NIGHT, PROFESSOR MICKELWHITE, OUR NEXT-DOOR NEIGHBOR, BEGAN PLAYING THE VIOLIN IN HIS LIVING ROOM.
HE OFTEN DOES THAT. GO FIGURE.
LUCKILY, THE MONROES WERE ASLEEP, AND SO WAS I.
BUT CHESTER, STILL STEWING OVER THE LOST MILK, WAS AWAKE.
BRAVELY IGNORING THE RUMBLING IN HIS STOMACH, CHESTER FOCUSED ON HIS BOOK.
Edgar Allan Poe
Edgar Allan Poe Fall of the House of Usher
FIRST, HE TUCKED INTO THE END OF EDGAR ALLAN POE'S *THE FALL OF THE HOUSE OF USHER*.

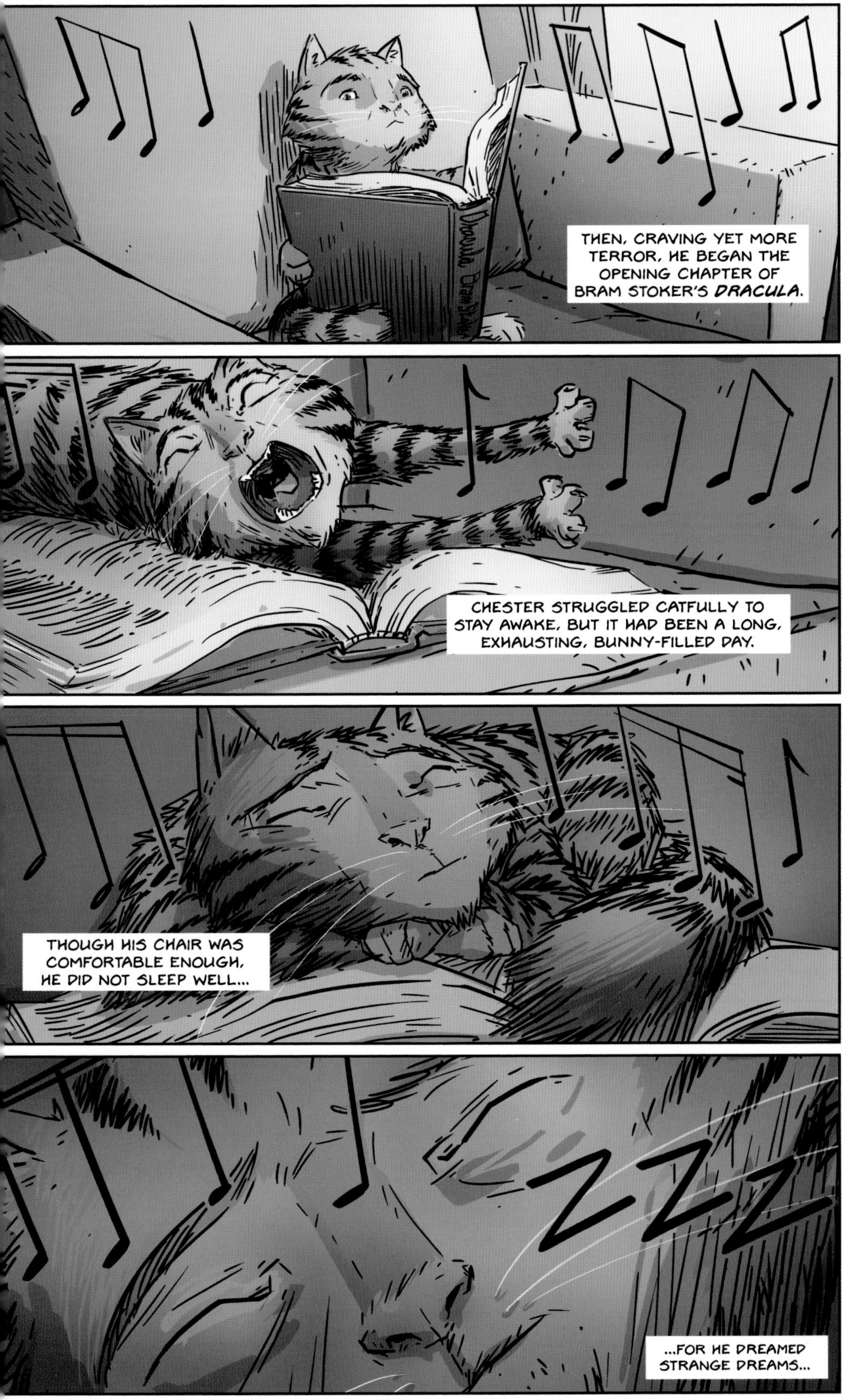
THEN, CRAVING YET MORE TERROR, HE BEGAN THE OPENING CHAPTER OF BRAM STOKER'S *DRACULA*.
CHESTER STRUGGLED CATFULLY TO STAY AWAKE, BUT IT HAD BEEN A LONG, EXHAUSTING, BUNNY-FILLED DAY.
THOUGH HIS CHAIR WAS COMFORTABLE ENOUGH, HE DID NOT SLEEP WELL...
ZZZ
...FOR HE DREAMED STRANGE DREAMS...

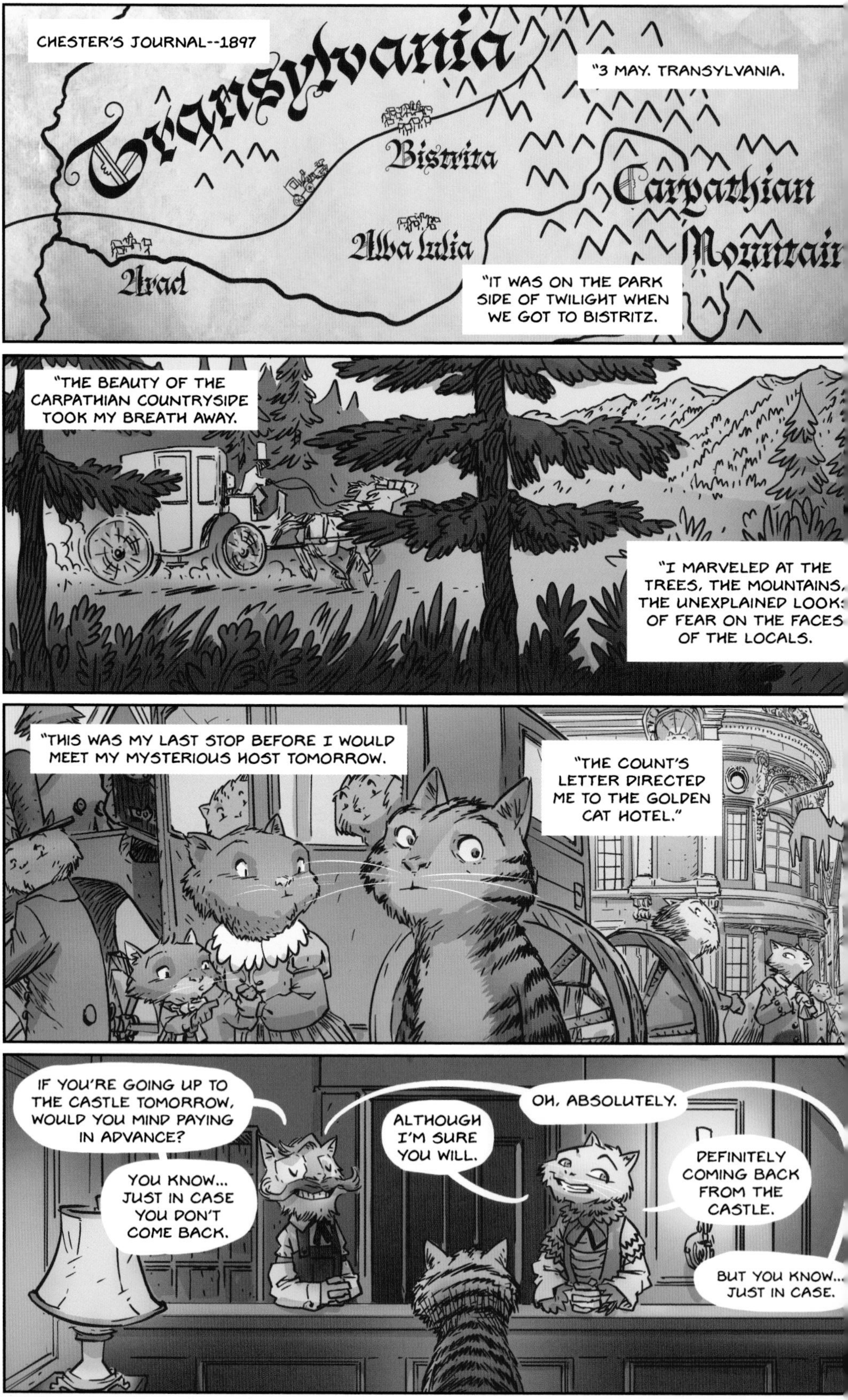
CHESTER'S JOURNAL--1897
Transylvania
Bistrita
Alba Iulia
Arad
Carpathian Mountain
"3 MAY. TRANSYLVANIA.
"IT WAS ON THE DARK SIDE OF TWILIGHT WHEN WE GOT TO BISTRITZ.
"THE BEAUTY OF THE CARPATHIAN COUNTRYSIDE TOOK MY BREATH AWAY.
"I MARVELED AT THE TREES, THE MOUNTAINS, THE UNEXPLAINED LOOK OF FEAR ON THE FACES OF THE LOCALS.
"THIS WAS MY LAST STOP BEFORE I WOULD MEET MY MYSTERIOUS HOST TOMORROW.
"THE COUNT'S LETTER DIRECTED ME TO THE GOLDEN CAT HOTEL."
IF YOU'RE GOING UP TO THE CASTLE TOMORROW, WOULD YOU MIND PAYING IN ADVANCE?
YOU KNOW... JUST IN CASE YOU DON'T COME BACK.
OH, ABSOLUTELY.
ALTHOUGH I'M SURE YOU WILL.
DEFINITELY COMING BACK FROM THE CASTLE.
BUT YOU KNOW... JUST IN CASE.

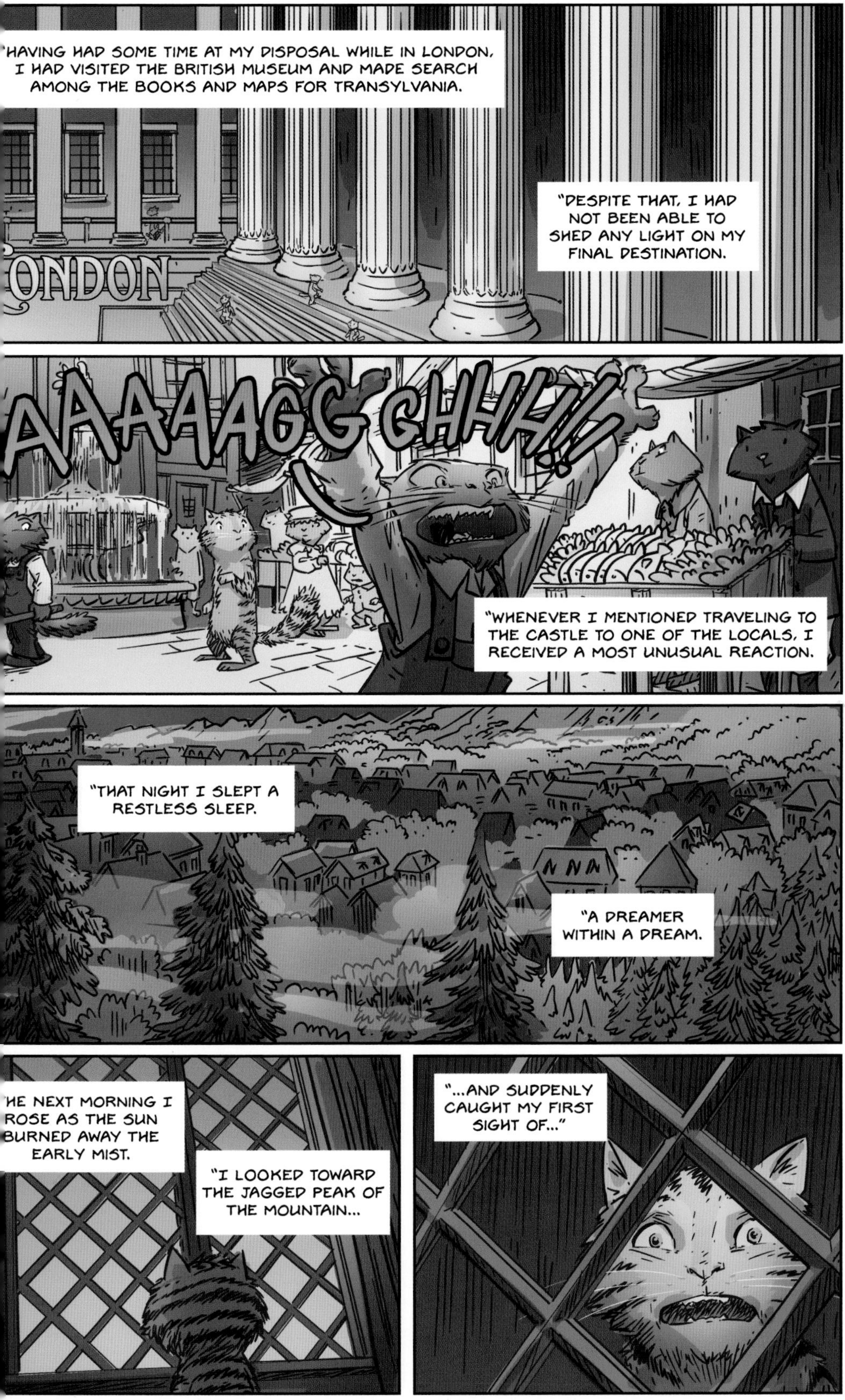
"HAVING HAD SOME TIME AT MY DISPOSAL WHILE IN LONDON, I HAD VISITED THE BRITISH MUSEUM AND MADE SEARCH AMONG THE BOOKS AND MAPS FOR TRANSYLVANIA.
LONDON
"DESPITE THAT, I HAD NOT BEEN ABLE TO SHED ANY LIGHT ON MY FINAL DESTINATION.
AAAAAAGGHHH!!
"WHENEVER I MENTIONED TRAVELING TO THE CASTLE TO ONE OF THE LOCALS, I RECEIVED A MOST UNUSUAL REACTION.
"THAT NIGHT I SLEPT A RESTLESS SLEEP.
"A DREAMER WITHIN A DREAM.
HE NEXT MORNING I ROSE AS THE SUN BURNED AWAY THE EARLY MIST.
"I LOOKED TOWARD THE JAGGED PEAK OF THE MOUNTAIN...
"...AND SUDDENLY CAUGHT MY FIRST SIGHT OF..."

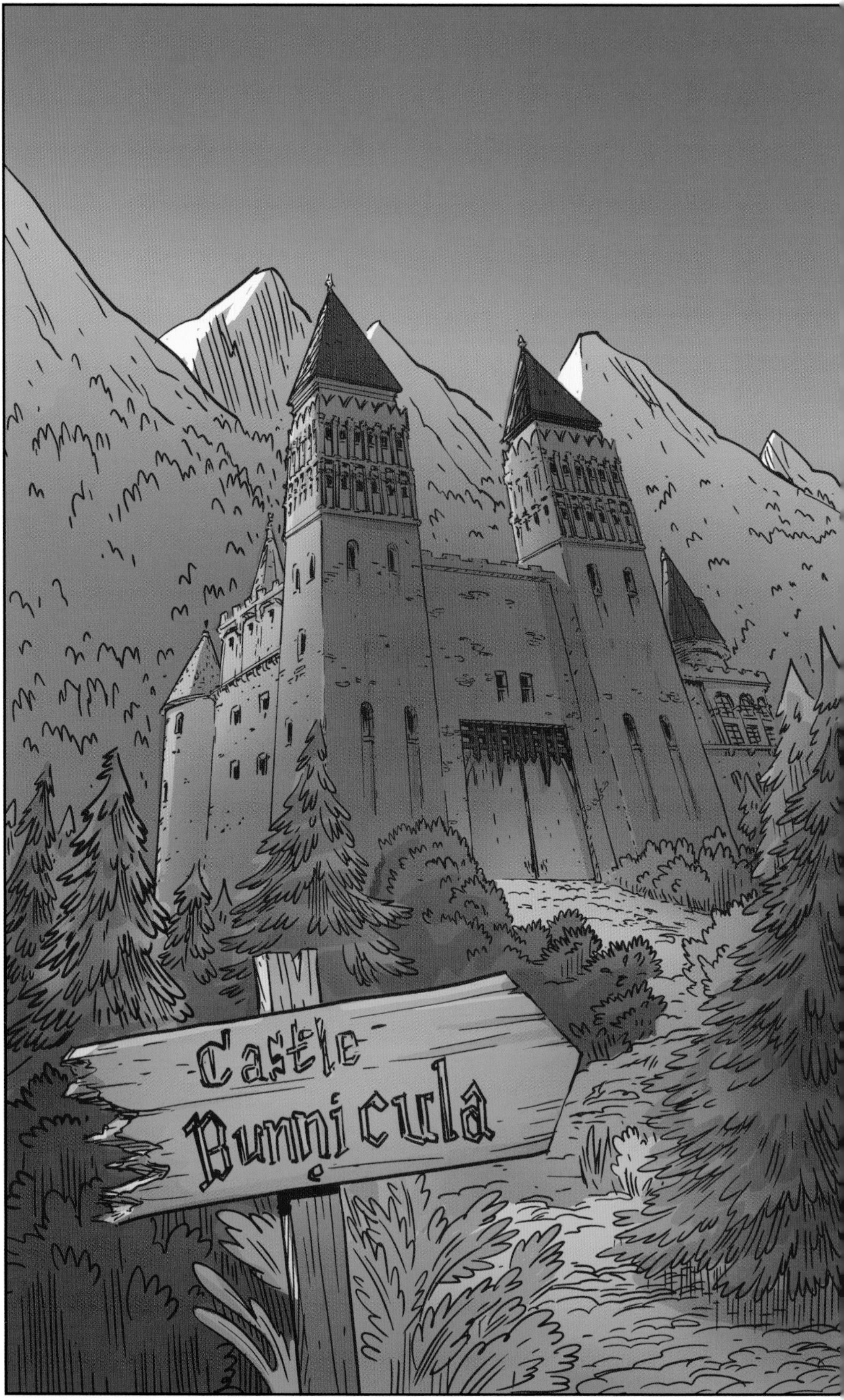
Castle
Bunnicula

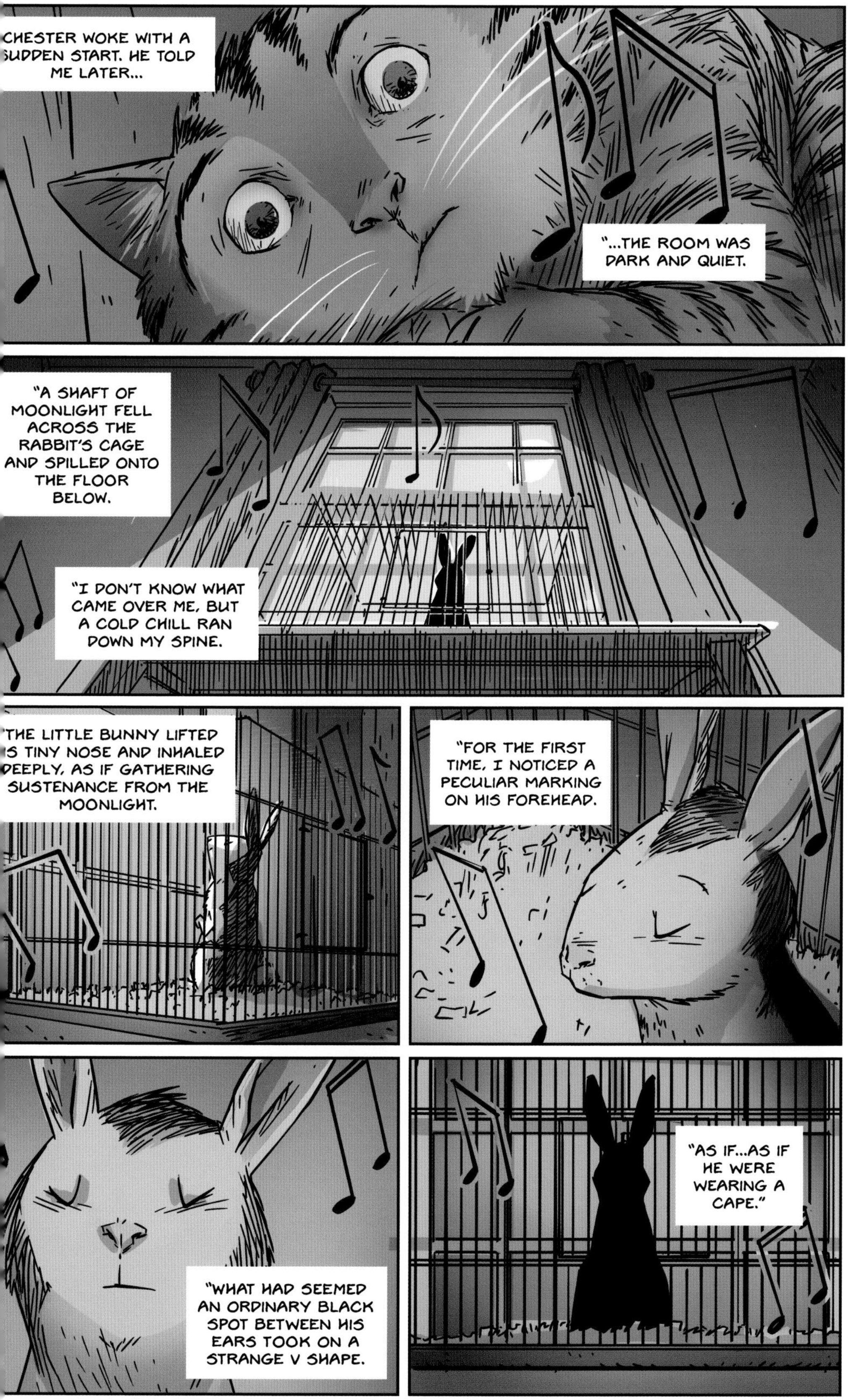
CHESTER WOKE WITH A SUDDEN START. HE TOLD ME LATER...
"...THE ROOM WAS DARK AND QUIET.
"A SHAFT OF MOONLIGHT FELL ACROSS THE RABBIT'S CAGE AND SPILLED ONTO THE FLOOR BELOW.
"I DON'T KNOW WHAT CAME OVER ME, BUT A COLD CHILL RAN DOWN MY SPINE.
"THE LITTLE BUNNY LIFTED HIS TINY NOSE AND INHALED DEEPLY, AS IF GATHERING SUSTENANCE FROM THE MOONLIGHT.
"FOR THE FIRST TIME, I NOTICED A PECULIAR MARKING ON HIS FOREHEAD.
"WHAT HAD SEEMED AN ORDINARY BLACK SPOT BETWEEN HIS EARS TOOK ON A STRANGE V SHAPE.
"AS IF...AS IF HE WERE WEARING A CAPE."

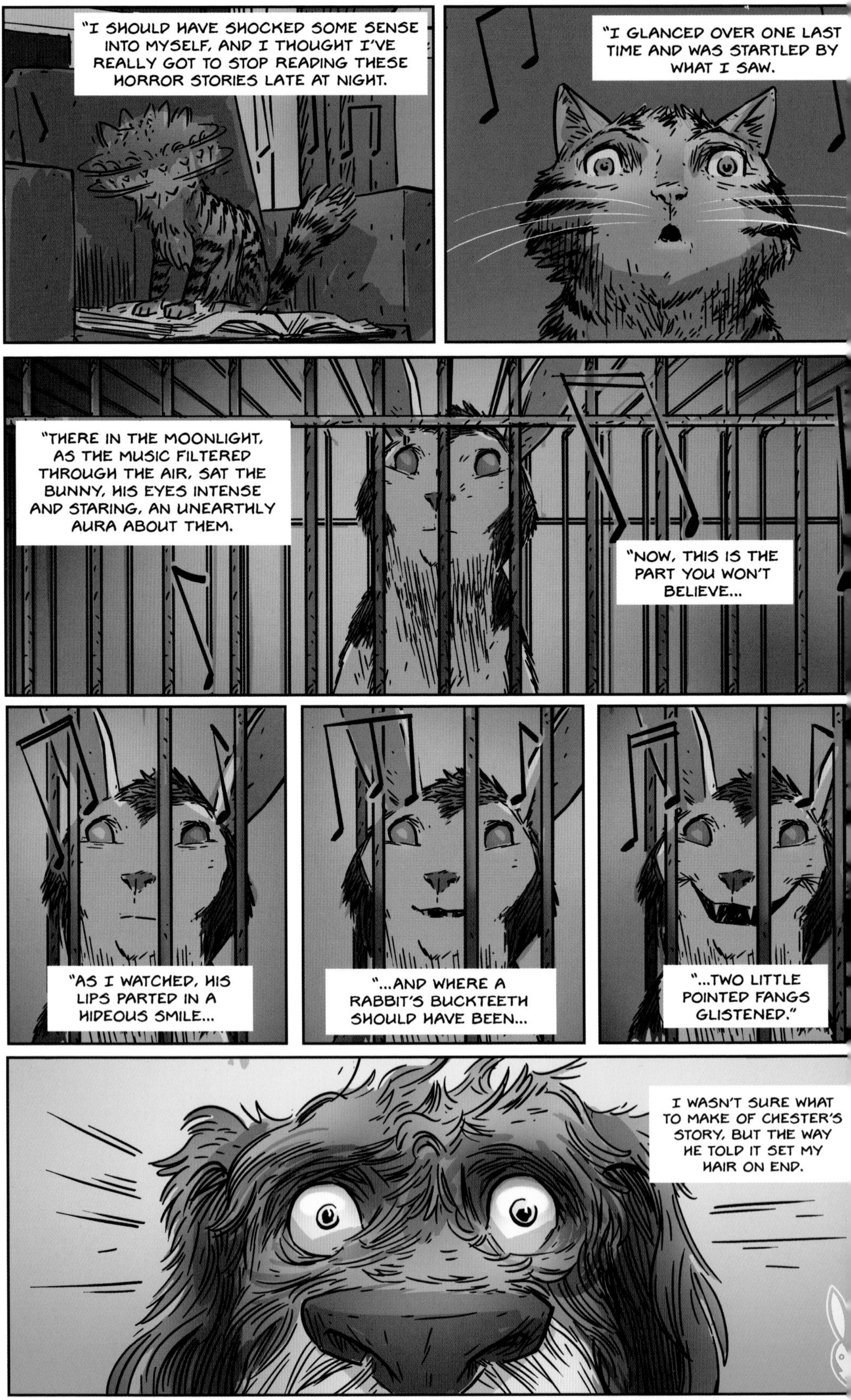
"I SHOULD HAVE SHOCKED SOME SENSE INTO MYSELF, AND I THOUGHT I'VE REALLY GOT TO STOP READING THESE HORROR STORIES LATE AT NIGHT.
"I GLANCED OVER ONE LAST TIME AND WAS STARTLED BY WHAT I SAW.
"THERE IN THE MOONLIGHT, AS THE MUSIC FILTERED THROUGH THE AIR, SAT THE BUNNY, HIS EYES INTENSE AND STARING, AN UNEARTHLY AURA ABOUT THEM.
"NOW, THIS IS THE PART YOU WON'T BELIEVE...
"AS I WATCHED, HIS LIPS PARTED IN A HIDEOUS SMILE...
"...AND WHERE A RABBIT'S BUCKTEETH SHOULD HAVE BEEN...
"...TWO LITTLE POINTED FANGS GLISTENED."
I WASN'T SURE WHAT TO MAKE OF CHESTER'S STORY, BUT THE WAY HE TOLD IT SET MY HAIR ON END.

CHAPTER 3
OME UNUSUAL GOINGS-ON

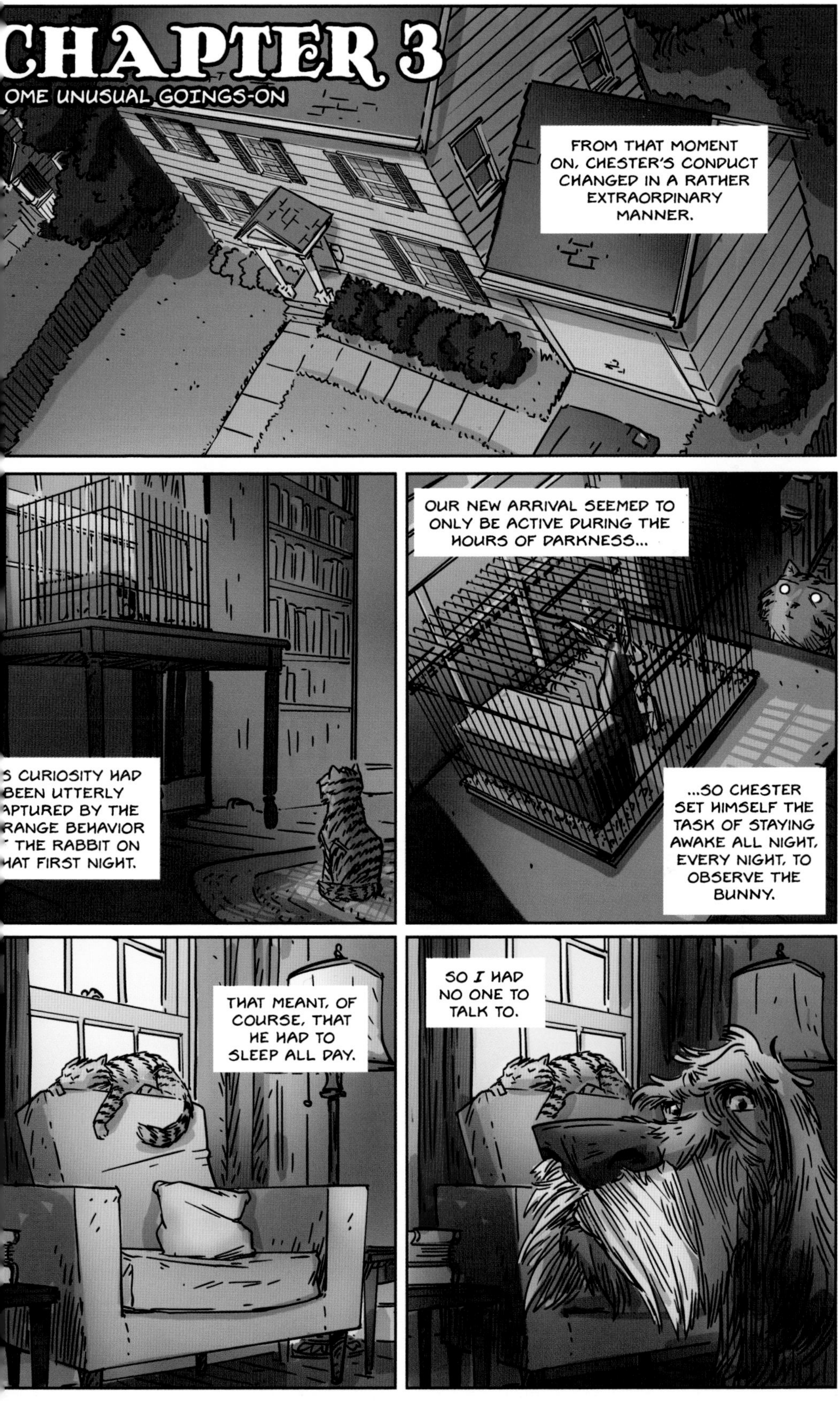
FROM THAT MOMENT ON, CHESTER'S CONDUCT CHANGED IN A RATHER EXTRAORDINARY MANNER.
S CURIOSITY HAD BEEN UTTERLY APTURED BY THE RANGE BEHAVIOR THE RABBIT ON HAT FIRST NIGHT.
OUR NEW ARRIVAL SEEMED TO ONLY BE ACTIVE DURING THE HOURS OF DARKNESS...
...SO CHESTER SET HIMSELF THE TASK OF STAYING AWAKE ALL NIGHT, EVERY NIGHT, TO OBSERVE THE BUNNY.
THAT MEANT, OF COURSE, THAT HE HAD TO SLEEP ALL DAY.
SO I HAD NO ONE TO TALK TO.

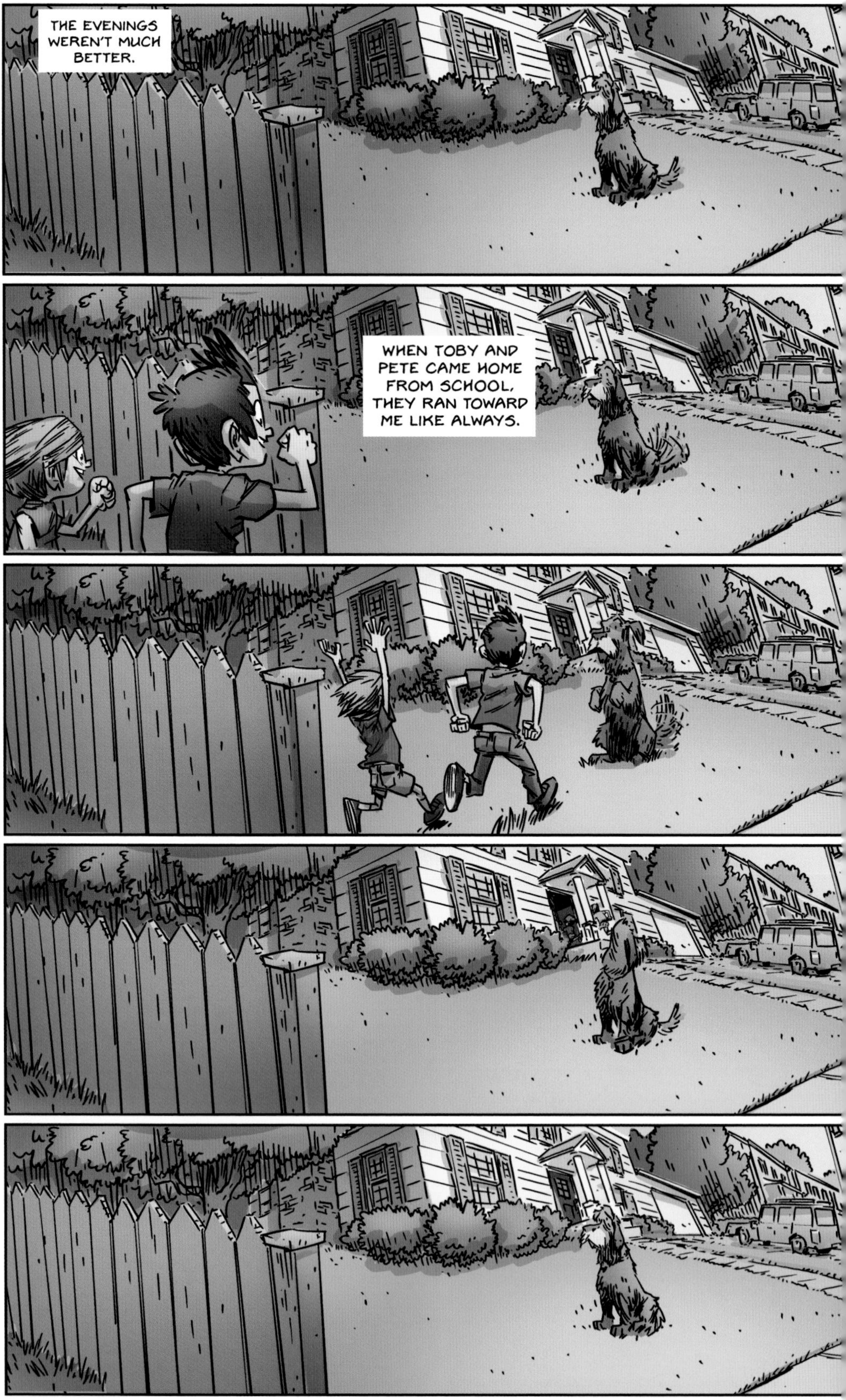
THE EVENINGS WEREN'T MUCH BETTER.
WHEN TOBY AND PETE CAME HOME FROM SCHOOL, THEY RAN TOWARD ME LIKE ALWAYS.

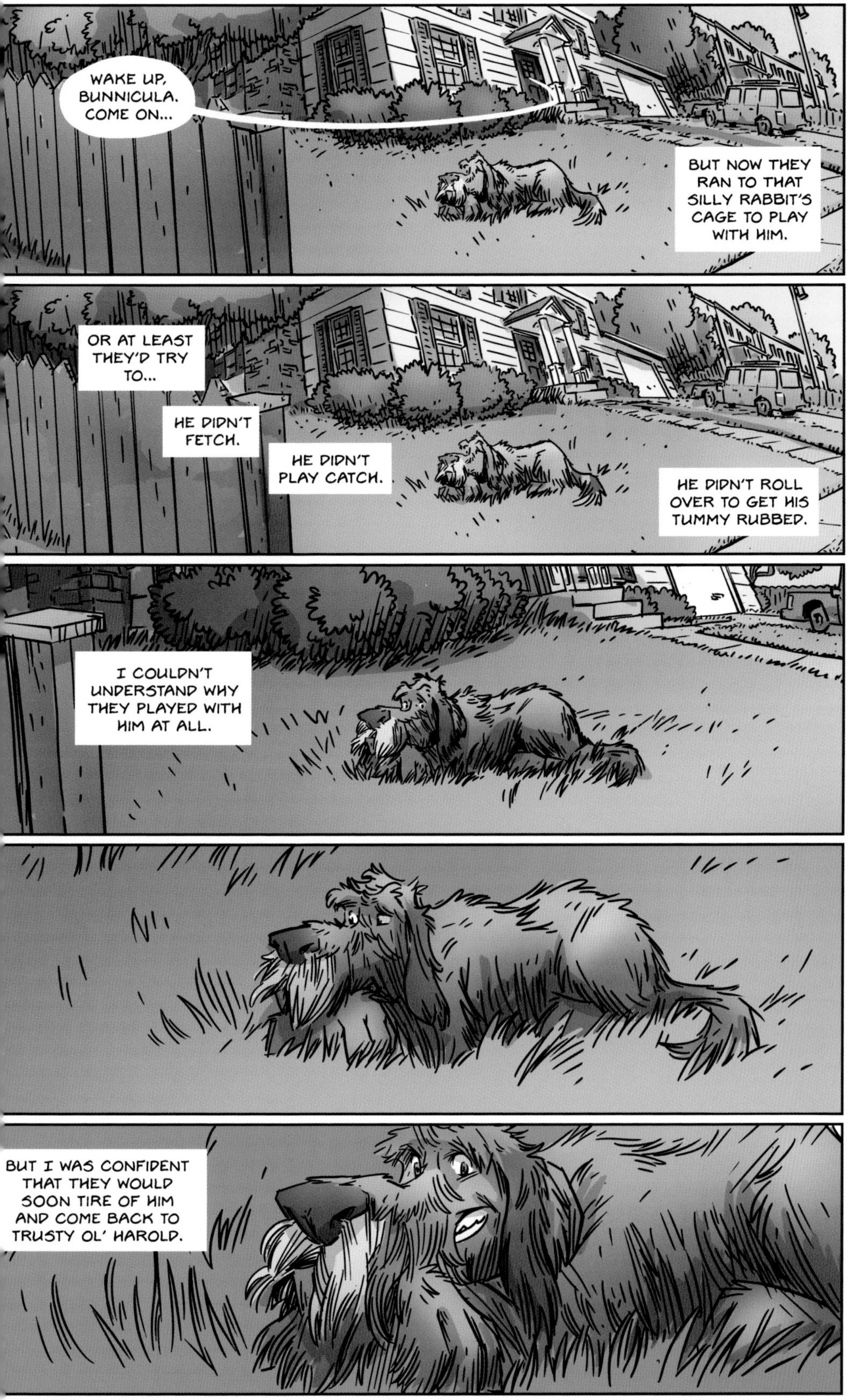
WAKE UP, BUNNICULA. COME ON...
BUT NOW THEY RAN TO THAT SILLY RABBIT'S CAGE TO PLAY WITH HIM.
OR AT LEAST THEY'D TRY TO...
HE DIDN'T FETCH.
HE DIDN'T PLAY CATCH.
HE DIDN'T ROLL OVER TO GET HIS TUMMY RUBBED.
I COULDN'T UNDERSTAND WHY THEY PLAYED WITH HIM AT ALL.
BUT I WAS CONFIDENT THAT THEY WOULD SOON TIRE OF HIM AND COME BACK TO TRUSTY OL' HAROLD.

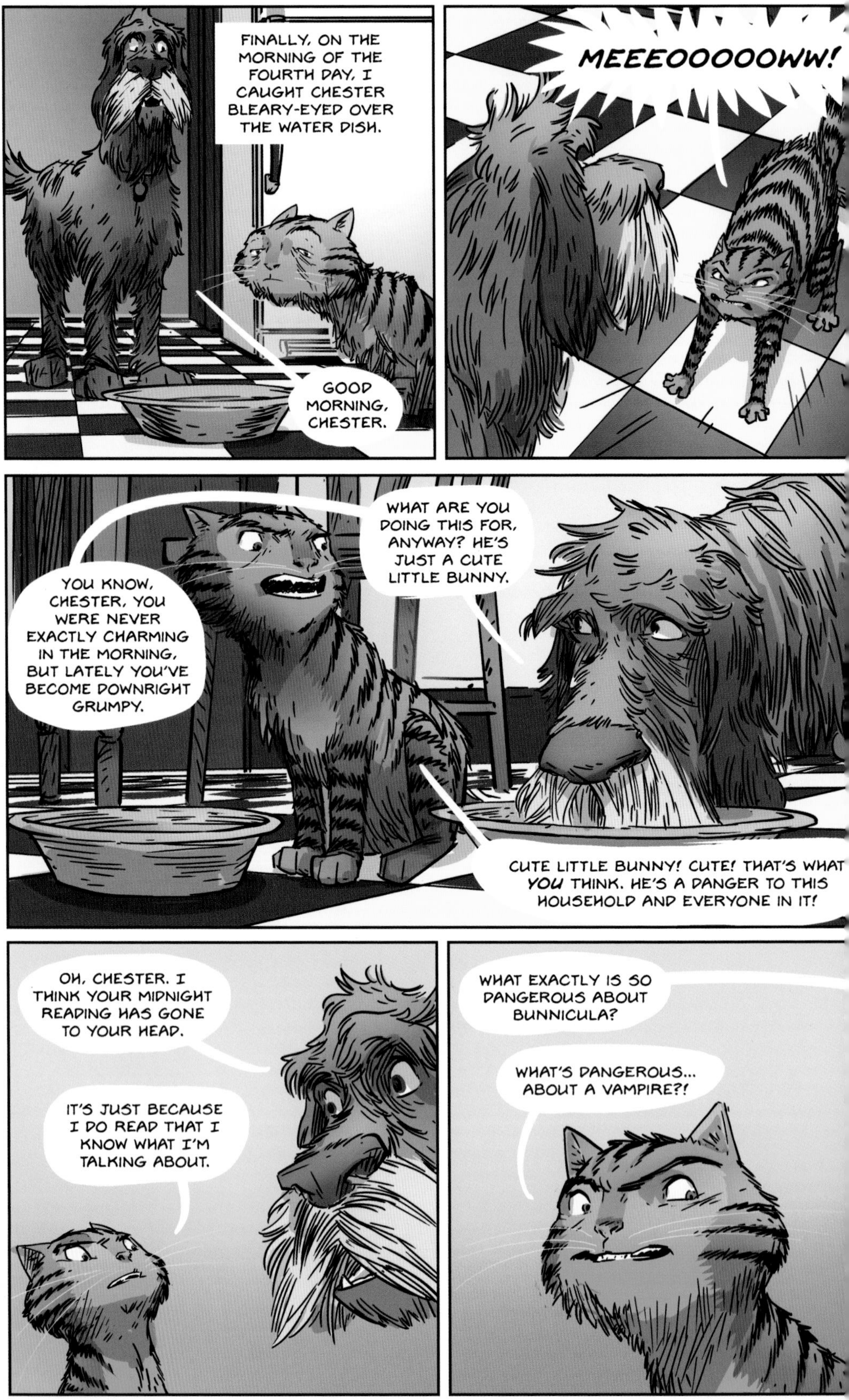

FINALLY, ON THE MORNING OF THE FOURTH DAY, I CAUGHT CHESTER BLEARY-EYED OVER THE WATER DISH.
GOOD MORNING, CHESTER.
MEEEOOOOOWW!
YOU KNOW, CHESTER, YOU WERE NEVER EXACTLY CHARMING IN THE MORNING, BUT LATELY YOU'VE BECOME DOWNRIGHT GRUMPY.
WHAT ARE YOU DOING THIS FOR, ANYWAY? HE'S JUST A CUTE LITTLE BUNNY.
CUTE LITTLE BUNNY! CUTE! THAT'S WHAT *YOU* THINK. HE'S A DANGER TO THIS HOUSEHOLD AND EVERYONE IN IT!
OH, CHESTER. I THINK YOUR MIDNIGHT READING HAS GONE TO YOUR HEAD.
IT'S JUST BECAUSE I DO READ THAT I KNOW WHAT I'M TALKING ABOUT.
WHAT EXACTLY IS SO DANGEROUS ABOUT BUNNICULA?
WHAT'S DANGEROUS... ABOUT A VAMPIRE?!

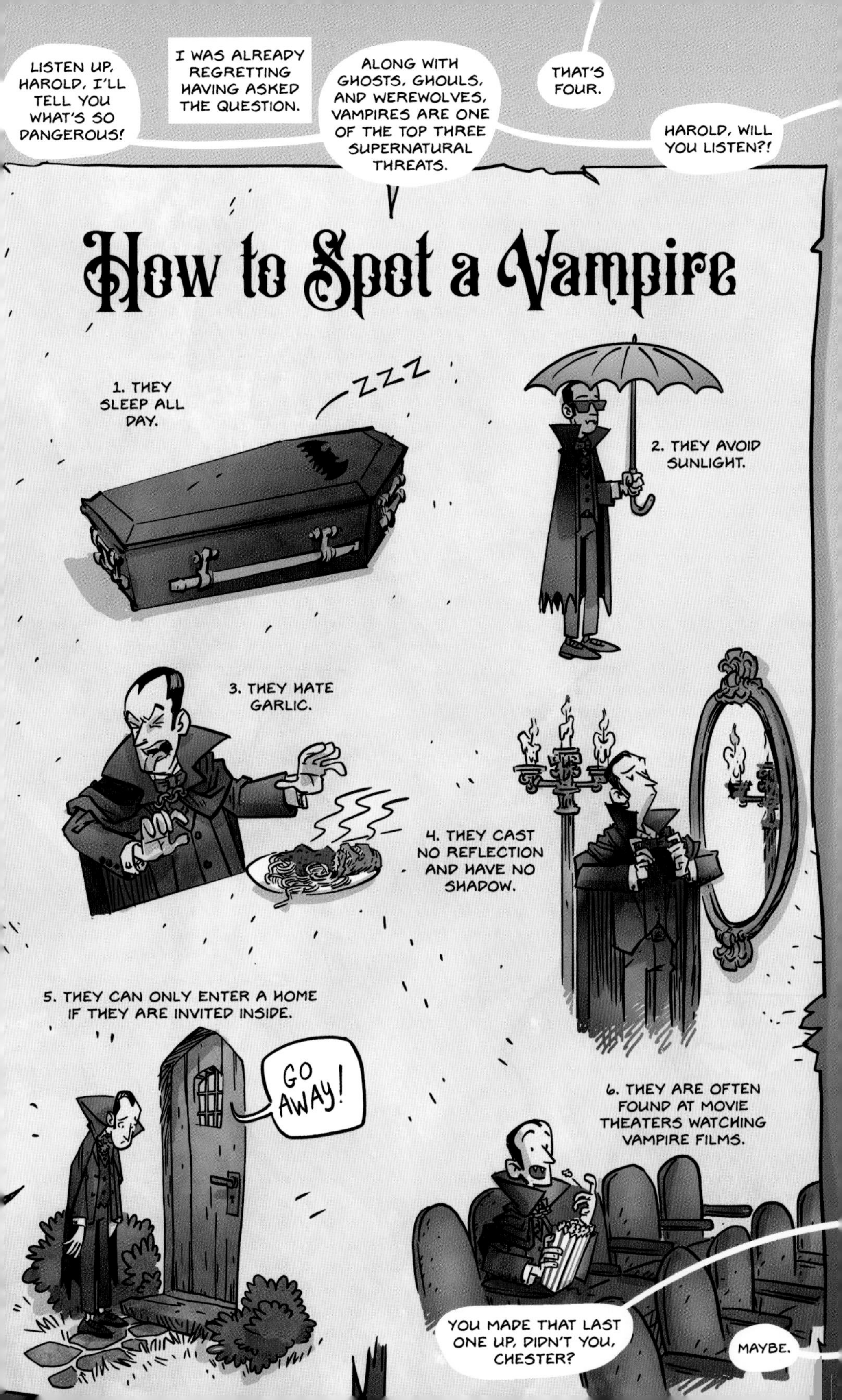

LISTEN UP, HAROLD, I'LL TELL YOU WHAT'S SO DANGEROUS!
I WAS ALREADY REGRETTING HAVING ASKED THE QUESTION.
ALONG WITH GHOSTS, GHOULS, AND WEREWOLVES, VAMPIRES ARE ONE OF THE TOP THREE SUPERNATURAL THREATS.
THAT'S FOUR.
HAROLD, WILL YOU LISTEN?!
How to Spot a Vampire
1. THEY SLEEP ALL DAY.
ZZZ
2. THEY AVOID SUNLIGHT.
3. THEY HATE GARLIC.
4. THEY CAST NO REFLECTION AND HAVE NO SHADOW.
5. THEY CAN ONLY ENTER A HOME IF THEY ARE INVITED INSIDE.
GO AWAY!
6. THEY ARE OFTEN FOUND AT MOVIE THEATERS WATCHING VAMPIRE FILMS.
YOU MADE THAT LAST ONE UP, DIDN'T YOU, CHESTER?
MAYBE.

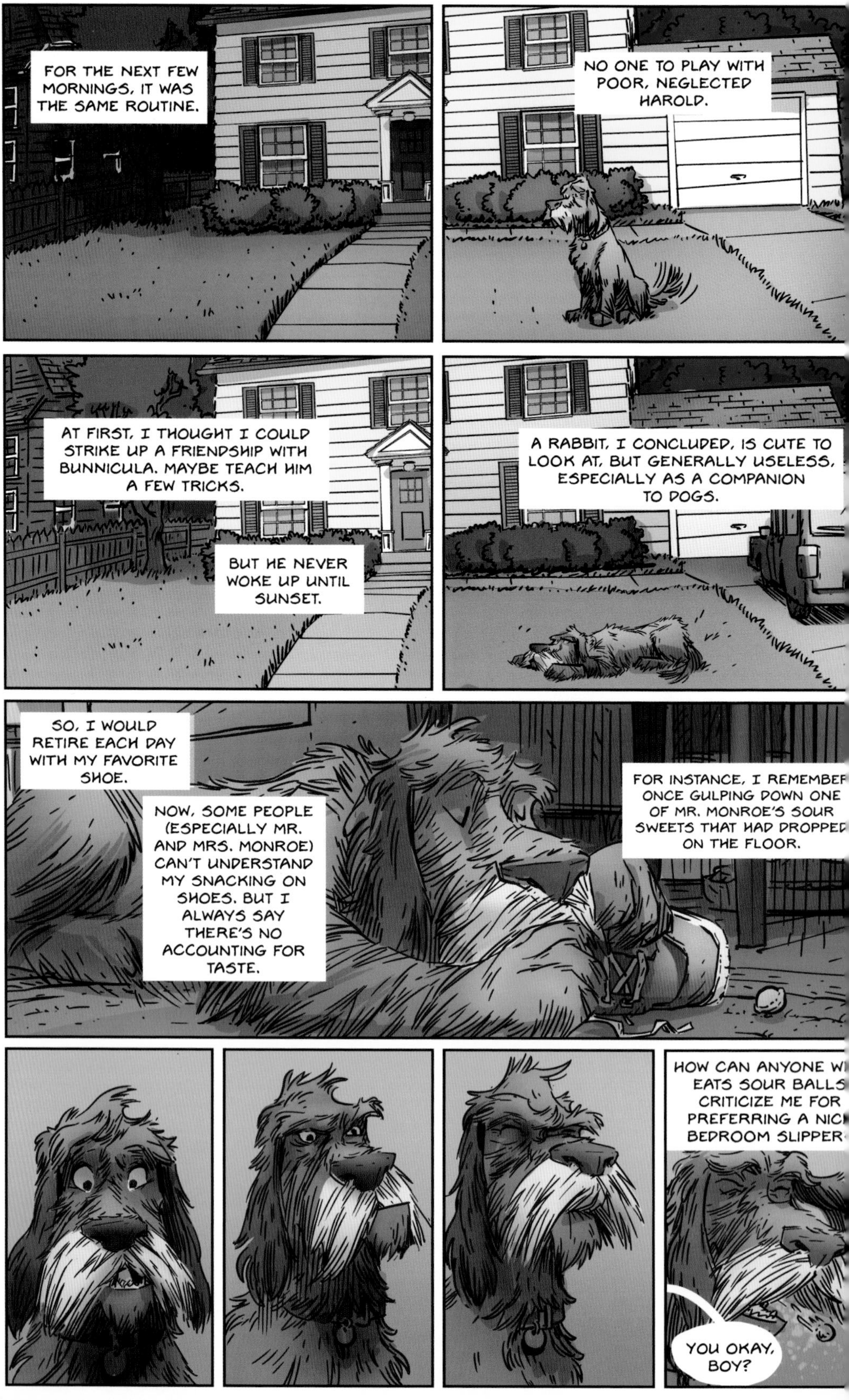

FOR THE NEXT FEW MORNINGS, IT WAS THE SAME ROUTINE.
NO ONE TO PLAY WITH POOR, NEGLECTED HAROLD.
AT FIRST, I THOUGHT I COULD STRIKE UP A FRIENDSHIP WITH BUNNICULA. MAYBE TEACH HIM A FEW TRICKS.
BUT HE NEVER WOKE UP UNTIL SUNSET.
A RABBIT, I CONCLUDED, IS CUTE TO LOOK AT, BUT GENERALLY USELESS, ESPECIALLY AS A COMPANION TO DOGS.
SO, I WOULD RETIRE EACH DAY WITH MY FAVORITE SHOE.
NOW, SOME PEOPLE (ESPECIALLY MR. AND MRS. MONROE) CAN'T UNDERSTAND MY SNACKING ON SHOES. BUT I ALWAYS SAY THERE'S NO ACCOUNTING FOR TASTE.
FOR INSTANCE, I REMEMBER ONCE GULPING DOWN ONE OF MR. MONROE'S SOUR SWEETS THAT HAD DROPPED ON THE FLOOR.
HOW CAN ANYONE W EATS SOUR BALLS CRITICIZE ME FOR PREFERRING A NIC BEDROOM SLIPPER
YOU OKAY, BOY?

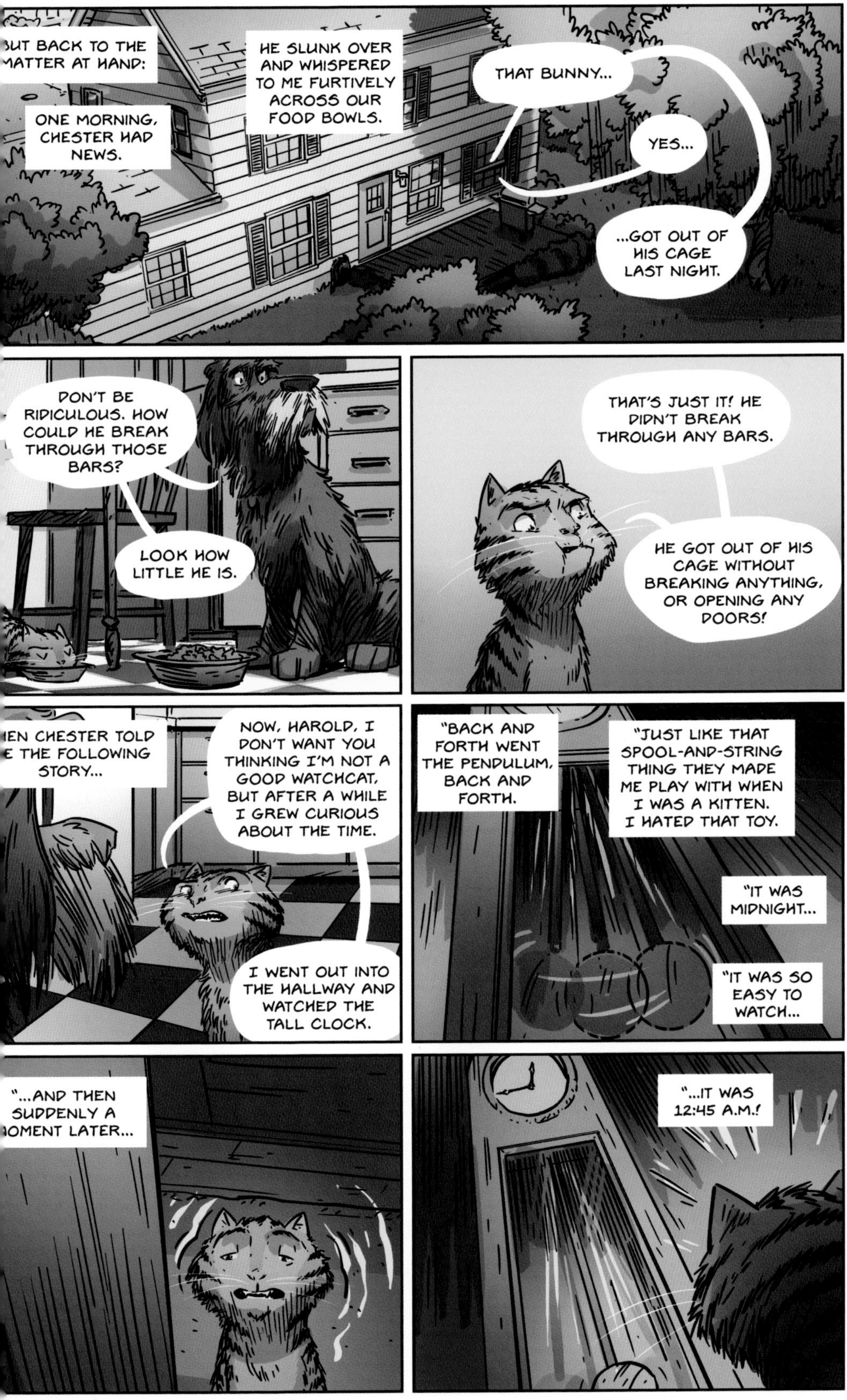
UT BACK TO THE
ATTER AT HAND:
ONE MORNING, CHESTER HAD NEWS.
HE SLUNK OVER AND WHISPERED TO ME FURTIVELY ACROSS OUR FOOD BOWLS.
THAT BUNNY...
YES...
...GOT OUT OF HIS CAGE LAST NIGHT.
DON'T BE RIDICULOUS. HOW COULD HE BREAK THROUGH THOSE BARS?
LOOK HOW LITTLE HE IS.
THAT'S JUST IT! HE DIDN'T BREAK THROUGH ANY BARS.
HE GOT OUT OF HIS CAGE WITHOUT BREAKING ANYTHING, OR OPENING ANY DOORS!
EN CHESTER TOLD
E THE FOLLOWING STORY...
NOW, HAROLD, I DON'T WANT YOU THINKING I'M NOT A GOOD WATCHCAT, BUT AFTER A WHILE I GREW CURIOUS ABOUT THE TIME.
I WENT OUT INTO THE HALLWAY AND WATCHED THE TALL CLOCK.
"BACK AND FORTH WENT THE PENDULUM, BACK AND FORTH.
"JUST LIKE THAT SPOOL-AND-STRING THING THEY MADE ME PLAY WITH WHEN I WAS A KITTEN. I HATED THAT TOY.
"IT WAS MIDNIGHT...
"IT WAS SO EASY TO WATCH...
"...AND THEN SUDDENLY A
OMENT LATER...
"...IT WAS 12:45 A.M.!

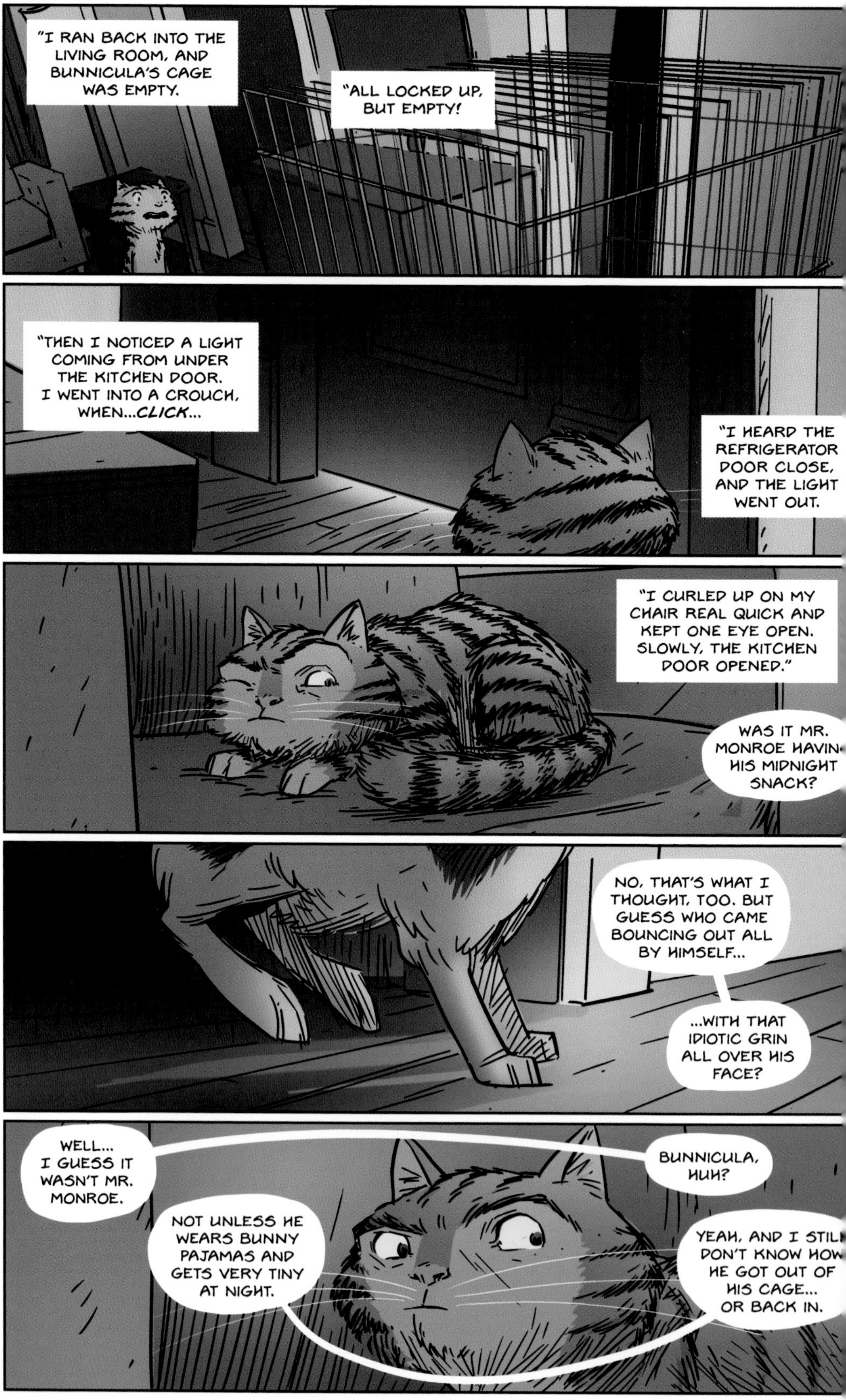
"I RAN BACK INTO THE LIVING ROOM, AND BUNNICULA'S CAGE WAS EMPTY.
"ALL LOCKED UP, BUT EMPTY!
"THEN I NOTICED A LIGHT COMING FROM UNDER THE KITCHEN DOOR. I WENT INTO A CROUCH, WHEN...*CLICK*...
"I HEARD THE REFRIGERATOR DOOR CLOSE, AND THE LIGHT WENT OUT.
"I CURLED UP ON MY CHAIR REAL QUICK AND KEPT ONE EYE OPEN. SLOWLY, THE KITCHEN DOOR OPENED."
WAS IT MR. MONROE HAVIN HIS MIDNIGHT SNACK?
NO, THAT'S WHAT I THOUGHT, TOO. BUT GUESS WHO CAME BOUNCING OUT ALL BY HIMSELF...
...WITH THAT IDIOTIC GRIN ALL OVER HIS FACE?
WELL... I GUESS IT WASN'T MR. MONROE.
NOT UNLESS HE WEARS BUNNY PAJAMAS AND GETS VERY TINY AT NIGHT.
BUNNICULA, HUH?
YEAH, AND I STIL DON'T KNOW HOW HE GOT OUT OF HIS CAGE... OR BACK IN.

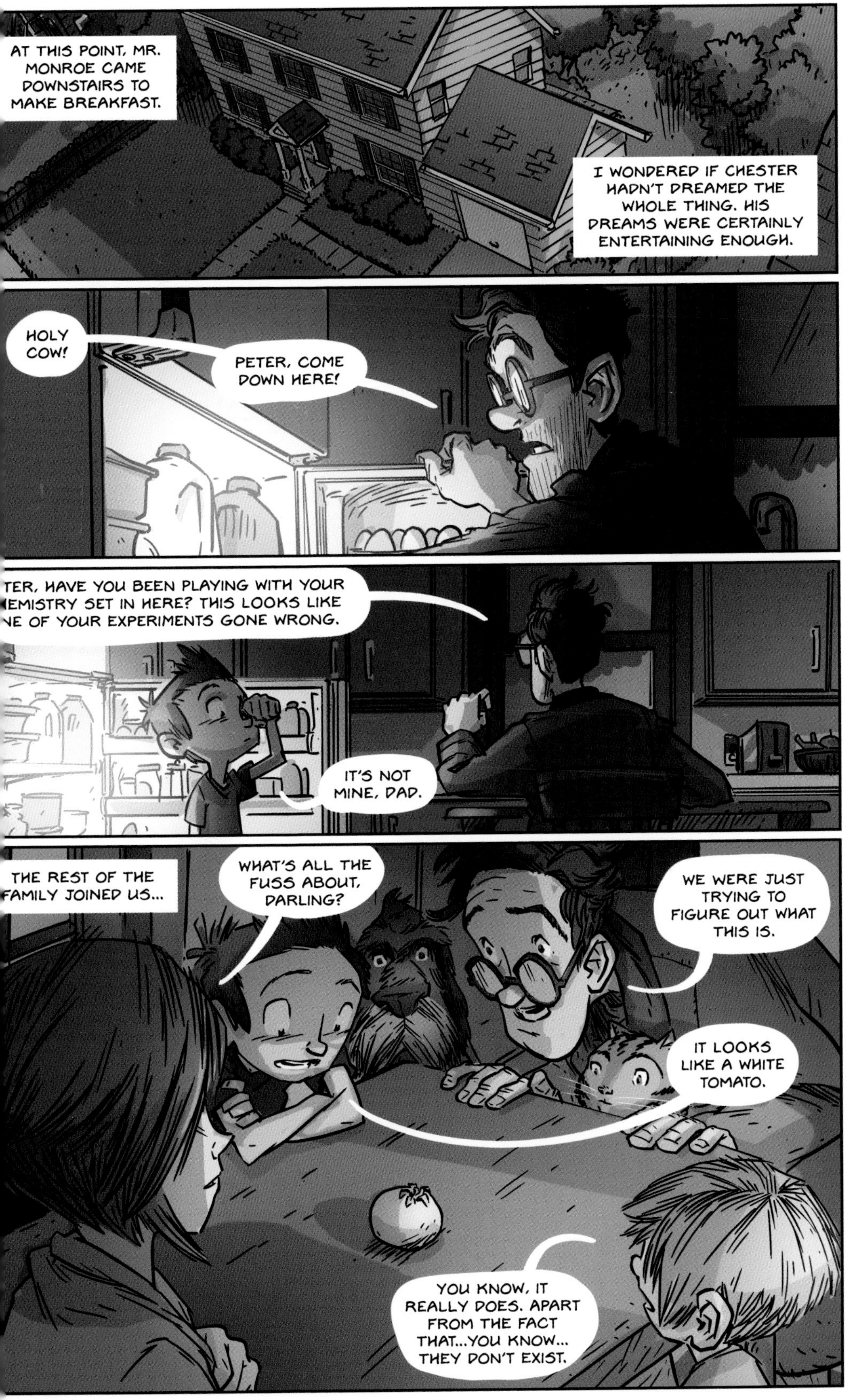
AT THIS POINT, MR. MONROE CAME DOWNSTAIRS TO MAKE BREAKFAST.
I WONDERED IF CHESTER HADN'T DREAMED THE WHOLE THING. HIS DREAMS WERE CERTAINLY ENTERTAINING ENOUGH.
HOLY COW!
PETER, COME DOWN HERE!
TER, HAVE YOU BEEN PLAYING WITH YOUR EMISTRY SET IN HERE? THIS LOOKS LIKE NE OF YOUR EXPERIMENTS GONE WRONG.
IT'S NOT MINE, DAD.
THE REST OF THE FAMILY JOINED US...
WHAT'S ALL THE FUSS ABOUT, DARLING?
WE WERE JUST TRYING TO FIGURE OUT WHAT THIS IS.
IT LOOKS LIKE A WHITE TOMATO.
YOU KNOW, IT REALLY DOES. APART FROM THE FACT THAT...YOU KNOW... THEY DON'T EXIST.

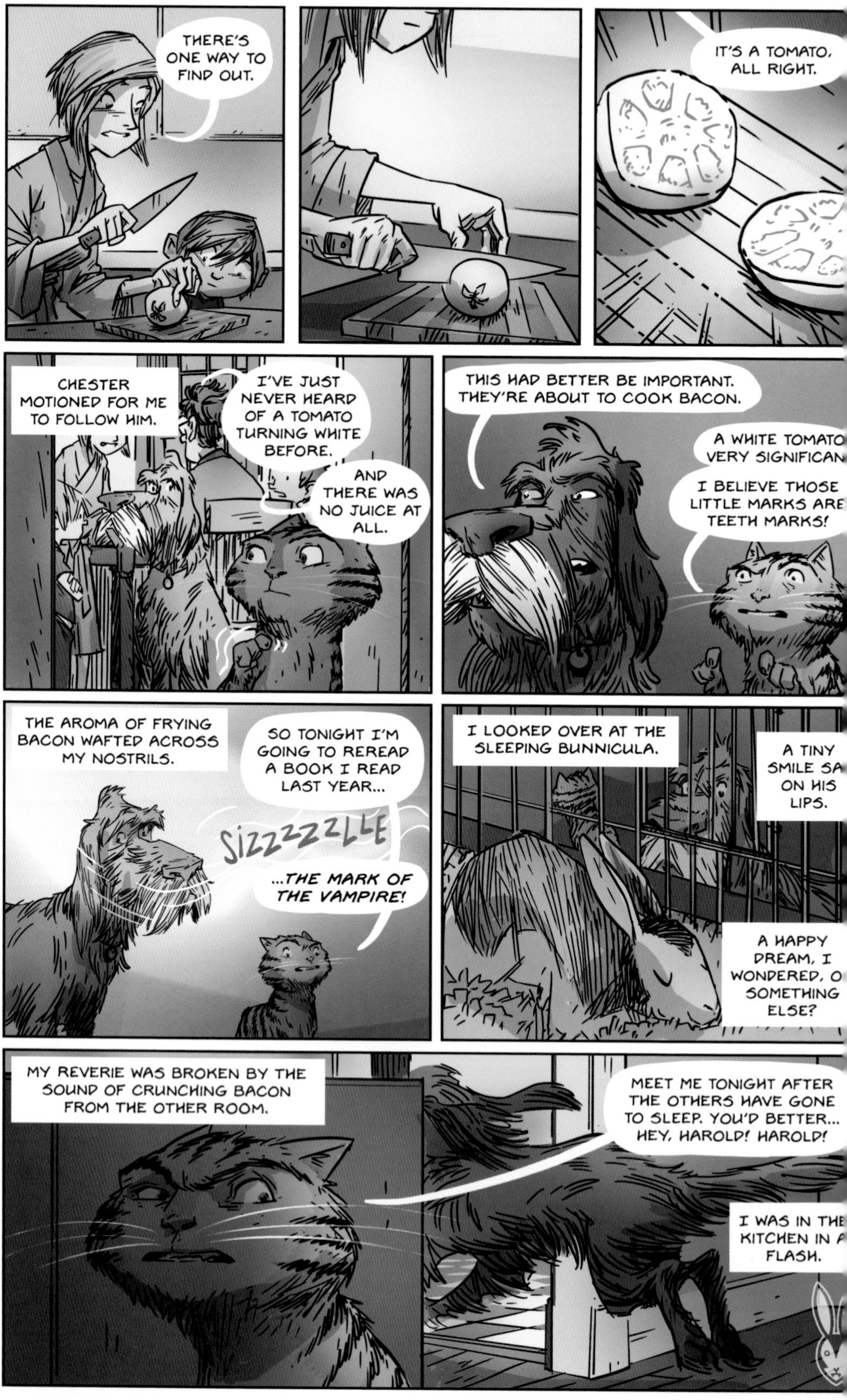
THERE'S ONE WAY TO FIND OUT.
IT'S A TOMATO, ALL RIGHT.
CHESTER MOTIONED FOR ME TO FOLLOW HIM.
I'VE JUST NEVER HEARD OF A TOMATO TURNING WHITE BEFORE.
AND THERE WAS NO JUICE AT ALL.
THIS HAD BETTER BE IMPORTANT. THEY'RE ABOUT TO COOK BACON.
A WHITE TOMATO
VERY SIGNIFICAN
I BELIEVE THOSE LITTLE MARKS ARE TEETH MARKS!
THE AROMA OF FRYING BACON WAFTED ACROSS MY NOSTRILS.
SO TONIGHT I'M GOING TO REREAD A BOOK I READ LAST YEAR...
SIZZZZZLLE
...THE MARK OF THE VAMPIRE!
I LOOKED OVER AT THE SLEEPING BUNNICULA.
A TINY SMILE SA ON HIS LIPS.
A HAPPY DREAM, I WONDERED, O SOMETHING ELSE?
MY REVERIE WAS BROKEN BY THE SOUND OF CRUNCHING BACON FROM THE OTHER ROOM.
MEET ME TONIGHT AFTER THE OTHERS HAVE GONE TO SLEEP. YOU'D BETTER... HEY, HAROLD! HAROLD!
I WAS IN THE KITCHEN IN A FLASH.

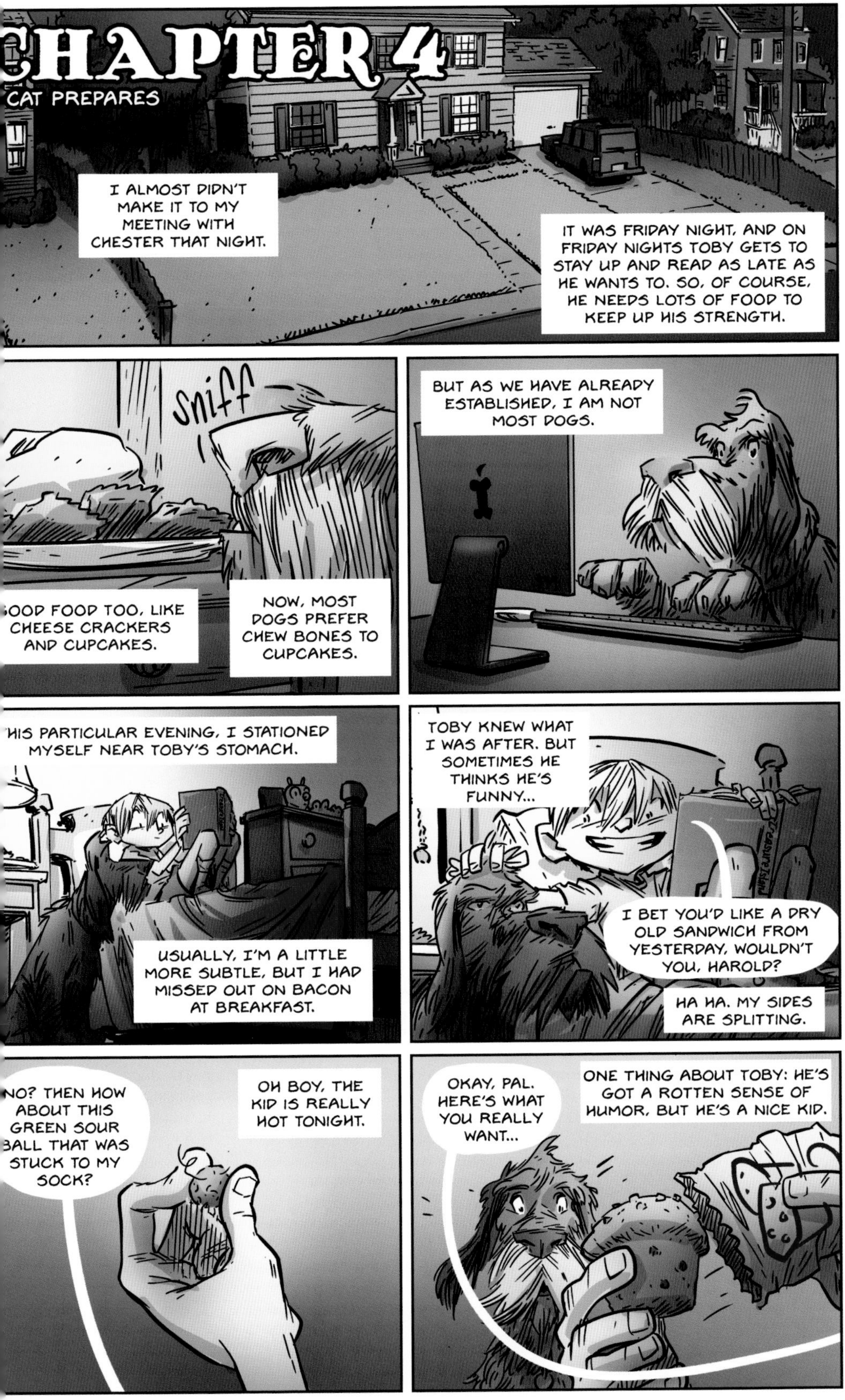
CHAPTER 4
CAT PREPARES
I ALMOST DIDN'T MAKE IT TO MY MEETING WITH CHESTER THAT NIGHT.
IT WAS FRIDAY NIGHT, AND ON FRIDAY NIGHTS TOBY GETS TO STAY UP AND READ AS LATE AS HE WANTS TO. SO, OF COURSE, HE NEEDS LOTS OF FOOD TO KEEP UP HIS STRENGTH.
SNIFF
OOD FOOD TOO, LIKE CHEESE CRACKERS AND CUPCAKES.
NOW, MOST DOGS PREFER CHEW BONES TO CUPCAKES.
BUT AS WE HAVE ALREADY ESTABLISHED, I AM NOT MOST DOGS.
HIS PARTICULAR EVENING, I STATIONED MYSELF NEAR TOBY'S STOMACH.
USUALLY, I'M A LITTLE MORE SUBTLE, BUT I HAD MISSED OUT ON BACON AT BREAKFAST.
TOBY KNEW WHAT I WAS AFTER. BUT SOMETIMES HE THINKS HE'S FUNNY...
Treasure Island
I BET YOU'D LIKE A DRY OLD SANDWICH FROM YESTERDAY, WOULDN'T YOU, HAROLD?
HA HA. MY SIDES ARE SPLITTING.
NO? THEN HOW ABOUT THIS GREEN SOUR BALL THAT WAS STUCK TO MY SOCK?
OH BOY, THE KID IS REALLY HOT TONIGHT.
OKAY, PAL. HERE'S WHAT YOU REALLY WANT...
ONE THING ABOUT TOBY: HE'S GOT A ROTTEN SENSE OF HUMOR, BUT HE'S A NICE KID.

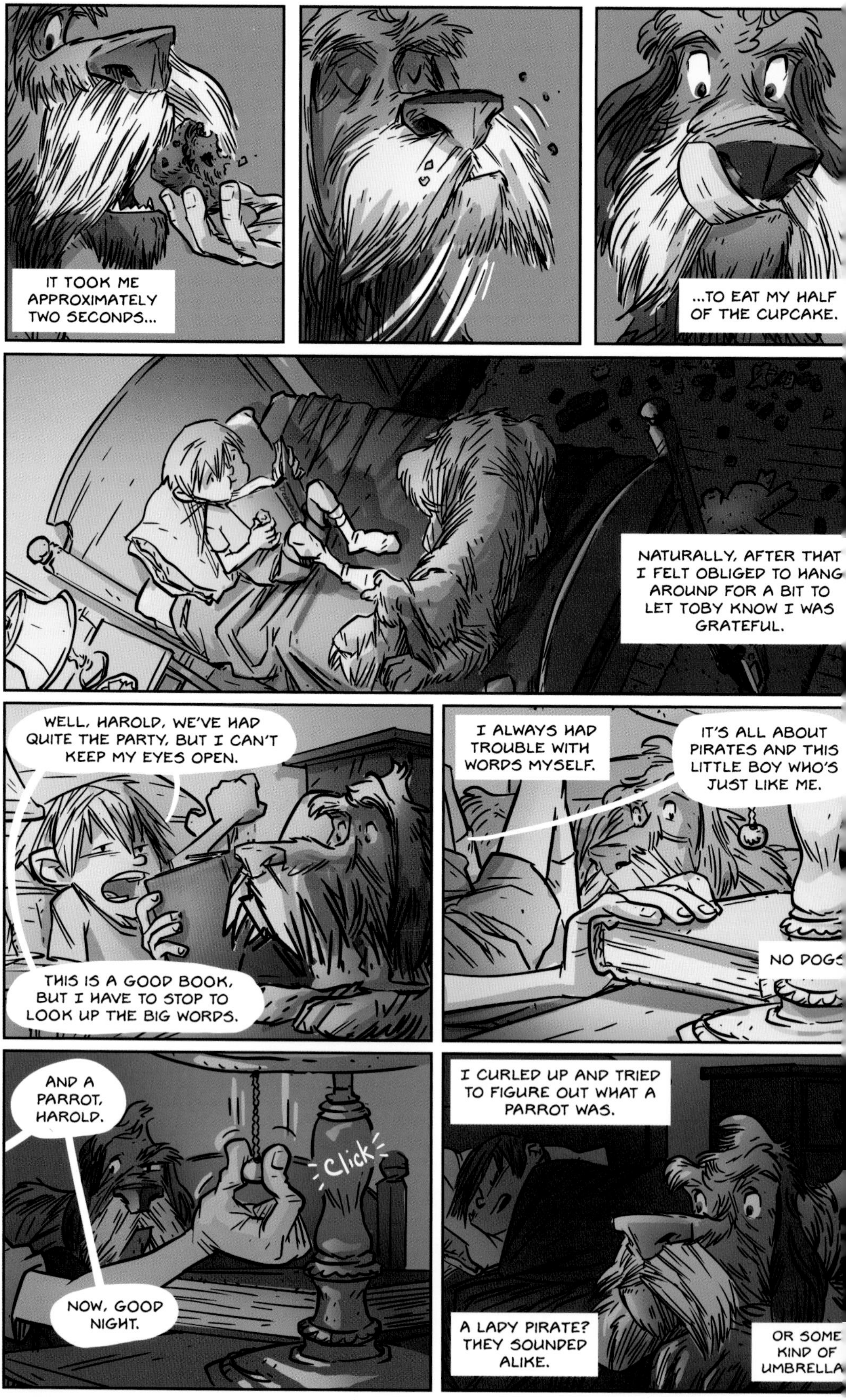
IT TOOK ME APPROXIMATELY TWO SECONDS...
...TO EAT MY HALF OF THE CUPCAKE.
NATURALLY, AFTER THAT I FELT OBLIGED TO HANG AROUND FOR A BIT TO LET TOBY KNOW I WAS GRATEFUL.
WELL, HAROLD, WE'VE HAD QUITE THE PARTY, BUT I CAN'T KEEP MY EYES OPEN.
THIS IS A GOOD BOOK, BUT I HAVE TO STOP TO LOOK UP THE BIG WORDS.
I ALWAYS HAD TROUBLE WITH WORDS MYSELF.
IT'S ALL ABOUT PIRATES AND THIS LITTLE BOY WHO'S JUST LIKE ME.
NO DOGS
AND A PARROT, HAROLD.
CLICK
NOW, GOOD NIGHT.
I CURLED UP AND TRIED TO FIGURE OUT WHAT A PARROT WAS.
A LADY PIRATE? THEY SOUNDED ALIKE.
OR SOME KIND OF UMBRELLA

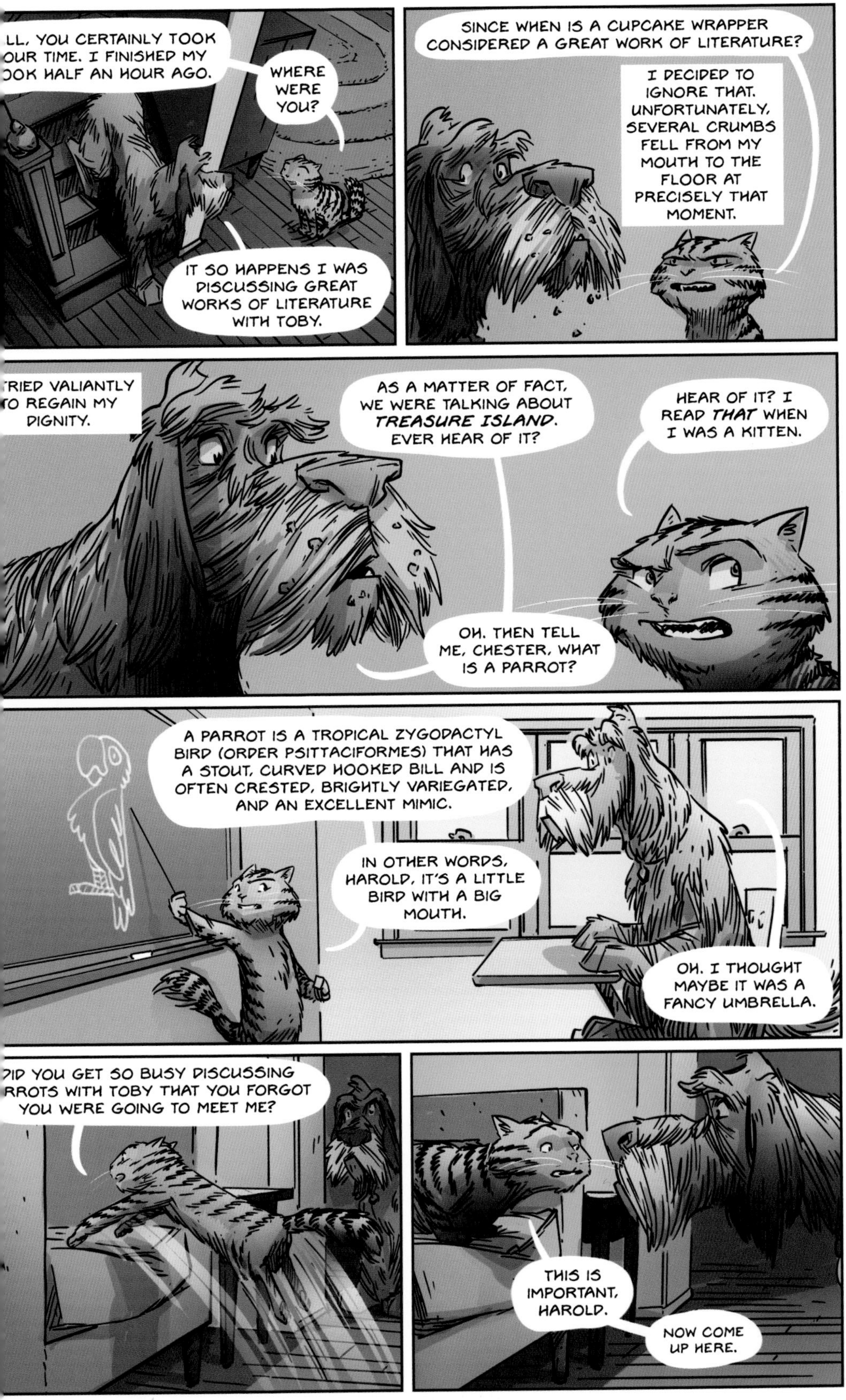
LL, YOU CERTAINLY TOOK OUR TIME. I FINISHED MY OOK HALF AN HOUR AGO.
WHERE WERE YOU?
IT SO HAPPENS I WAS DISCUSSING GREAT WORKS OF LITERATURE WITH TOBY.
SINCE WHEN IS A CUPCAKE WRAPPER CONSIDERED A GREAT WORK OF LITERATURE?
I DECIDED TO IGNORE THAT. UNFORTUNATELY, SEVERAL CRUMBS FELL FROM MY MOUTH TO THE FLOOR AT PRECISELY THAT MOMENT.
TRIED VALIANTLY O REGAIN MY DIGNITY.
AS A MATTER OF FACT, WE WERE TALKING ABOUT *TREASURE ISLAND*. EVER HEAR OF IT?
HEAR OF IT? I READ *THAT* WHEN I WAS A KITTEN.
OH. THEN TELL ME, CHESTER, WHAT IS A PARROT?
A PARROT IS A TROPICAL ZYGODACTYL BIRD (ORDER PSITTACIFORMES) THAT HAS A STOUT, CURVED HOOKED BILL AND IS OFTEN CRESTED, BRIGHTLY VARIEGATED, AND AN EXCELLENT MIMIC.
IN OTHER WORDS, HAROLD, IT'S A LITTLE BIRD WITH A BIG MOUTH.
OH. I THOUGHT MAYBE IT WAS A FANCY UMBRELLA.
DID YOU GET SO BUSY DISCUSSING RROTS WITH TOBY THAT YOU FORGOT YOU WERE GOING TO MEET ME?
THIS IS IMPORTANT, HAROLD.
NOW COME UP HERE.

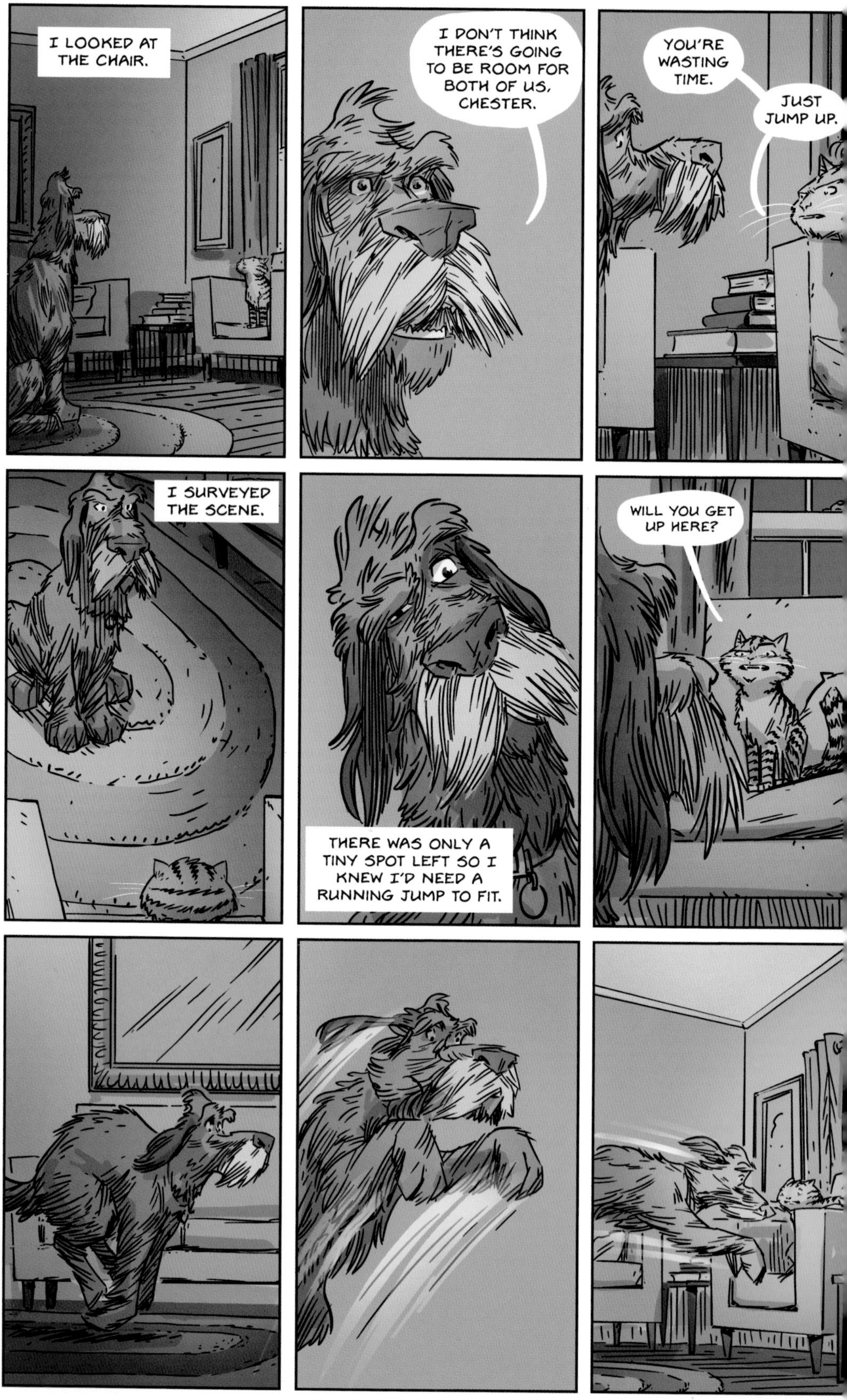
I LOOKED AT THE CHAIR.
I DON'T THINK THERE'S GOING TO BE ROOM FOR BOTH OF US, CHESTER.
YOU'RE WASTING TIME.
JUST JUMP UP.
I SURVEYED THE SCENE.
THERE WAS ONLY A TINY SPOT LEFT SO I KNEW I'D NEED A RUNNING JUMP TO FIT.
WILL YOU GET UP HERE?

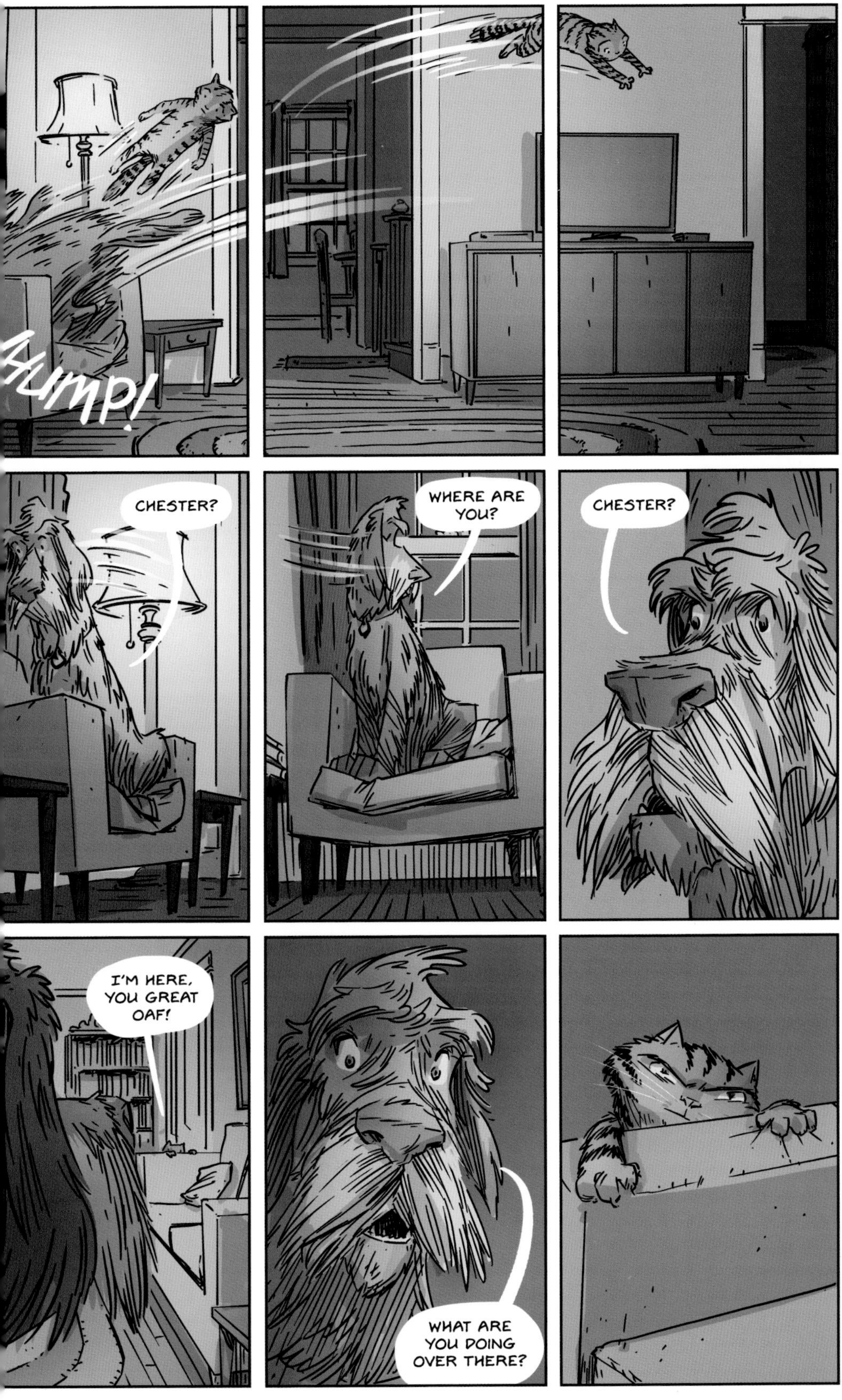

HUMP!
CHESTER?
WHERE ARE YOU?
CHESTER?
I'M HERE, YOU GREAT OAF!
WHAT ARE YOU DOING OVER THERE?

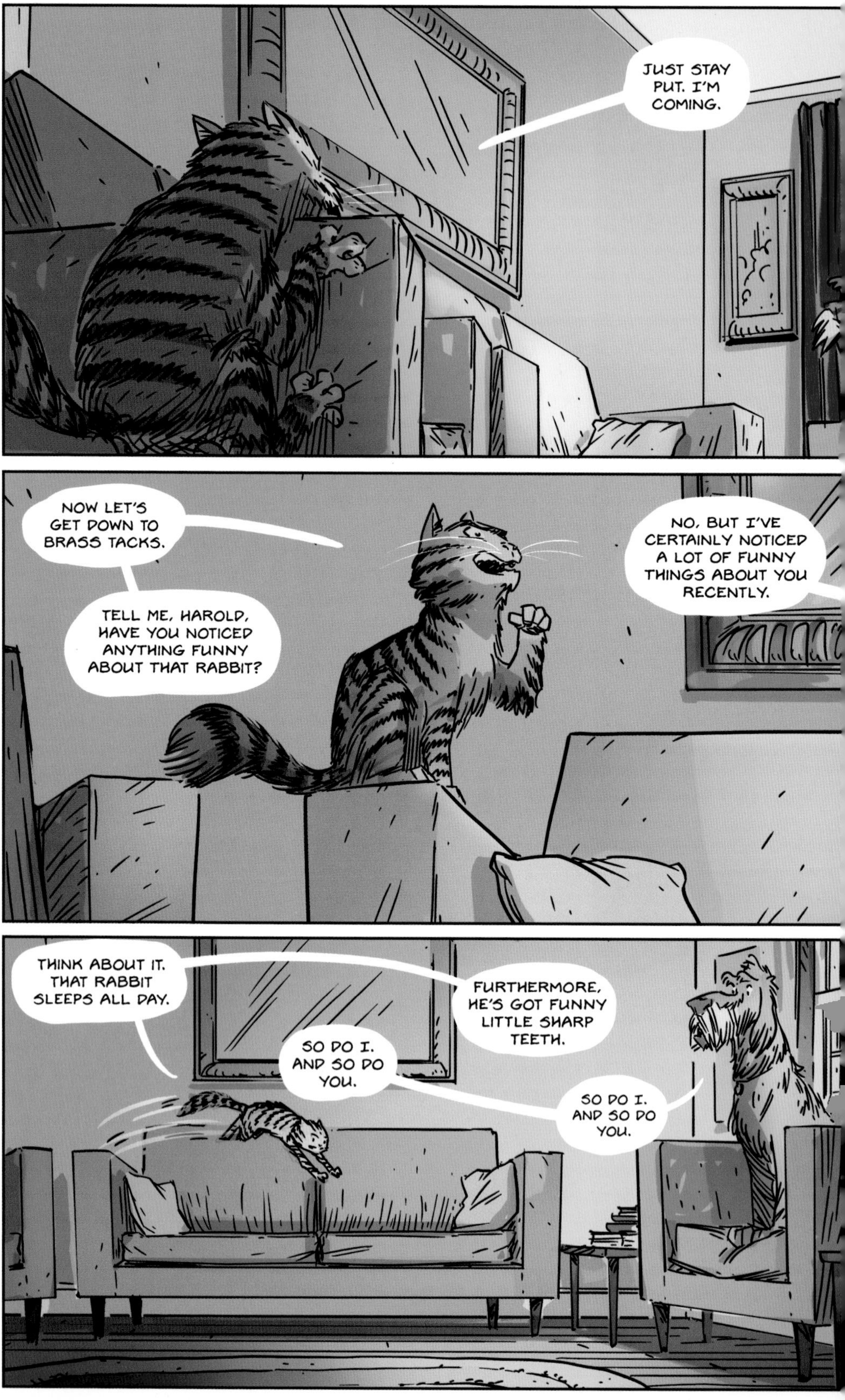
JUST STAY PUT. I'M COMING.
NOW LET'S GET DOWN TO BRASS TACKS.
TELL ME, HAROLD, HAVE YOU NOTICED ANYTHING FUNNY ABOUT THAT RABBIT?
NO, BUT I'VE CERTAINLY NOTICED A LOT OF FUNNY THINGS ABOUT YOU RECENTLY.
THINK ABOUT IT. THAT RABBIT SLEEPS ALL DAY.
SO DO I. AND SO DO YOU.
FURTHERMORE, HE'S GOT FUNNY LITTLE SHARP TEETH.
SO DO I. AND SO DO YOU.

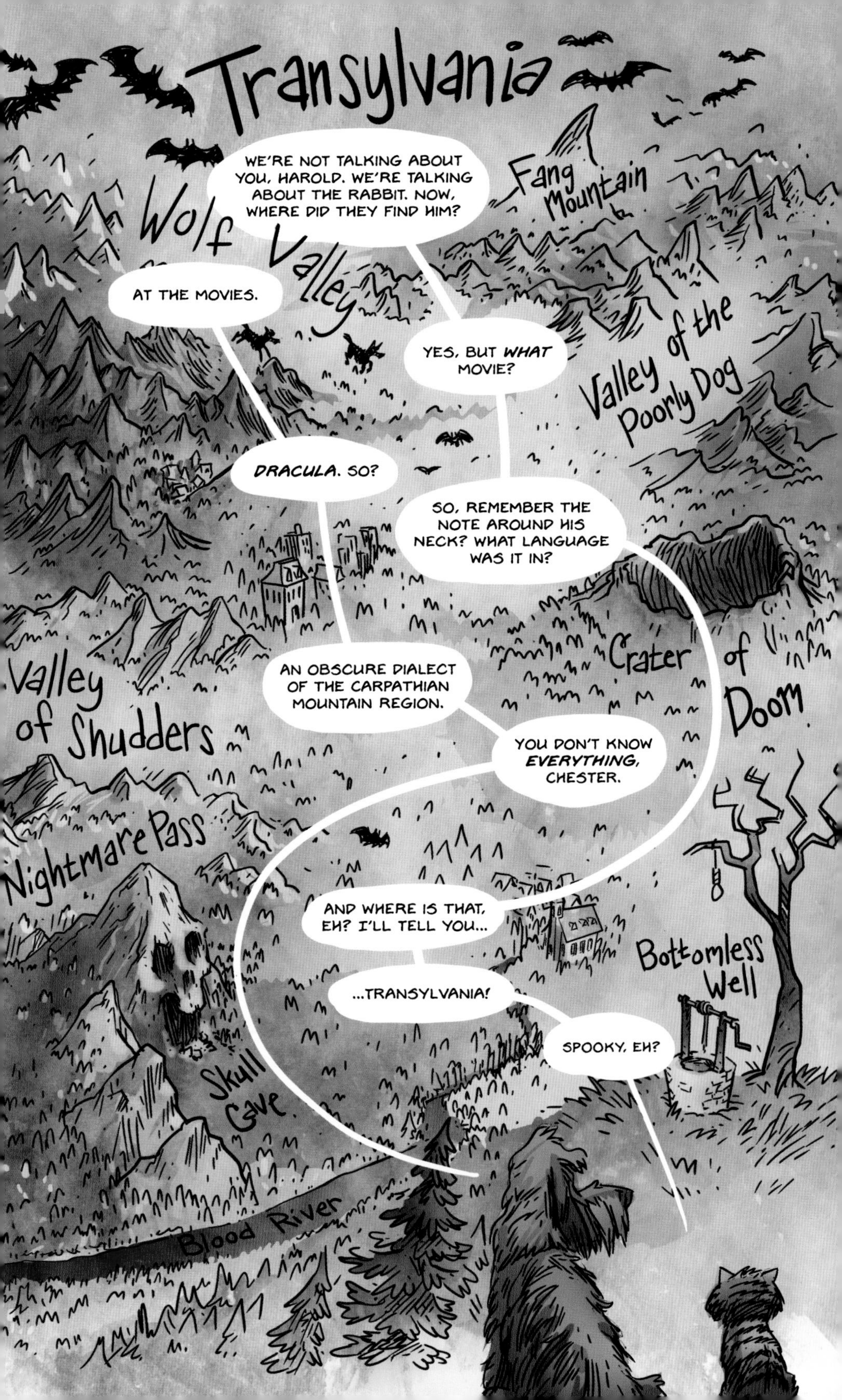

Transylvania
Fang Mountain
Wolf Valley
WE'RE NOT TALKING ABOUT YOU, HAROLD. WE'RE TALKING ABOUT THE RABBIT. NOW, WHERE DID THEY FIND HIM?
AT THE MOVIES.
YES, BUT *WHAT* MOVIE?
Valley of the Poorly Dog
DRACULA. SO?
SO, REMEMBER THE NOTE AROUND HIS NECK? WHAT LANGUAGE WAS IT IN?
AN OBSCURE DIALECT OF THE CARPATHIAN MOUNTAIN REGION.
Crater of Doom
Valley of Shudders
YOU DON'T KNOW *EVERYTHING*, CHESTER.
Nightmare Pass
AND WHERE IS THAT, EH? I'LL TELL YOU...
Bottomless Well
...TRANSYLVANIA!
SPOOKY, EH?
Skull Cave
Blood River

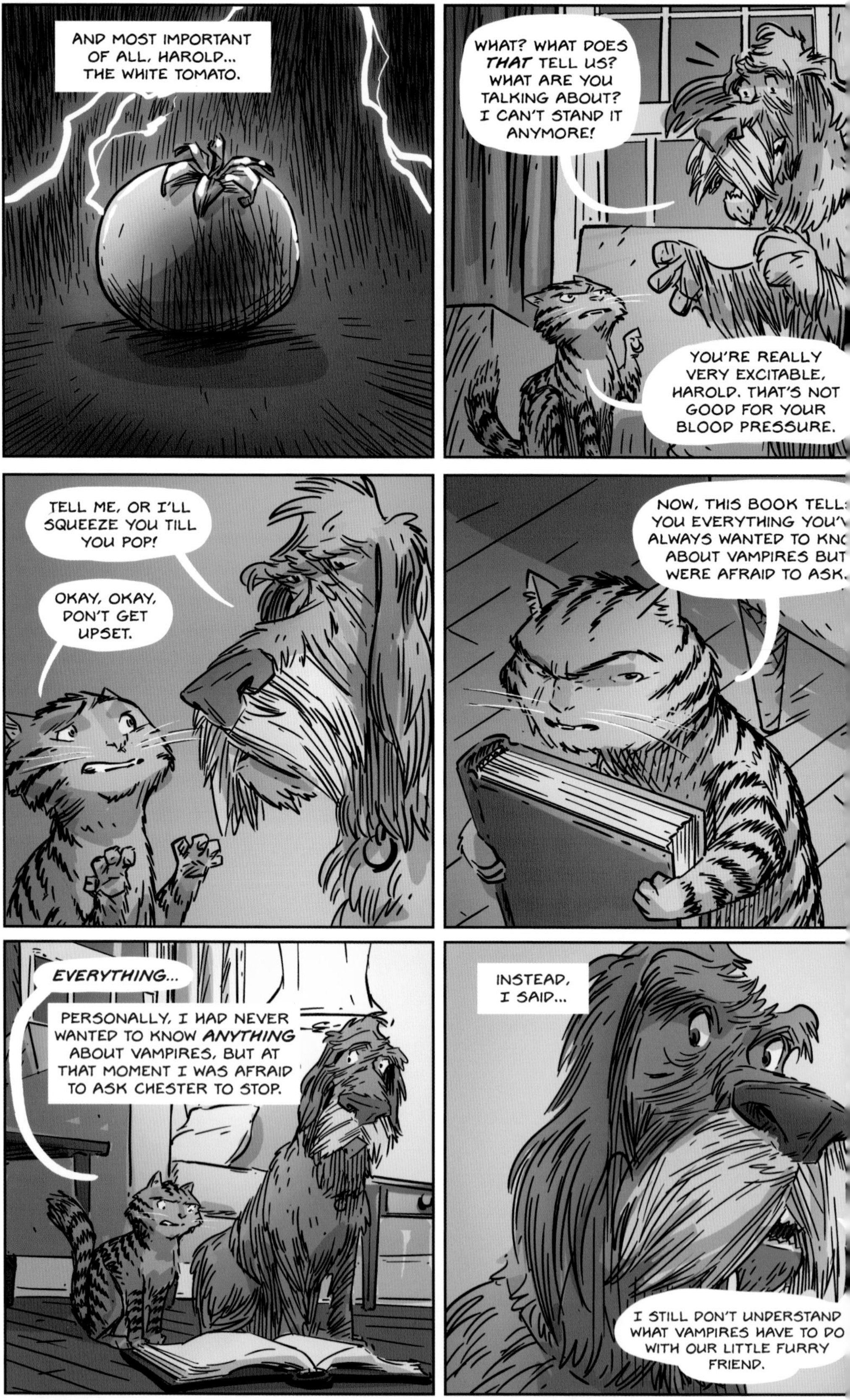
AND MOST IMPORTANT OF ALL, HAROLD... THE WHITE TOMATO.
WHAT? WHAT DOES *THAT* TELL US? WHAT ARE YOU TALKING ABOUT? I CAN'T STAND IT ANYMORE!
YOU'RE REALLY VERY EXCITABLE, HAROLD. THAT'S NOT GOOD FOR YOUR BLOOD PRESSURE.
TELL ME, OR I'LL SQUEEZE YOU TILL YOU POP!
OKAY, OKAY, DON'T GET UPSET.
NOW, THIS BOOK TELL YOU EVERYTHING YOU' ALWAYS WANTED TO KN ABOUT VAMPIRES BUT WERE AFRAID TO ASK.
EVERYTHING...
PERSONALLY, I HAD NEVER WANTED TO KNOW *ANYTHING* ABOUT VAMPIRES, BUT AT THAT MOMENT I WAS AFRAID TO ASK CHESTER TO STOP.
INSTEAD, I SAID...
I STILL DON'T UNDERSTAND WHAT VAMPIRES HAVE TO DO WITH OUR LITTLE FURRY FRIEND.

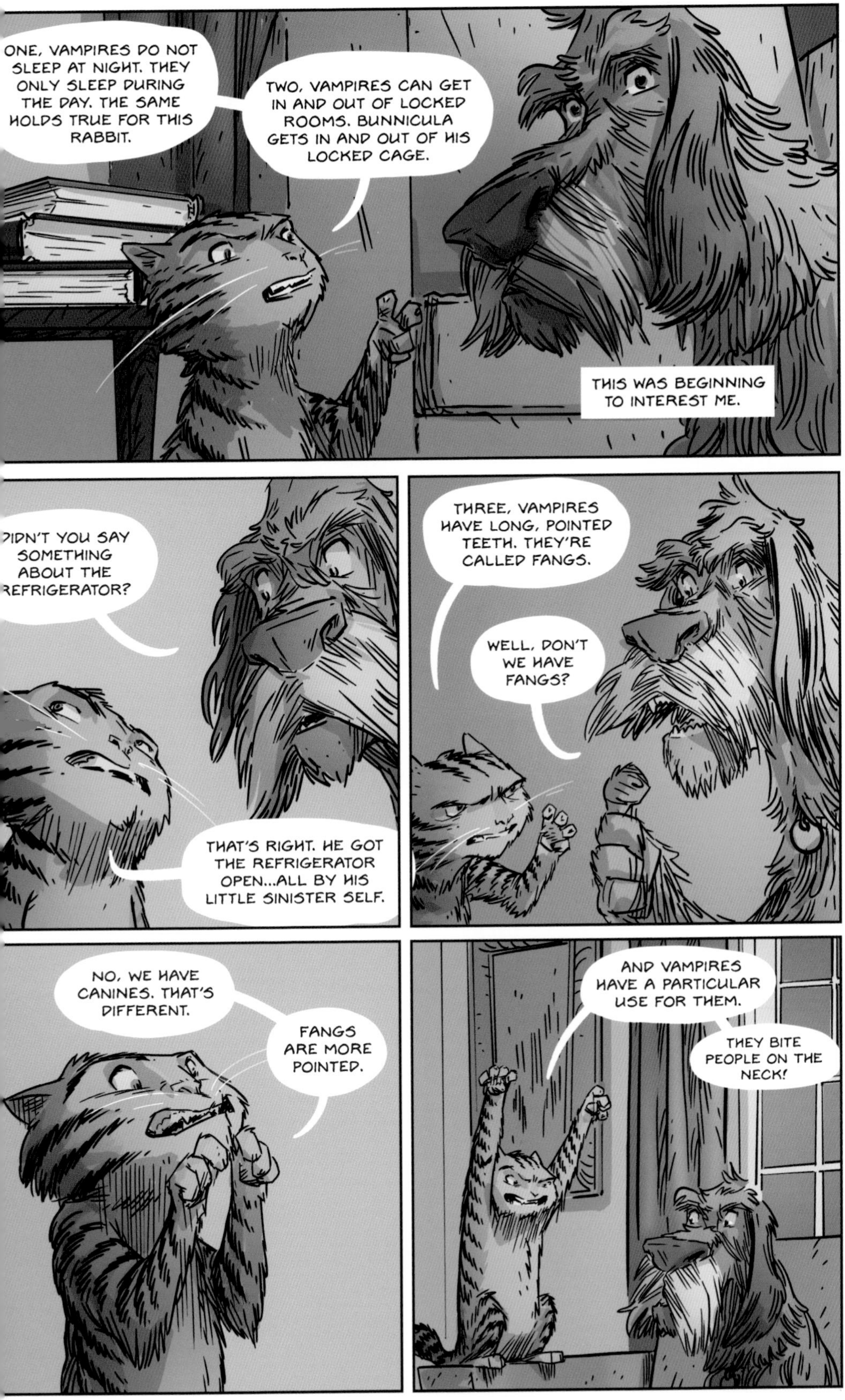

ONE, VAMPIRES DO NOT SLEEP AT NIGHT. THEY ONLY SLEEP DURING THE DAY. THE SAME HOLDS TRUE FOR THIS RABBIT.
TWO, VAMPIRES CAN GET IN AND OUT OF LOCKED ROOMS. BUNNICULA GETS IN AND OUT OF HIS LOCKED CAGE.
THIS WAS BEGINNING TO INTEREST ME.
DIDN'T YOU SAY SOMETHING ABOUT THE REFRIGERATOR?
THAT'S RIGHT. HE GOT THE REFRIGERATOR OPEN...ALL BY HIS LITTLE SINISTER SELF.
THREE, VAMPIRES HAVE LONG, POINTED TEETH. THEY'RE CALLED FANGS.
WELL, DON'T WE HAVE FANGS?
NO, WE HAVE CANINES. THAT'S DIFFERENT.
FANGS ARE MORE POINTED.
AND VAMPIRES HAVE A PARTICULAR USE FOR THEM.
THEY BITE PEOPLE ON THE NECK!

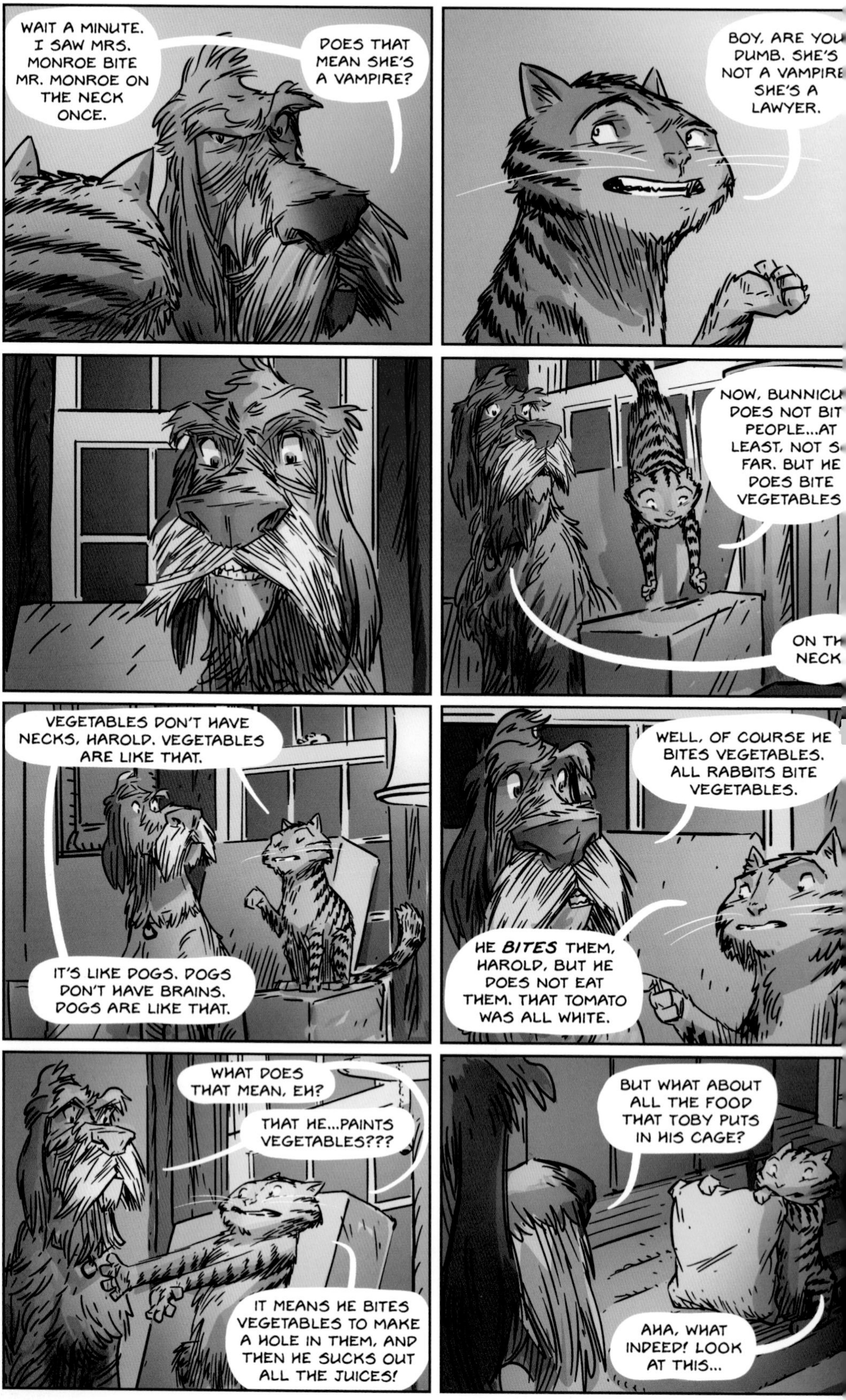
WAIT A MINUTE. I SAW MRS. MONROE BITE MR. MONROE ON THE NECK ONCE.
DOES THAT MEAN SHE'S A VAMPIRE?
BOY, ARE YOU DUMB. SHE'S NOT A VAMPIRE. SHE'S A LAWYER.
NOW, BUNNICULA DOES NOT BITE PEOPLE...AT LEAST, NOT SO FAR. BUT HE DOES BITE VEGETABLES
ON THE NECK
VEGETABLES DON'T HAVE NECKS, HAROLD. VEGETABLES ARE LIKE THAT.
IT'S LIKE DOGS. DOGS DON'T HAVE BRAINS. DOGS ARE LIKE THAT.
WELL, OF COURSE HE BITES VEGETABLES. ALL RABBITS BITE VEGETABLES.
HE *BITES* THEM, HAROLD, BUT HE DOES NOT EAT THEM. THAT TOMATO WAS ALL WHITE.
WHAT DOES THAT MEAN, EH?
THAT HE...PAINTS VEGETABLES???
IT MEANS HE BITES VEGETABLES TO MAKE A HOLE IN THEM, AND THEN HE SUCKS OUT ALL THE JUICES!
BUT WHAT ABOUT ALL THE FOOD THAT TOBY PUTS IN HIS CAGE?
AHA, WHAT INDEED! LOOK AT THIS...

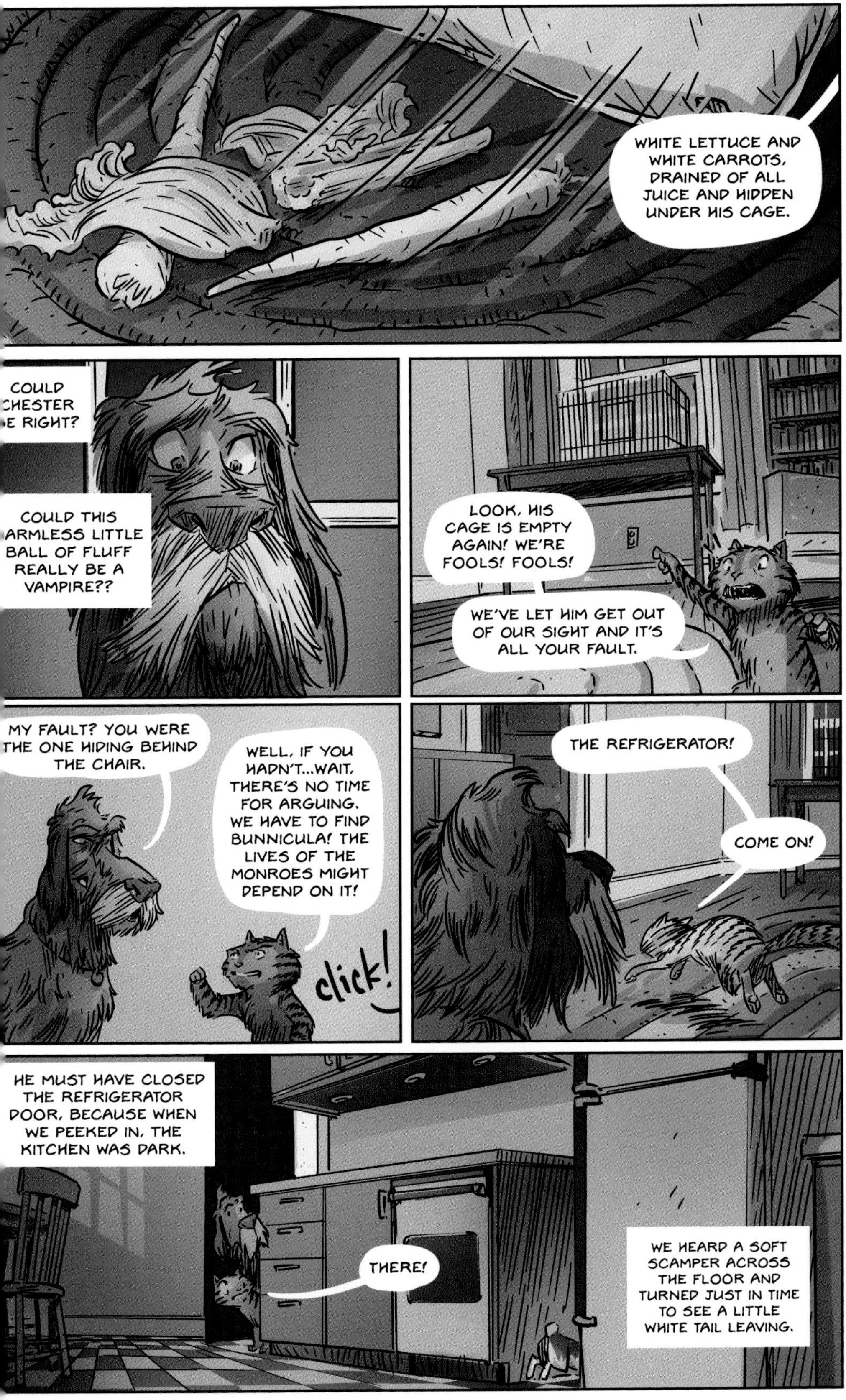

WHITE LETTUCE AND WHITE CARROTS, DRAINED OF ALL JUICE AND HIDDEN UNDER HIS CAGE.
COULD CHESTER BE RIGHT?
COULD THIS HARMLESS LITTLE BALL OF FLUFF REALLY BE A VAMPIRE??
LOOK, HIS CAGE IS EMPTY AGAIN! WE'RE FOOLS! FOOLS!
WE'VE LET HIM GET OUT OF OUR SIGHT AND IT'S ALL YOUR FAULT.
MY FAULT? YOU WERE THE ONE HIDING BEHIND THE CHAIR.
WELL, IF YOU HADN'T...WAIT, THERE'S NO TIME FOR ARGUING. WE HAVE TO FIND BUNNICULA! THE LIVES OF THE MONROES MIGHT DEPEND ON IT!
click!
THE REFRIGERATOR!
COME ON!
HE MUST HAVE CLOSED THE REFRIGERATOR DOOR, BECAUSE WHEN WE PEEKED IN, THE KITCHEN WAS DARK.
THERE!
WE HEARD A SOFT SCAMPER ACROSS THE FLOOR AND TURNED JUST IN TIME TO SEE A LITTLE WHITE TAIL LEAVING.

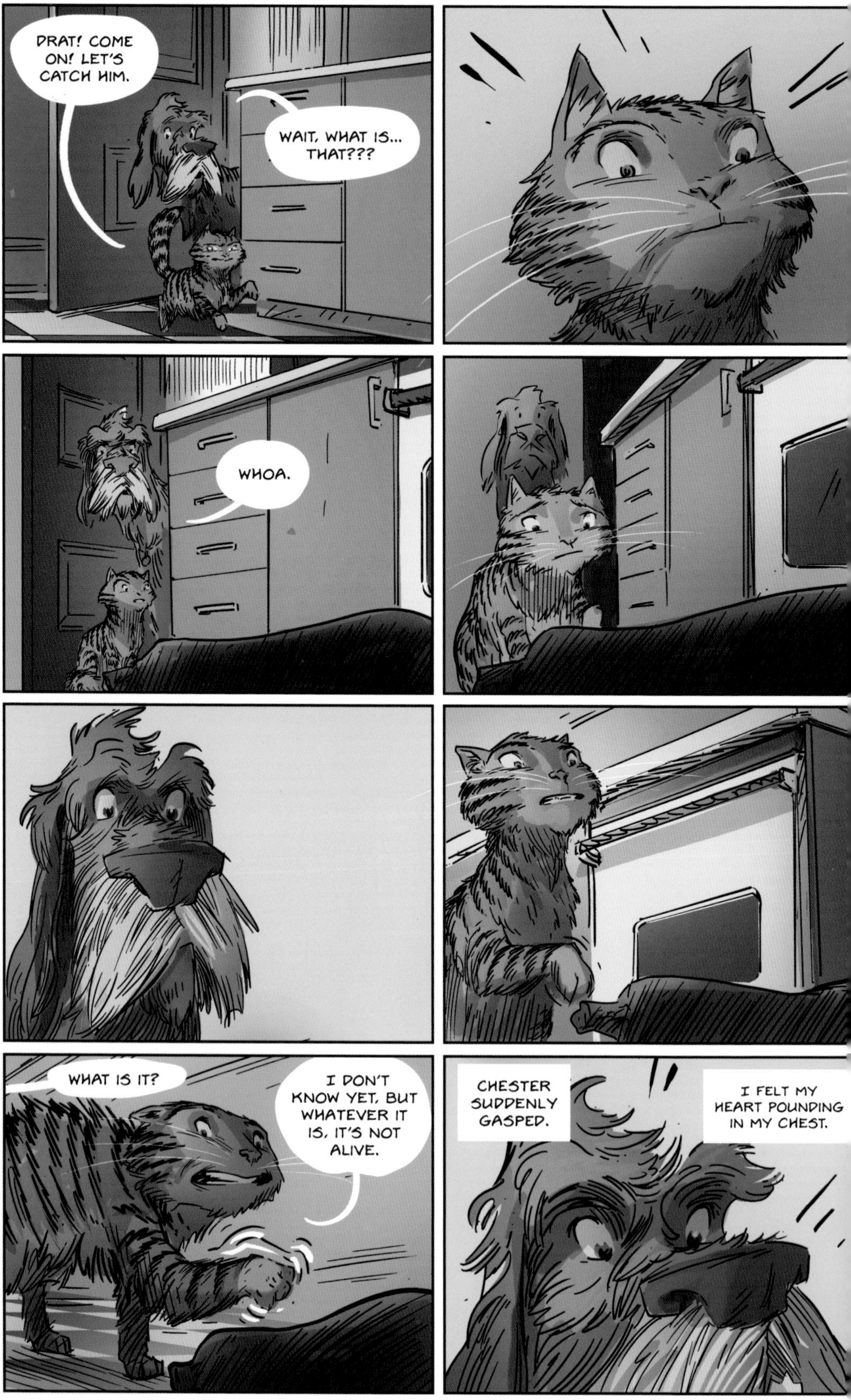
DRAT! COME ON! LET'S CATCH HIM.
WAIT, WHAT IS... THAT???
WHOA.
WHAT IS IT?
I DON'T KNOW YET, BUT WHATEVER IT IS, IT'S NOT ALIVE.
CHESTER SUDDENLY GASPED.
I FELT MY HEART POUNDING IN MY CHEST.

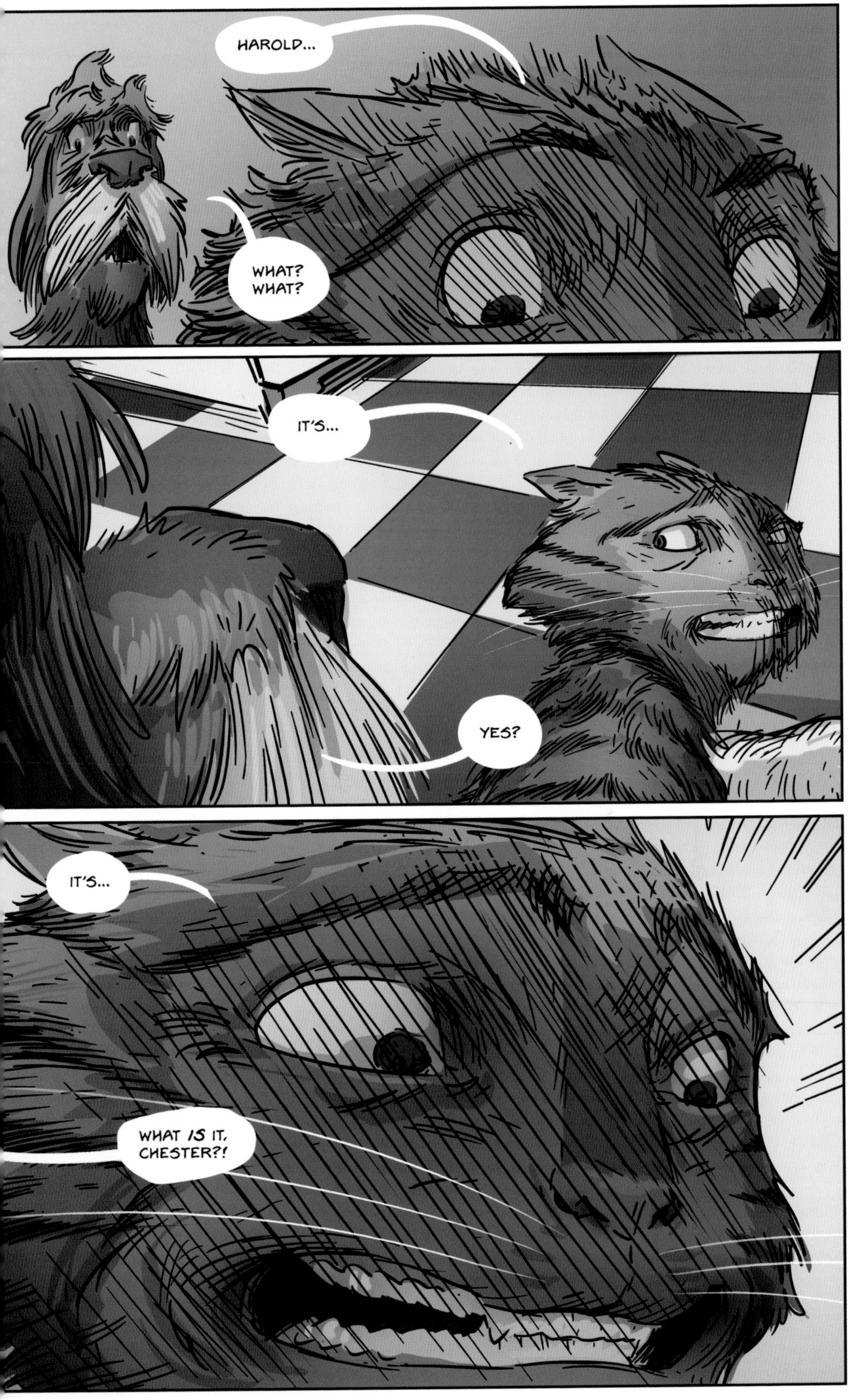
HAROLD...
WHAT? WHAT?
IT'S...
YES?
IT'S...
WHAT *IS* IT, CHESTER?!

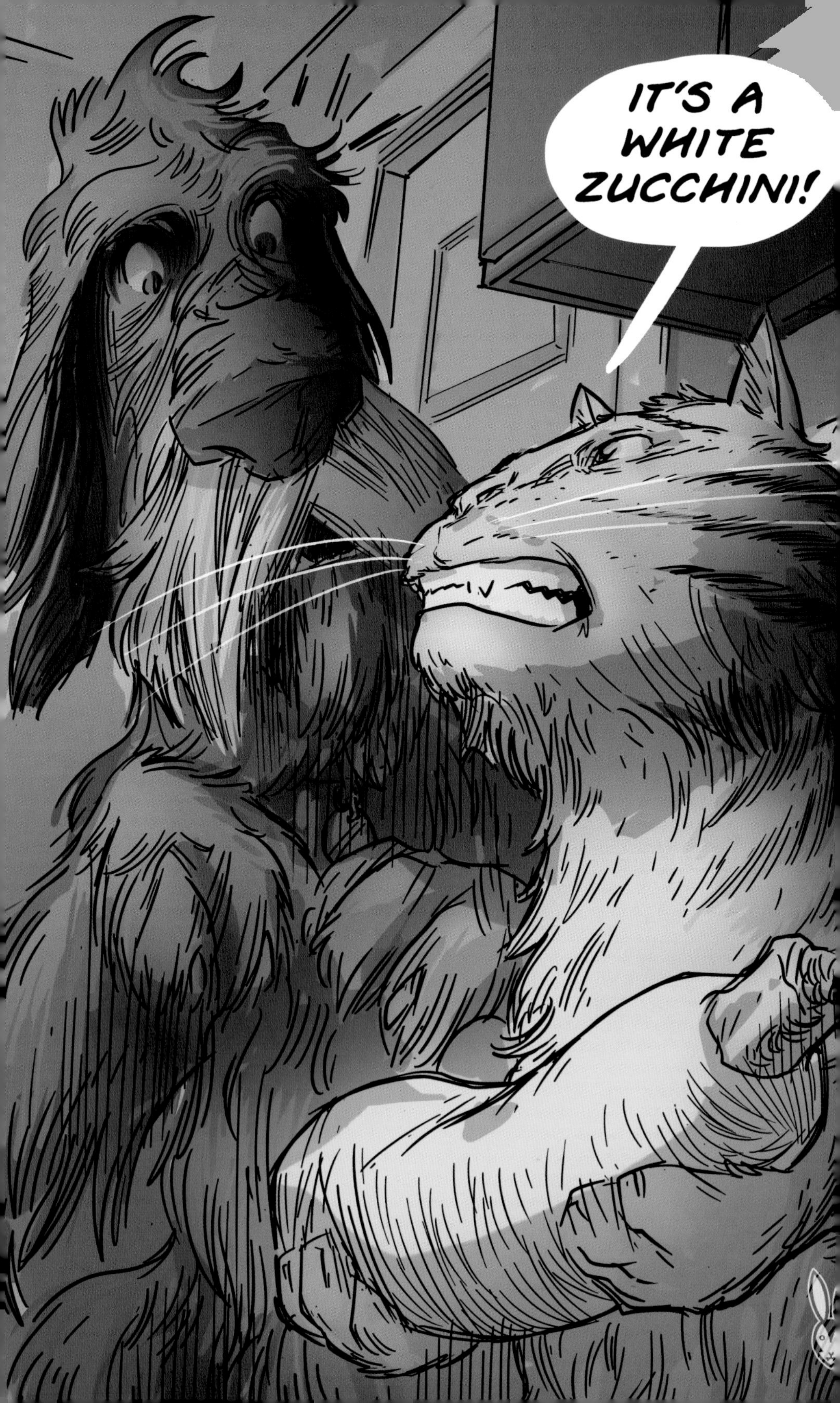
IT'S A WHITE ZUCCHINI!

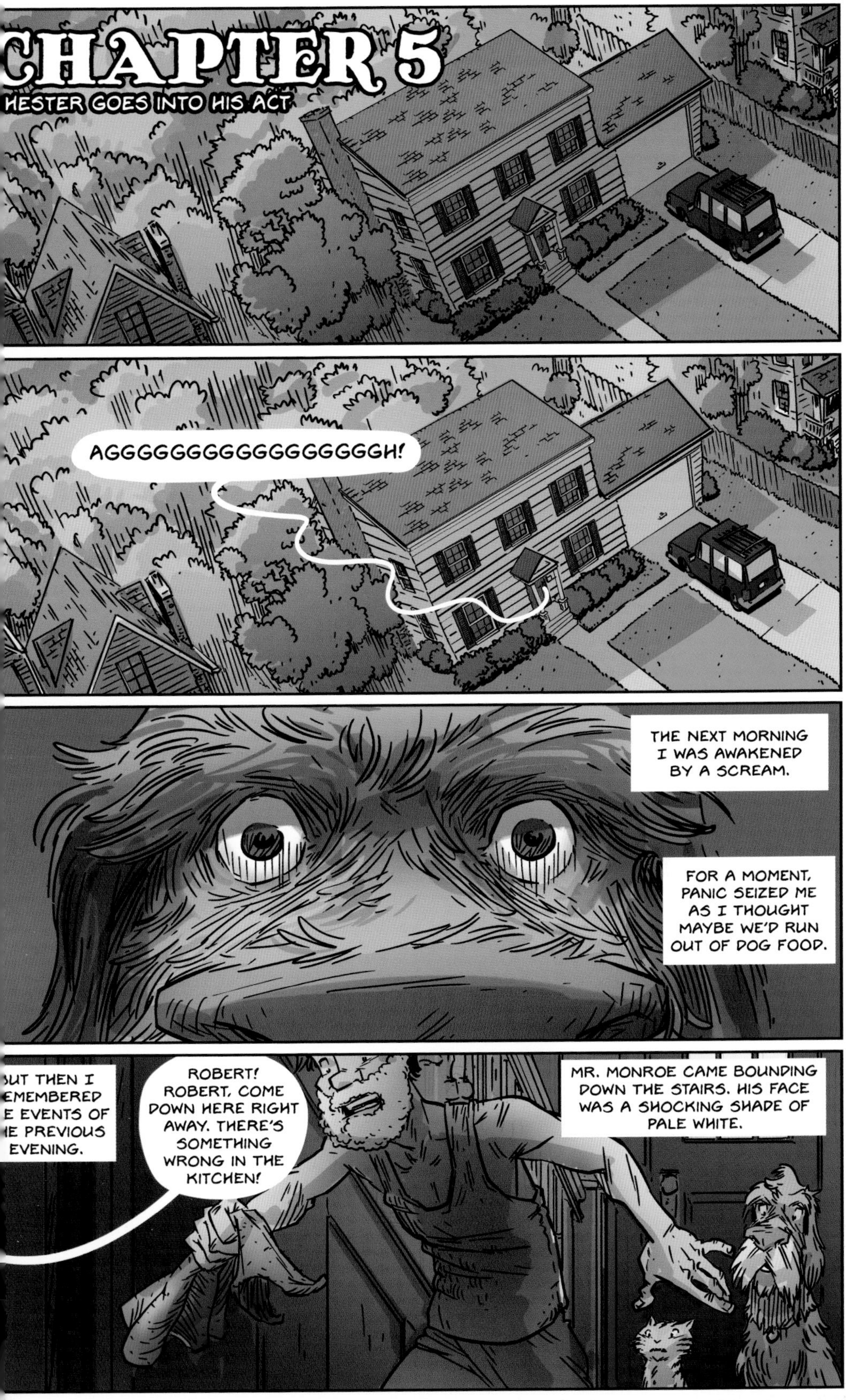
CHAPTER 5
HESTER GOES INTO HIS ACT
AGGGGGGGGGGGGGGGGH!
THE NEXT MORNING I WAS AWAKENED BY A SCREAM.
FOR A MOMENT, PANIC SEIZED ME AS I THOUGHT MAYBE WE'D RUN OUT OF DOG FOOD.
UT THEN I EMEMBERED E EVENTS OF E PREVIOUS EVENING.
ROBERT! ROBERT, COME DOWN HERE RIGHT AWAY. THERE'S SOMETHING WRONG IN THE KITCHEN!
MR. MONROE CAME BOUNDING DOWN THE STAIRS. HIS FACE WAS A SHOCKING SHADE OF PALE WHITE.

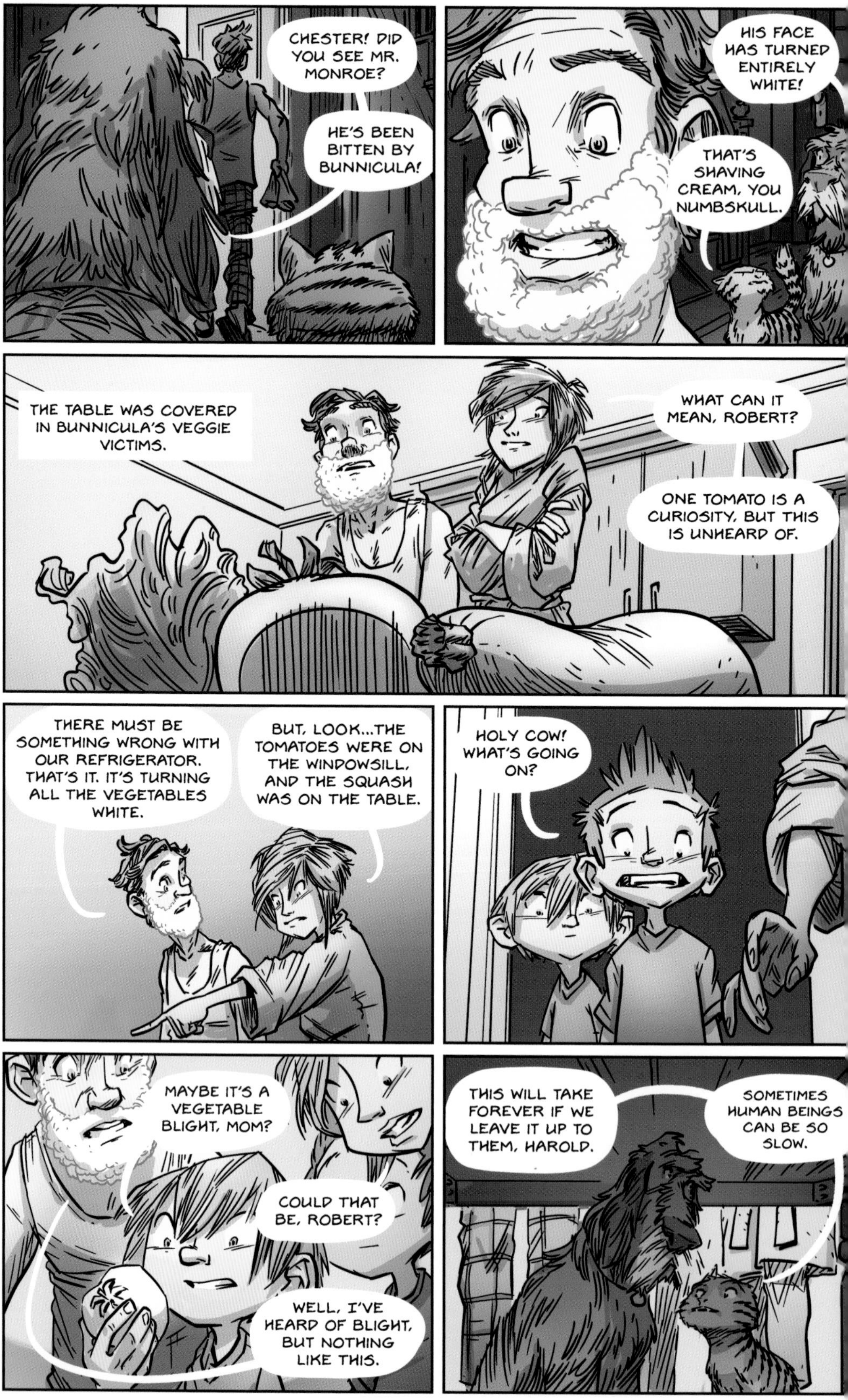

CHESTER! DID YOU SEE MR. MONROE?
HE'S BEEN BITTEN BY BUNNICULA!
HIS FACE HAS TURNED ENTIRELY WHITE!
THAT'S SHAVING CREAM, YOU NUMBSKULL.
THE TABLE WAS COVERED IN BUNNICULA'S VEGGIE VICTIMS.
WHAT CAN IT MEAN, ROBERT?
ONE TOMATO IS A CURIOSITY, BUT THIS IS UNHEARD OF.
THERE MUST BE SOMETHING WRONG WITH OUR REFRIGERATOR. THAT'S IT. IT'S TURNING ALL THE VEGETABLES WHITE.
BUT, LOOK...THE TOMATOES WERE ON THE WINDOWSILL, AND THE SQUASH WAS ON THE TABLE.
HOLY COW! WHAT'S GOING ON?
MAYBE IT'S A VEGETABLE BLIGHT, MOM?
COULD THAT BE, ROBERT?
WELL, I'VE HEARD OF BLIGHT, BUT NOTHING LIKE THIS.
THIS WILL TAKE FOREVER IF WE LEAVE IT UP TO THEM, HAROLD.
SOMETIMES HUMAN BEINGS CAN BE SO SLOW.

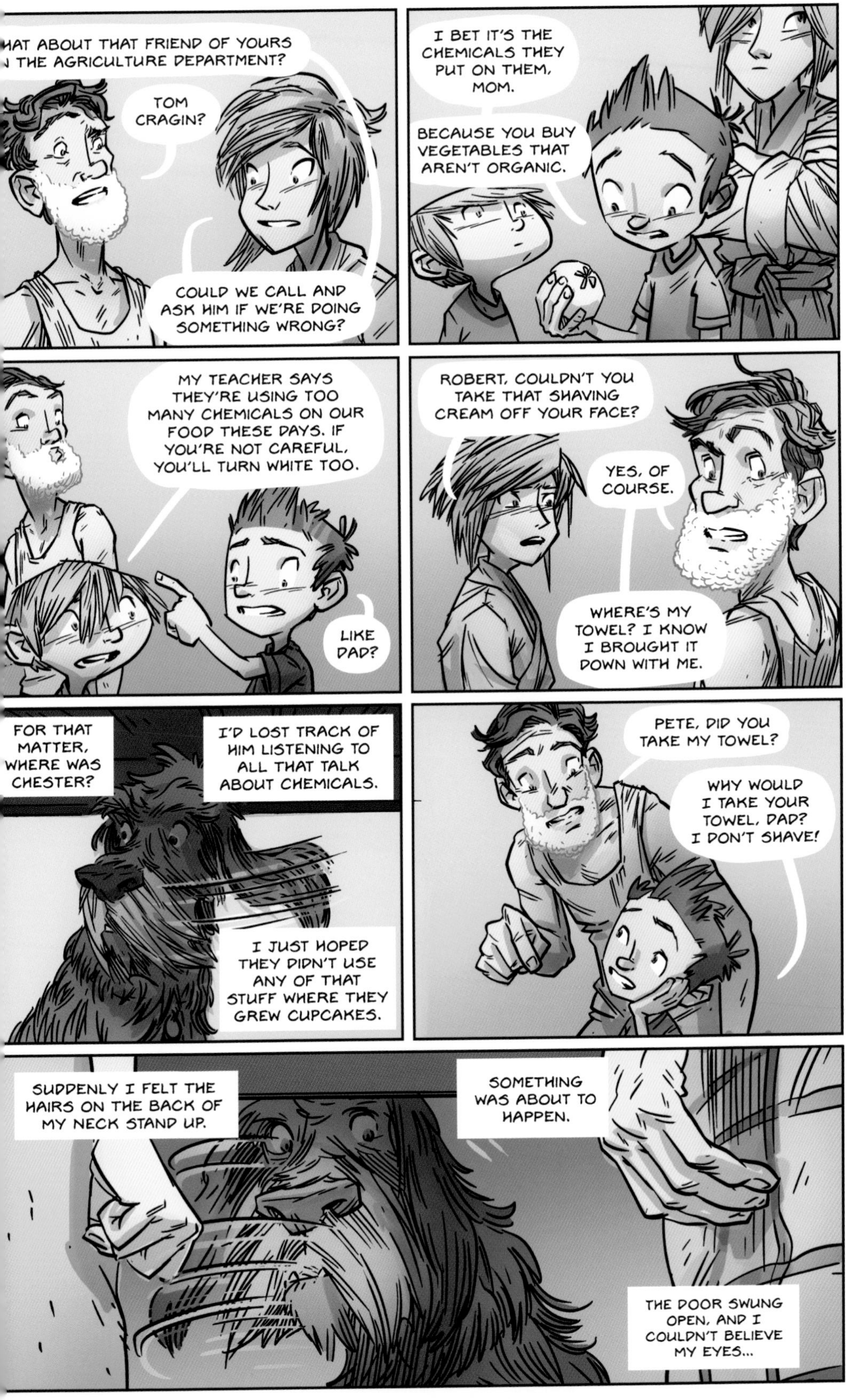
HAT ABOUT THAT FRIEND OF YOURS
N THE AGRICULTURE DEPARTMENT?
TOM CRAGIN?
COULD WE CALL AND ASK HIM IF WE'RE DOING SOMETHING WRONG?
I BET IT'S THE CHEMICALS THEY PUT ON THEM, MOM.
BECAUSE YOU BUY VEGETABLES THAT AREN'T ORGANIC.
MY TEACHER SAYS THEY'RE USING TOO MANY CHEMICALS ON OUR FOOD THESE DAYS. IF YOU'RE NOT CAREFUL, YOU'LL TURN WHITE TOO.
LIKE DAD?
ROBERT, COULDN'T YOU TAKE THAT SHAVING CREAM OFF YOUR FACE?
YES, OF COURSE.
WHERE'S MY TOWEL? I KNOW I BROUGHT IT DOWN WITH ME.
FOR THAT MATTER, WHERE WAS CHESTER?
I'D LOST TRACK OF HIM LISTENING TO ALL THAT TALK ABOUT CHEMICALS.
I JUST HOPED THEY DIDN'T USE ANY OF THAT STUFF WHERE THEY GREW CUPCAKES.
PETE, DID YOU TAKE MY TOWEL?
WHY WOULD I TAKE YOUR TOWEL, DAD? I DON'T SHAVE!
SUDDENLY I FELT THE HAIRS ON THE BACK OF MY NECK STAND UP.
SOMETHING WAS ABOUT TO HAPPEN.
THE DOOR SWUNG OPEN, AND I COULDN'T BELIEVE MY EYES...

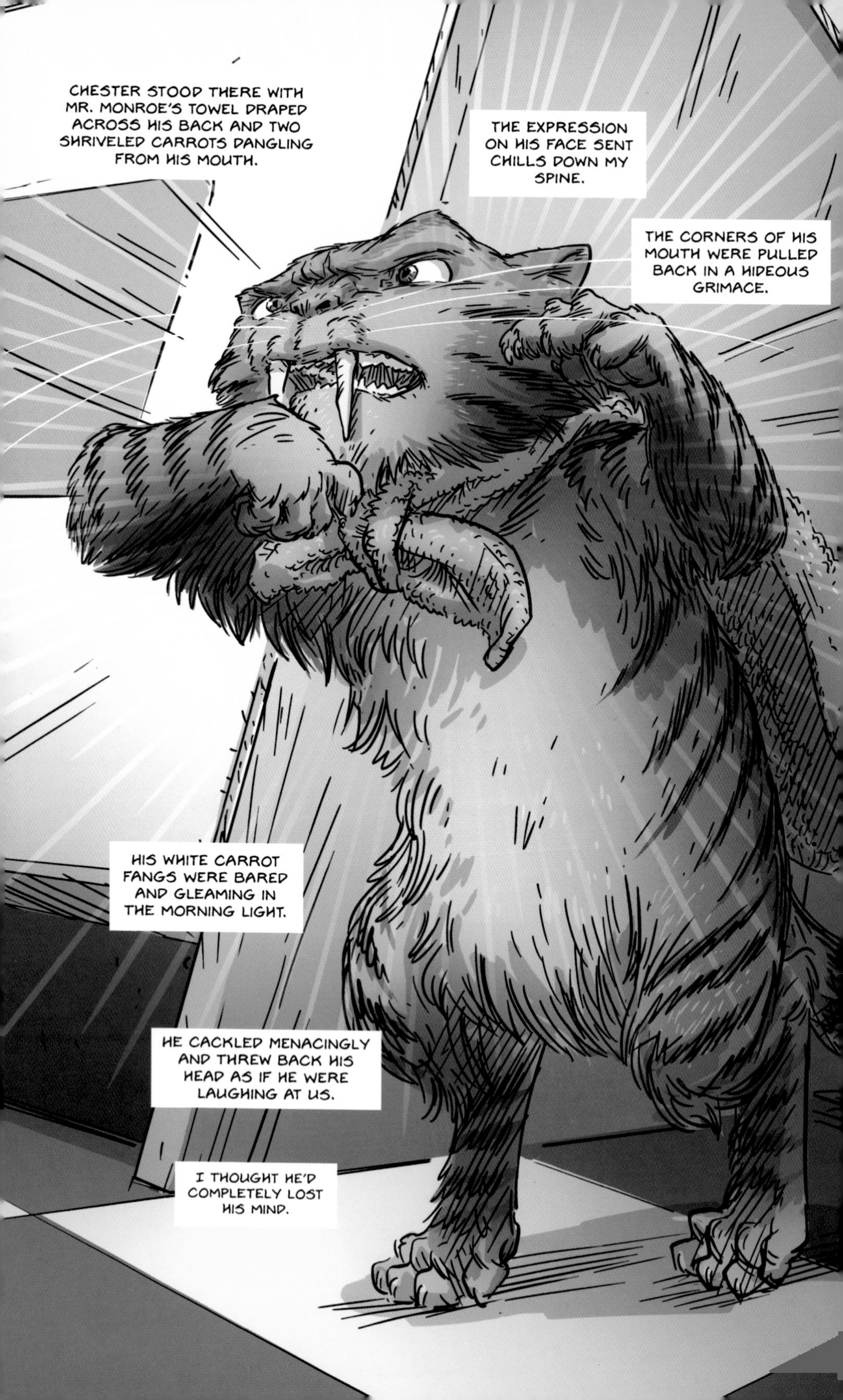
CHESTER STOOD THERE WITH MR. MONROE'S TOWEL DRAPED ACROSS HIS BACK AND TWO SHRIVELED CARROTS DANGLING FROM HIS MOUTH.
THE EXPRESSION ON HIS FACE SENT CHILLS DOWN MY SPINE.
THE CORNERS OF HIS MOUTH WERE PULLED BACK IN A HIDEOUS GRIMACE.
HIS WHITE CARROT FANGS WERE BARED AND GLEAMING IN THE MORNING LIGHT.
HE CACKLED MENACINGLY AND THREW BACK HIS HEAD AS IF HE WERE LAUGHING AT US.
I THOUGHT HE'D COMPLETELY LOST HIS MIND.

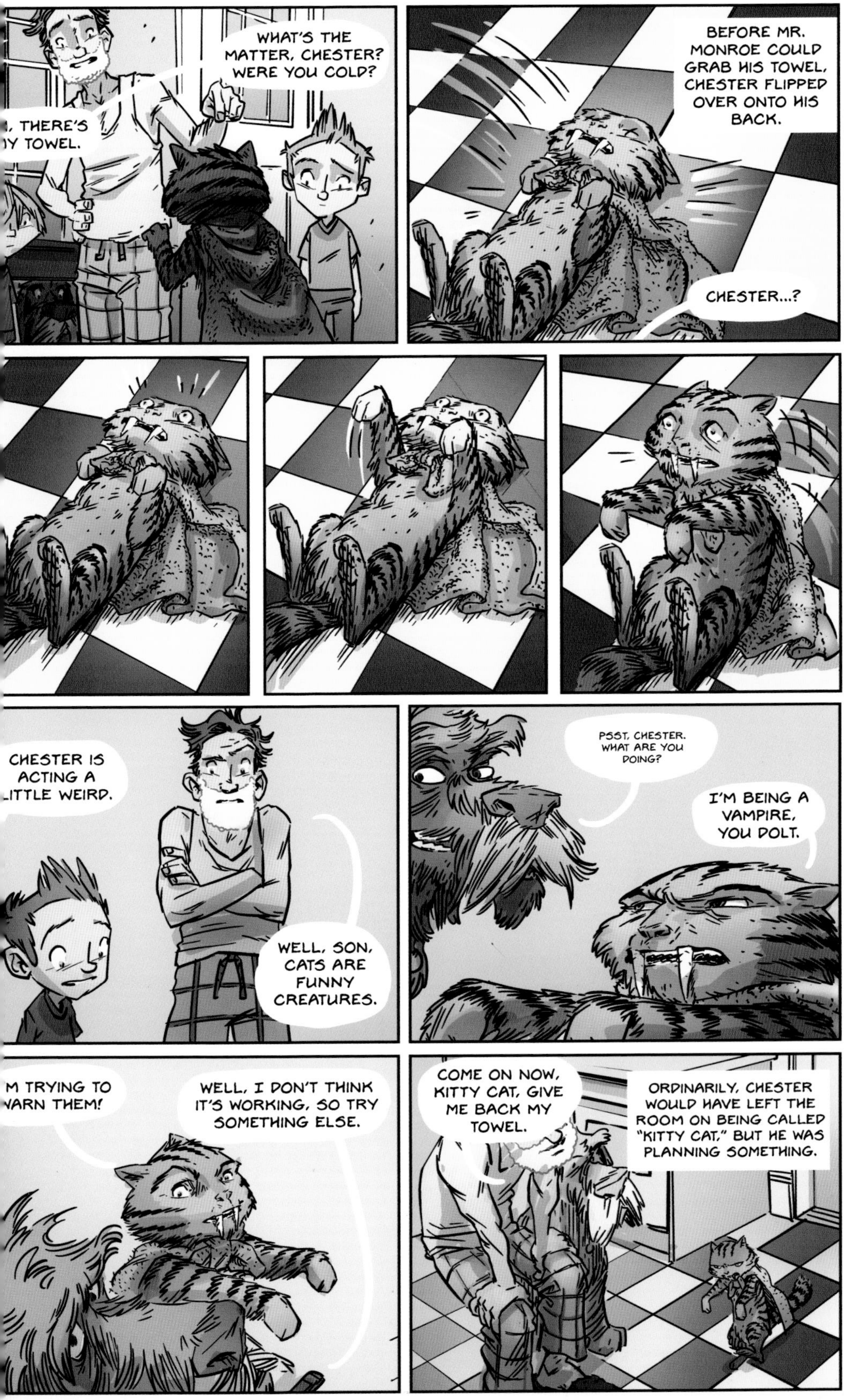

, THERE'S
Y TOWEL.
WHAT'S THE MATTER, CHESTER? WERE YOU COLD?
BEFORE MR. MONROE COULD GRAB HIS TOWEL, CHESTER FLIPPED OVER ONTO HIS BACK.
CHESTER...?
CHESTER IS ACTING A
ITTLE WEIRD.
WELL, SON, CATS ARE FUNNY CREATURES.
PSST, CHESTER. WHAT ARE YOU DOING?
I'M BEING A VAMPIRE, YOU DOLT.
M TRYING TO
ARN THEM!
WELL, I DON'T THINK IT'S WORKING, SO TRY SOMETHING ELSE.
COME ON NOW, KITTY CAT, GIVE ME BACK MY TOWEL.
ORDINARILY, CHESTER WOULD HAVE LEFT THE ROOM ON BEING CALLED "KITTY CAT," BUT HE WAS PLANNING SOMETHING.

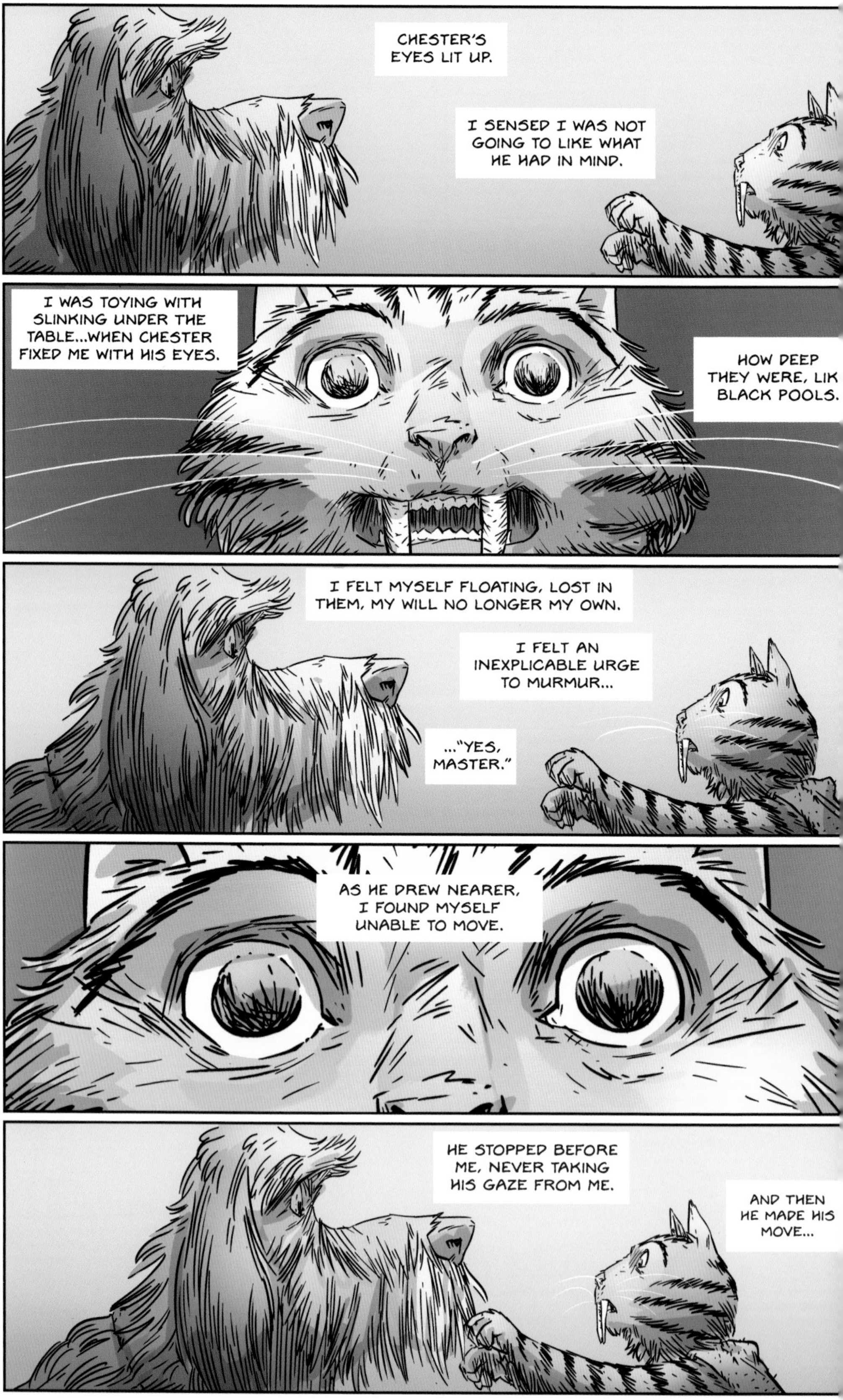

CHESTER'S EYES LIT UP.
I SENSED I WAS NOT GOING TO LIKE WHAT HE HAD IN MIND.
I WAS TOYING WITH SLINKING UNDER THE TABLE...WHEN CHESTER FIXED ME WITH HIS EYES.
HOW DEEP THEY WERE, LIK BLACK POOLS.
I FELT MYSELF FLOATING, LOST IN THEM, MY WILL NO LONGER MY OWN.
I FELT AN INEXPLICABLE URGE TO MURMUR...
..."YES, MASTER."
AS HE DREW NEARER, I FOUND MYSELF UNABLE TO MOVE.
HE STOPPED BEFORE ME, NEVER TAKING HIS GAZE FROM ME.
AND THEN HE MADE HIS MOVE...

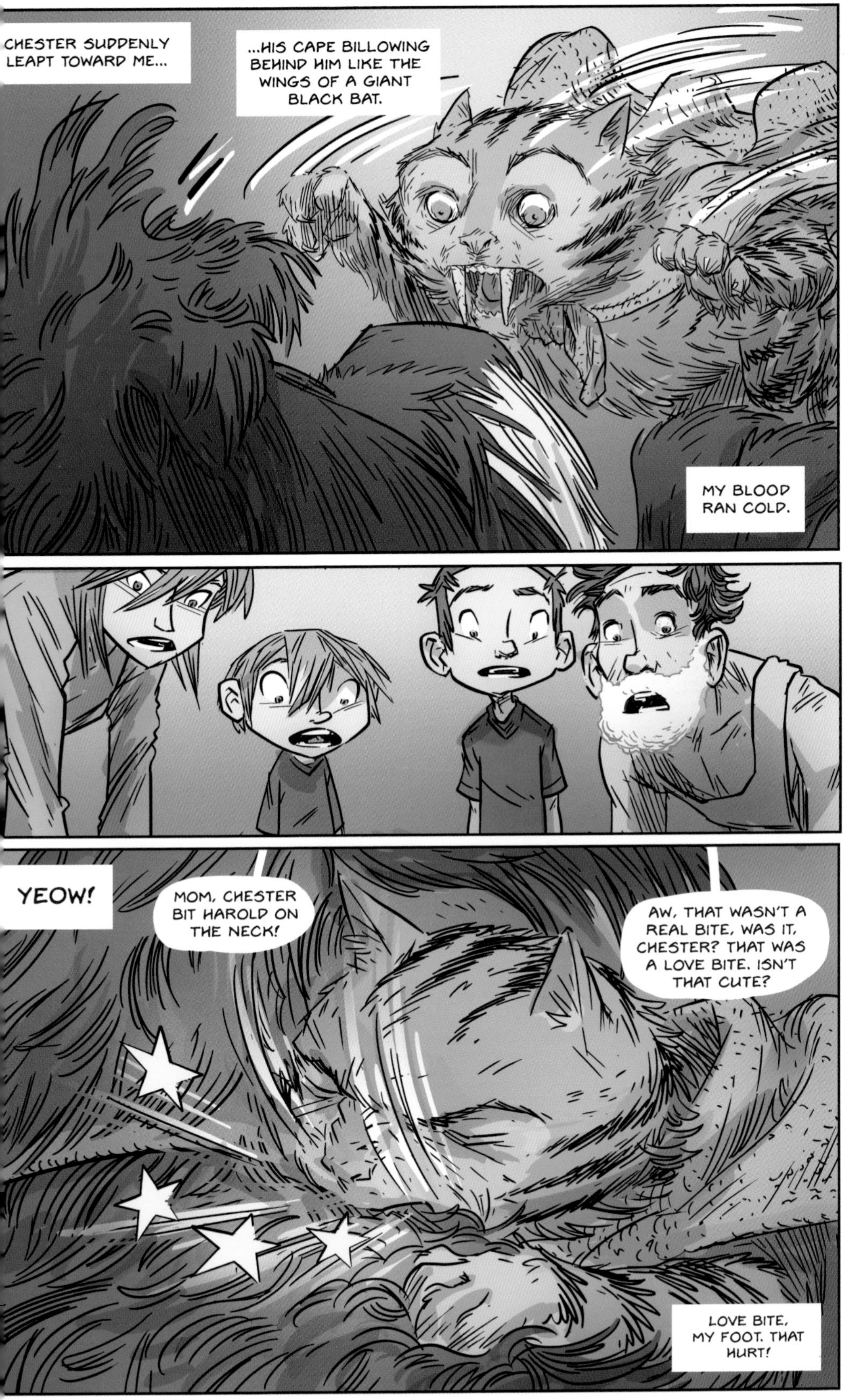
CHESTER SUDDENLY LEAPT TOWARD ME...
...HIS CAPE BILLOWING BEHIND HIM LIKE THE WINGS OF A GIANT BLACK BAT.
MY BLOOD RAN COLD.
YEOW!
MOM, CHESTER BIT HAROLD ON THE NECK!
AW, THAT WASN'T A REAL BITE, WAS IT, CHESTER? THAT WAS A LOVE BITE. ISN'T THAT CUTE?
LOVE BITE, MY FOOT. THAT HURT!

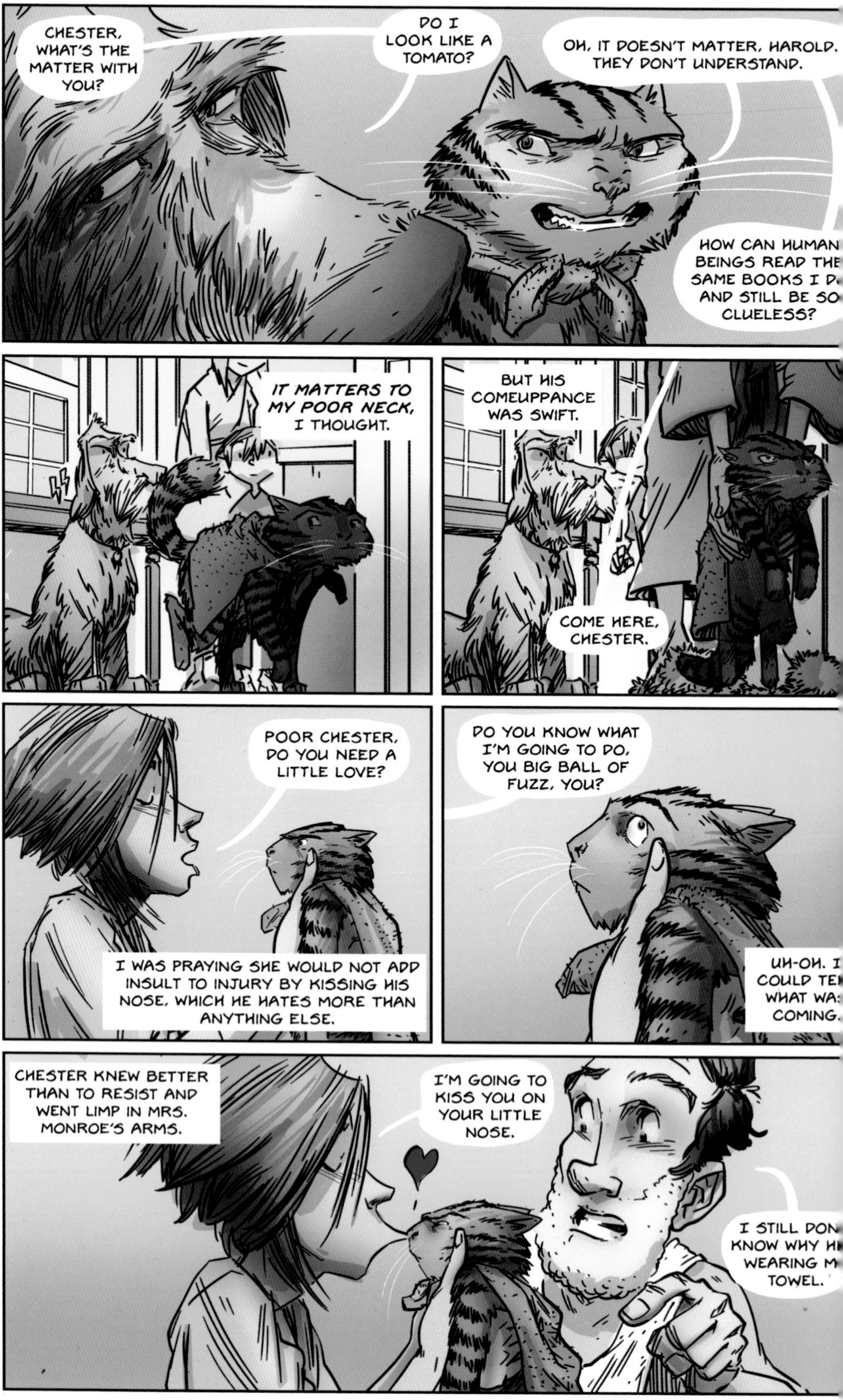
CHESTER, WHAT'S THE MATTER WITH YOU?
DO I LOOK LIKE A TOMATO?
OH, IT DOESN'T MATTER, HAROLD. THEY DON'T UNDERSTAND.
HOW CAN HUMAN BEINGS READ THE SAME BOOKS I D. AND STILL BE SO CLUELESS?
IT MATTERS TO MY POOR NECK, I THOUGHT.
BUT HIS COMEUPPANCE WAS SWIFT.
COME HERE, CHESTER.
POOR CHESTER, DO YOU NEED A LITTLE LOVE?
I WAS PRAYING SHE WOULD NOT ADD INSULT TO INJURY BY KISSING HIS NOSE, WHICH HE HATES MORE THAN ANYTHING ELSE.
DO YOU KNOW WHAT I'M GOING TO DO, YOU BIG BALL OF FUZZ, YOU?
UH-OH. I COULD TE WHAT WA COMING.
CHESTER KNEW BETTER THAN TO RESIST AND WENT LIMP IN MRS. MONROE'S ARMS.
I'M GOING TO KISS YOU ON YOUR LITTLE NOSE.
I STILL DON KNOW WHY H WEARING M TOWEL.

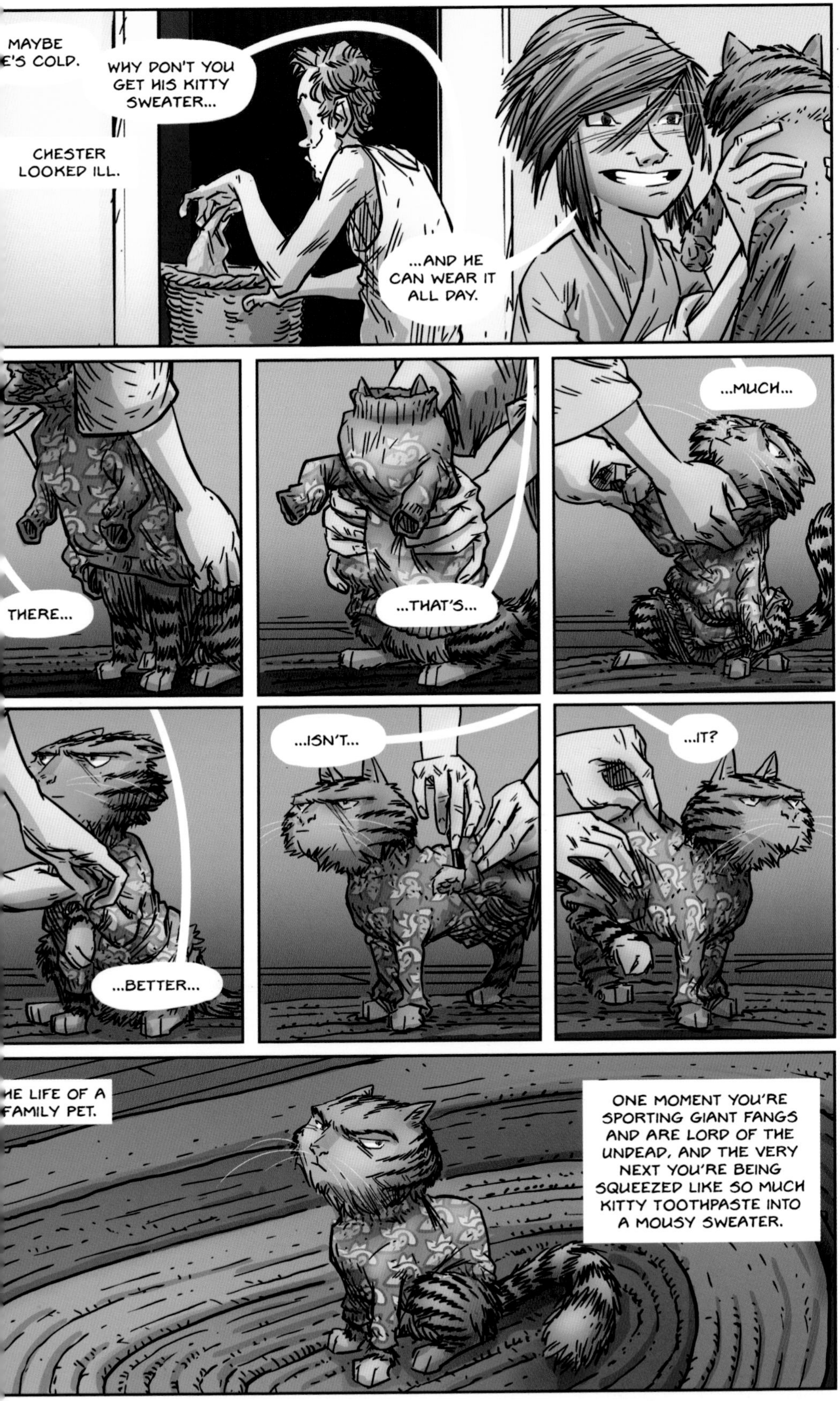
MAYBE
E'S COLD.
WHY DON'T YOU GET HIS KITTY SWEATER...
CHESTER LOOKED ILL.
...AND HE CAN WEAR IT ALL DAY.
THERE...
...THAT'S...
...MUCH...
...BETTER...
...ISN'T...
...IT?
HE LIFE OF A FAMILY PET.
ONE MOMENT YOU'RE SPORTING GIANT FANGS AND ARE LORD OF THE UNDEAD, AND THE VERY NEXT YOU'RE BEING SQUEEZED LIKE SO MUCH KITTY TOOTHPASTE INTO A MOUSY SWEATER.

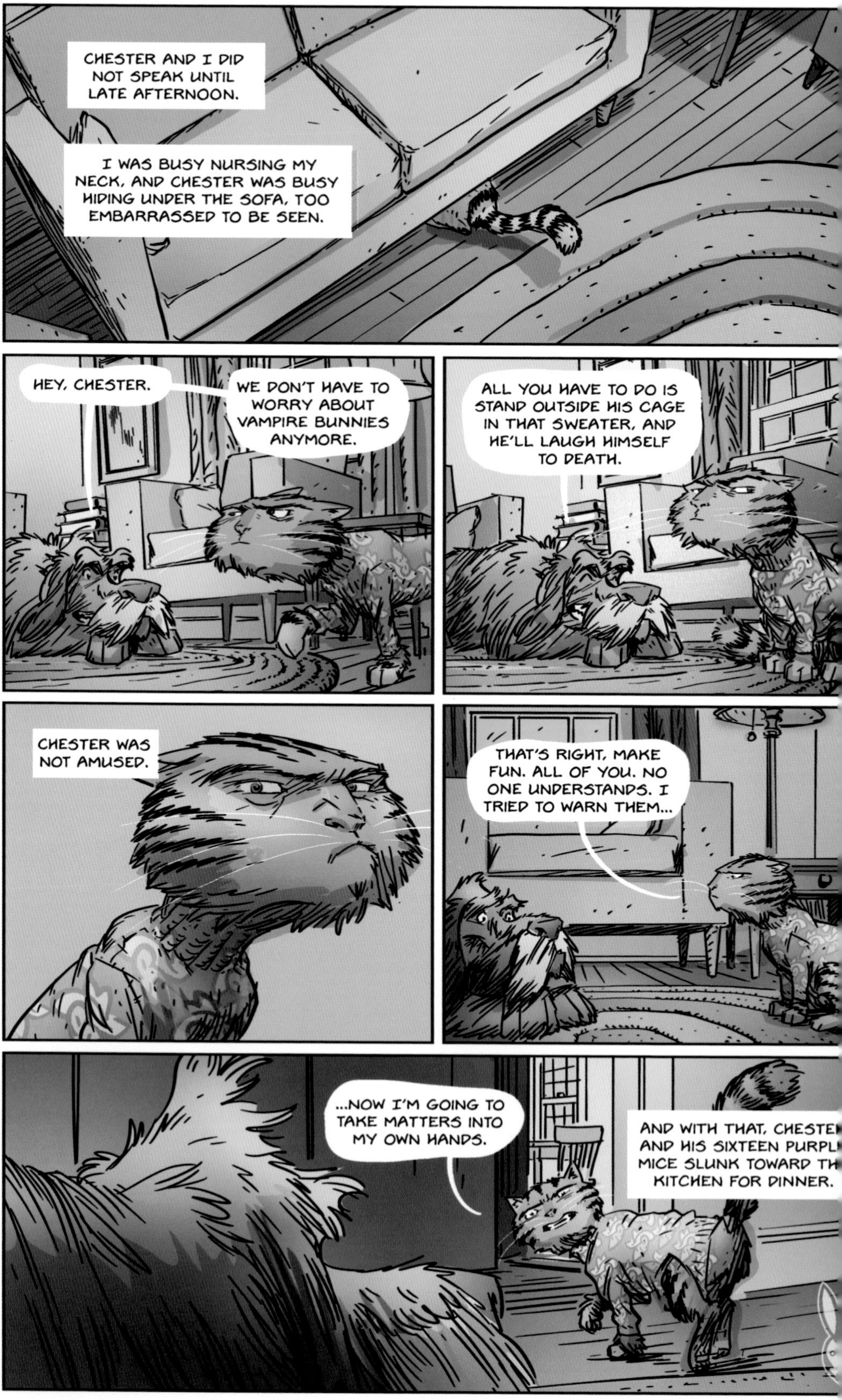
CHESTER AND I DID NOT SPEAK UNTIL LATE AFTERNOON.
I WAS BUSY NURSING MY NECK, AND CHESTER WAS BUSY HIDING UNDER THE SOFA, TOO EMBARRASSED TO BE SEEN.
HEY, CHESTER.
WE DON'T HAVE TO WORRY ABOUT VAMPIRE BUNNIES ANYMORE.
ALL YOU HAVE TO DO IS STAND OUTSIDE HIS CAGE IN THAT SWEATER, AND HE'LL LAUGH HIMSELF TO DEATH.
CHESTER WAS NOT AMUSED.
THAT'S RIGHT, MAKE FUN. ALL OF YOU. NO ONE UNDERSTANDS. I TRIED TO WARN THEM...
...NOW I'M GOING TO TAKE MATTERS INTO MY OWN HANDS.
AND WITH THAT, CHESTER AND HIS SIXTEEN PURPLE MICE SLUNK TOWARD THE KITCHEN FOR DINNER.

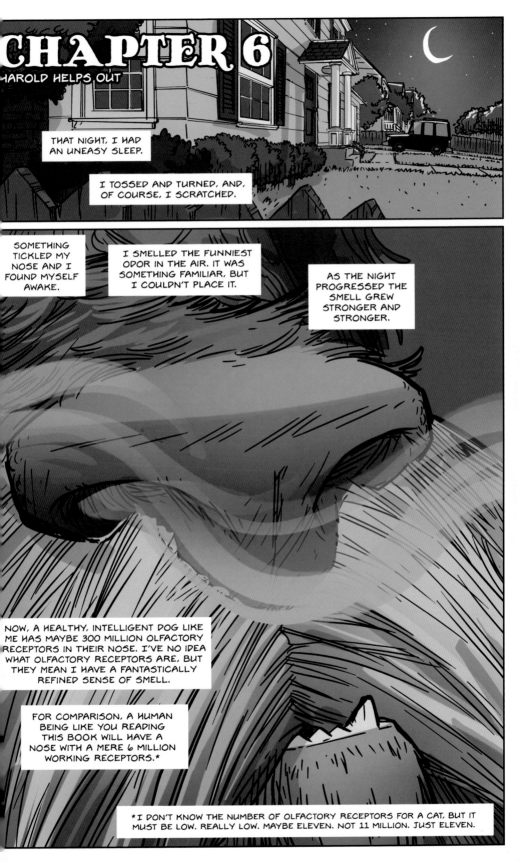

CHAPTER 6
HAROLD HELPS OUT

THAT NIGHT, I HAD AN UNEASY SLEEP.

I TOSSED AND TURNED, AND, OF COURSE, I SCRATCHED.

SOMETHING TICKLED MY NOSE AND I FOUND MYSELF AWAKE.

I SMELLED THE FUNNIEST ODOR IN THE AIR. IT WAS SOMETHING FAMILIAR, BUT I COULDN'T PLACE IT.

AS THE NIGHT PROGRESSED THE SMELL GREW STRONGER AND STRONGER.

NOW, A HEALTHY, INTELLIGENT DOG LIKE ME HAS MAYBE 300 MILLION OLFACTORY RECEPTORS IN THEIR NOSE. I'VE NO IDEA WHAT OLFACTORY RECEPTORS ARE, BUT THEY MEAN I HAVE A FANTASTICALLY REFINED SENSE OF SMELL.

FOR COMPARISON, A HUMAN BEING LIKE YOU READING THIS BOOK WILL HAVE A NOSE WITH A MERE 6 MILLION WORKING RECEPTORS.*

*I DON'T KNOW THE NUMBER OF OLFACTORY RECEPTORS FOR A CAT, BUT IT MUST BE LOW. REALLY LOW. MAYBE ELEVEN. NOT 11 MILLION. JUST ELEVEN.

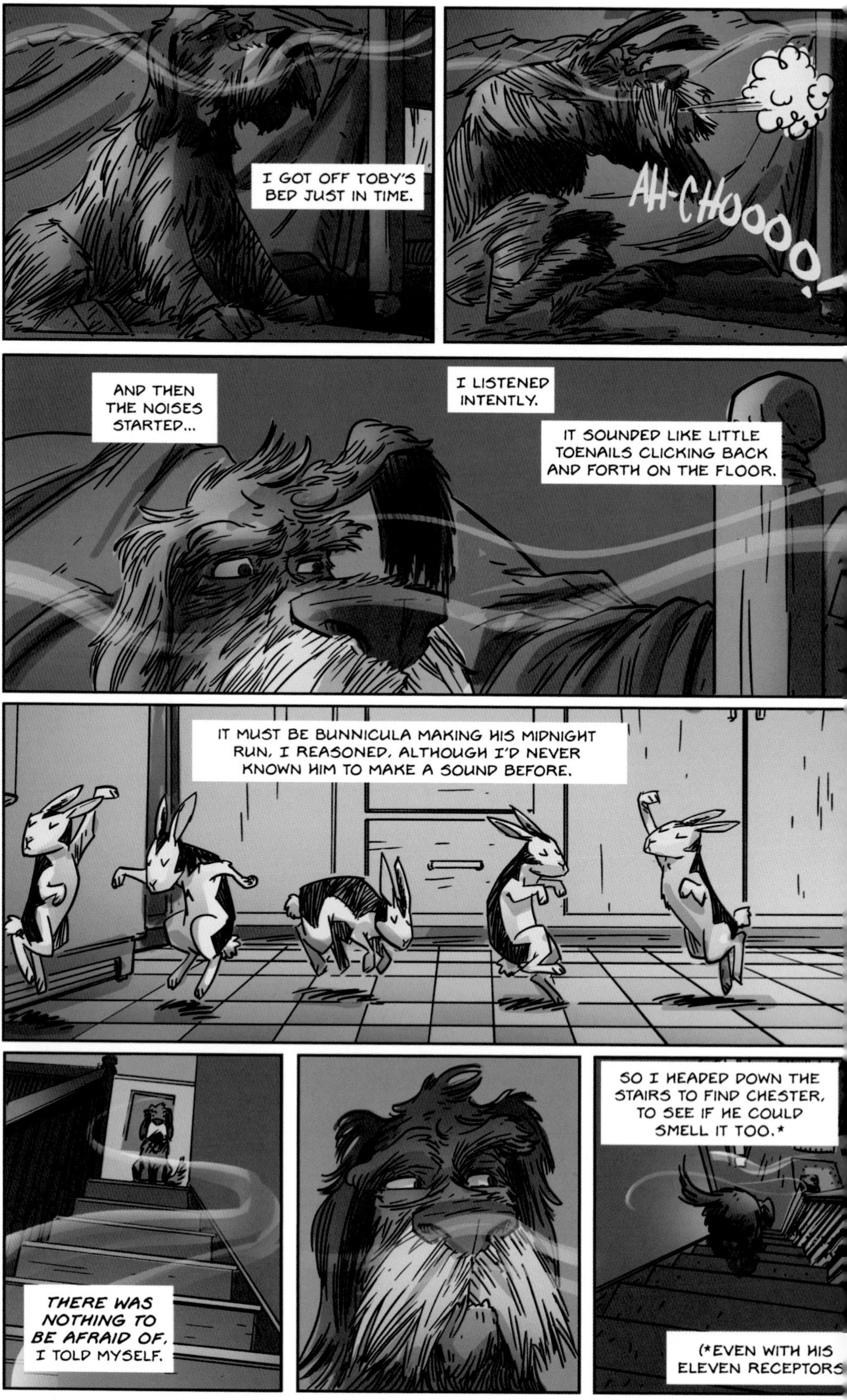
I GOT OFF TOBY'S BED JUST IN TIME.
AH-CHOOOO!
AND THEN THE NOISES STARTED...
I LISTENED INTENTLY.
IT SOUNDED LIKE LITTLE TOENAILS CLICKING BACK AND FORTH ON THE FLOOR.
IT MUST BE BUNNICULA MAKING HIS MIDNIGHT RUN, I REASONED, ALTHOUGH I'D NEVER KNOWN HIM TO MAKE A SOUND BEFORE.
THERE WAS NOTHING TO BE AFRAID OF, I TOLD MYSELF.
SO I HEADED DOWN THE STAIRS TO FIND CHESTER, TO SEE IF HE COULD SMELL IT TOO.*
(*EVEN WITH HIS ELEVEN RECEPTORS

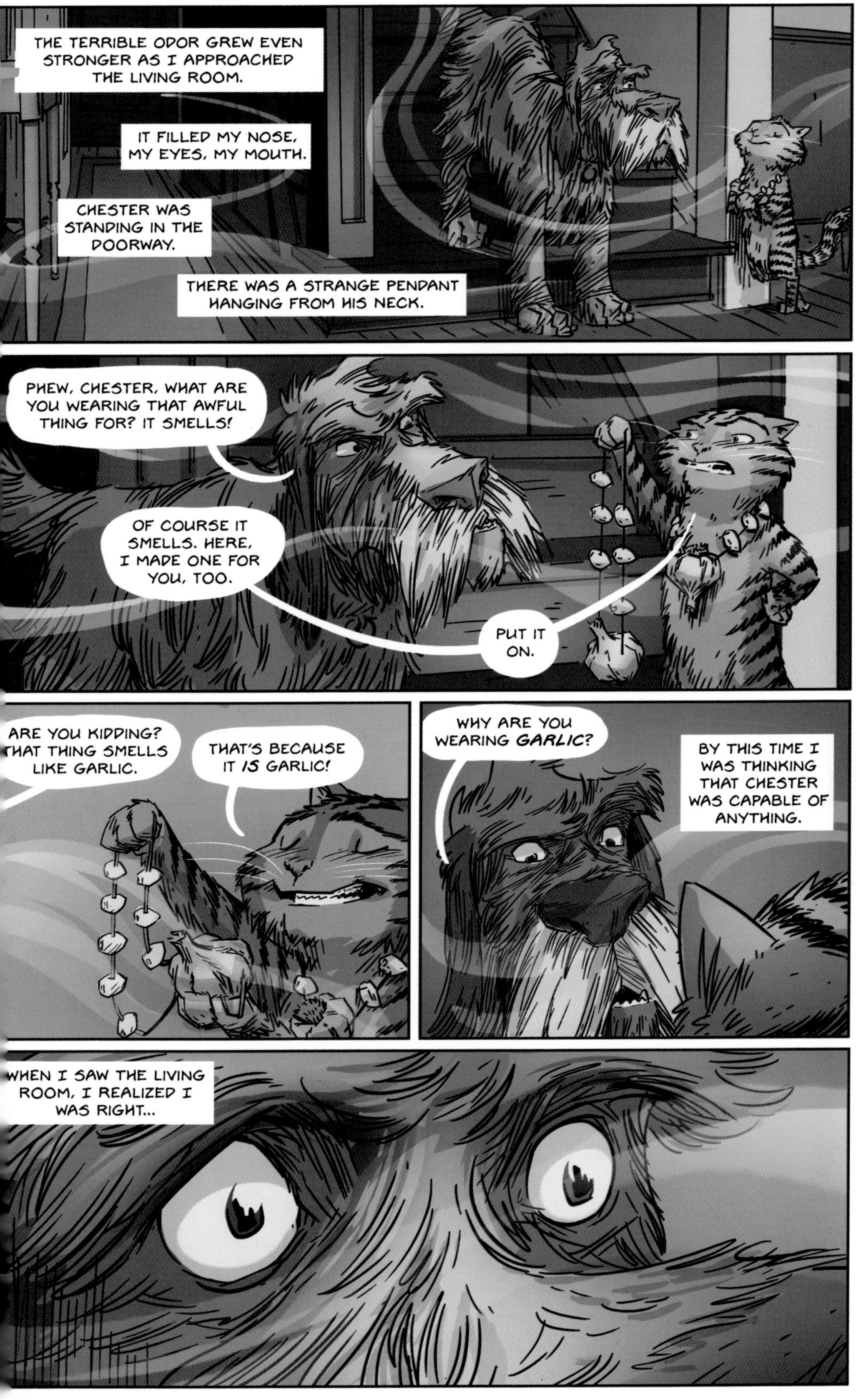
THE TERRIBLE ODOR GREW EVEN STRONGER AS I APPROACHED THE LIVING ROOM.
IT FILLED MY NOSE, MY EYES, MY MOUTH.
CHESTER WAS STANDING IN THE DOORWAY.
THERE WAS A STRANGE PENDANT HANGING FROM HIS NECK.
PHEW, CHESTER, WHAT ARE YOU WEARING THAT AWFUL THING FOR? IT SMELLS!
OF COURSE IT SMELLS. HERE, I MADE ONE FOR YOU, TOO.
PUT IT ON.
ARE YOU KIDDING? THAT THING SMELLS LIKE GARLIC.
THAT'S BECAUSE IT *IS* GARLIC!
WHY ARE YOU WEARING ***GARLIC***?
BY THIS TIME I WAS THINKING THAT CHESTER WAS CAPABLE OF ANYTHING.
WHEN I SAW THE LIVING ROOM, I REALIZED I WAS RIGHT...

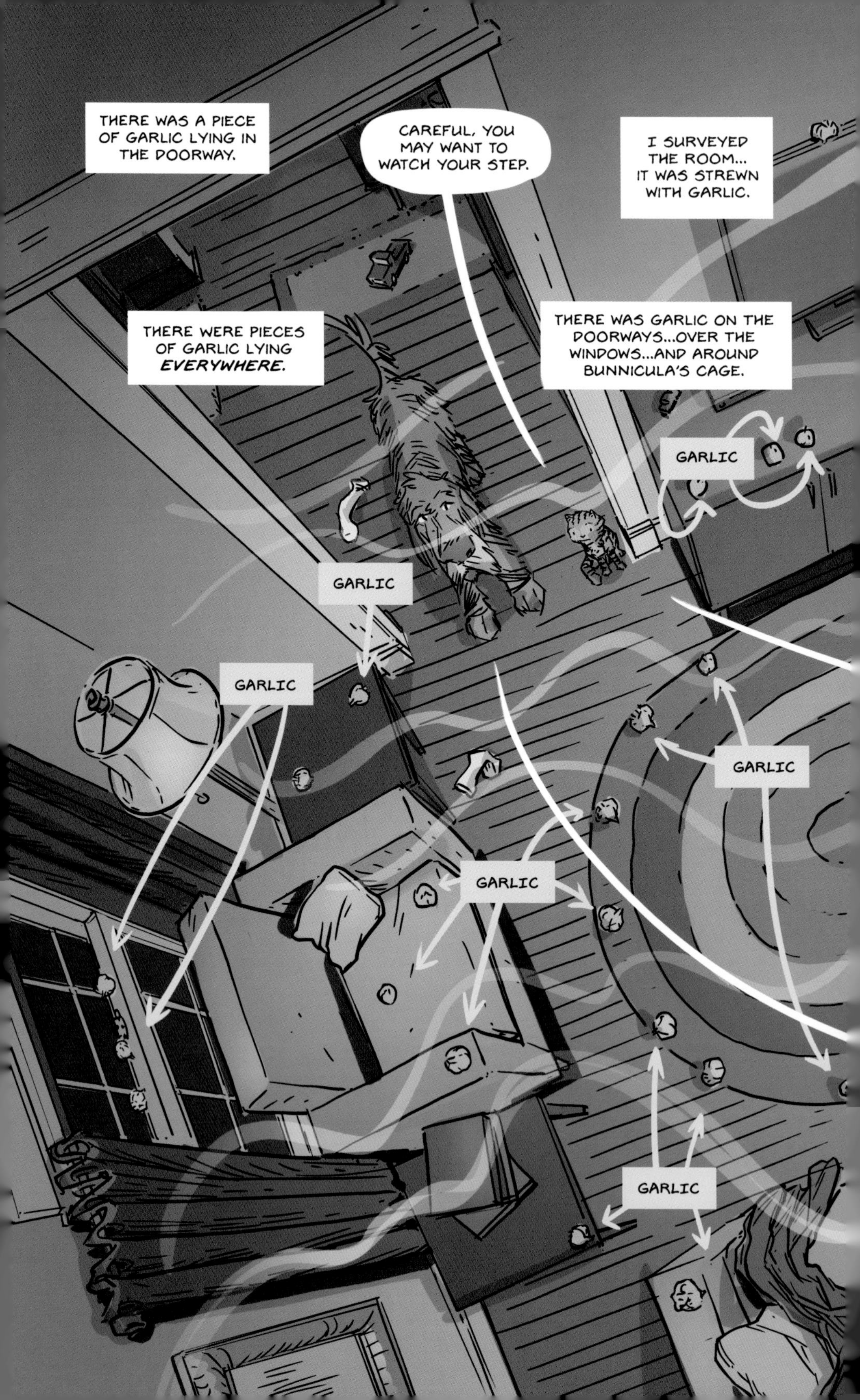
THERE WAS A PIECE OF GARLIC LYING IN THE DOORWAY.
CAREFUL, YOU MAY WANT TO WATCH YOUR STEP.
I SURVEYED THE ROOM... IT WAS STREWN WITH GARLIC.
THERE WERE PIECES OF GARLIC LYING *EVERYWHERE.*
THERE WAS GARLIC ON THE DOORWAYS...OVER THE WINDOWS...AND AROUND BUNNICULA'S CAGE.
GARLIC
GARLIC
GARLIC
GARLIC
GARLIC
GARLIC

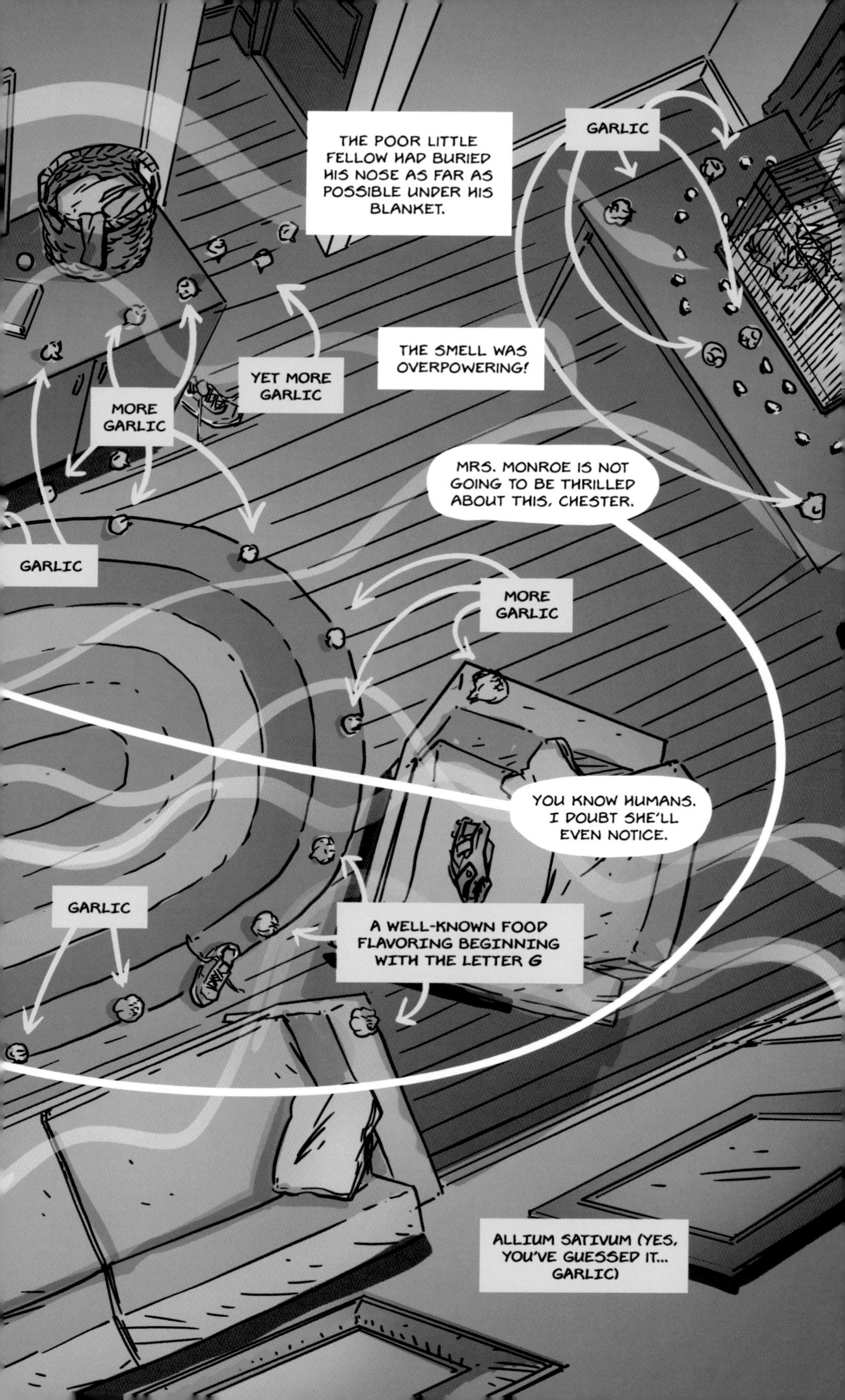
THE POOR LITTLE FELLOW HAD BURIED HIS NOSE AS FAR AS POSSIBLE UNDER HIS BLANKET.
GARLIC
MORE GARLIC
YET MORE GARLIC
THE SMELL WAS OVERPOWERING!
GARLIC
MRS. MONROE IS NOT GOING TO BE THRILLED ABOUT THIS, CHESTER.
MORE GARLIC
YOU KNOW HUMANS. I DOUBT SHE'LL EVEN NOTICE.
GARLIC
A WELL-KNOWN FOOD FLAVORING BEGINNING WITH THE LETTER G
ALLIUM SATIVUM (YES, YOU'VE GUESSED IT... GARLIC)

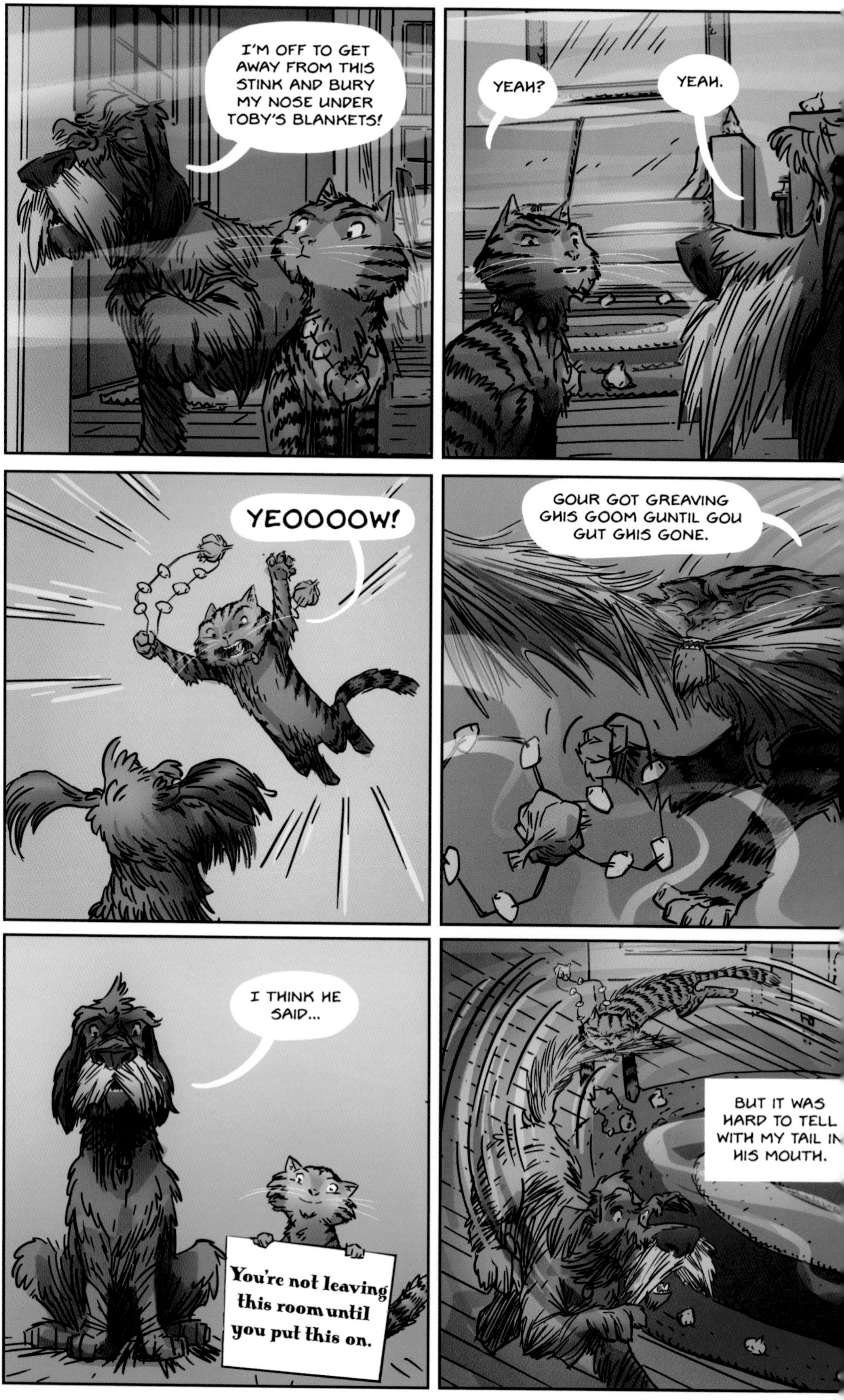
I'M OFF TO GET AWAY FROM THIS STINK AND BURY MY NOSE UNDER TOBY'S BLANKETS!
YEAH?
YEAH.
YEOOOOW!
GOUR GOT GREAVING GHIS GOOM GUNTIL GOU GUT GHIS GONE.
I THINK HE SAID...
You're not leaving this room until you put this on.
BUT IT WAS HARD TO TELL WITH MY TAIL IN HIS MOUTH.

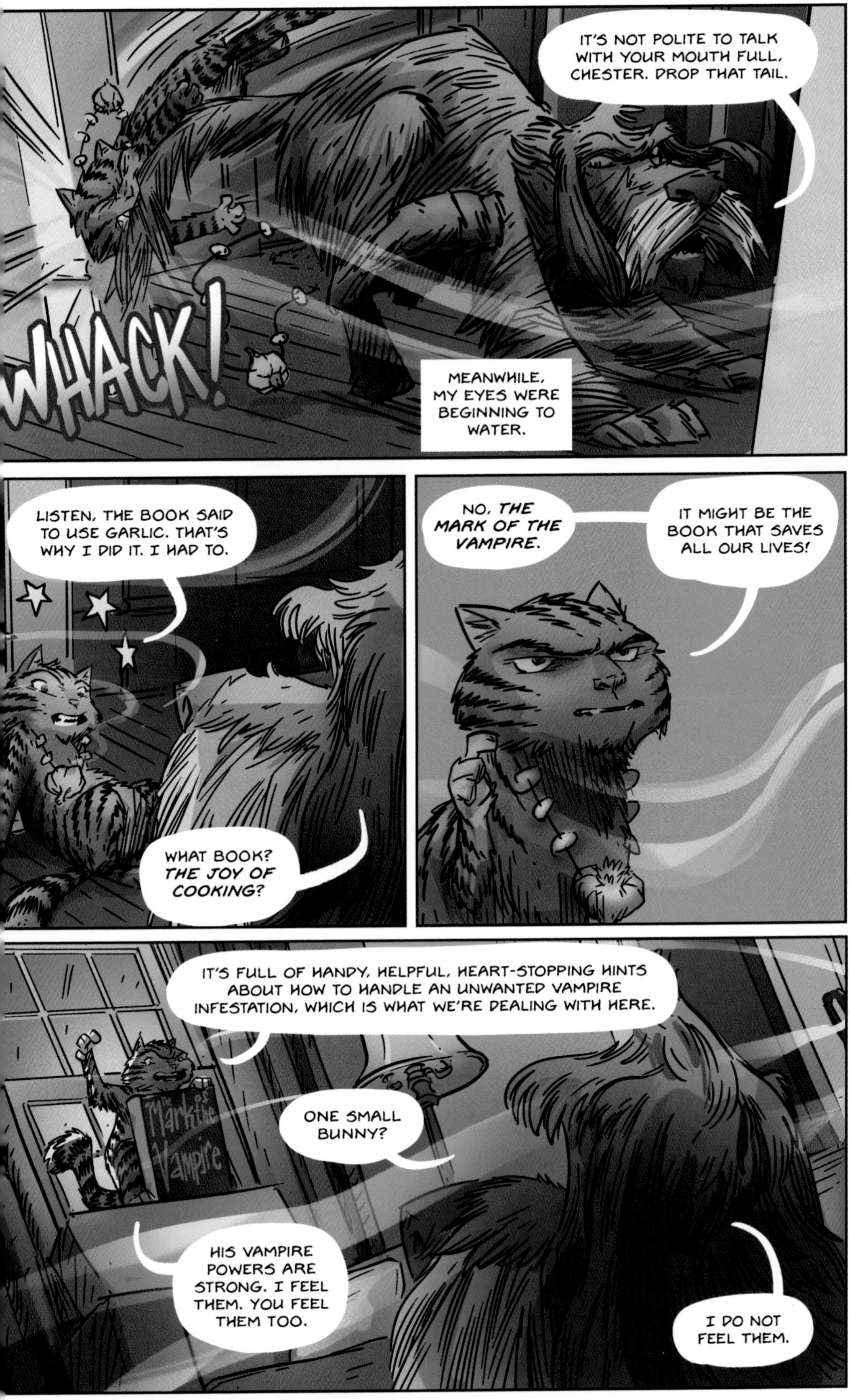
IT'S NOT POLITE TO TALK WITH YOUR MOUTH FULL, CHESTER. DROP THAT TAIL.
WHACK!
MEANWHILE, MY EYES WERE BEGINNING TO WATER.
LISTEN, THE BOOK SAID TO USE GARLIC. THAT'S WHY I DID IT. I HAD TO.
WHAT BOOK? *THE JOY OF COOKING*?
NO, *THE MARK OF THE VAMPIRE*.
IT MIGHT BE THE BOOK THAT SAVES ALL OUR LIVES!
IT'S FULL OF HANDY, HELPFUL, HEART-STOPPING HINTS ABOUT HOW TO HANDLE AN UNWANTED VAMPIRE INFESTATION, WHICH IS WHAT WE'RE DEALING WITH HERE.
The Mark of the Vampire
ONE SMALL BUNNY?
HIS VAMPIRE POWERS ARE STRONG. I FEEL THEM. YOU FEEL THEM TOO.
I DO NOT FEEL THEM.

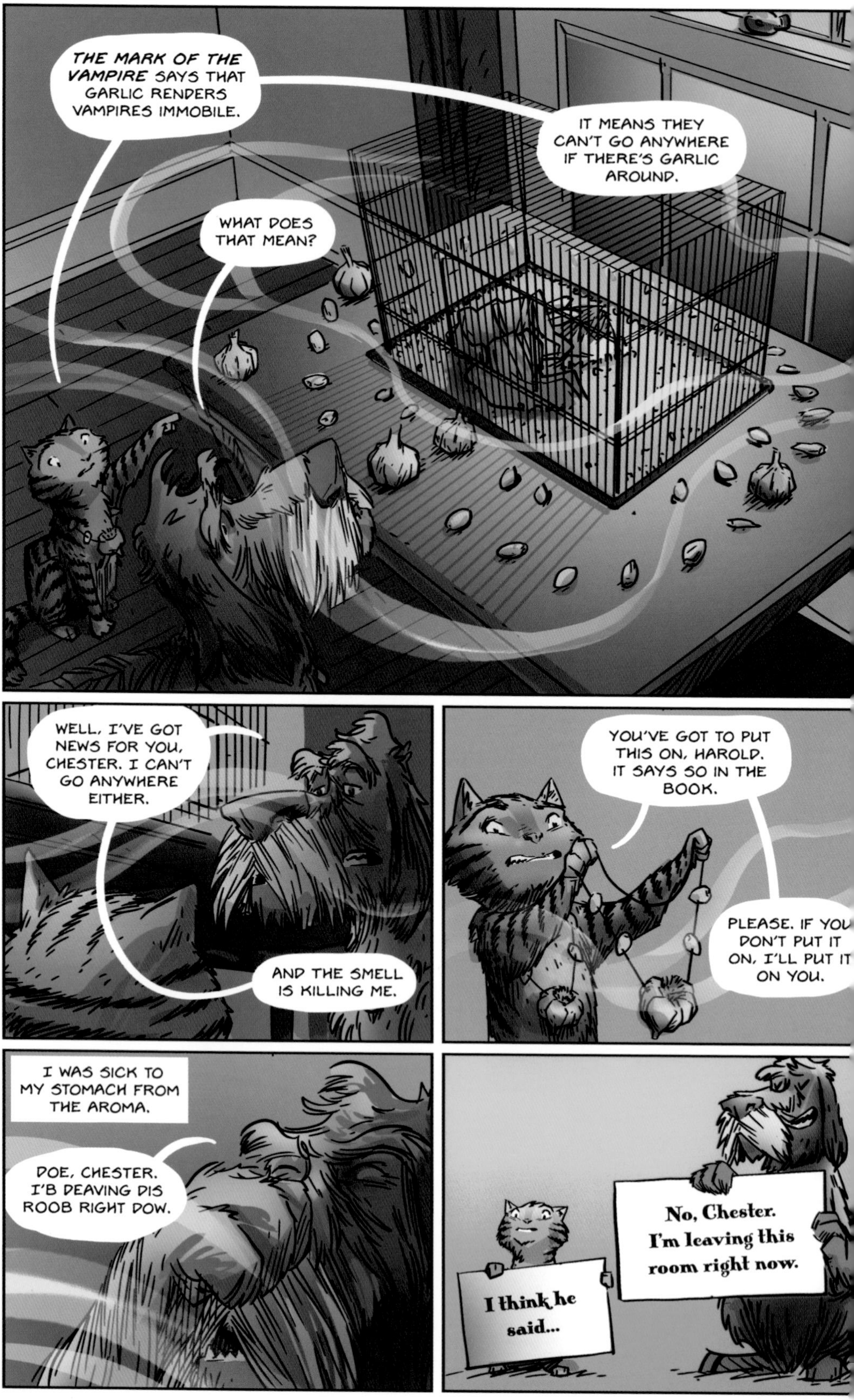
THE MARK OF THE VAMPIRE SAYS THAT GARLIC RENDERS VAMPIRES IMMOBILE.
WHAT DOES THAT MEAN?
IT MEANS THEY CAN'T GO ANYWHERE IF THERE'S GARLIC AROUND.
WELL, I'VE GOT NEWS FOR YOU, CHESTER. I CAN'T GO ANYWHERE EITHER.
AND THE SMELL IS KILLING ME.
YOU'VE GOT TO PUT THIS ON, HAROLD. IT SAYS SO IN THE BOOK.
PLEASE. IF YOU DON'T PUT IT ON, I'LL PUT IT ON YOU.
I WAS SICK TO MY STOMACH FROM THE AROMA.
DOE, CHESTER. I'B DEAVING DIS ROOB RIGHT DOW.
I think he said...
No, Chester. I'm leaving this room right now.

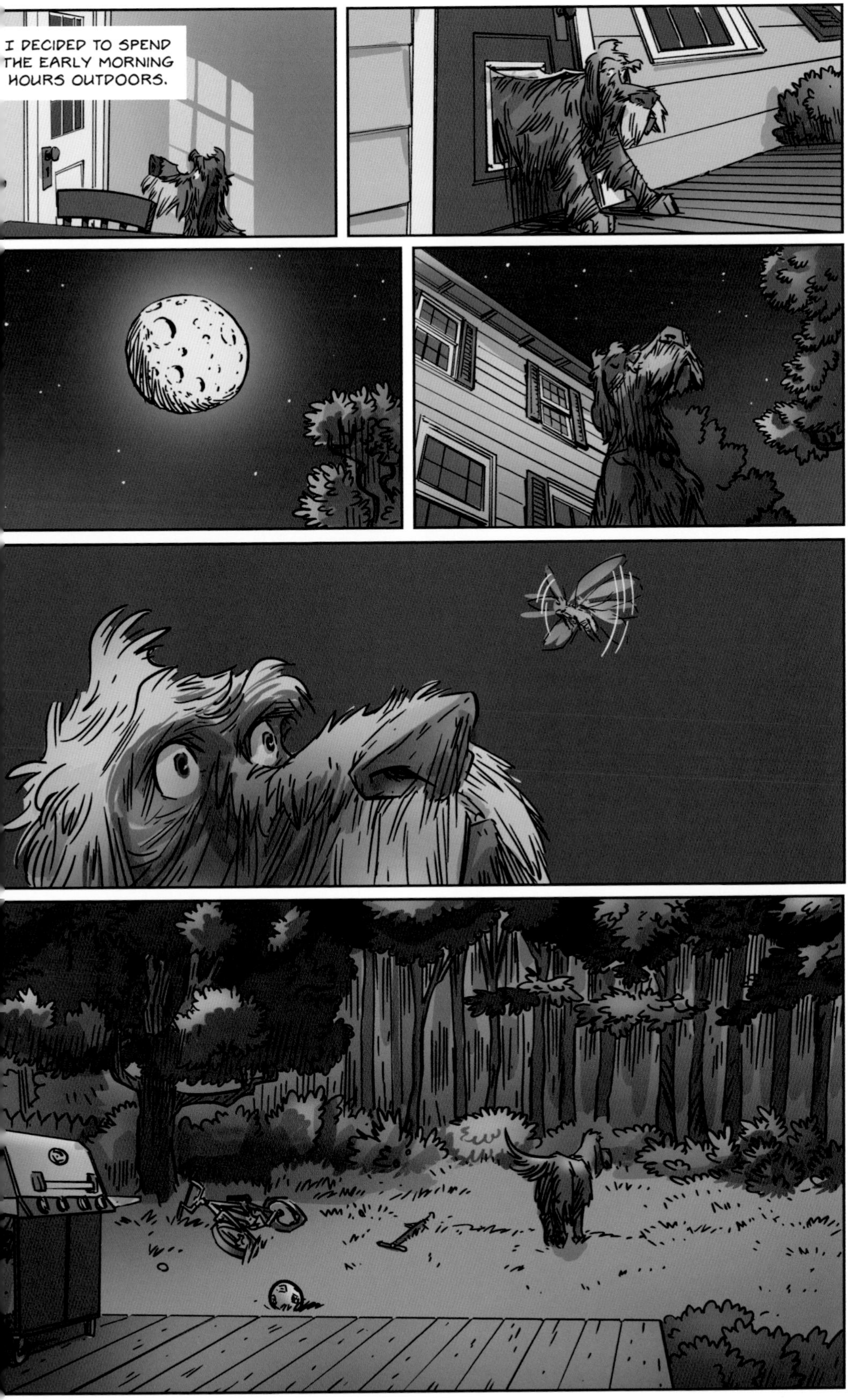
I DECIDED TO SPEND THE EARLY MORNING HOURS OUTDOORS.

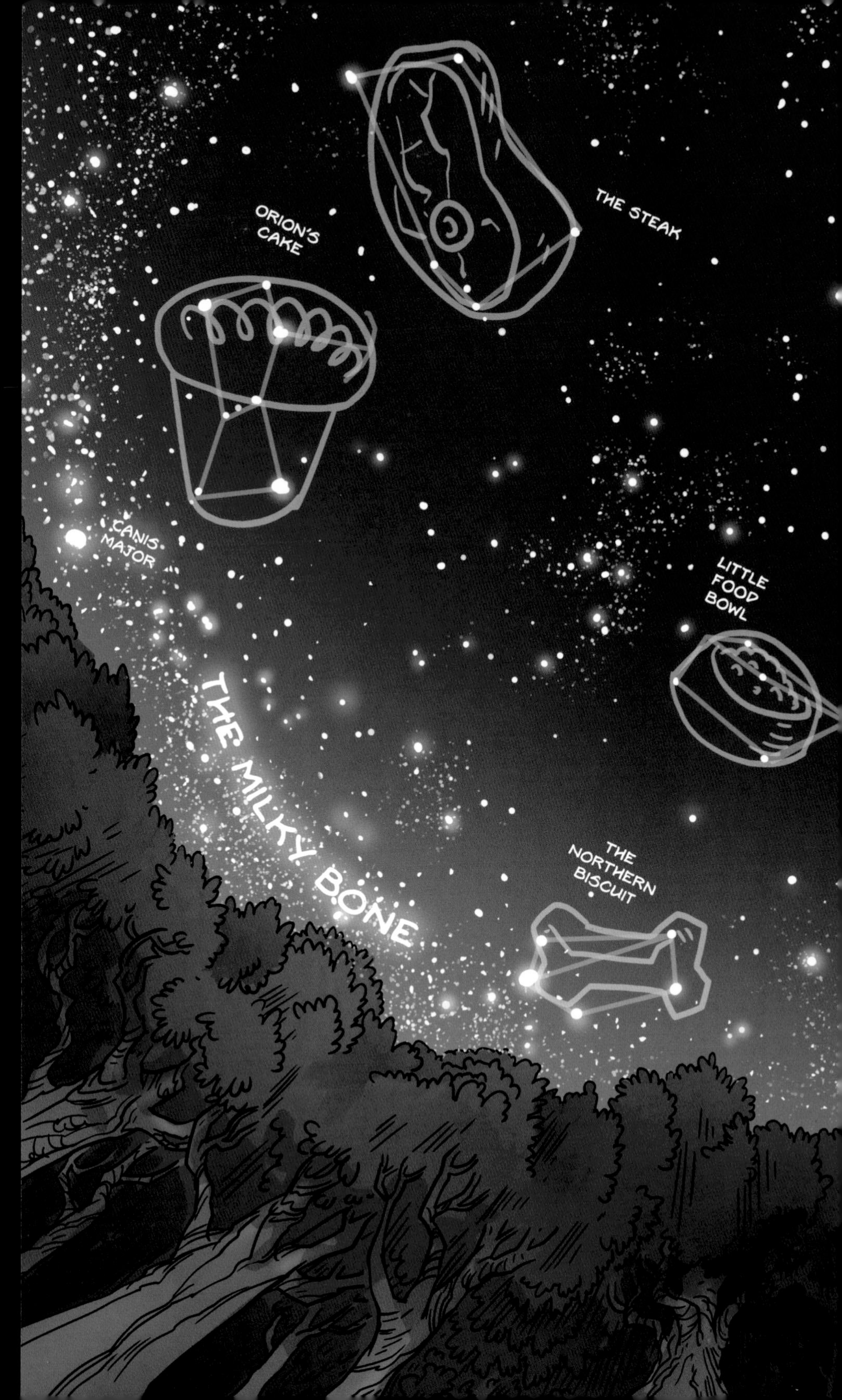

ORION'S CAKE
THE STEAK
CANIS MAJOR
LITTLE FOOD BOWL
THE MILKY BONE
THE NORTHERN BISCUIT

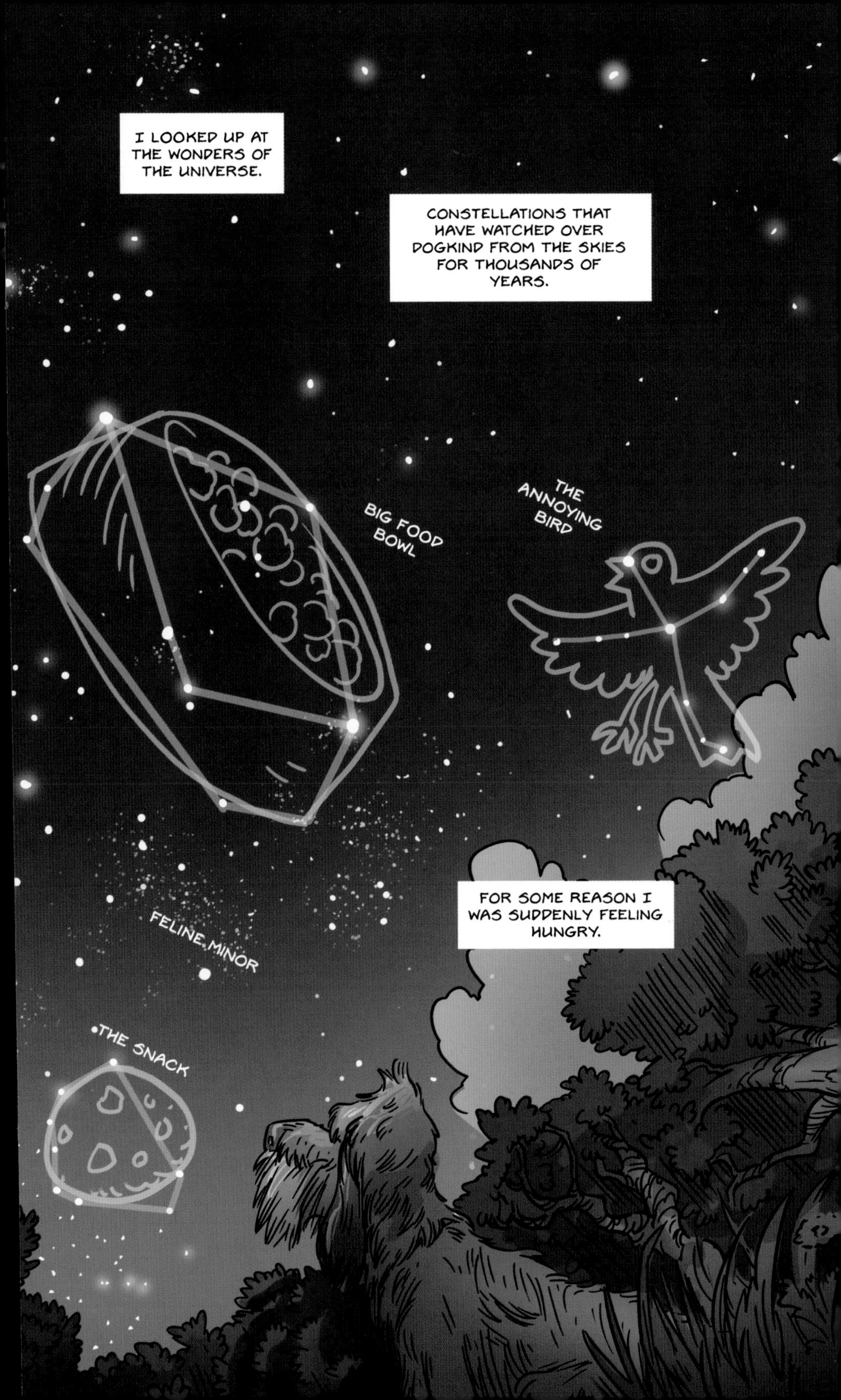
I LOOKED UP AT THE WONDERS OF THE UNIVERSE.
CONSTELLATIONS THAT HAVE WATCHED OVER DOGKIND FROM THE SKIES FOR THOUSANDS OF YEARS.
BIG FOOD BOWL
THE ANNOYING BIRD
FELINE MINOR
THE SNACK
FOR SOME REASON I WAS SUDDENLY FEELING HUNGRY.

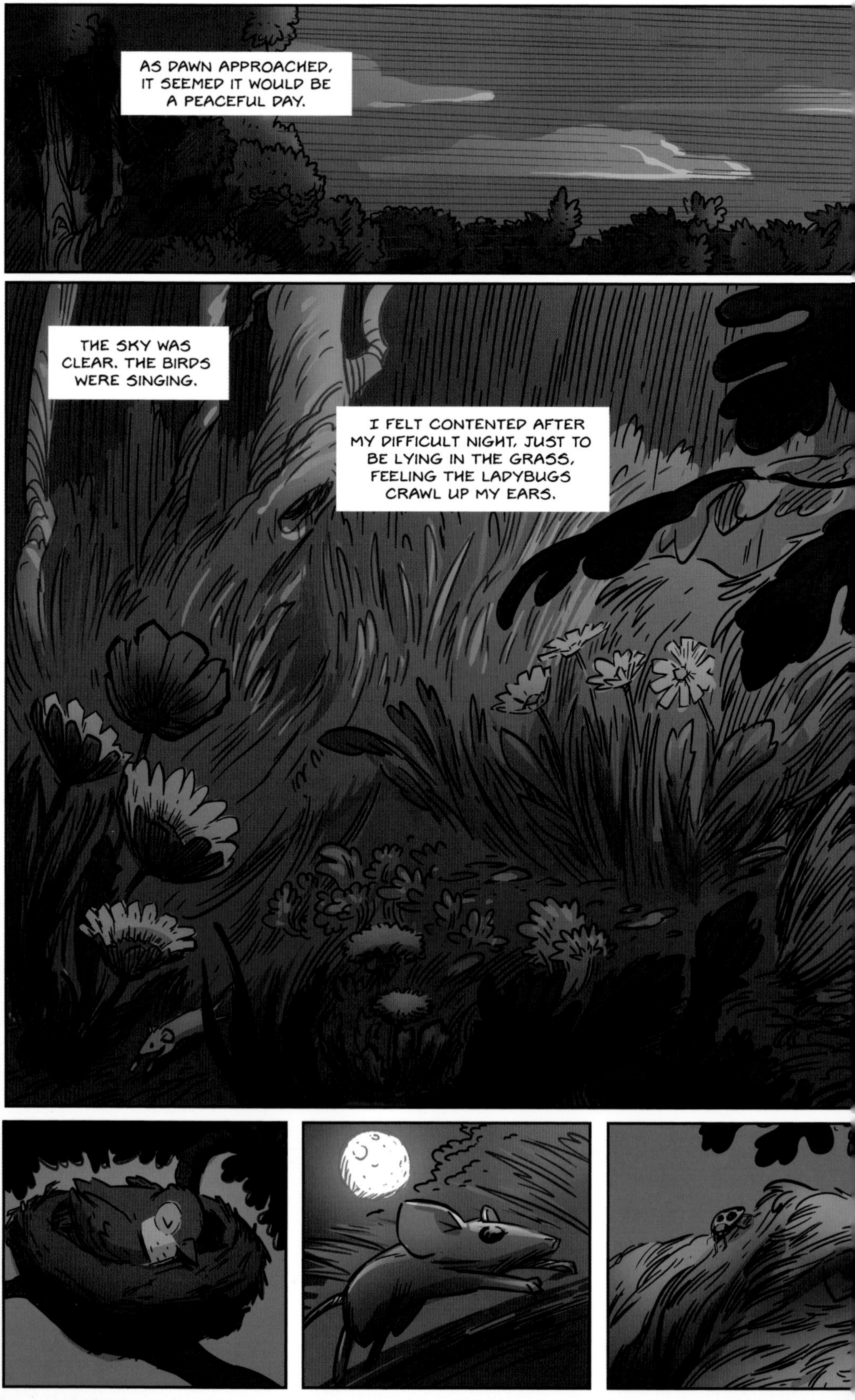
AS DAWN APPROACHED, IT SEEMED IT WOULD BE A PEACEFUL DAY.
THE SKY WAS CLEAR. THE BIRDS WERE SINGING.
I FELT CONTENTED AFTER MY DIFFICULT NIGHT, JUST TO BE LYING IN THE GRASS, FEELING THE LADYBUGS CRAWL UP MY EARS.

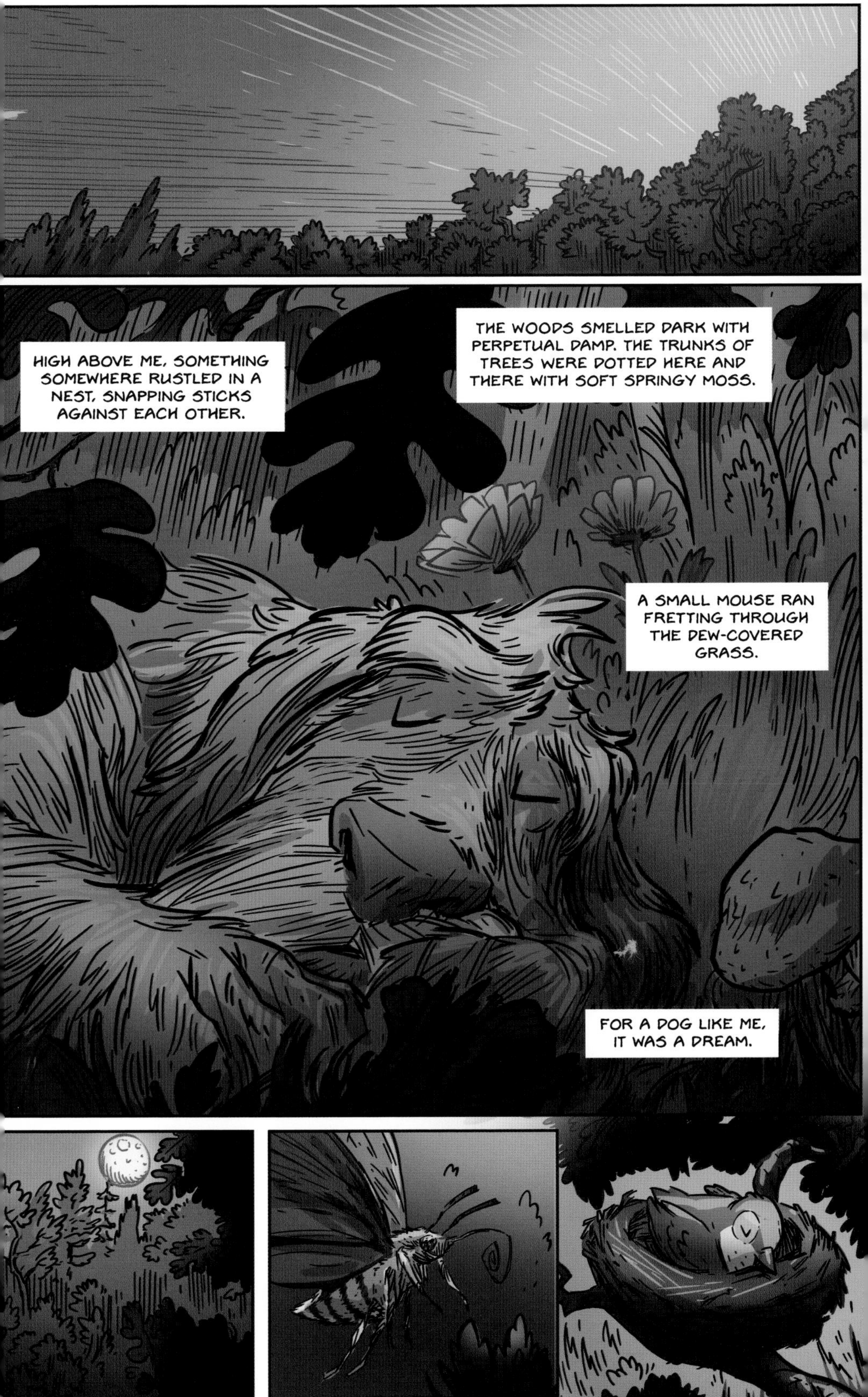
HIGH ABOVE ME, SOMETHING SOMEWHERE RUSTLED IN A NEST, SNAPPING STICKS AGAINST EACH OTHER.
THE WOODS SMELLED DARK WITH PERPETUAL DAMP. THE TRUNKS OF TREES WERE DOTTED HERE AND THERE WITH SOFT SPRINGY MOSS.
A SMALL MOUSE RAN FRETTING THROUGH THE DEW-COVERED GRASS.
FOR A DOG LIKE ME, IT WAS A DREAM.

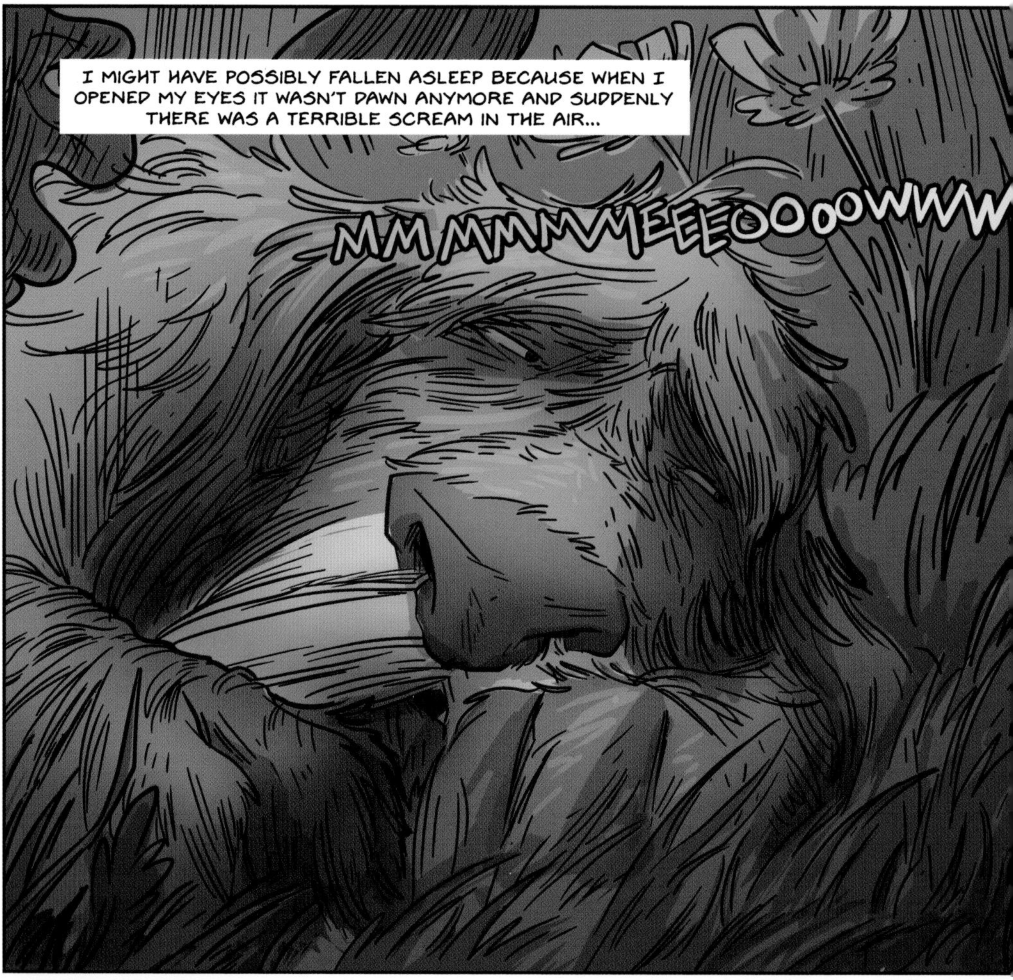
I MIGHT HAVE POSSIBLY FALLEN ASLEEP BECAUSE WHEN I OPENED MY EYES IT WASN'T DAWN ANYMORE AND SUDDENLY THERE WAS A TERRIBLE SCREAM IN THE AIR...
MM MMMMEEEOOooOWWW

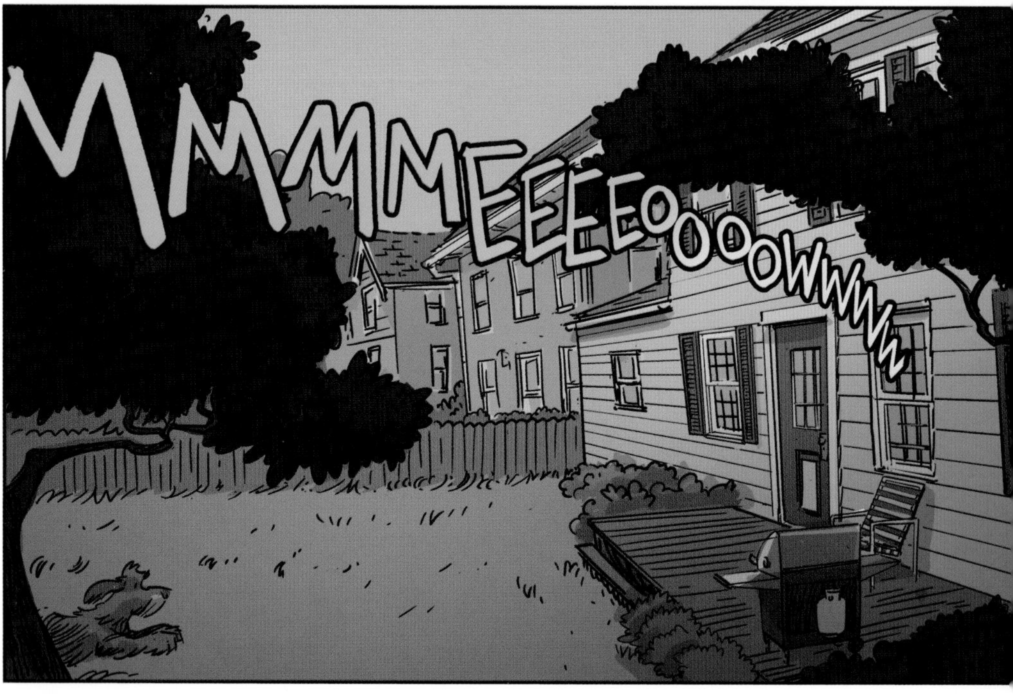
MMMMEEEEOOOOWWWW

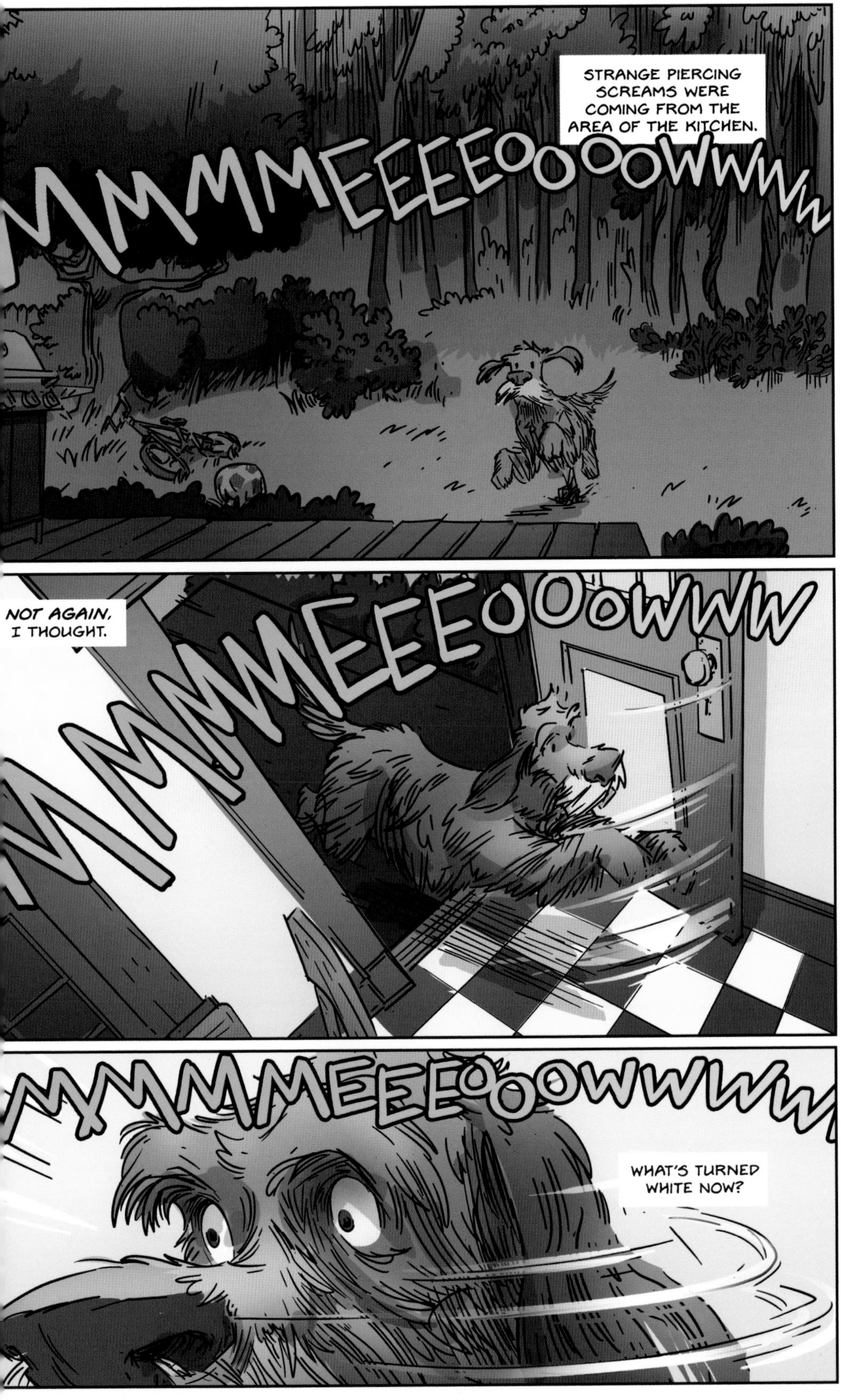
STRANGE PIERCING SCREAMS WERE COMING FROM THE AREA OF THE KITCHEN.
MMMMEEEEEOOOOWWWW
NOT AGAIN, I THOUGHT.
MMMMEEEEOOOOWWW
MMMMEEEEOOOOWWWW
WHAT'S TURNED WHITE NOW?

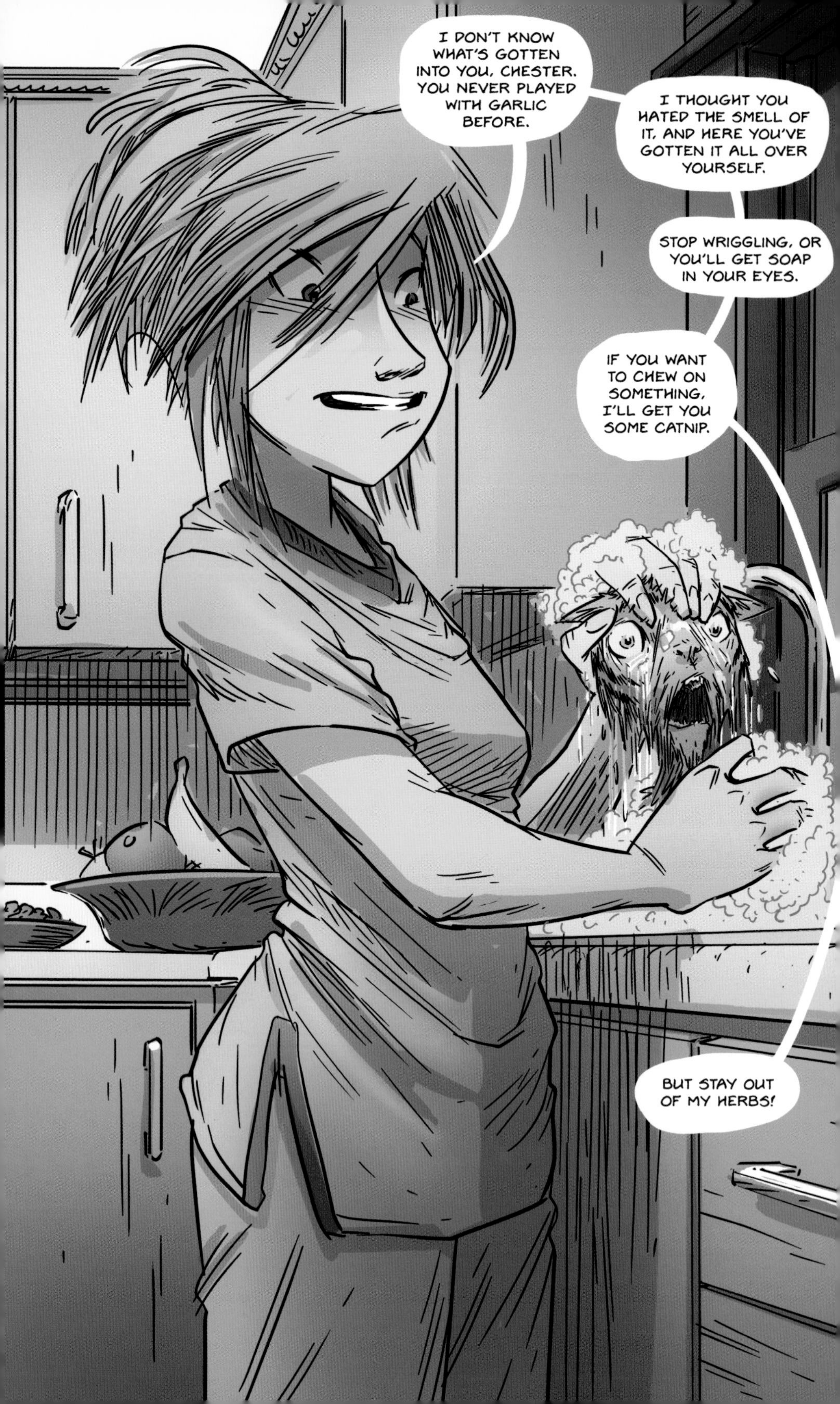
I DON'T KNOW WHAT'S GOTTEN INTO YOU, CHESTER. YOU NEVER PLAYED WITH GARLIC BEFORE.
I THOUGHT YOU HATED THE SMELL OF IT, AND HERE YOU'VE GOTTEN IT ALL OVER YOURSELF.
STOP WRIGGLING, OR YOU'LL GET SOAP IN YOUR EYES.
IF YOU WANT TO CHEW ON SOMETHING, I'LL GET YOU SOME CATNIP.
BUT STAY OUT OF MY HERBS!

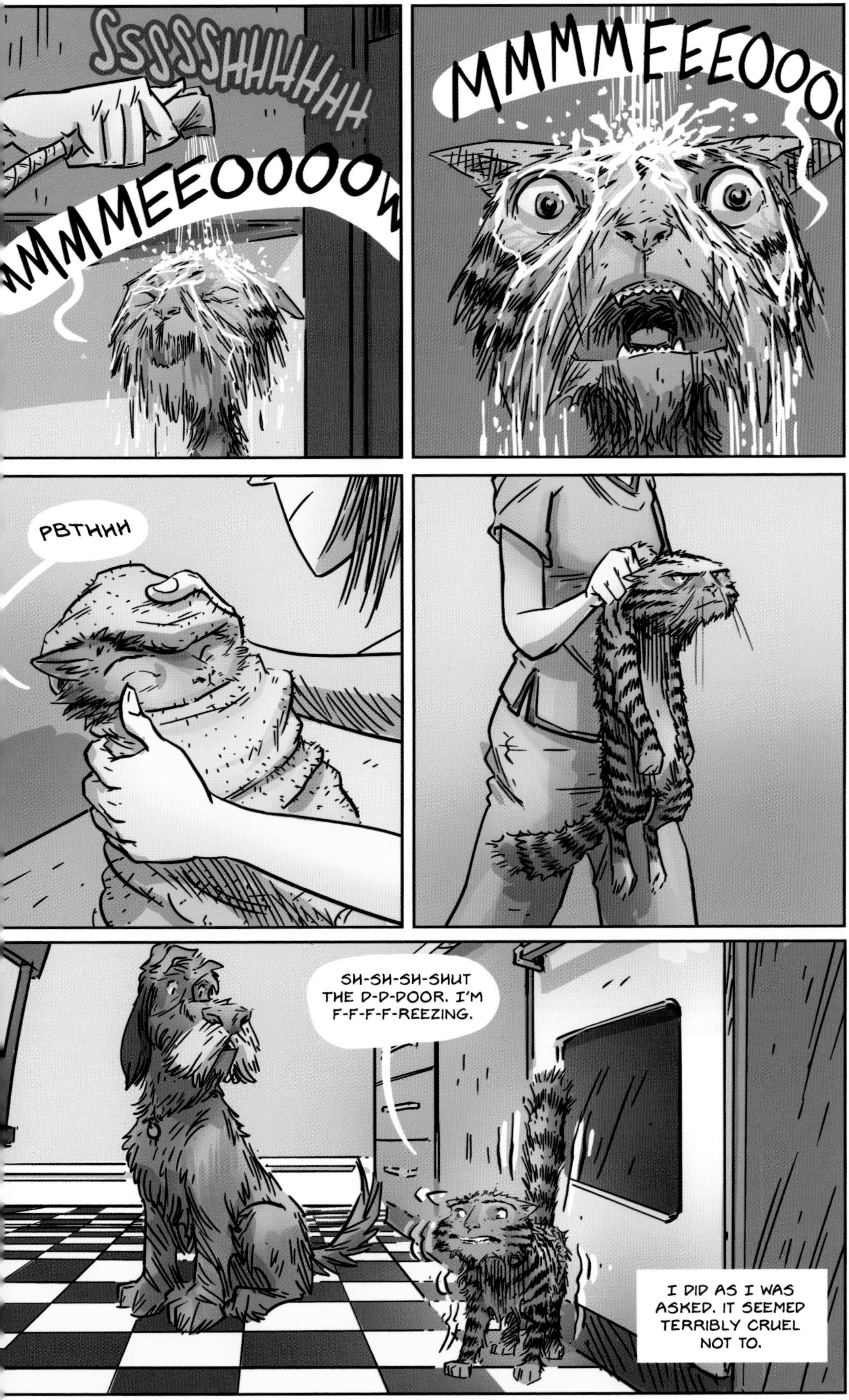
SSSSSHHHHHHH
MMMEEOOOOW
MMMMEEEOOO
PBTHHH
SH-SH-SH-SHUT THE D-D-DOOR. I'M F-F-F-F-REEZING.
I DID AS I WAS ASKED. IT SEEMED TERRIBLY CRUEL NOT TO.

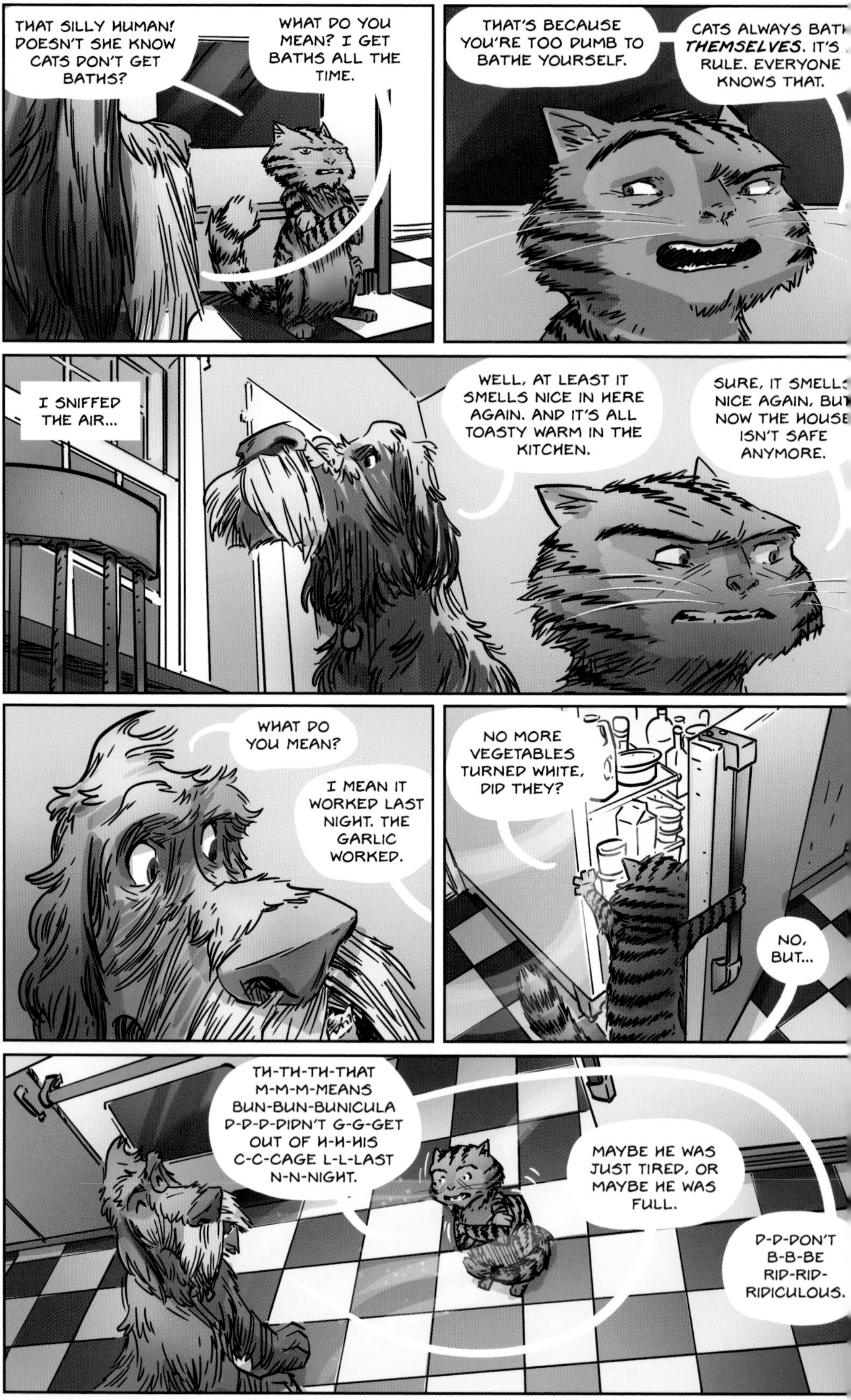
THAT SILLY HUMAN! DOESN'T SHE KNOW CATS DON'T GET BATHS?
WHAT DO YOU MEAN? I GET BATHS ALL THE TIME.
THAT'S BECAUSE YOU'RE TOO DUMB TO BATHE YOURSELF.
CATS ALWAYS BATHE *THEMSELVES*. IT'S A RULE. EVERYONE KNOWS THAT.
I SNIFFED THE AIR...
WELL, AT LEAST IT SMELLS NICE IN HERE AGAIN. AND IT'S ALL TOASTY WARM IN THE KITCHEN.
SURE, IT SMELLS NICE AGAIN, BUT NOW THE HOUSE ISN'T SAFE ANYMORE.
WHAT DO YOU MEAN?
I MEAN IT WORKED LAST NIGHT. THE GARLIC WORKED.
NO MORE VEGETABLES TURNED WHITE, DID THEY?
NO, BUT...
TH-TH-TH-THAT M-M-M-MEANS BUN-BUN-BUNICULA D-D-D-DIDN'T G-G-GET OUT OF H-H-HIS C-C-CAGE L-L-LAST N-N-NIGHT.
MAYBE HE WAS JUST TIRED, OR MAYBE HE WAS FULL.
D-D-DON'T B-B-BE RID-RID-RIDICULOUS.

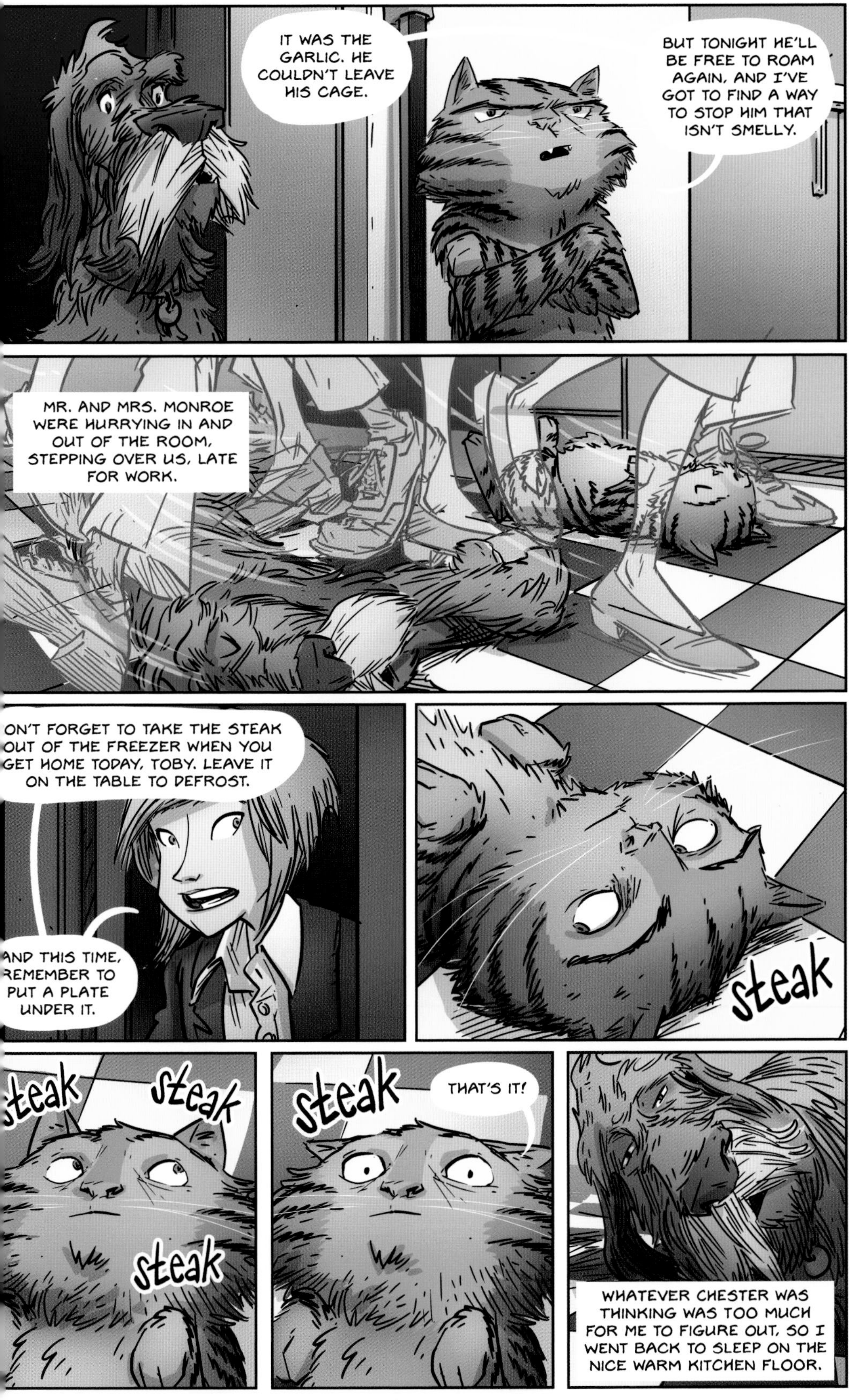

IT WAS THE GARLIC. HE COULDN'T LEAVE HIS CAGE.
BUT TONIGHT HE'LL BE FREE TO ROAM AGAIN, AND I'VE GOT TO FIND A WAY TO STOP HIM THAT ISN'T SMELLY.
MR. AND MRS. MONROE WERE HURRYING IN AND OUT OF THE ROOM, STEPPING OVER US, LATE FOR WORK.
ON'T FORGET TO TAKE THE STEAK OUT OF THE FREEZER WHEN YOU GET HOME TODAY, TOBY. LEAVE IT ON THE TABLE TO DEFROST.
AND THIS TIME, REMEMBER TO PUT A PLATE UNDER IT.
steak
steak
steak
steak
steak
THAT'S IT!
WHATEVER CHESTER WAS THINKING WAS TOO MUCH FOR ME TO FIGURE OUT, SO I WENT BACK TO SLEEP ON THE NICE WARM KITCHEN FLOOR.

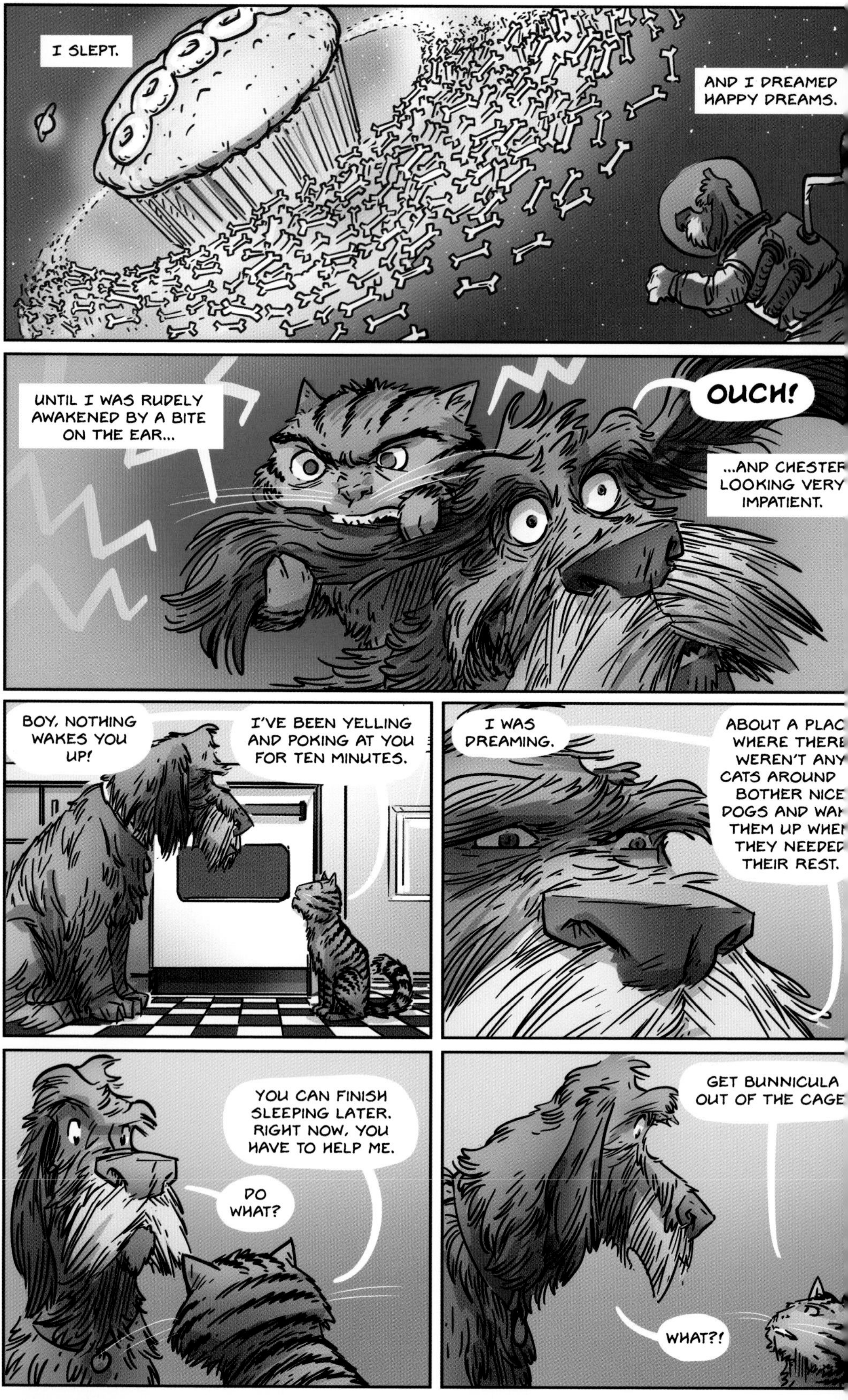

I SLEPT.
AND I DREAMED HAPPY DREAMS.
UNTIL I WAS RUDELY AWAKENED BY A BITE ON THE EAR...
OUCH!
...AND CHESTER LOOKING VERY IMPATIENT.
BOY, NOTHING WAKES YOU UP!
I'VE BEEN YELLING AND POKING AT YOU FOR TEN MINUTES.
I WAS DREAMING.
ABOUT A PLAC WHERE THERE WEREN'T ANY CATS AROUND BOTHER NICE DOGS AND WAK THEM UP WHEN THEY NEEDED THEIR REST.
YOU CAN FINISH SLEEPING LATER. RIGHT NOW, YOU HAVE TO HELP ME.
DO WHAT?
GET BUNNICULA OUT OF THE CAGE
WHAT?!

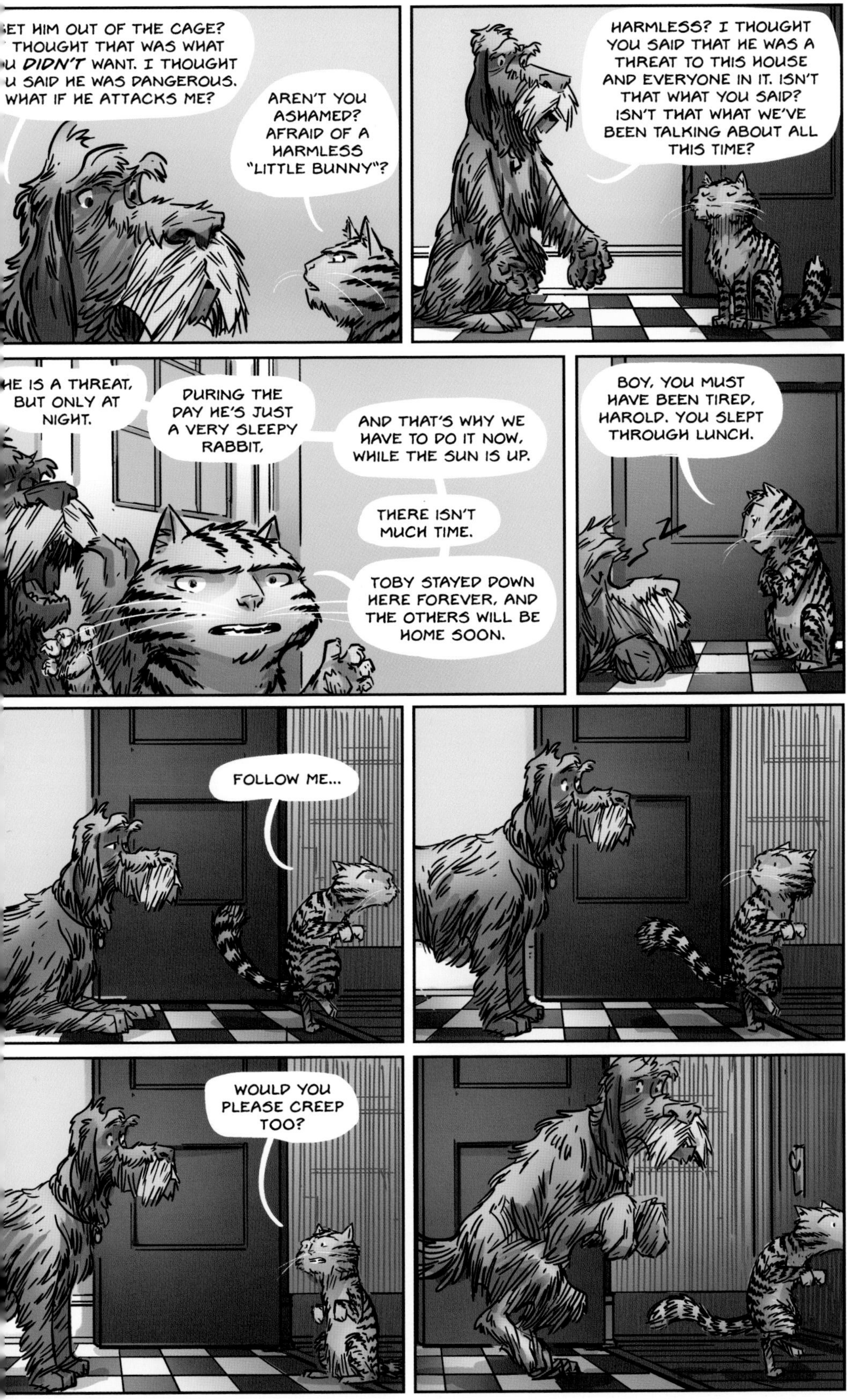
GET HIM OUT OF THE CAGE? I THOUGHT THAT WAS WHAT YOU *DIDN'T* WANT. I THOUGHT YOU SAID HE WAS DANGEROUS. WHAT IF HE ATTACKS ME?
AREN'T YOU ASHAMED? AFRAID OF A HARMLESS "LITTLE BUNNY"?
HARMLESS? I THOUGHT YOU SAID THAT HE WAS A THREAT TO THIS HOUSE AND EVERYONE IN IT. ISN'T THAT WHAT YOU SAID? ISN'T THAT WHAT WE'VE BEEN TALKING ABOUT ALL THIS TIME?
HE IS A THREAT, BUT ONLY AT NIGHT.
DURING THE DAY HE'S JUST A VERY SLEEPY RABBIT.
AND THAT'S WHY WE HAVE TO DO IT NOW, WHILE THE SUN IS UP.
THERE ISN'T MUCH TIME.
TOBY STAYED DOWN HERE FOREVER, AND THE OTHERS WILL BE HOME SOON.
BOY, YOU MUST HAVE BEEN TIRED, HAROLD. YOU SLEPT THROUGH LUNCH.
FOLLOW ME...
WOULD YOU PLEASE CREEP TOO?

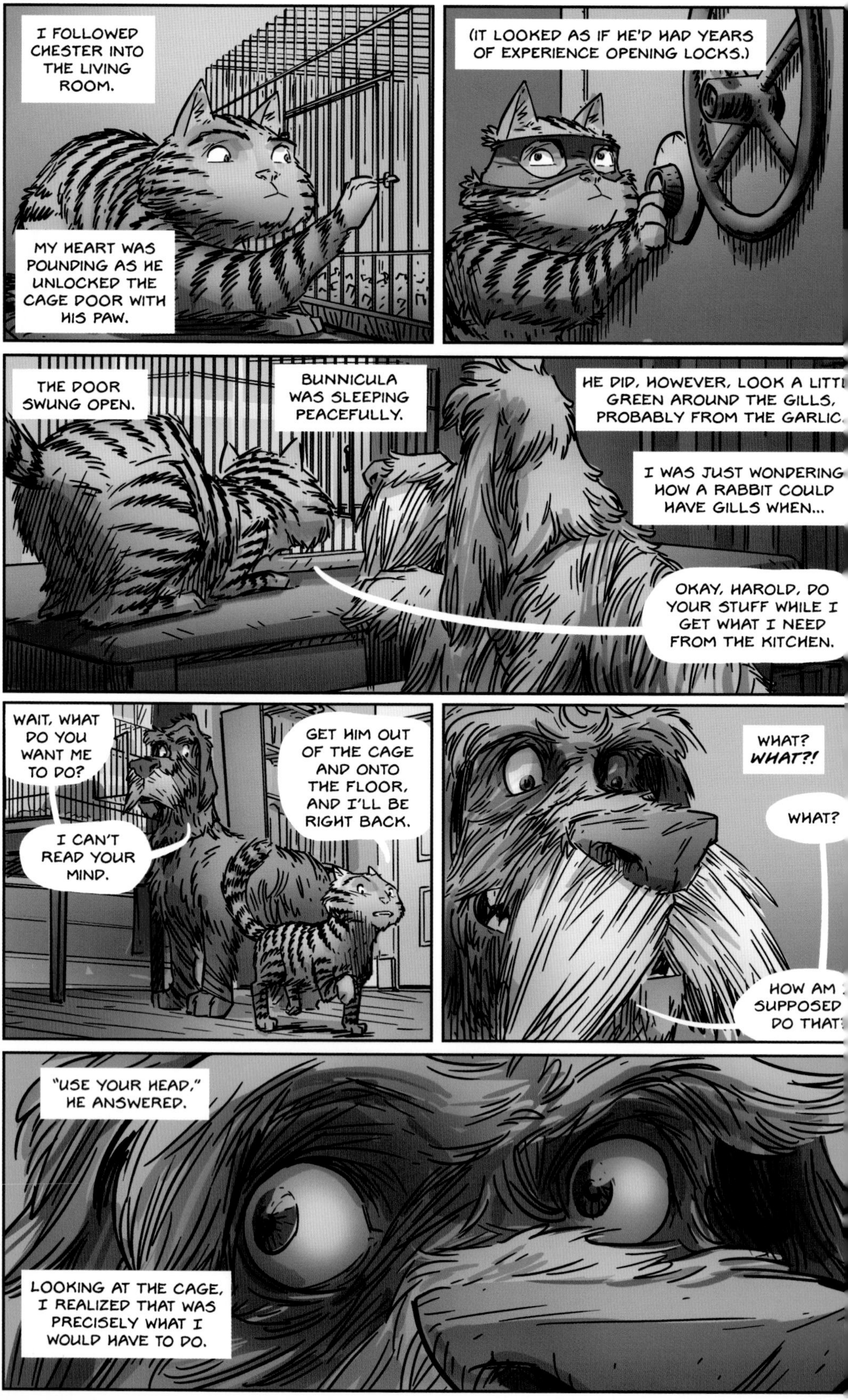
I FOLLOWED CHESTER INTO THE LIVING ROOM.
MY HEART WAS POUNDING AS HE UNLOCKED THE CAGE DOOR WITH HIS PAW.
(IT LOOKED AS IF HE'D HAD YEARS OF EXPERIENCE OPENING LOCKS.)
THE DOOR SWUNG OPEN.
BUNNICULA WAS SLEEPING PEACEFULLY.
HE DID, HOWEVER, LOOK A LITT GREEN AROUND THE GILLS, PROBABLY FROM THE GARLIC.
I WAS JUST WONDERING HOW A RABBIT COULD HAVE GILLS WHEN...
OKAY, HAROLD, DO YOUR STUFF WHILE I GET WHAT I NEED FROM THE KITCHEN.
WAIT, WHAT DO YOU WANT ME TO DO?
I CAN'T READ YOUR MIND.
GET HIM OUT OF THE CAGE AND ONTO THE FLOOR, AND I'LL BE RIGHT BACK.
WHAT? *WHAT?!*
WHAT?
HOW AM SUPPOSED DO THAT
"USE YOUR HEAD," HE ANSWERED.
LOOKING AT THE CAGE, I REALIZED THAT WAS PRECISELY WHAT I WOULD HAVE TO DO.

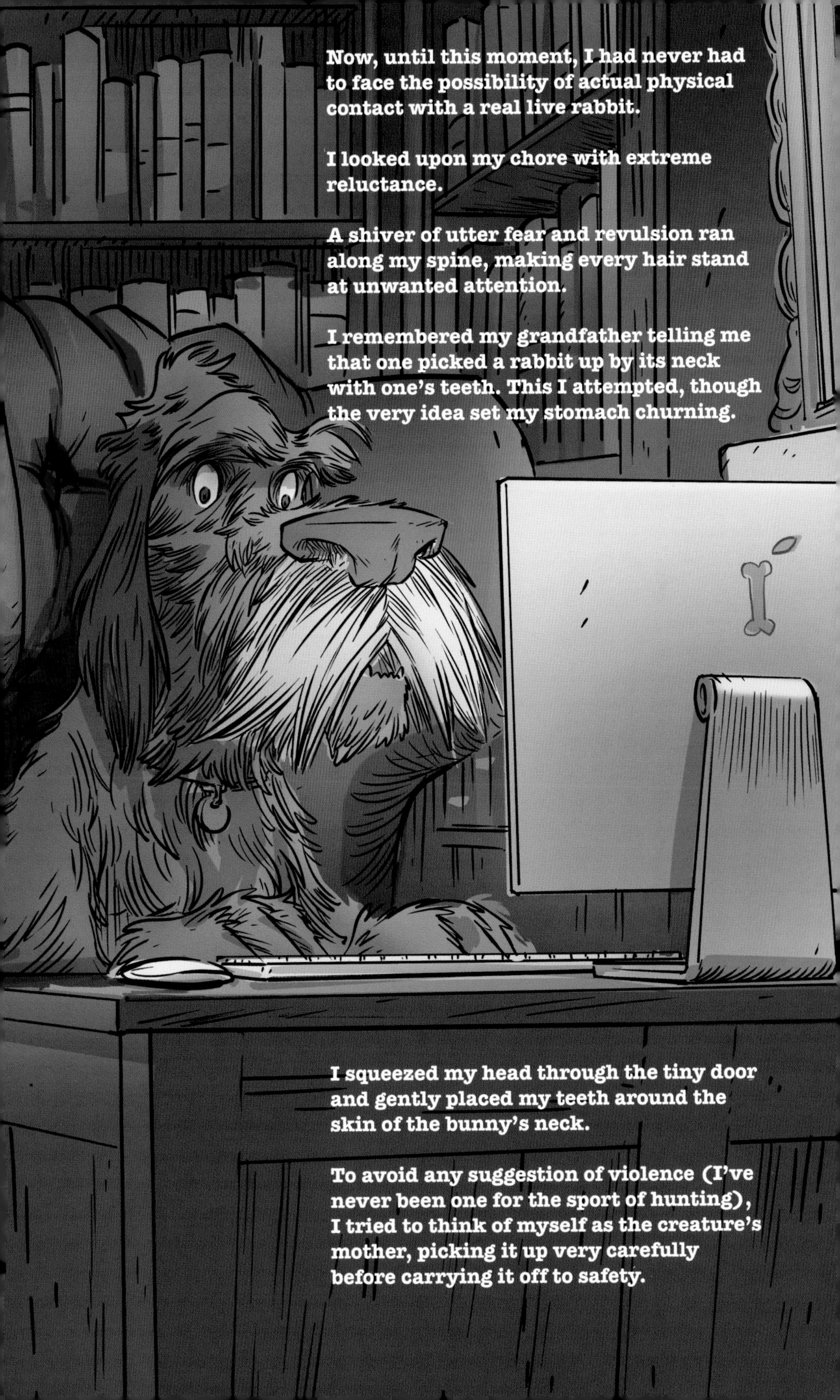

Now, until this moment, I had never had to face the possibility of actual physical contact with a real live rabbit.

I looked upon my chore with extreme reluctance.

A shiver of utter fear and revulsion ran along my spine, making every hair stand at unwanted attention.

I remembered my grandfather telling me that one picked a rabbit up by its neck with one's teeth. This I attempted, though the very idea set my stomach churning.

I squeezed my head through the tiny door and gently placed my teeth around the skin of the bunny's neck.

To avoid any suggestion of violence (I've never been one for the sport of hunting), I tried to think of myself as the creature's mother, picking it up very carefully before carrying it off to safety.

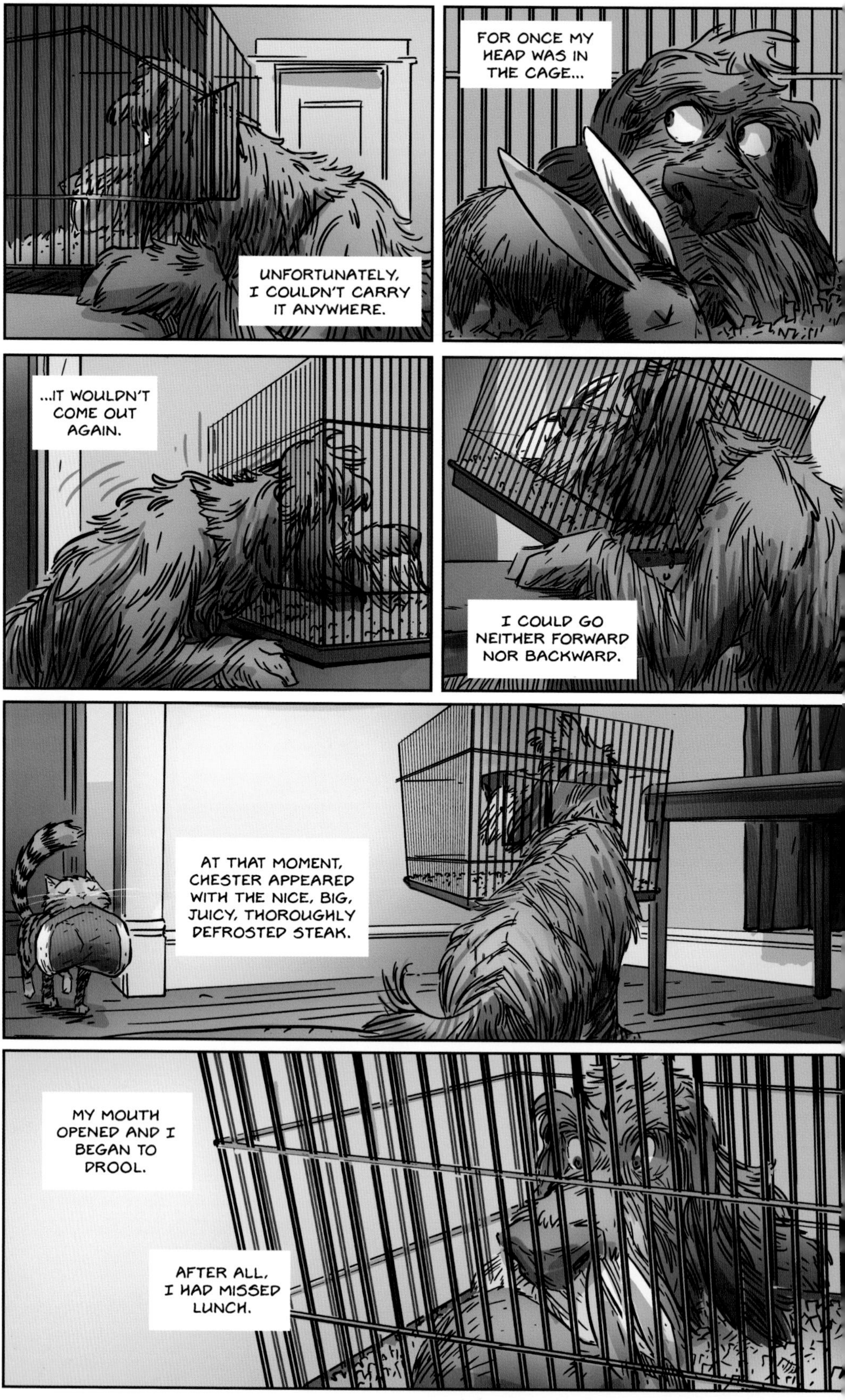
UNFORTUNATELY, I COULDN'T CARRY IT ANYWHERE.
FOR ONCE MY HEAD WAS IN THE CAGE...
...IT WOULDN'T COME OUT AGAIN.
I COULD GO NEITHER FORWARD NOR BACKWARD.
AT THAT MOMENT, CHESTER APPEARED WITH THE NICE, BIG, JUICY, THOROUGHLY DEFROSTED STEAK.
MY MOUTH OPENED AND I BEGAN TO DROOL.
AFTER ALL, I HAD MISSED LUNCH.

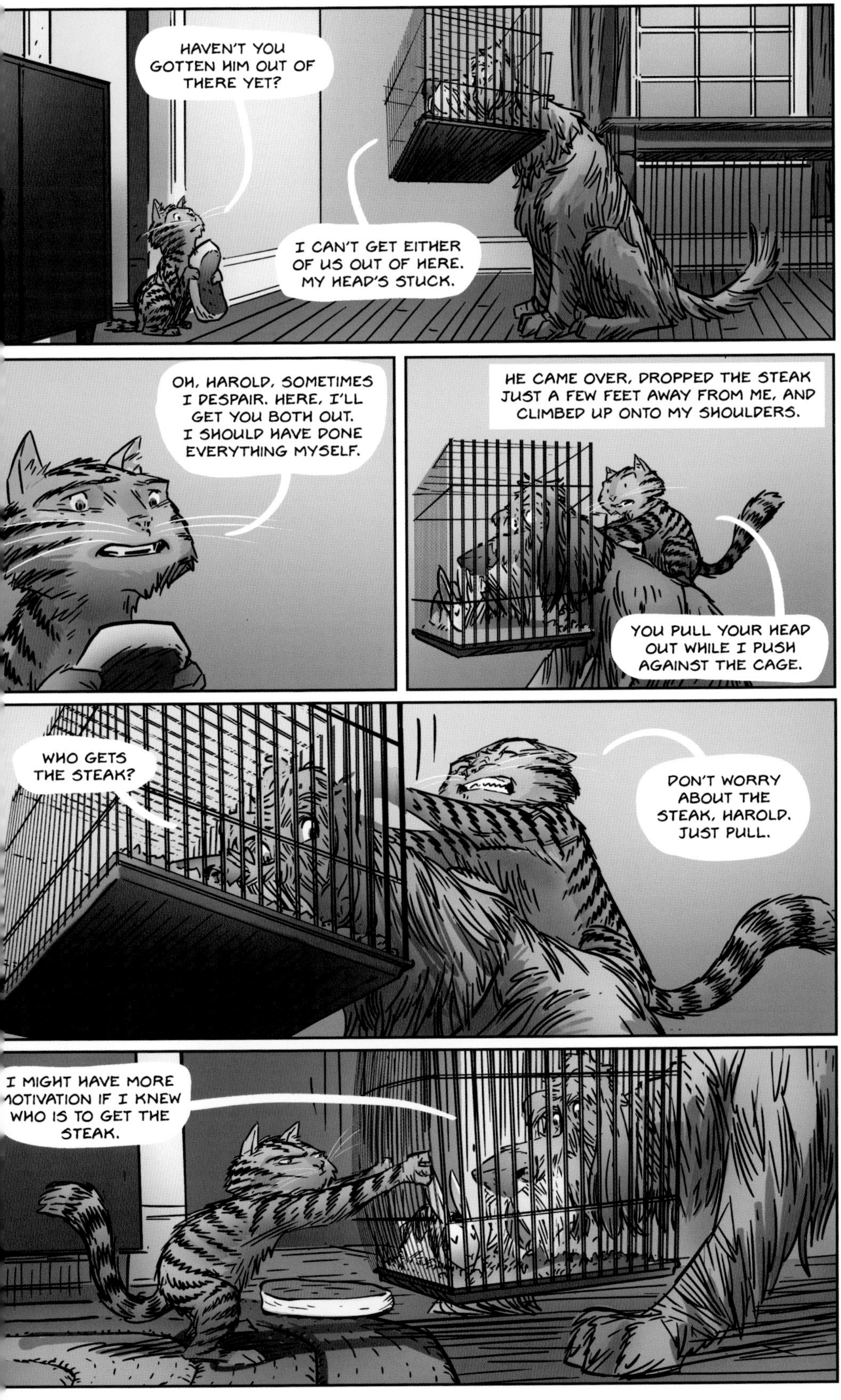
HAVEN'T YOU GOTTEN HIM OUT OF THERE YET?
I CAN'T GET EITHER OF US OUT OF HERE. MY HEAD'S STUCK.
OH, HAROLD, SOMETIMES I DESPAIR. HERE, I'LL GET YOU BOTH OUT. I SHOULD HAVE DONE EVERYTHING MYSELF.
HE CAME OVER, DROPPED THE STEAK JUST A FEW FEET AWAY FROM ME, AND CLIMBED UP ONTO MY SHOULDERS.
YOU PULL YOUR HEAD OUT WHILE I PUSH AGAINST THE CAGE.
WHO GETS THE STEAK?
DON'T WORRY ABOUT THE STEAK, HAROLD. JUST PULL.
I MIGHT HAVE MORE MOTIVATION IF I KNEW WHO IS TO GET THE STEAK.

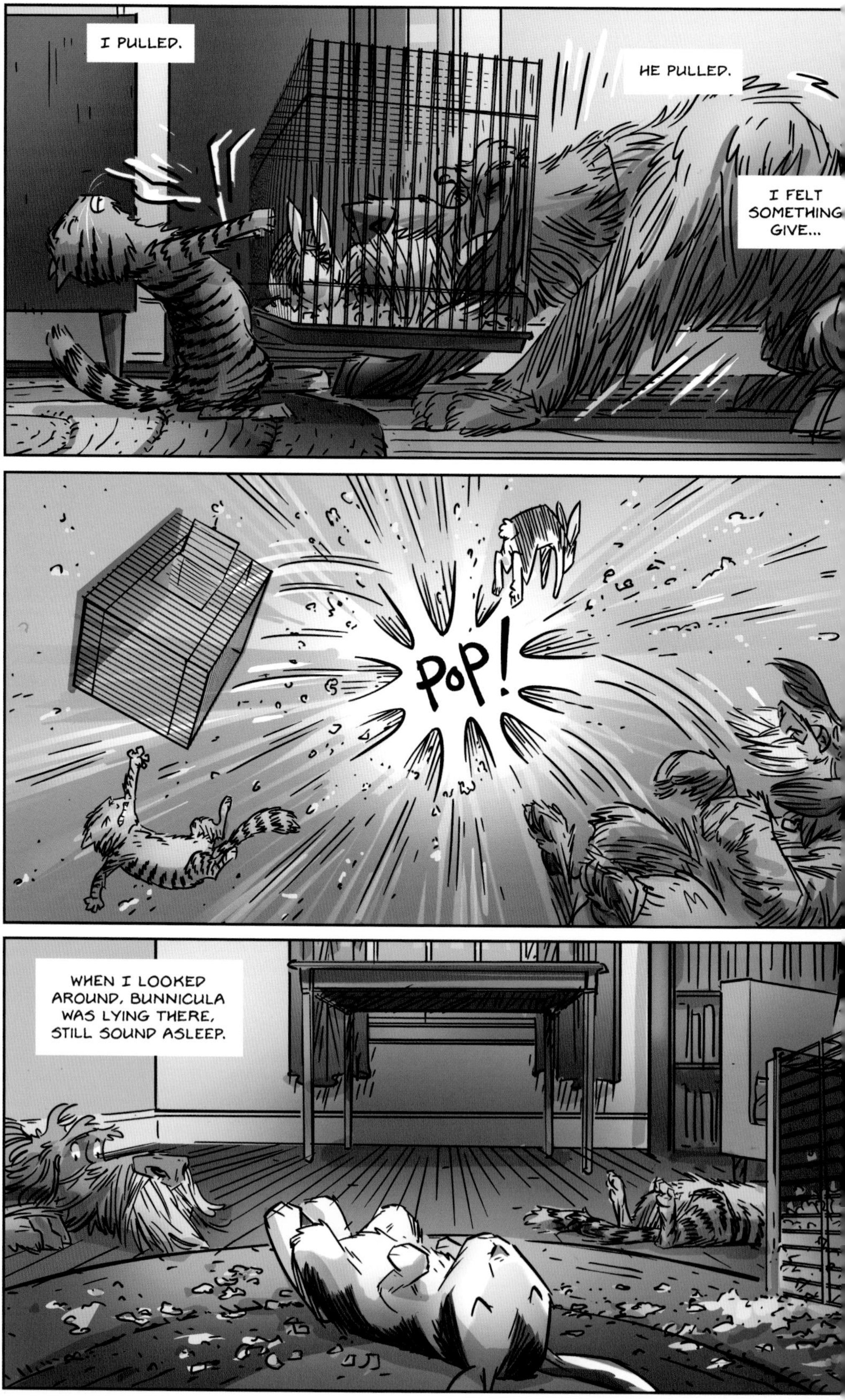

I PULLED.
HE PULLED.
I FELT SOMETHING GIVE...
POP!
WHEN I LOOKED AROUND, BUNNICULA WAS LYING THERE, STILL SOUND ASLEEP.

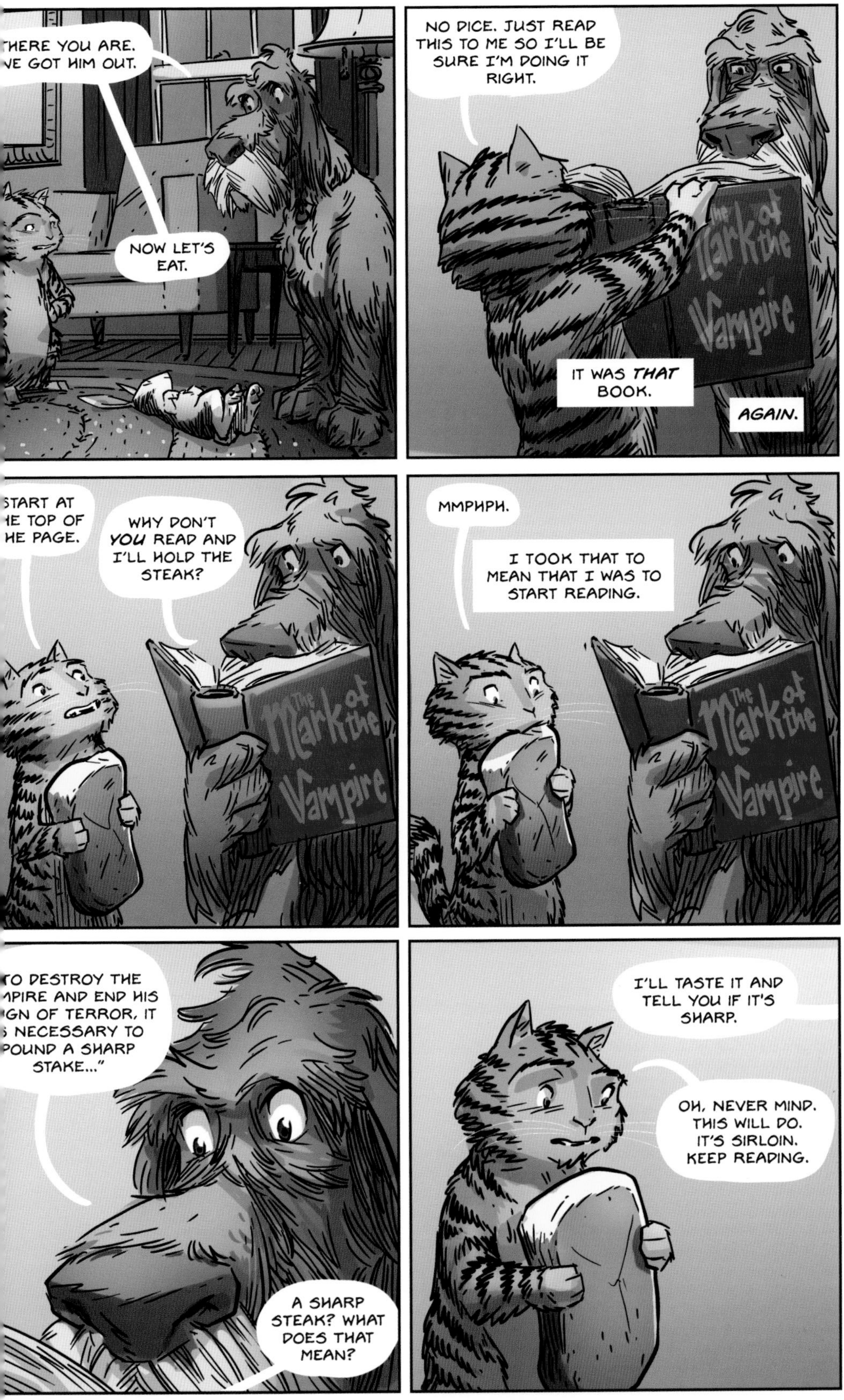
THERE YOU ARE. VE GOT HIM OUT.
NOW LET'S EAT.
NO DICE. JUST READ THIS TO ME SO I'LL BE SURE I'M DOING IT RIGHT.
IT WAS *THAT* BOOK.
AGAIN.
The Mark of the Vampire
START AT HE TOP OF HE PAGE.
WHY DON'T *YOU* READ AND I'LL HOLD THE STEAK?
The Mark of the Vampire
MMPHPH.
I TOOK THAT TO MEAN THAT I WAS TO START READING.
The Mark of the Vampire
TO DESTROY THE MPIRE AND END HIS GN OF TERROR, IT NECESSARY TO POUND A SHARP STAKE..."
A SHARP STEAK? WHAT DOES THAT MEAN?
I'LL TASTE IT AND TELL YOU IF IT'S SHARP.
OH, NEVER MIND. THIS WILL DO. IT'S SIRLOIN. KEEP READING.

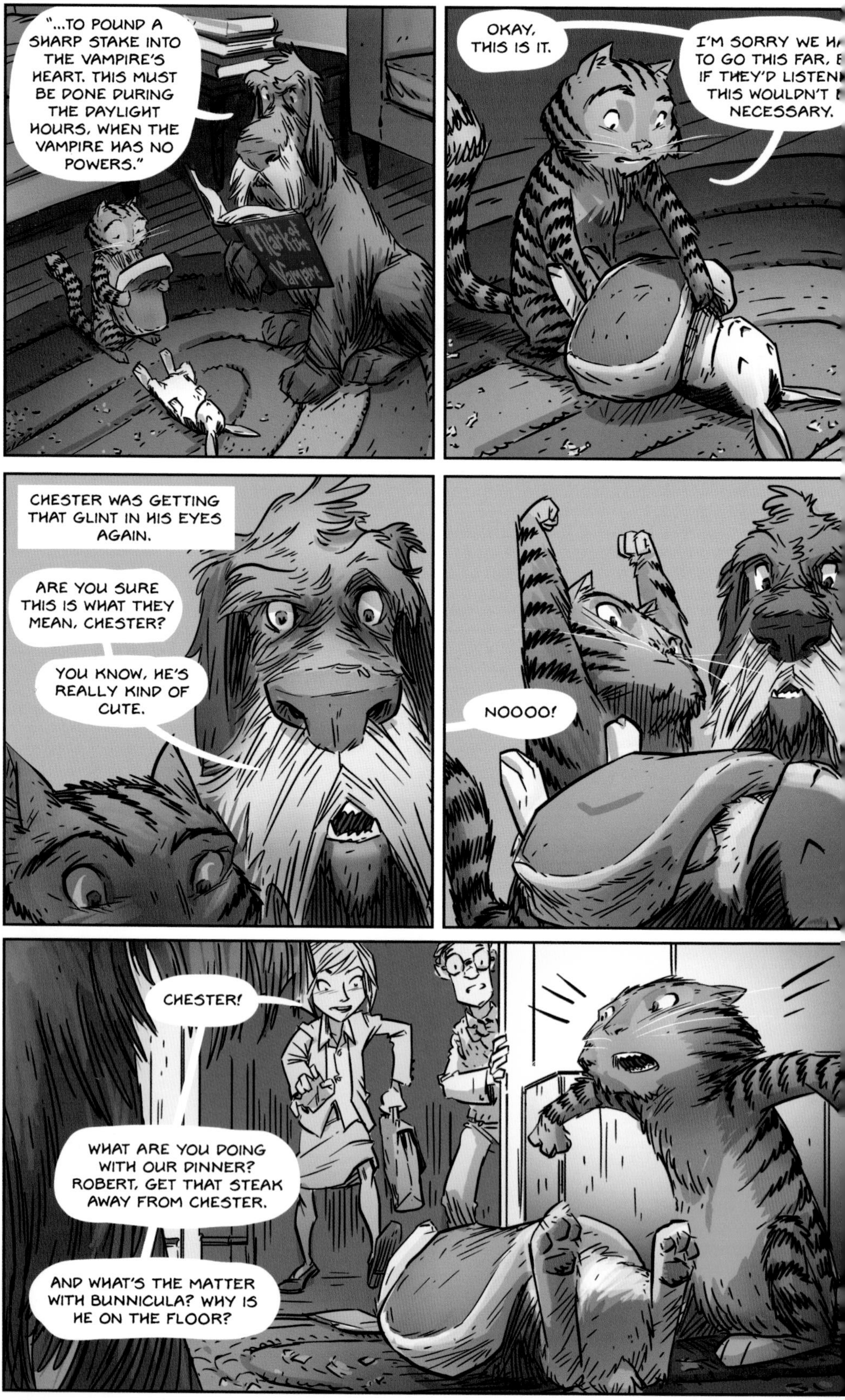
"...TO POUND A SHARP STAKE INTO THE VAMPIRE'S HEART. THIS MUST BE DONE DURING THE DAYLIGHT HOURS, WHEN THE VAMPIRE HAS NO POWERS."
The Mark of the Vampire
OKAY, THIS IS IT.
I'M SORRY WE HA TO GO THIS FAR, B IF THEY'D LISTEN THIS WOULDN'T B NECESSARY.
CHESTER WAS GETTING THAT GLINT IN HIS EYES AGAIN.
ARE YOU SURE THIS IS WHAT THEY MEAN, CHESTER?
YOU KNOW, HE'S REALLY KIND OF CUTE.
NOOOO!
CHESTER!
WHAT ARE YOU DOING WITH OUR DINNER? ROBERT, GET THAT STEAK AWAY FROM CHESTER.
AND WHAT'S THE MATTER WITH BUNNICULA? WHY IS HE ON THE FLOOR?

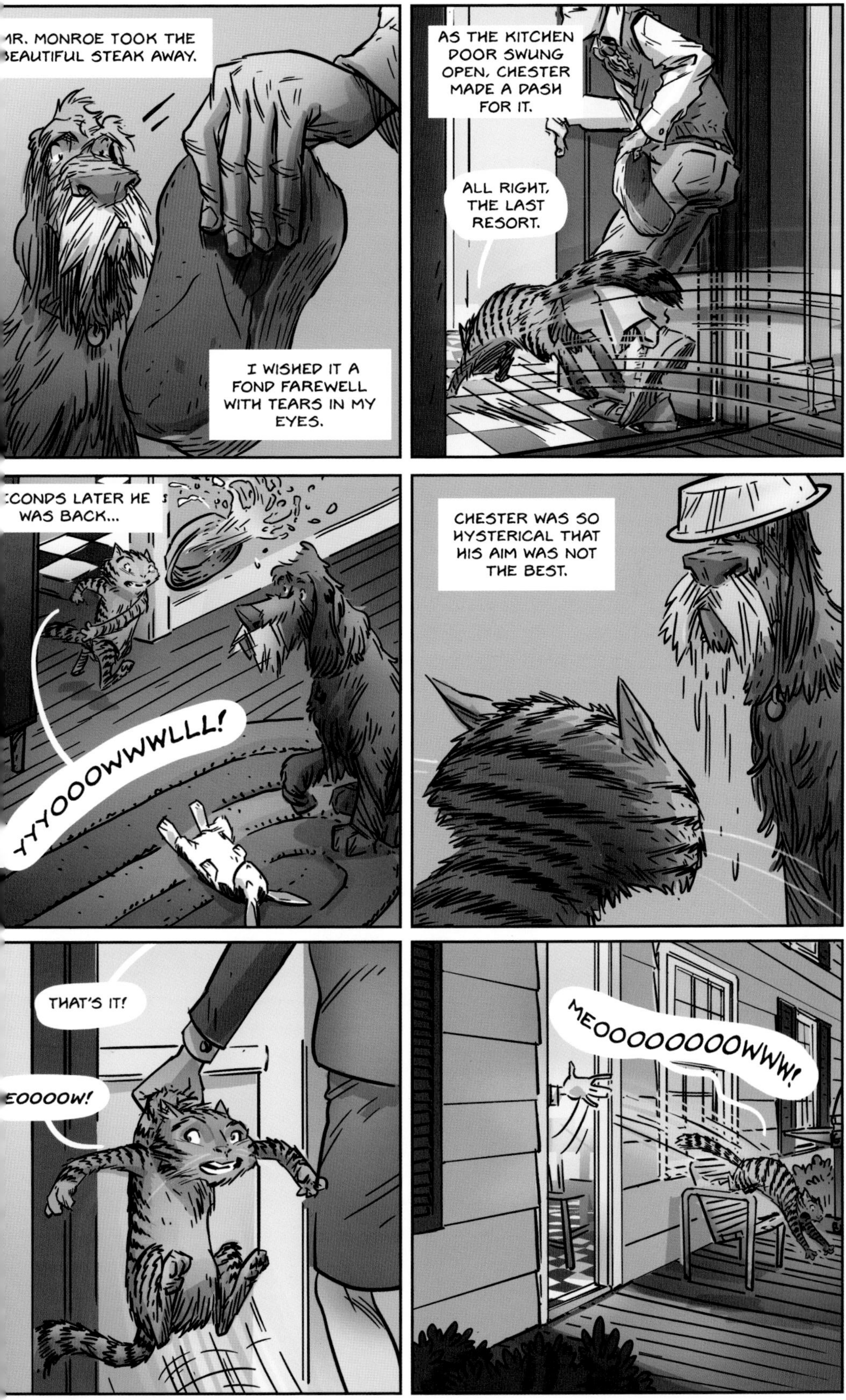
R. MONROE TOOK THE
EAUTIFUL STEAK AWAY.
I WISHED IT A FOND FAREWELL WITH TEARS IN MY EYES.
AS THE KITCHEN DOOR SWUNG OPEN, CHESTER MADE A DASH FOR IT.
ALL RIGHT, THE LAST RESORT.
CONDS LATER HE WAS BACK...
YYYOOOWWWLLL!
CHESTER WAS SO HYSTERICAL THAT HIS AIM WAS NOT THE BEST.
THAT'S IT!
EOOOOW!
MEOOOOOOOOWWW!

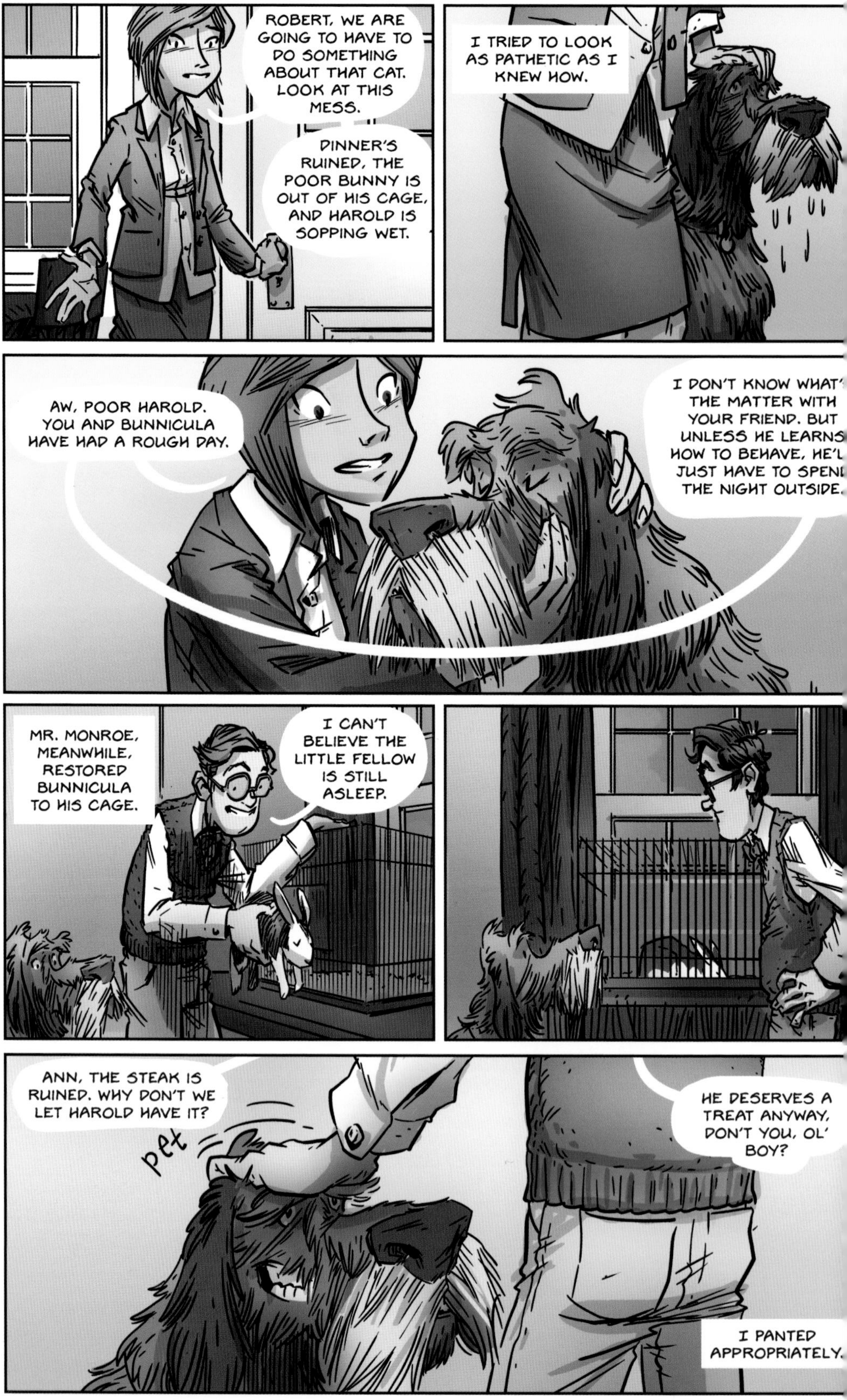
ROBERT, WE ARE GOING TO HAVE TO DO SOMETHING ABOUT THAT CAT. LOOK AT THIS MESS.
DINNER'S RUINED, THE POOR BUNNY IS OUT OF HIS CAGE, AND HAROLD IS SOPPING WET.
I TRIED TO LOOK AS PATHETIC AS I KNEW HOW.
AW, POOR HAROLD. YOU AND BUNNICULA HAVE HAD A ROUGH DAY.
I DON'T KNOW WHAT' THE MATTER WITH YOUR FRIEND. BUT UNLESS HE LEARNS HOW TO BEHAVE, HE'L JUST HAVE TO SPEN THE NIGHT OUTSIDE.
MR. MONROE, MEANWHILE, RESTORED BUNNICULA TO HIS CAGE.
I CAN'T BELIEVE THE LITTLE FELLOW IS STILL ASLEEP.
ANN, THE STEAK IS RUINED. WHY DON'T WE LET HAROLD HAVE IT?
pet
HE DESERVES A TREAT ANYWAY, DON'T YOU, OL' BOY?
I PANTED APPROPRIATELY.

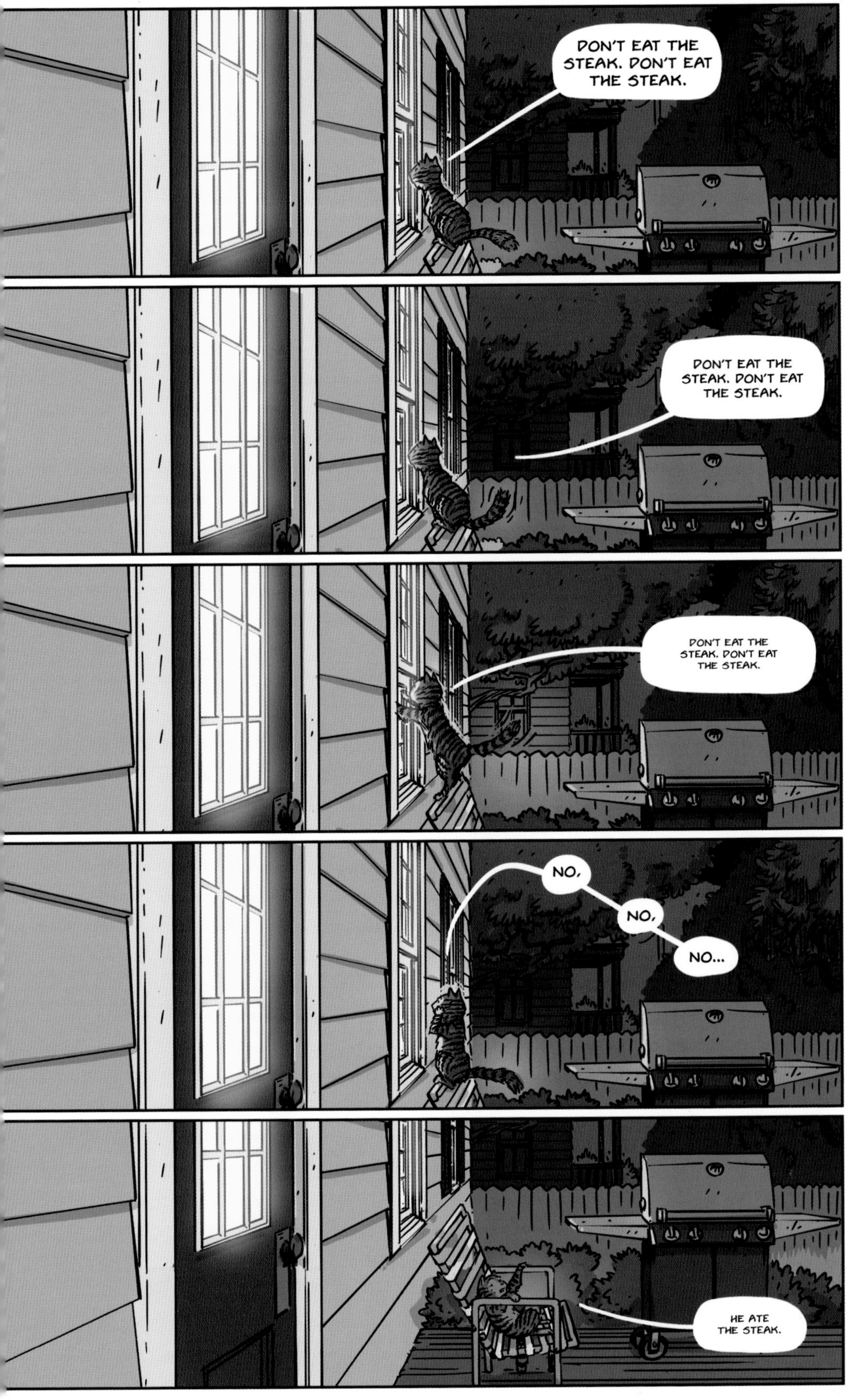
DON'T EAT THE STEAK. DON'T EAT THE STEAK.
DON'T EAT THE STEAK. DON'T EAT THE STEAK.
DON'T EAT THE STEAK. DON'T EAT THE STEAK.
NO,
NO,
NO...
HE ATE THE STEAK.

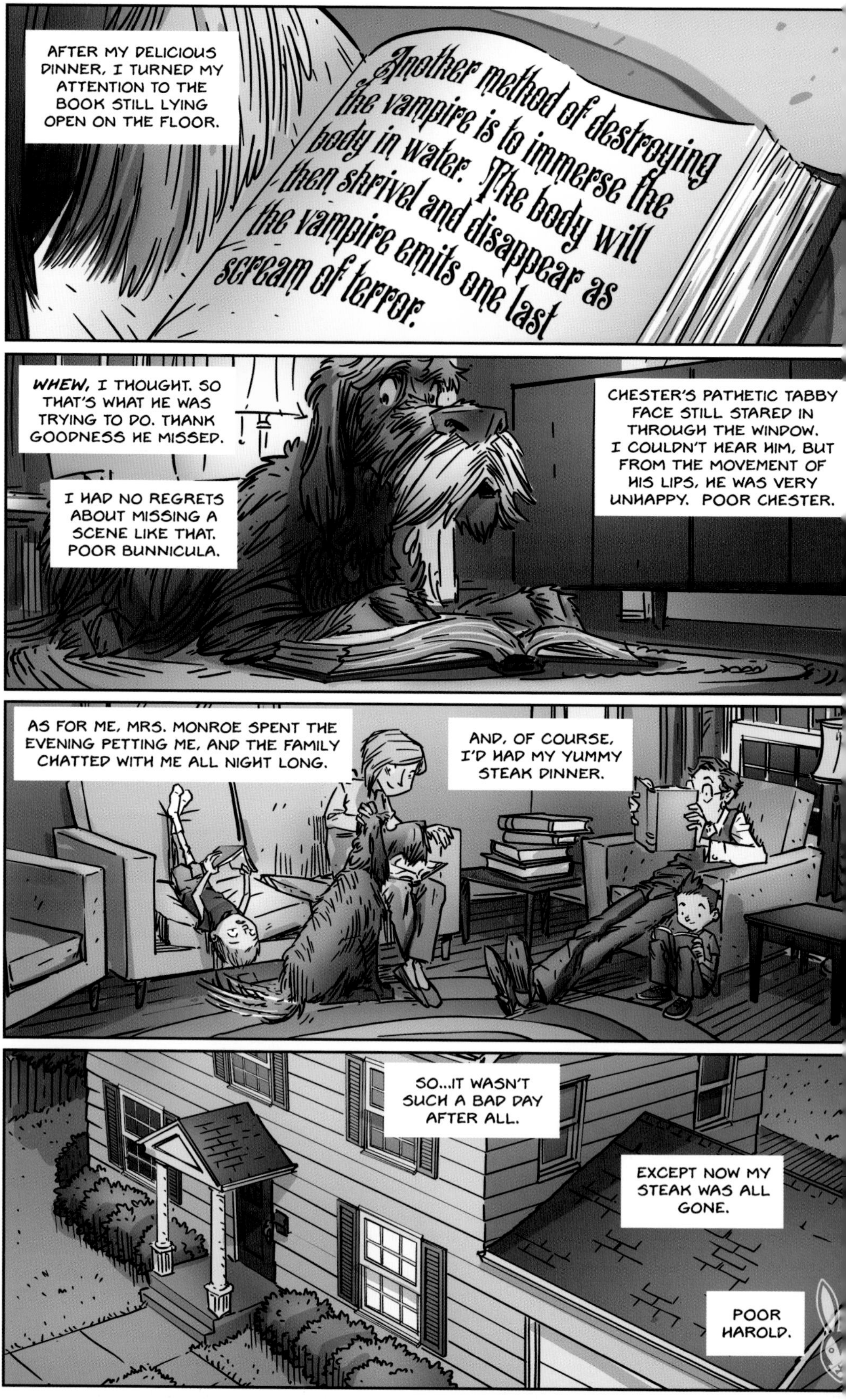
AFTER MY DELICIOUS DINNER, I TURNED MY ATTENTION TO THE BOOK STILL LYING OPEN ON THE FLOOR.
Another method of destroying the vampire is to immerse the body in water. The body will then shrivel and disappear as the vampire emits one last scream of terror.
WHEW, I THOUGHT. SO THAT'S WHAT HE WAS TRYING TO DO. THANK GOODNESS HE MISSED.
I HAD NO REGRETS ABOUT MISSING A SCENE LIKE THAT. POOR BUNNICULA.
CHESTER'S PATHETIC TABBY FACE STILL STARED IN THROUGH THE WINDOW. I COULDN'T HEAR HIM, BUT FROM THE MOVEMENT OF HIS LIPS, HE WAS VERY UNHAPPY. POOR CHESTER.
AS FOR ME, MRS. MONROE SPENT THE EVENING PETTING ME, AND THE FAMILY CHATTED WITH ME ALL NIGHT LONG.
AND, OF COURSE, I'D HAD MY YUMMY STEAK DINNER.
SO...IT WASN'T SUCH A BAD DAY AFTER ALL.
EXCEPT NOW MY STEAK WAS ALL GONE.
POOR HAROLD.

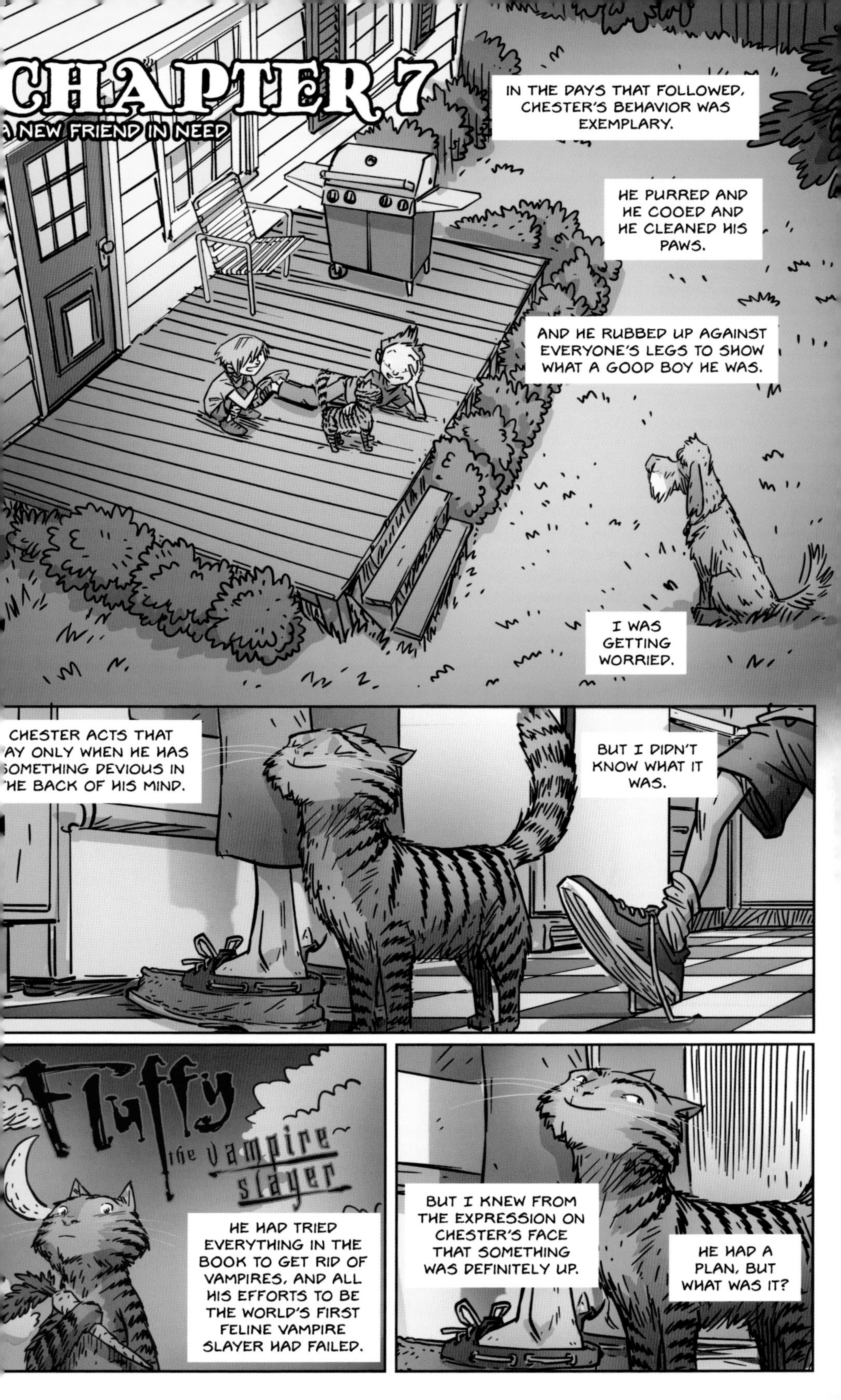
CHAPTER 7
A NEW FRIEND IN NEED
IN THE DAYS THAT FOLLOWED, CHESTER'S BEHAVIOR WAS EXEMPLARY.
HE PURRED AND HE COOED AND HE CLEANED HIS PAWS.
AND HE RUBBED UP AGAINST EVERYONE'S LEGS TO SHOW WHAT A GOOD BOY HE WAS.
I WAS GETTING WORRIED.
CHESTER ACTS THAT WAY ONLY WHEN HE HAS SOMETHING DEVIOUS IN THE BACK OF HIS MIND.
BUT I DIDN'T KNOW WHAT IT WAS.
Fluffy the Vampire slayer
HE HAD TRIED EVERYTHING IN THE BOOK TO GET RID OF VAMPIRES, AND ALL HIS EFFORTS TO BE THE WORLD'S FIRST FELINE VAMPIRE SLAYER HAD FAILED.
BUT I KNEW FROM THE EXPRESSION ON CHESTER'S FACE THAT SOMETHING WAS DEFINITELY UP.
HE HAD A PLAN, BUT WHAT WAS IT?

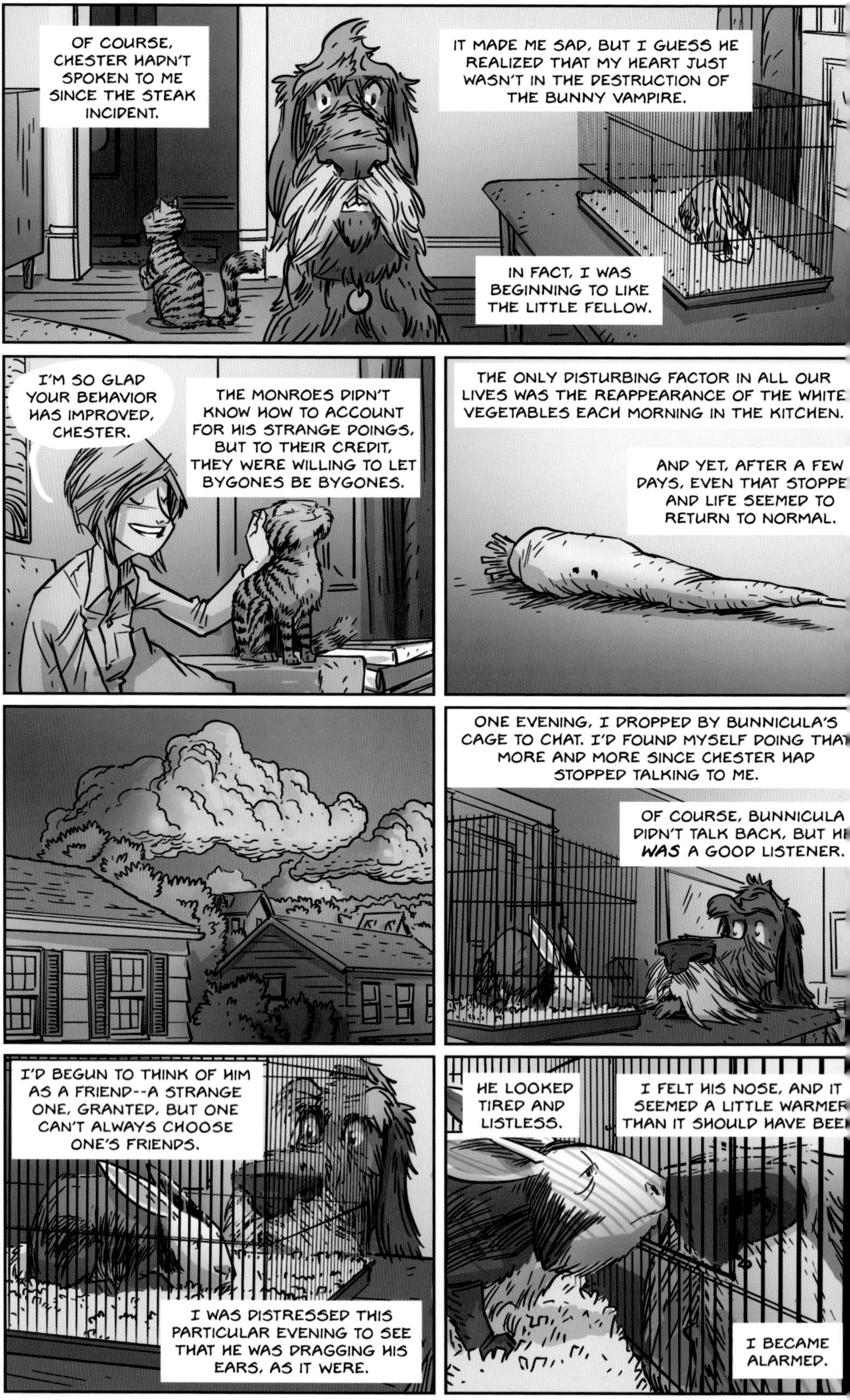

OF COURSE, CHESTER HADN'T SPOKEN TO ME SINCE THE STEAK INCIDENT.
IT MADE ME SAD, BUT I GUESS HE REALIZED THAT MY HEART JUST WASN'T IN THE DESTRUCTION OF THE BUNNY VAMPIRE.
IN FACT, I WAS BEGINNING TO LIKE THE LITTLE FELLOW.
I'M SO GLAD YOUR BEHAVIOR HAS IMPROVED, CHESTER.
THE MONROES DIDN'T KNOW HOW TO ACCOUNT FOR HIS STRANGE DOINGS, BUT TO THEIR CREDIT, THEY WERE WILLING TO LET BYGONES BE BYGONES.
THE ONLY DISTURBING FACTOR IN ALL OUR LIVES WAS THE REAPPEARANCE OF THE WHITE VEGETABLES EACH MORNING IN THE KITCHEN.
AND YET, AFTER A FEW DAYS, EVEN THAT STOPPE AND LIFE SEEMED TO RETURN TO NORMAL.
ONE EVENING, I DROPPED BY BUNNICULA'S CAGE TO CHAT. I'D FOUND MYSELF DOING THAT MORE AND MORE SINCE CHESTER HAD STOPPED TALKING TO ME.
OF COURSE, BUNNICULA DIDN'T TALK BACK, BUT H *WAS* A GOOD LISTENER.
I'D BEGUN TO THINK OF HIM AS A FRIEND--A STRANGE ONE, GRANTED, BUT ONE CAN'T ALWAYS CHOOSE ONE'S FRIENDS.
I WAS DISTRESSED THIS PARTICULAR EVENING TO SEE THAT HE WAS DRAGGING HIS EARS, AS IT WERE.
HE LOOKED TIRED AND LISTLESS.
I FELT HIS NOSE, AND IT SEEMED A LITTLE WARMER THAN IT SHOULD HAVE BEE
I BECAME ALARMED.

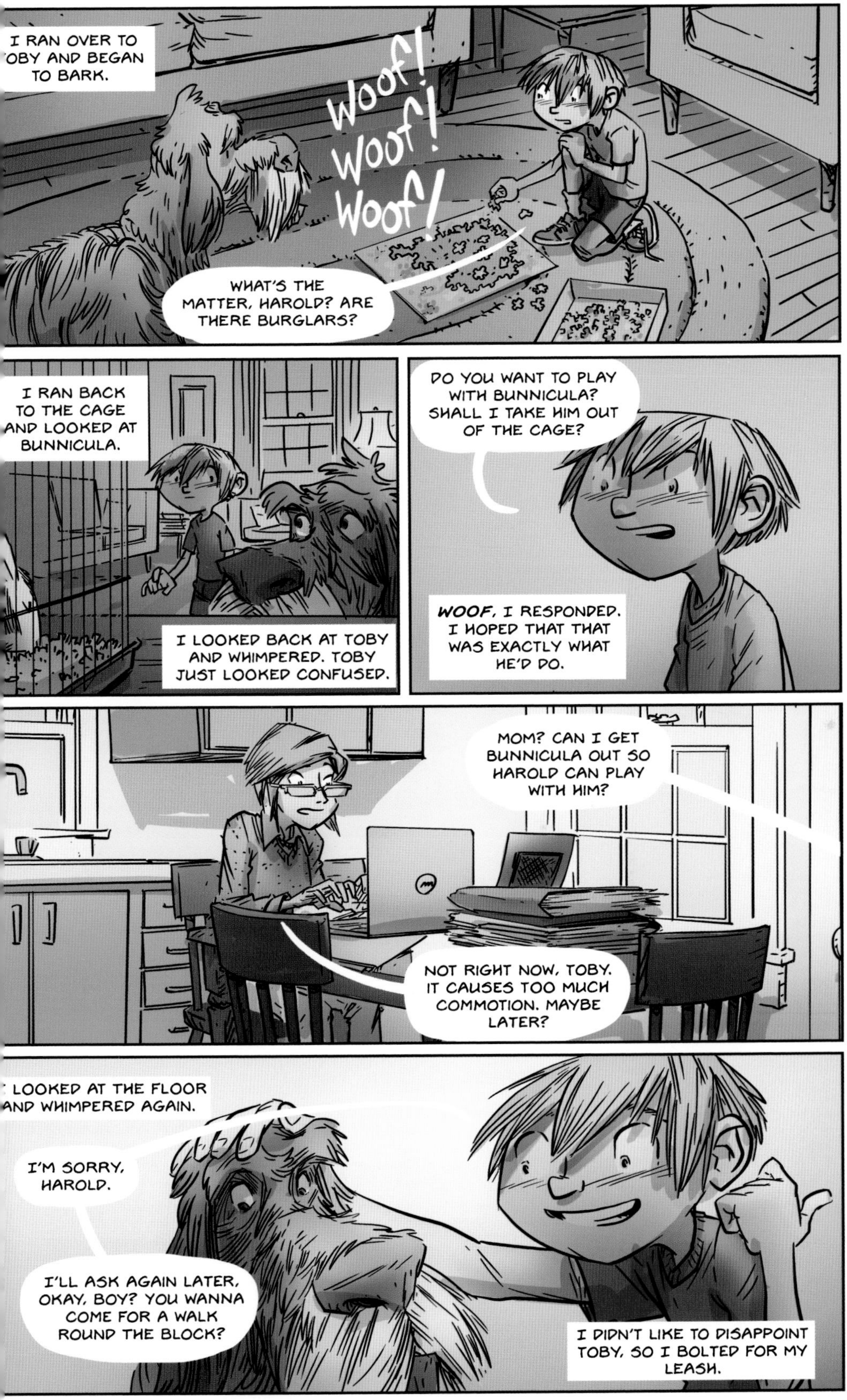

I RAN OVER TO
OBY AND BEGAN TO BARK.
Woof! Woof! Woof!
WHAT'S THE MATTER, HAROLD? ARE THERE BURGLARS?
I RAN BACK TO THE CAGE AND LOOKED AT BUNNICULA.
I LOOKED BACK AT TOBY AND WHIMPERED. TOBY JUST LOOKED CONFUSED.
DO YOU WANT TO PLAY WITH BUNNICULA? SHALL I TAKE HIM OUT OF THE CAGE?
WOOF, I RESPONDED. I HOPED THAT THAT WAS EXACTLY WHAT HE'D DO.
MOM? CAN I GET BUNNICULA OUT SO HAROLD CAN PLAY WITH HIM?
NOT RIGHT NOW, TOBY. IT CAUSES TOO MUCH COMMOTION. MAYBE LATER?
LOOKED AT THE FLOOR AND WHIMPERED AGAIN.
I'M SORRY, HAROLD.
I'LL ASK AGAIN LATER, OKAY, BOY? YOU WANNA COME FOR A WALK ROUND THE BLOCK?
I DIDN'T LIKE TO DISAPPOINT TOBY, SO I BOLTED FOR MY LEASH.

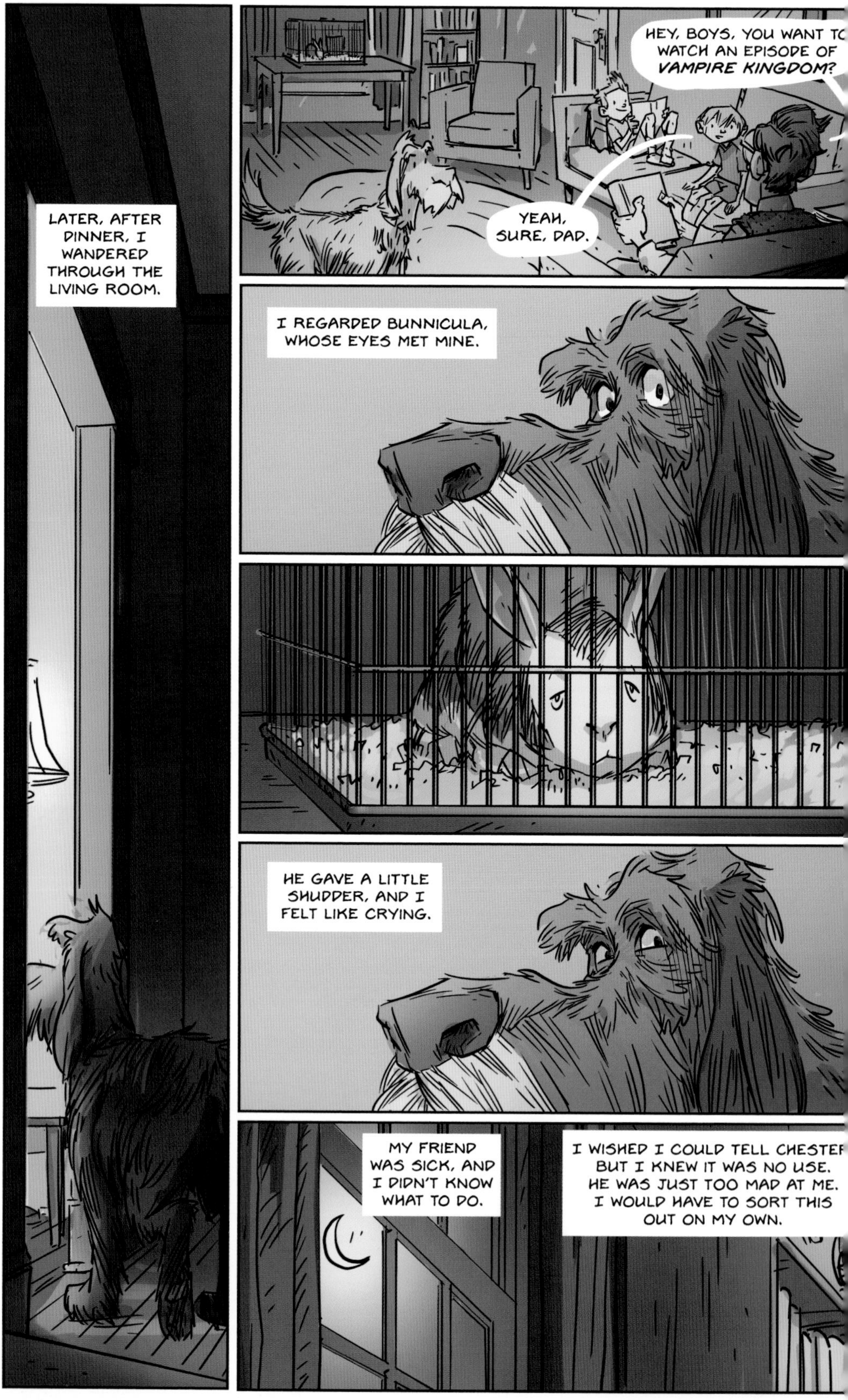
LATER, AFTER DINNER, I WANDERED THROUGH THE LIVING ROOM.
HEY, BOYS, YOU WANT TO WATCH AN EPISODE OF *VAMPIRE KINGDOM*?
YEAH, SURE, DAD.
I REGARDED BUNNICULA, WHOSE EYES MET MINE.
HE GAVE A LITTLE SHUDDER, AND I FELT LIKE CRYING.
MY FRIEND WAS SICK, AND I DIDN'T KNOW WHAT TO DO.
I WISHED I COULD TELL CHESTER BUT I KNEW IT WAS NO USE. HE WAS JUST TOO MAD AT ME. I WOULD HAVE TO SORT THIS OUT ON MY OWN.

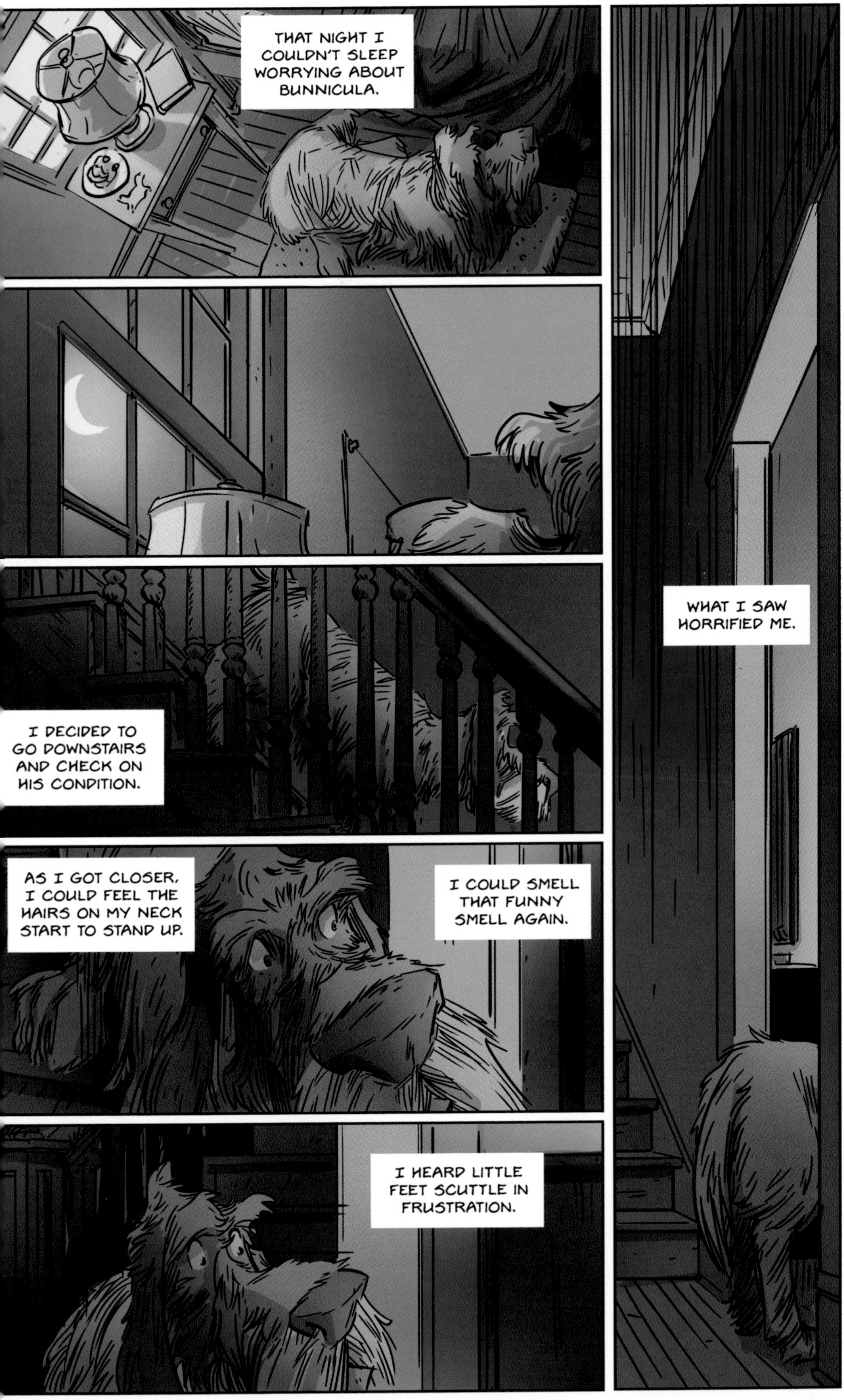
THAT NIGHT I COULDN'T SLEEP WORRYING ABOUT BUNNICULA.
I DECIDED TO GO DOWNSTAIRS AND CHECK ON HIS CONDITION.
AS I GOT CLOSER, I COULD FEEL THE HAIRS ON MY NECK START TO STAND UP.
I COULD SMELL THAT FUNNY SMELL AGAIN.
I HEARD LITTLE FEET SCUTTLE IN FRUSTRATION.
WHAT I SAW HORRIFIED ME.

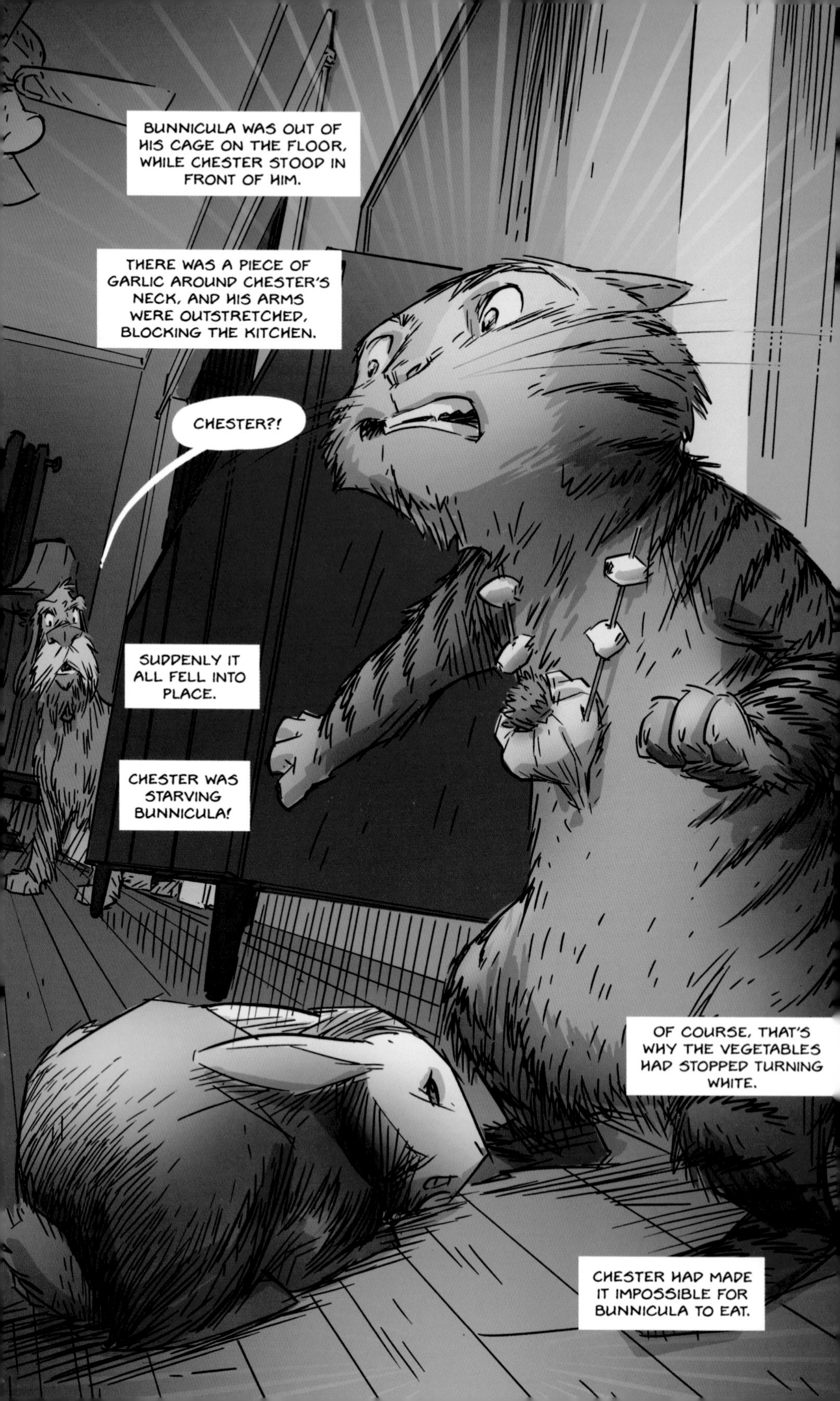
BUNNICULA WAS OUT OF HIS CAGE ON THE FLOOR, WHILE CHESTER STOOD IN FRONT OF HIM.
THERE WAS A PIECE OF GARLIC AROUND CHESTER'S NECK, AND HIS ARMS WERE OUTSTRETCHED, BLOCKING THE KITCHEN.
CHESTER?!
SUDDENLY IT ALL FELL INTO PLACE.
CHESTER WAS STARVING BUNNICULA!
OF COURSE, THAT'S WHY THE VEGETABLES HAD STOPPED TURNING WHITE.
CHESTER HAD MADE IT IMPOSSIBLE FOR BUNNICULA TO EAT.

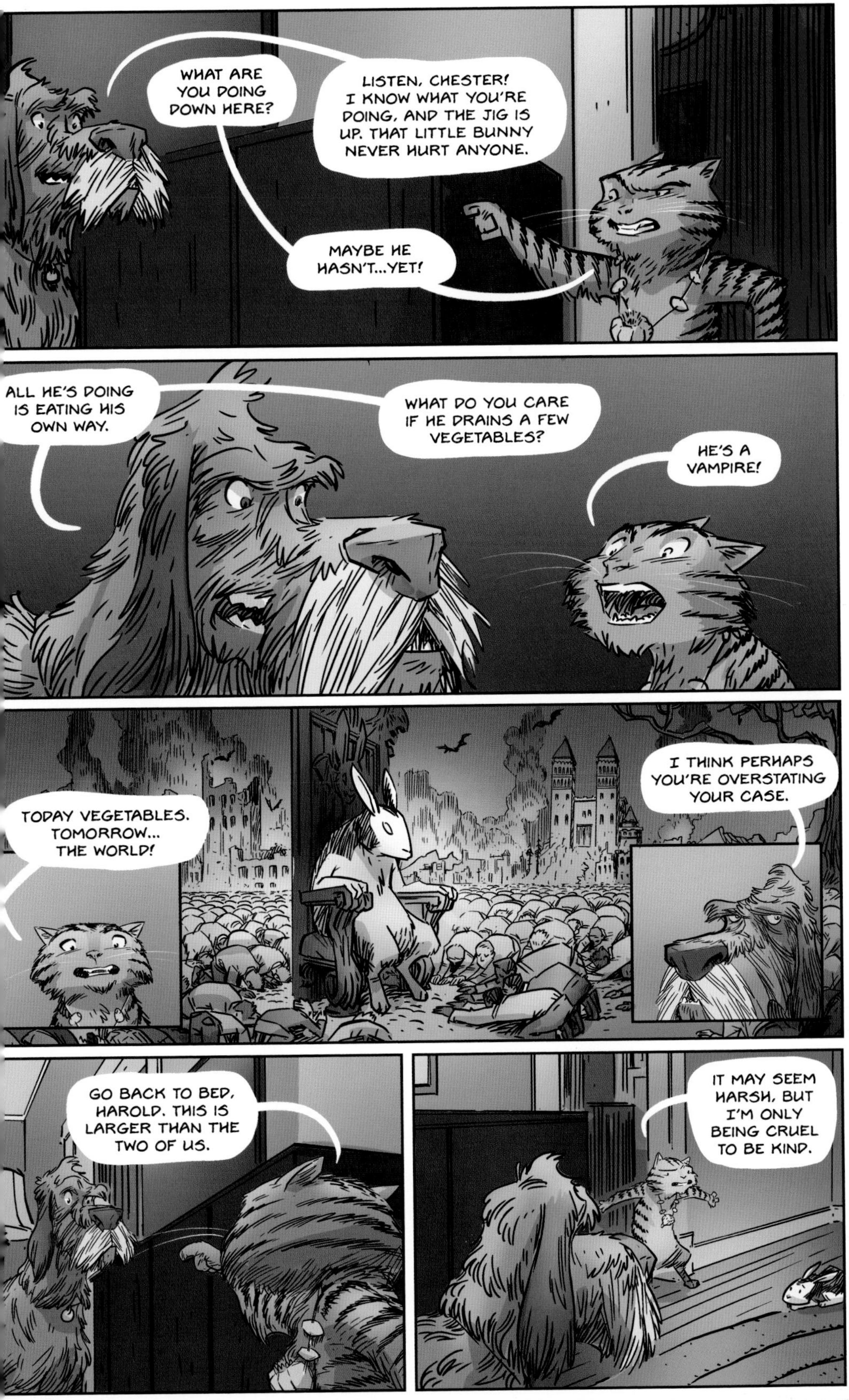
WHAT ARE YOU DOING DOWN HERE?
LISTEN, CHESTER! I KNOW WHAT YOU'RE DOING, AND THE JIG IS UP. THAT LITTLE BUNNY NEVER HURT ANYONE.
MAYBE HE HASN'T...YET!
ALL HE'S DOING IS EATING HIS OWN WAY.
WHAT DO YOU CARE IF HE DRAINS A FEW VEGETABLES?
HE'S A VAMPIRE!
TODAY VEGETABLES. TOMORROW... THE WORLD!
I THINK PERHAPS YOU'RE OVERSTATING YOUR CASE.
GO BACK TO BED, HAROLD. THIS IS LARGER THAN THE TWO OF US.
IT MAY SEEM HARSH, BUT I'M ONLY BEING CRUEL TO BE KIND.

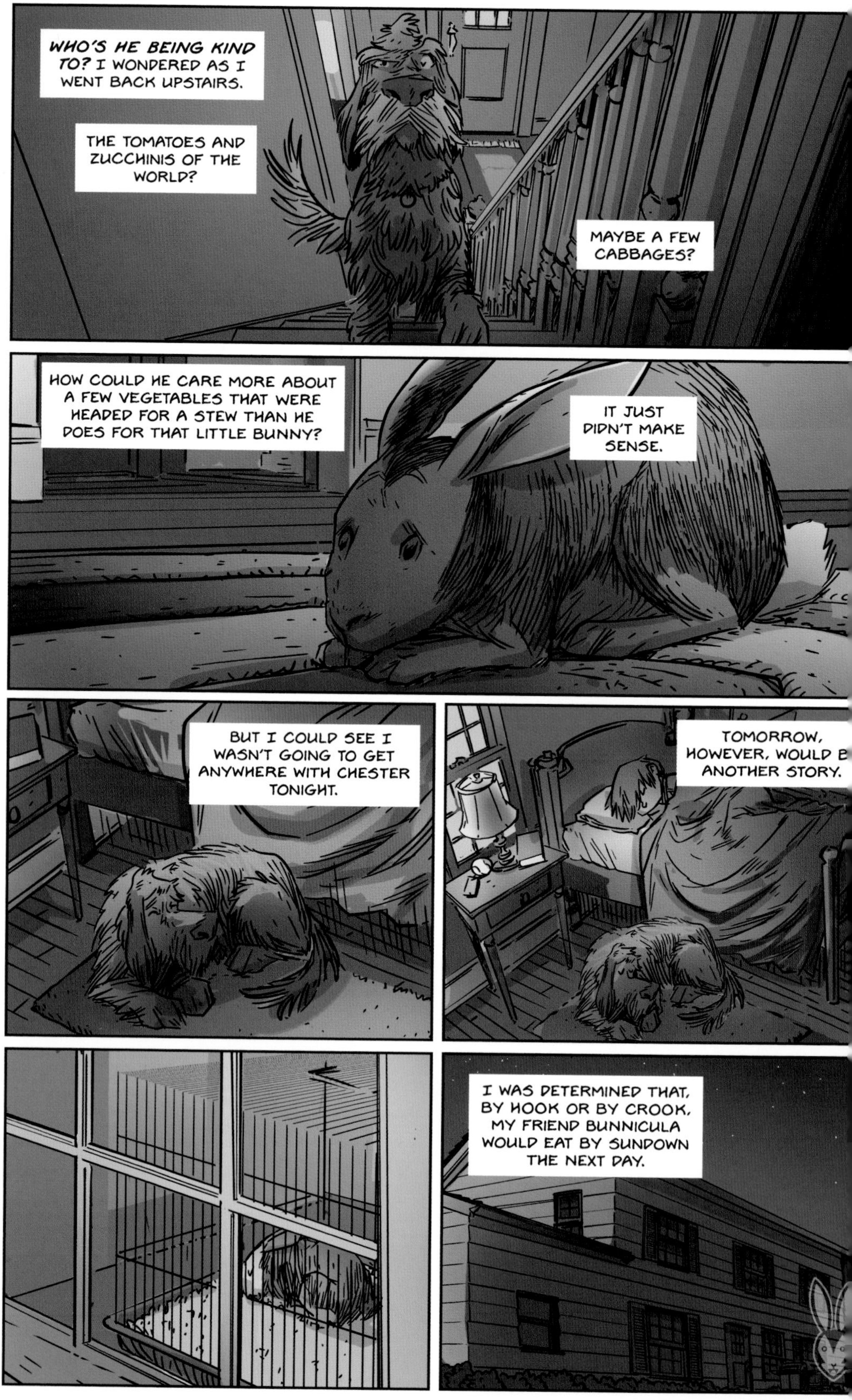
WHO'S HE BEING KIND TO? I WONDERED AS I WENT BACK UPSTAIRS.
THE TOMATOES AND ZUCCHINIS OF THE WORLD?
MAYBE A FEW CABBAGES?
HOW COULD HE CARE MORE ABOUT A FEW VEGETABLES THAT WERE HEADED FOR A STEW THAN HE DOES FOR THAT LITTLE BUNNY?
IT JUST DIDN'T MAKE SENSE.
BUT I COULD SEE I WASN'T GOING TO GET ANYWHERE WITH CHESTER TONIGHT.
TOMORROW, HOWEVER, WOULD B ANOTHER STORY.
I WAS DETERMINED THAT, BY HOOK OR BY CROOK, MY FRIEND BUNNICULA WOULD EAT BY SUNDOWN THE NEXT DAY.

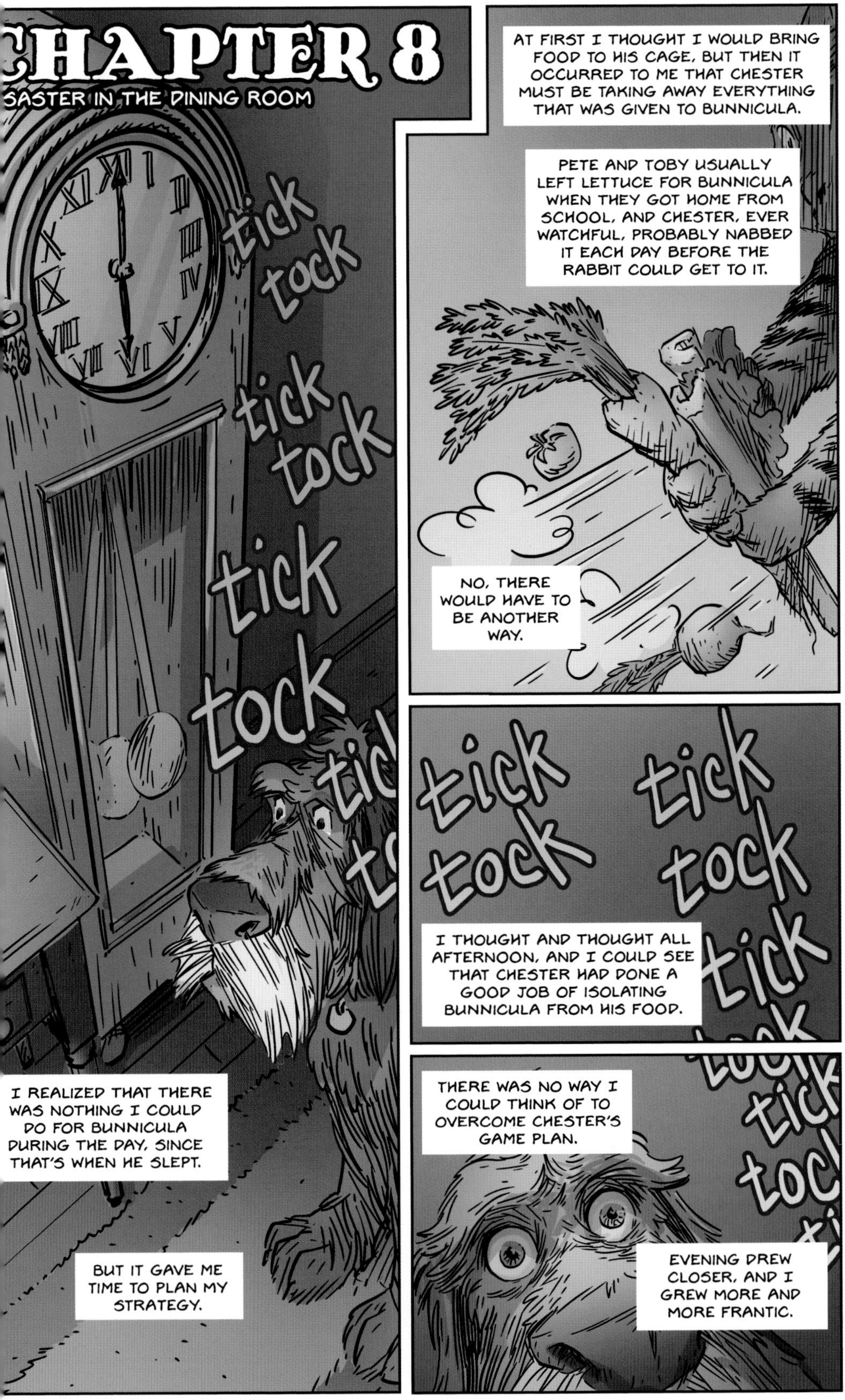
CHAPTER 8
SASTER IN THE DINING ROOM
tick tock
tick tock
tick tock
I REALIZED THAT THERE WAS NOTHING I COULD DO FOR BUNNICULA DURING THE DAY, SINCE THAT'S WHEN HE SLEPT.
BUT IT GAVE ME TIME TO PLAN MY STRATEGY.
AT FIRST I THOUGHT I WOULD BRING FOOD TO HIS CAGE, BUT THEN IT OCCURRED TO ME THAT CHESTER MUST BE TAKING AWAY EVERYTHING THAT WAS GIVEN TO BUNNICULA.
PETE AND TOBY USUALLY LEFT LETTUCE FOR BUNNICULA WHEN THEY GOT HOME FROM SCHOOL, AND CHESTER, EVER WATCHFUL, PROBABLY NABBED IT EACH DAY BEFORE THE RABBIT COULD GET TO IT.
NO, THERE WOULD HAVE TO BE ANOTHER WAY.
tick tock
tick tock
tick
I THOUGHT AND THOUGHT ALL AFTERNOON, AND I COULD SEE THAT CHESTER HAD DONE A GOOD JOB OF ISOLATING BUNNICULA FROM HIS FOOD.
THERE WAS NO WAY I COULD THINK OF TO OVERCOME CHESTER'S GAME PLAN.
tick
EVENING DREW CLOSER, AND I GREW MORE AND MORE FRANTIC.

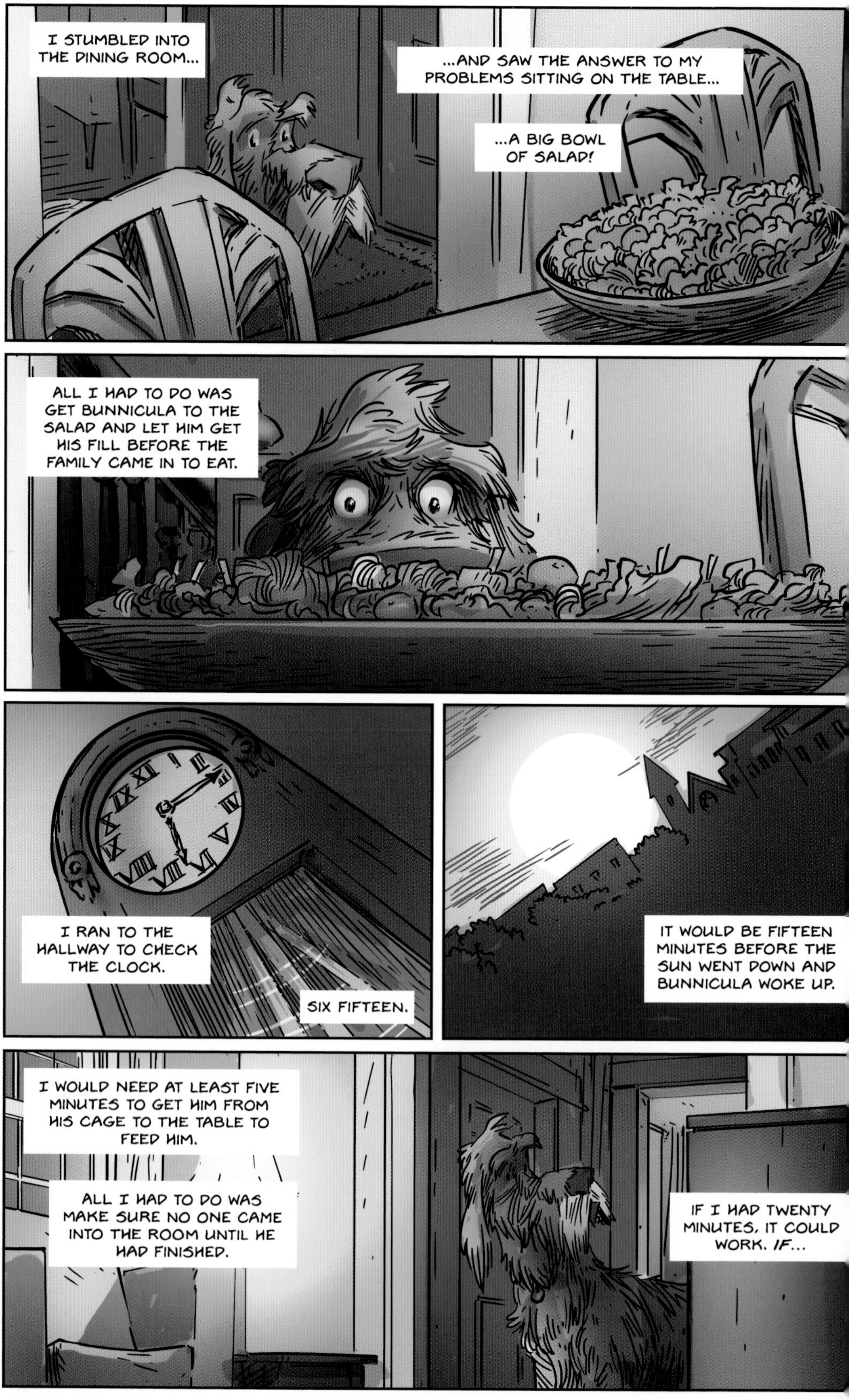
I STUMBLED INTO THE DINING ROOM...
...AND SAW THE ANSWER TO MY PROBLEMS SITTING ON THE TABLE...
...A BIG BOWL OF SALAD!
ALL I HAD TO DO WAS GET BUNNICULA TO THE SALAD AND LET HIM GET HIS FILL BEFORE THE FAMILY CAME IN TO EAT.
I RAN TO THE HALLWAY TO CHECK THE CLOCK.
SIX FIFTEEN.
IT WOULD BE FIFTEEN MINUTES BEFORE THE SUN WENT DOWN AND BUNNICULA WOKE UP.
I WOULD NEED AT LEAST FIVE MINUTES TO GET HIM FROM HIS CAGE TO THE TABLE TO FEED HIM.
ALL I HAD TO DO WAS MAKE SURE NO ONE CAME INTO THE ROOM UNTIL HE HAD FINISHED.
IF I HAD TWENTY MINUTES, IT COULD WORK. *IF*...

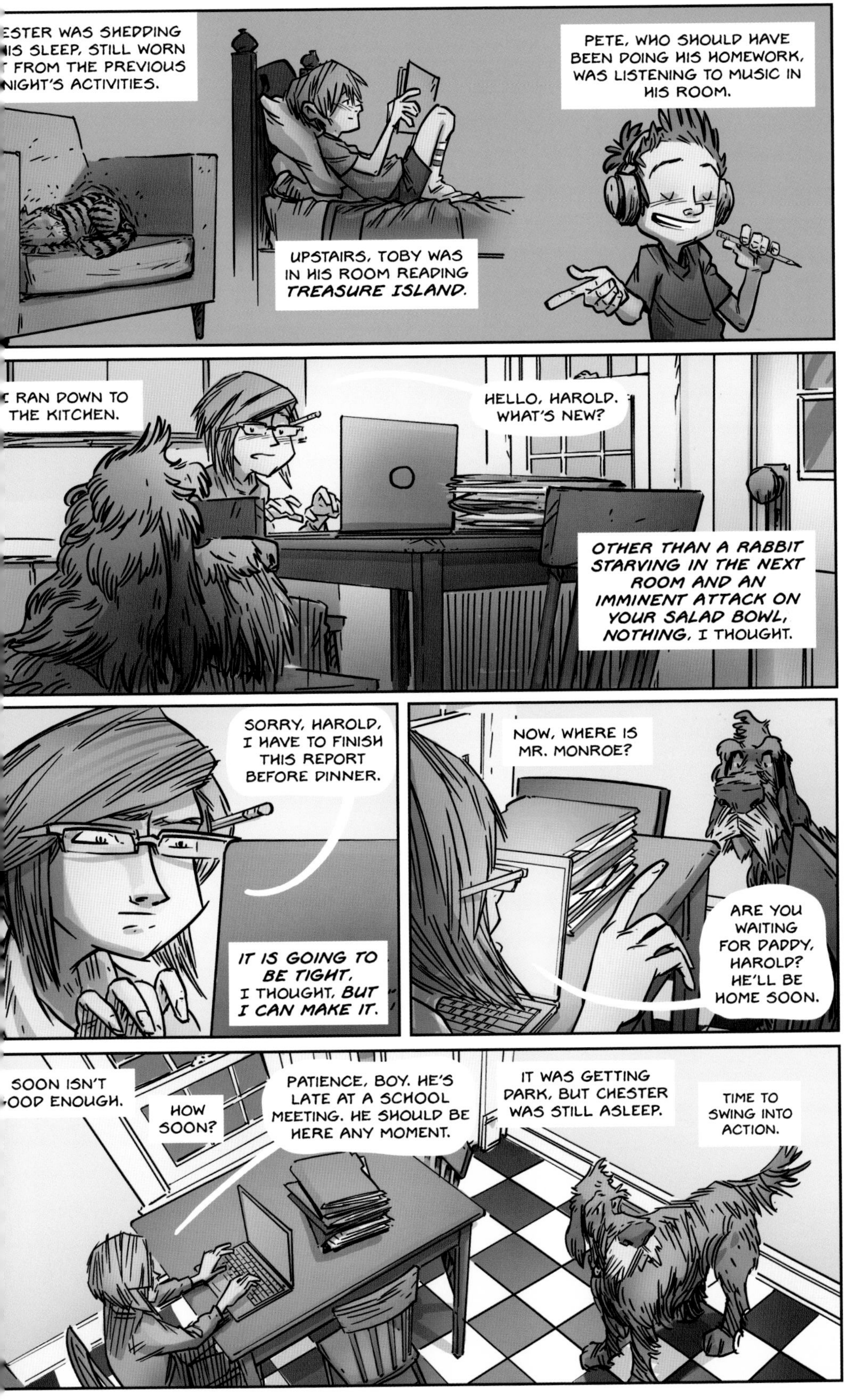
ESTER WAS SHEDDING
IIS SLEEP, STILL WORN
FROM THE PREVIOUS
NIGHT'S ACTIVITIES.
UPSTAIRS, TOBY WAS IN HIS ROOM READING *TREASURE ISLAND*.
PETE, WHO SHOULD HAVE BEEN DOING HIS HOMEWORK, WAS LISTENING TO MUSIC IN HIS ROOM.
RAN DOWN TO THE KITCHEN.
HELLO, HAROLD. WHAT'S NEW?
OTHER THAN A RABBIT STARVING IN THE NEXT ROOM AND AN IMMINENT ATTACK ON YOUR SALAD BOWL, NOTHING, I THOUGHT.
SORRY, HAROLD, I HAVE TO FINISH THIS REPORT BEFORE DINNER.
IT IS GOING TO BE TIGHT, I THOUGHT, *BUT I CAN MAKE IT*.
NOW, WHERE IS MR. MONROE?
ARE YOU WAITING FOR DADDY, HAROLD? HE'LL BE HOME SOON.
SOON ISN'T
OOD ENOUGH.
HOW SOON?
PATIENCE, BOY. HE'S LATE AT A SCHOOL MEETING. HE SHOULD BE HERE ANY MOMENT.
IT WAS GETTING DARK, BUT CHESTER WAS STILL ASLEEP.
TIME TO SWING INTO ACTION.

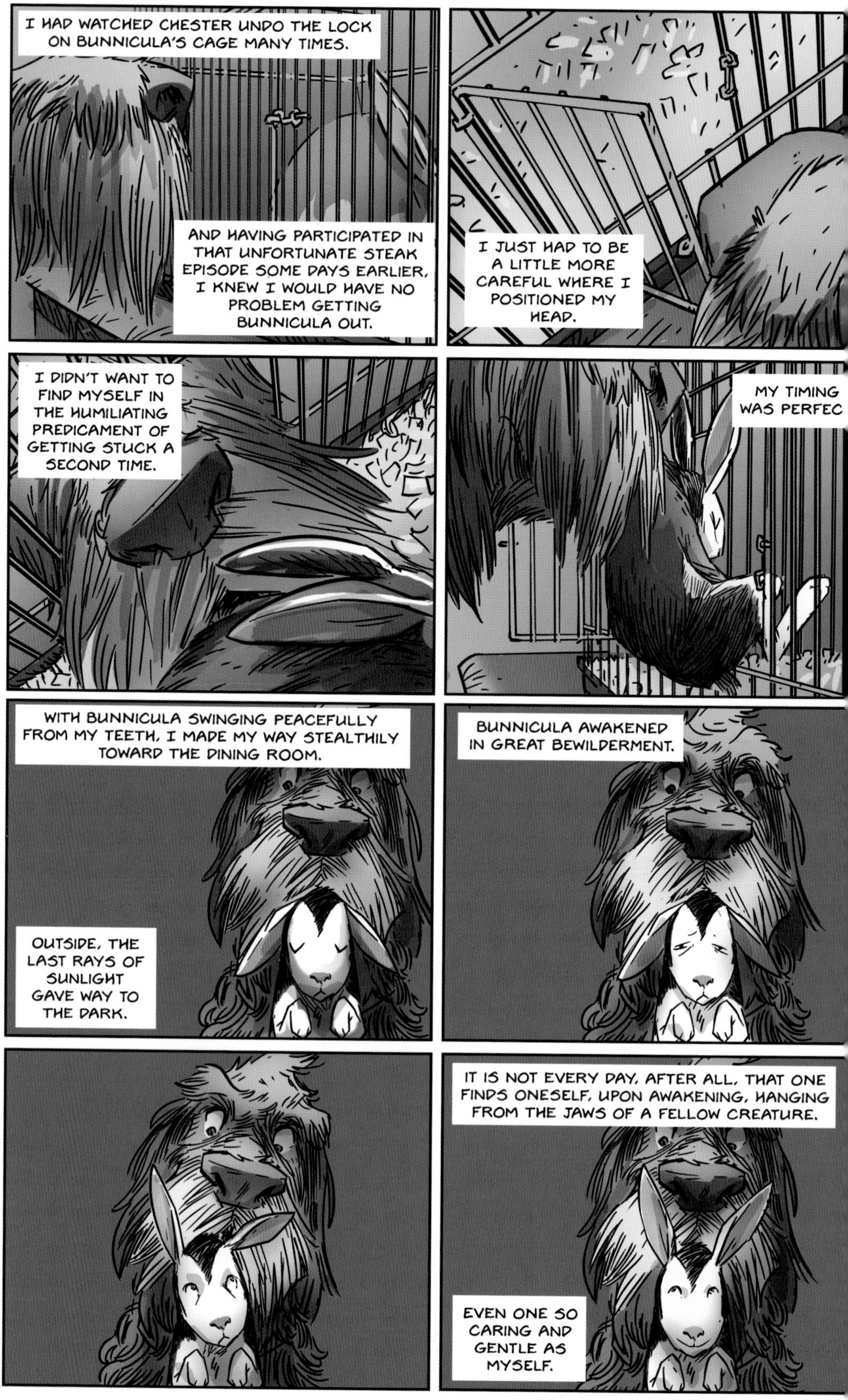
I HAD WATCHED CHESTER UNDO THE LOCK ON BUNNICULA'S CAGE MANY TIMES.
AND HAVING PARTICIPATED IN THAT UNFORTUNATE STEAK EPISODE SOME DAYS EARLIER, I KNEW I WOULD HAVE NO PROBLEM GETTING BUNNICULA OUT.
I JUST HAD TO BE A LITTLE MORE CAREFUL WHERE I POSITIONED MY HEAD.
I DIDN'T WANT TO FIND MYSELF IN THE HUMILIATING PREDICAMENT OF GETTING STUCK A SECOND TIME.
MY TIMING WAS PERFEC
WITH BUNNICULA SWINGING PEACEFULLY FROM MY TEETH, I MADE MY WAY STEALTHILY TOWARD THE DINING ROOM.
OUTSIDE, THE LAST RAYS OF SUNLIGHT GAVE WAY TO THE DARK.
BUNNICULA AWAKENED IN GREAT BEWILDERMENT.
IT IS NOT EVERY DAY, AFTER ALL, THAT ONE FINDS ONESELF, UPON AWAKENING, HANGING FROM THE JAWS OF A FELLOW CREATURE.
EVEN ONE SO CARING AND GENTLE AS MYSELF.

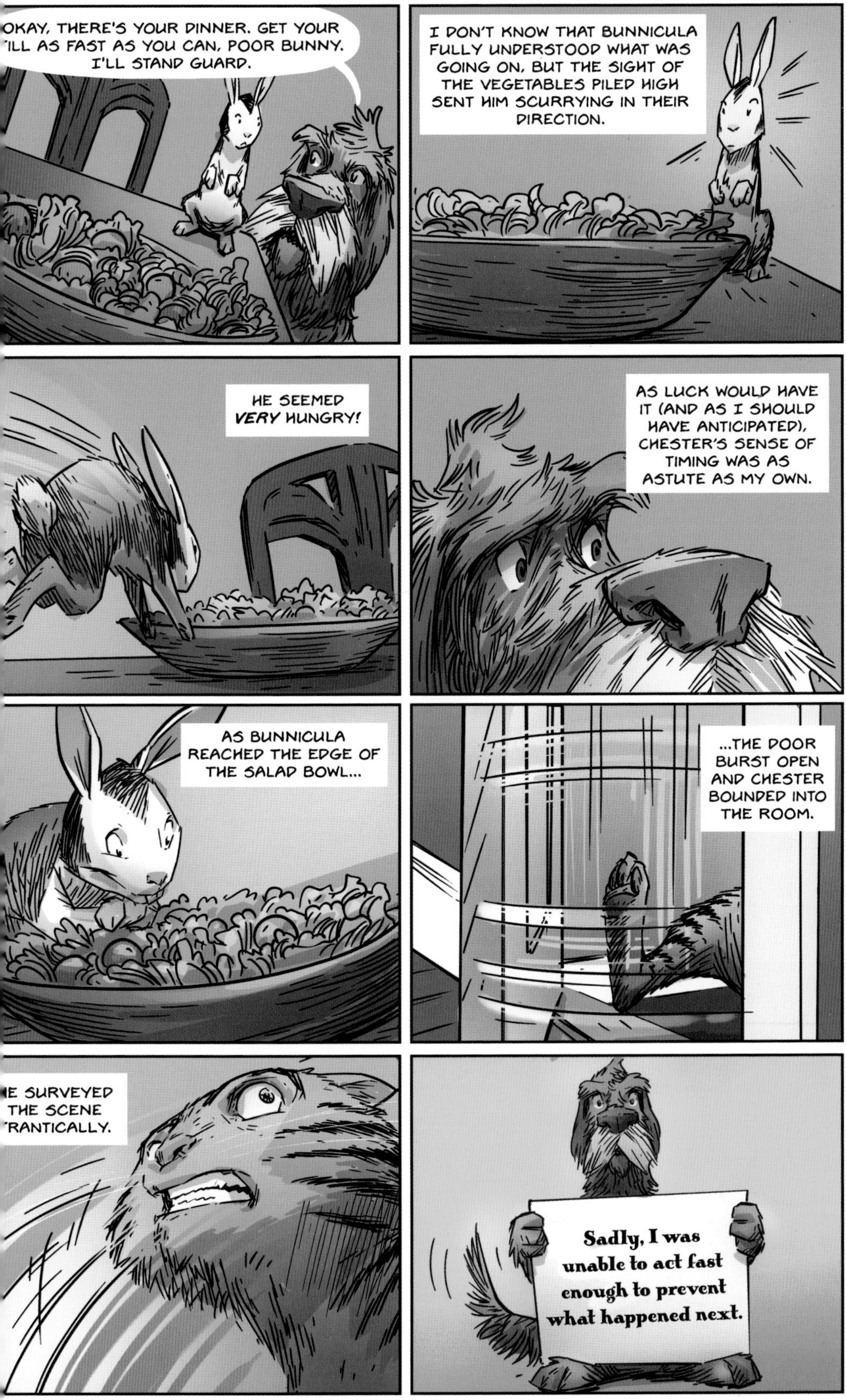
OKAY, THERE'S YOUR DINNER. GET YOUR FILL AS FAST AS YOU CAN, POOR BUNNY. I'LL STAND GUARD.
I DON'T KNOW THAT BUNNICULA FULLY UNDERSTOOD WHAT WAS GOING ON, BUT THE SIGHT OF THE VEGETABLES PILED HIGH SENT HIM SCURRYING IN THEIR DIRECTION.
HE SEEMED VERY HUNGRY!
AS LUCK WOULD HAVE IT (AND AS I SHOULD HAVE ANTICIPATED), CHESTER'S SENSE OF TIMING WAS AS ASTUTE AS MY OWN.
AS BUNNICULA REACHED THE EDGE OF THE SALAD BOWL...
...THE DOOR BURST OPEN AND CHESTER BOUNDED INTO THE ROOM.
HE SURVEYED THE SCENE FRANTICALLY.
Sadly, I was unable to act fast enough to prevent what happened next.

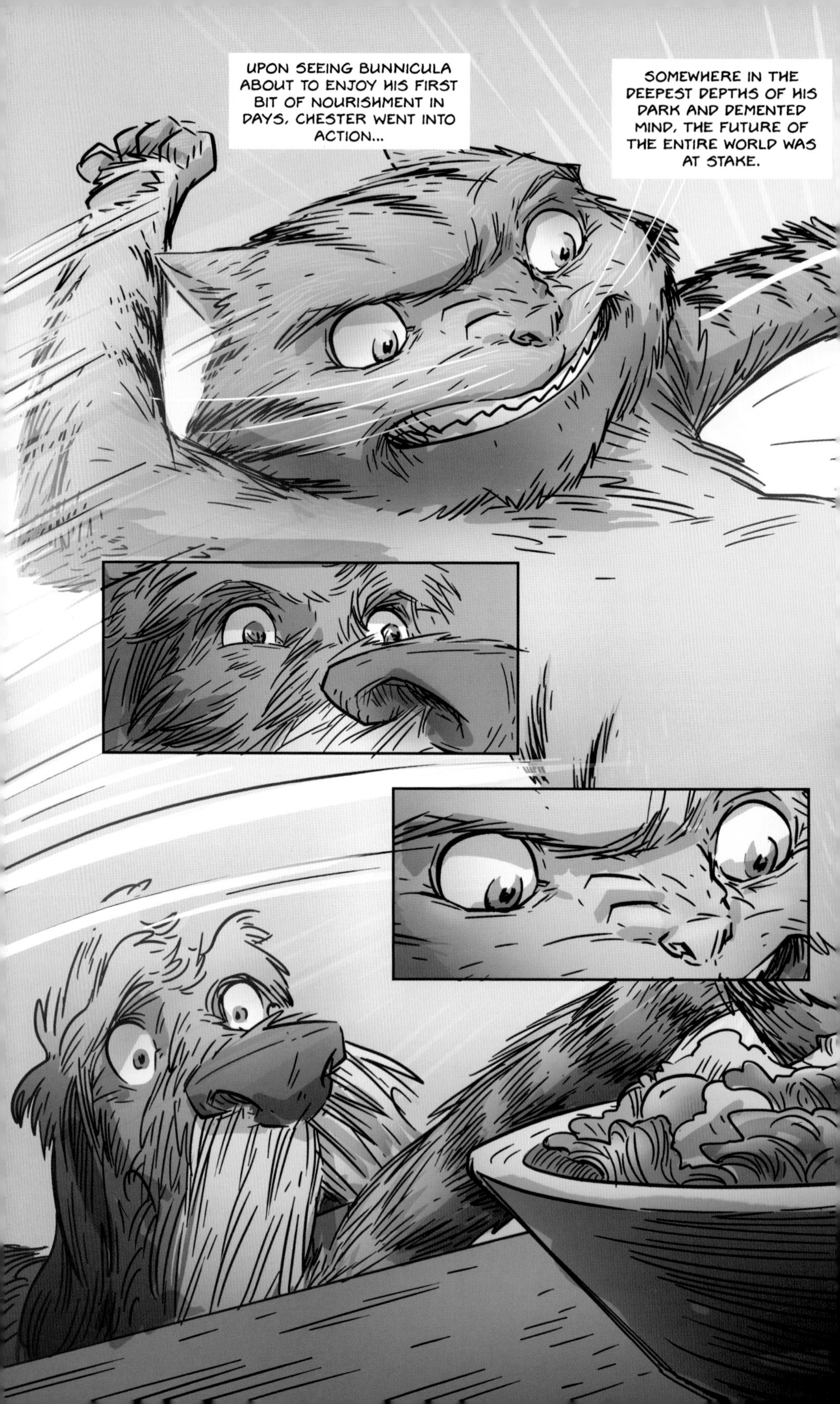

UPON SEEING BUNNICULA ABOUT TO ENJOY HIS FIRST BIT OF NOURISHMENT IN DAYS, CHESTER WENT INTO ACTION...
SOMEWHERE IN THE DEEPEST DEPTHS OF HIS DARK AND DEMENTED MIND, THE FUTURE OF THE ENTIRE WORLD WAS AT STAKE.

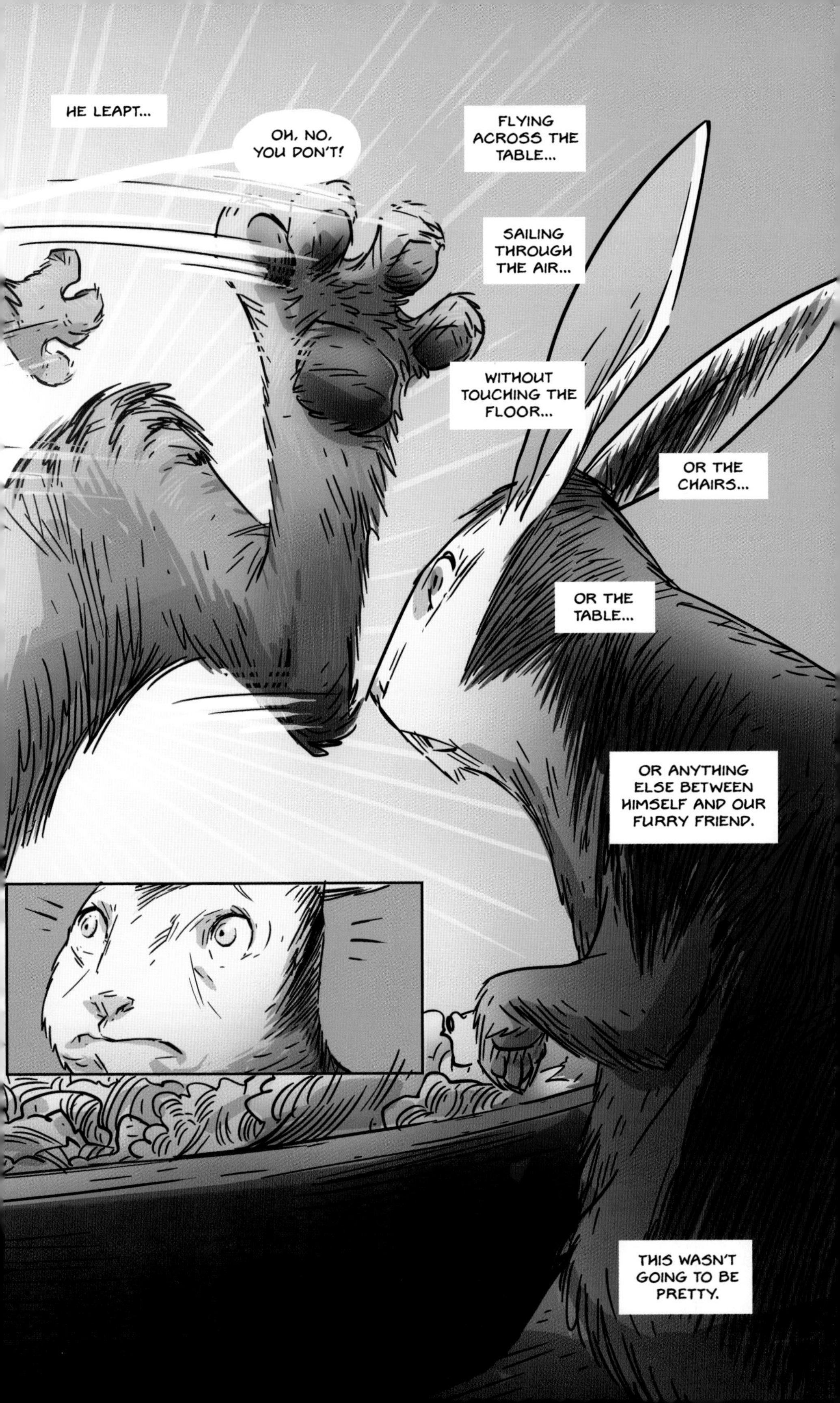
HE LEAPT...
OH, NO, YOU DON'T!
FLYING ACROSS THE TABLE...
SAILING THROUGH THE AIR...
WITHOUT TOUCHING THE FLOOR...
OR THE CHAIRS...
OR THE TABLE...
OR ANYTHING ELSE BETWEEN HIMSELF AND OUR FURRY FRIEND.
THIS WASN'T GOING TO BE PRETTY.

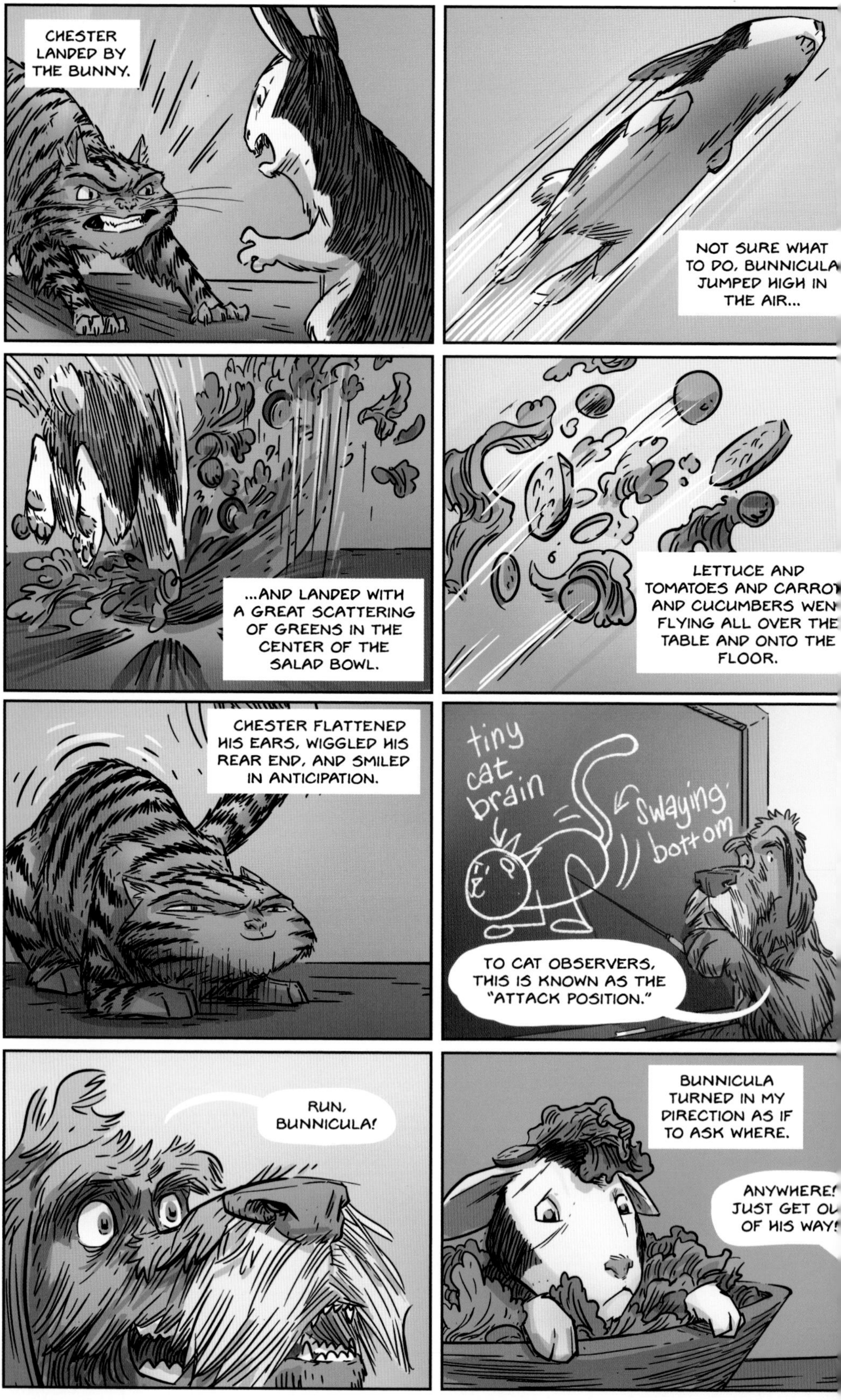

CHESTER LANDED BY THE BUNNY.
NOT SURE WHAT TO DO, BUNNICULA JUMPED HIGH IN THE AIR...
...AND LANDED WITH A GREAT SCATTERING OF GREENS IN THE CENTER OF THE SALAD BOWL.
LETTUCE AND TOMATOES AND CARRO AND CUCUMBERS WEN FLYING ALL OVER THE TABLE AND ONTO THE FLOOR.
CHESTER FLATTENED HIS EARS, WIGGLED HIS REAR END, AND SMILED IN ANTICIPATION.
tiny cat brain
swaying bottom
TO CAT OBSERVERS, THIS IS KNOWN AS THE "ATTACK POSITION."
RUN, BUNNICULA!
BUNNICULA TURNED IN MY DIRECTION AS IF TO ASK WHERE.
ANYWHERE! JUST GET OU OF HIS WAY!

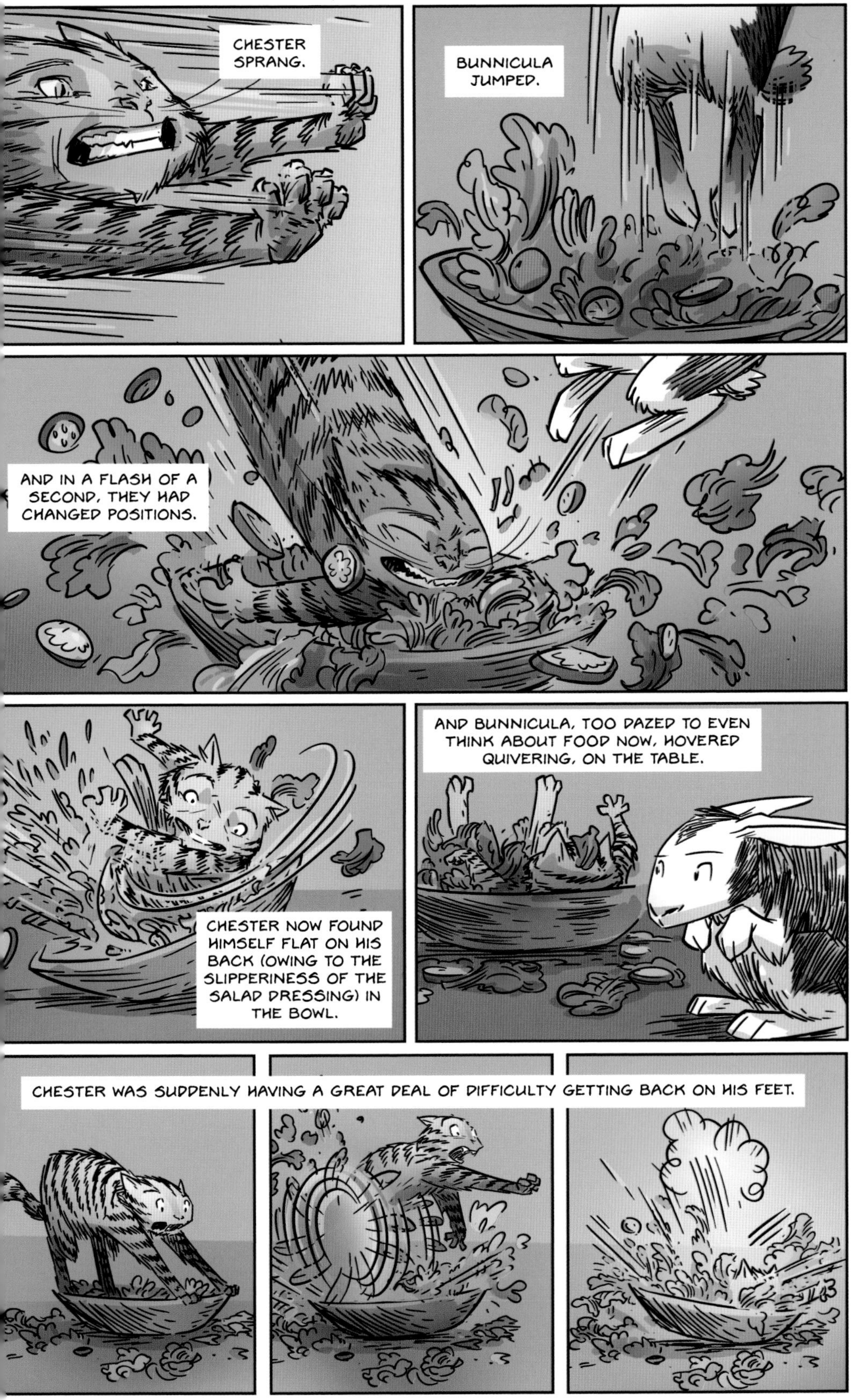
CHESTER SPRANG.
BUNNICULA JUMPED.
AND IN A FLASH OF A SECOND, THEY HAD CHANGED POSITIONS.
CHESTER NOW FOUND HIMSELF FLAT ON HIS BACK (OWING TO THE SLIPPERINESS OF THE SALAD DRESSING) IN THE BOWL.
AND BUNNICULA, TOO DAZED TO EVEN THINK ABOUT FOOD NOW, HOVERED QUIVERING, ON THE TABLE.
CHESTER WAS SUDDENLY HAVING A GREAT DEAL OF DIFFICULTY GETTING BACK ON HIS FEET.

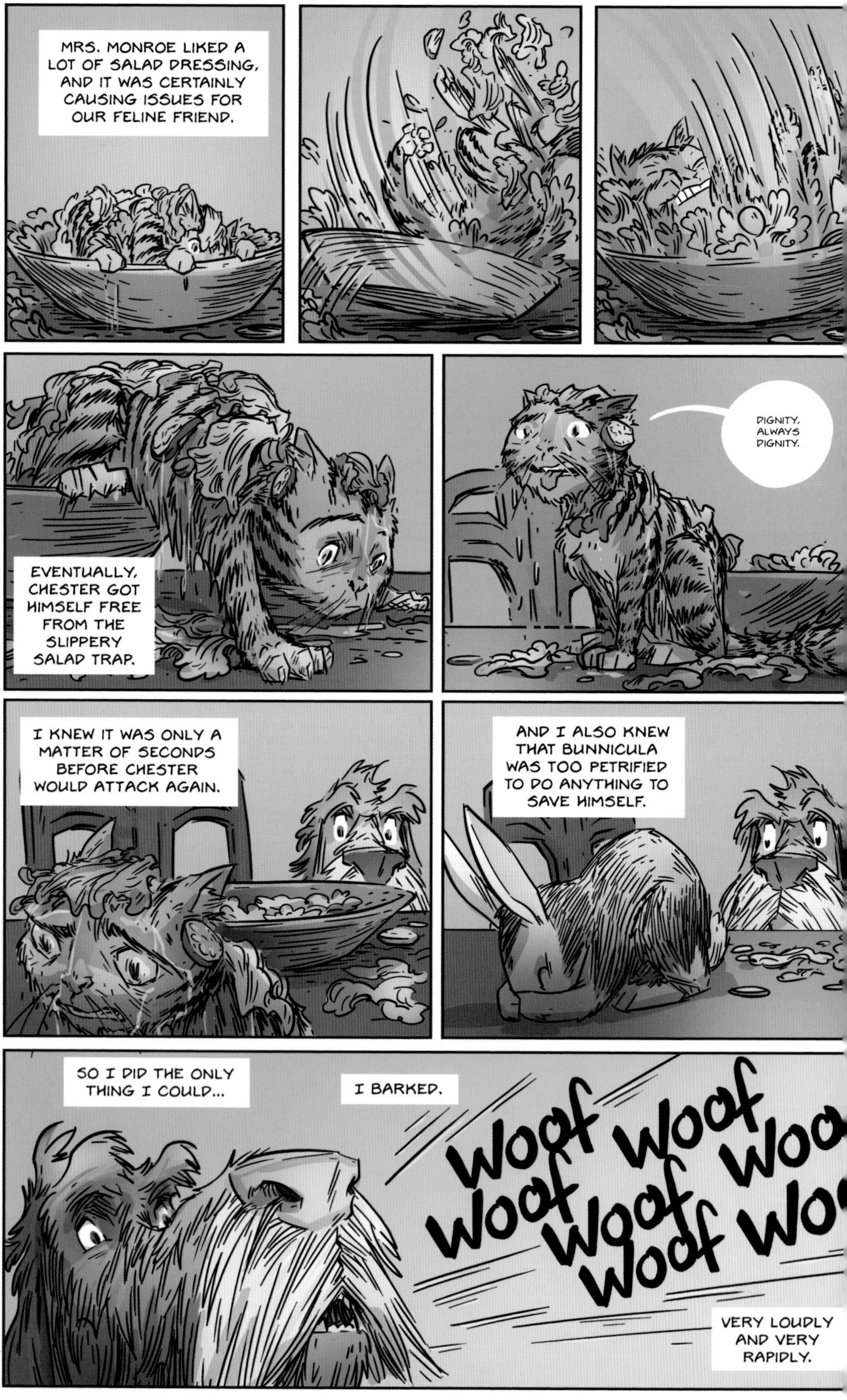
MRS. MONROE LIKED A LOT OF SALAD DRESSING, AND IT WAS CERTAINLY CAUSING ISSUES FOR OUR FELINE FRIEND.
EVENTUALLY, CHESTER GOT HIMSELF FREE FROM THE SLIPPERY SALAD TRAP.
DIGNITY. ALWAYS DIGNITY.
I KNEW IT WAS ONLY A MATTER OF SECONDS BEFORE CHESTER WOULD ATTACK AGAIN.
AND I ALSO KNEW THAT BUNNICULA WAS TOO PETRIFIED TO DO ANYTHING TO SAVE HIMSELF.
SO I DID THE ONLY THING I COULD...
I BARKED.
woof woof
woof woof
woof
woof
VERY LOUDLY AND VERY RAPIDLY.

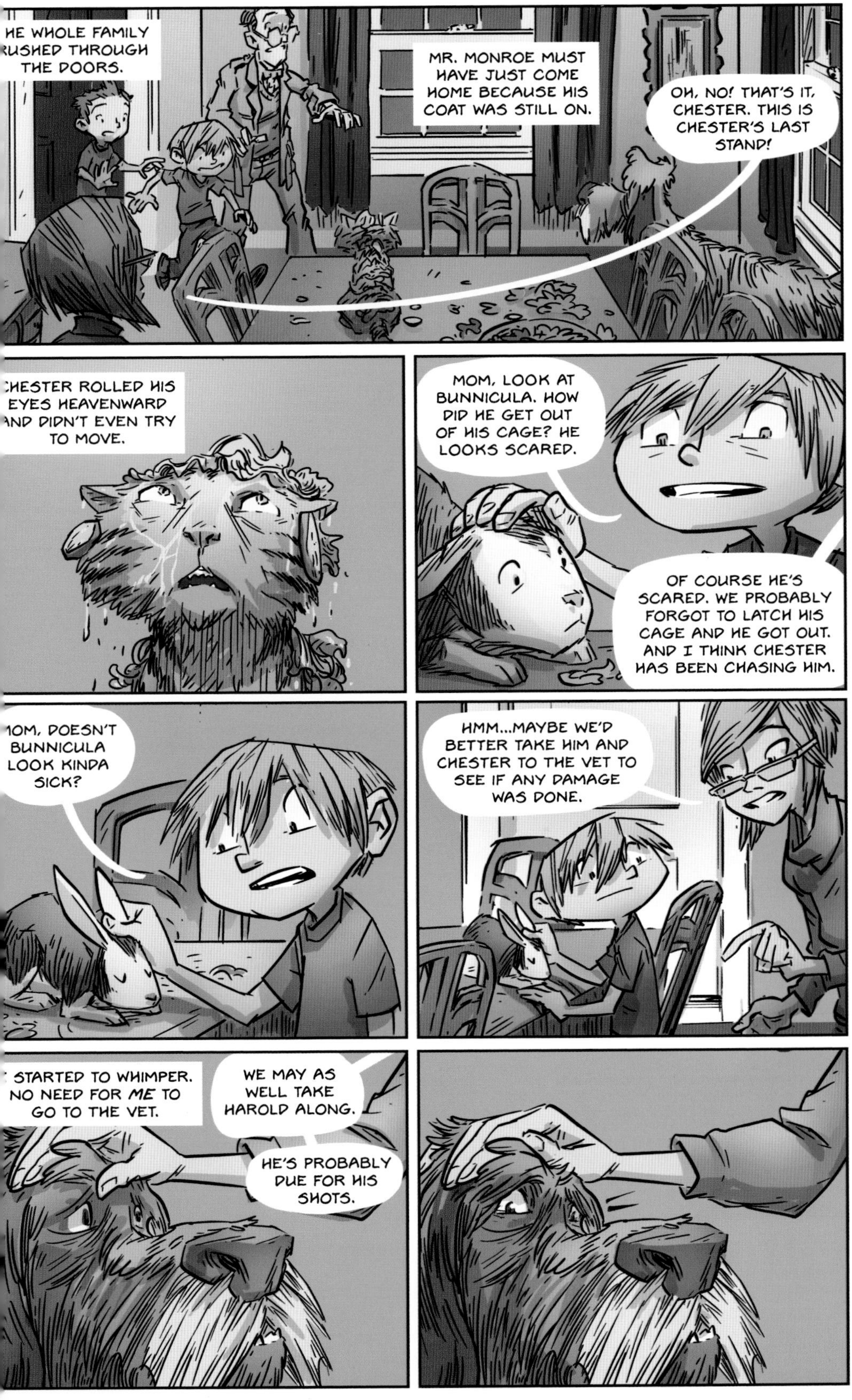
HE WHOLE FAMILY RUSHED THROUGH THE DOORS.
MR. MONROE MUST HAVE JUST COME HOME BECAUSE HIS COAT WAS STILL ON.
OH, NO! THAT'S IT, CHESTER. THIS IS CHESTER'S LAST STAND!
HESTER ROLLED HIS EYES HEAVENWARD AND DIDN'T EVEN TRY TO MOVE.
MOM, LOOK AT BUNNICULA. HOW DID HE GET OUT OF HIS CAGE? HE LOOKS SCARED.
OF COURSE HE'S SCARED. WE PROBABLY FORGOT TO LATCH HIS CAGE AND HE GOT OUT. AND I THINK CHESTER HAS BEEN CHASING HIM.
MOM, DOESN'T BUNNICULA LOOK KINDA SICK?
HMM...MAYBE WE'D BETTER TAKE HIM AND CHESTER TO THE VET TO SEE IF ANY DAMAGE WAS DONE.
STARTED TO WHIMPER. NO NEED FOR *ME* TO GO TO THE VET.
WE MAY AS WELL TAKE HAROLD ALONG.
HE'S PROBABLY DUE FOR HIS SHOTS.

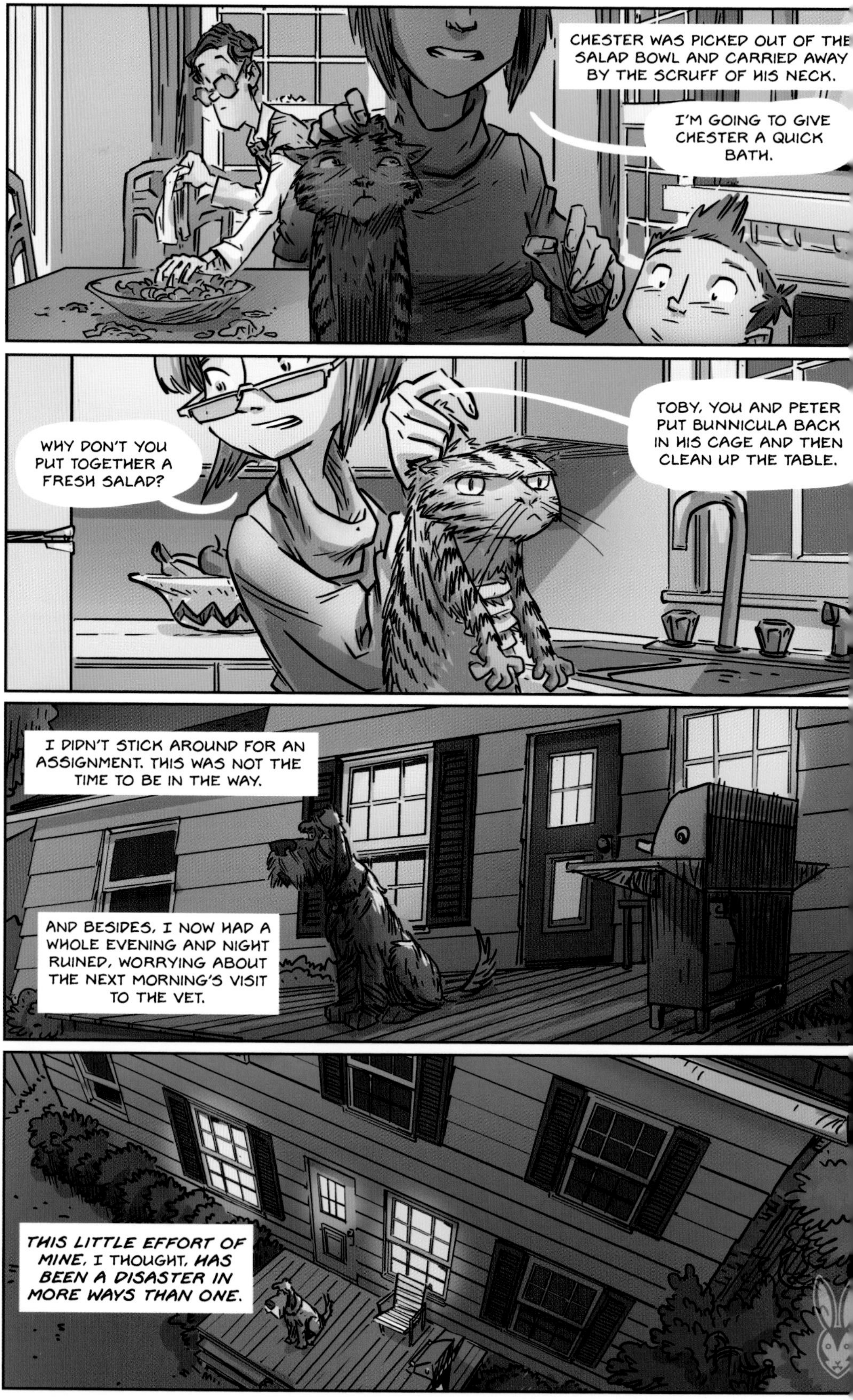
CHESTER WAS PICKED OUT OF THE SALAD BOWL AND CARRIED AWAY BY THE SCRUFF OF HIS NECK.
I'M GOING TO GIVE CHESTER A QUICK BATH.
WHY DON'T YOU PUT TOGETHER A FRESH SALAD?
TOBY, YOU AND PETER PUT BUNNICULA BACK IN HIS CAGE AND THEN CLEAN UP THE TABLE.
I DIDN'T STICK AROUND FOR AN ASSIGNMENT. THIS WAS NOT THE TIME TO BE IN THE WAY.
AND BESIDES, I NOW HAD A WHOLE EVENING AND NIGHT RUINED, WORRYING ABOUT THE NEXT MORNING'S VISIT TO THE VET.
THIS LITTLE EFFORT OF MINE, I THOUGHT, *HAS BEEN A DISASTER IN MORE WAYS THAN ONE*.

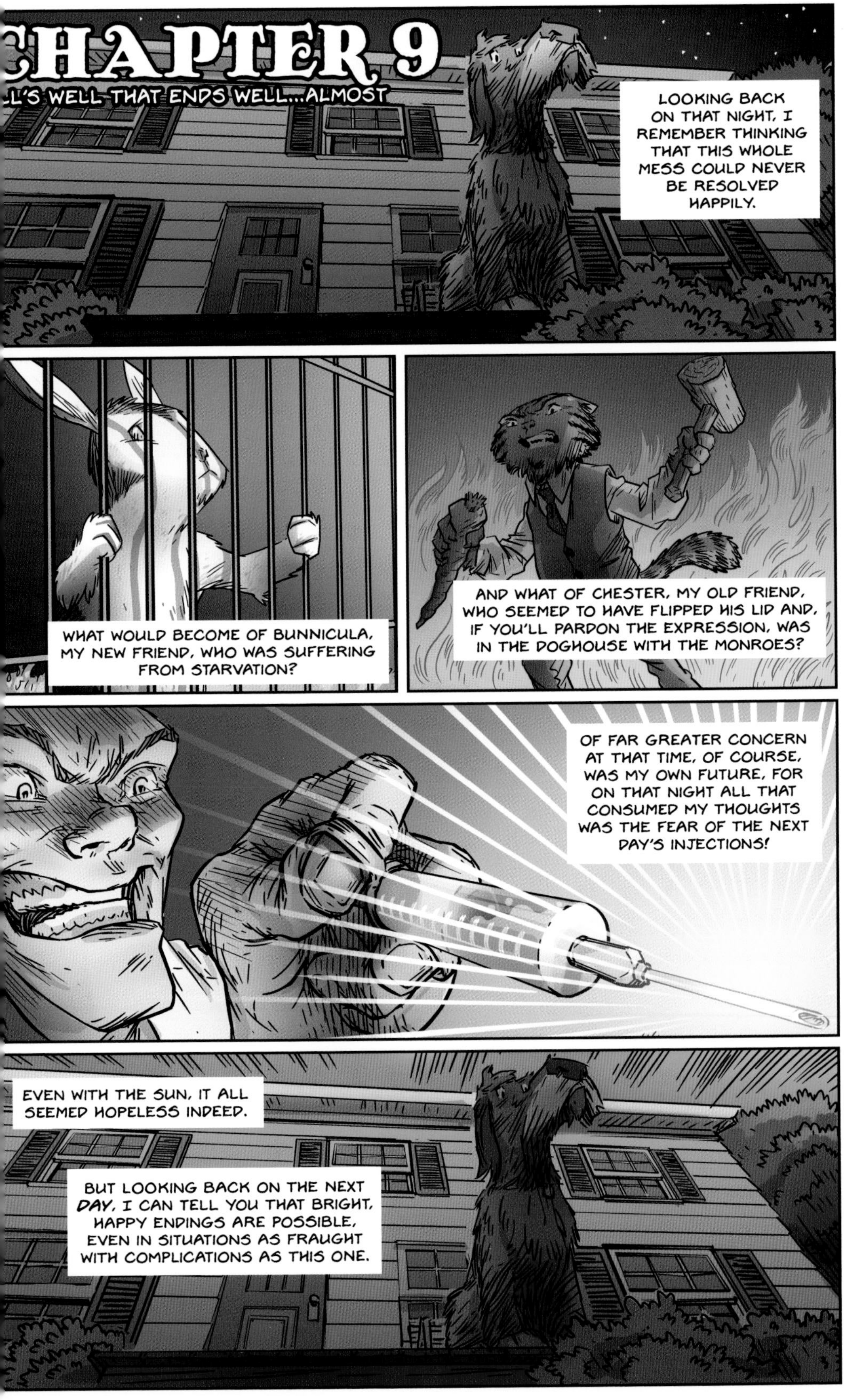
CHAPTER 9
...L'S WELL THAT ENDS WELL...ALMOST
LOOKING BACK ON THAT NIGHT, I REMEMBER THINKING THAT THIS WHOLE MESS COULD NEVER BE RESOLVED HAPPILY.
WHAT WOULD BECOME OF BUNNICULA, MY NEW FRIEND, WHO WAS SUFFERING FROM STARVATION?
AND WHAT OF CHESTER, MY OLD FRIEND, WHO SEEMED TO HAVE FLIPPED HIS LID AND, IF YOU'LL PARDON THE EXPRESSION, WAS IN THE DOGHOUSE WITH THE MONROES?
OF FAR GREATER CONCERN AT THAT TIME, OF COURSE, WAS MY OWN FUTURE, FOR ON THAT NIGHT ALL THAT CONSUMED MY THOUGHTS WAS THE FEAR OF THE NEXT DAY'S INJECTIONS!
EVEN WITH THE SUN, IT ALL SEEMED HOPELESS INDEED.
BUT LOOKING BACK ON THE NEXT DAY, I CAN TELL YOU THAT BRIGHT, HAPPY ENDINGS ARE POSSIBLE, EVEN IN SITUATIONS AS FRAUGHT WITH COMPLICATIONS AS THIS ONE.

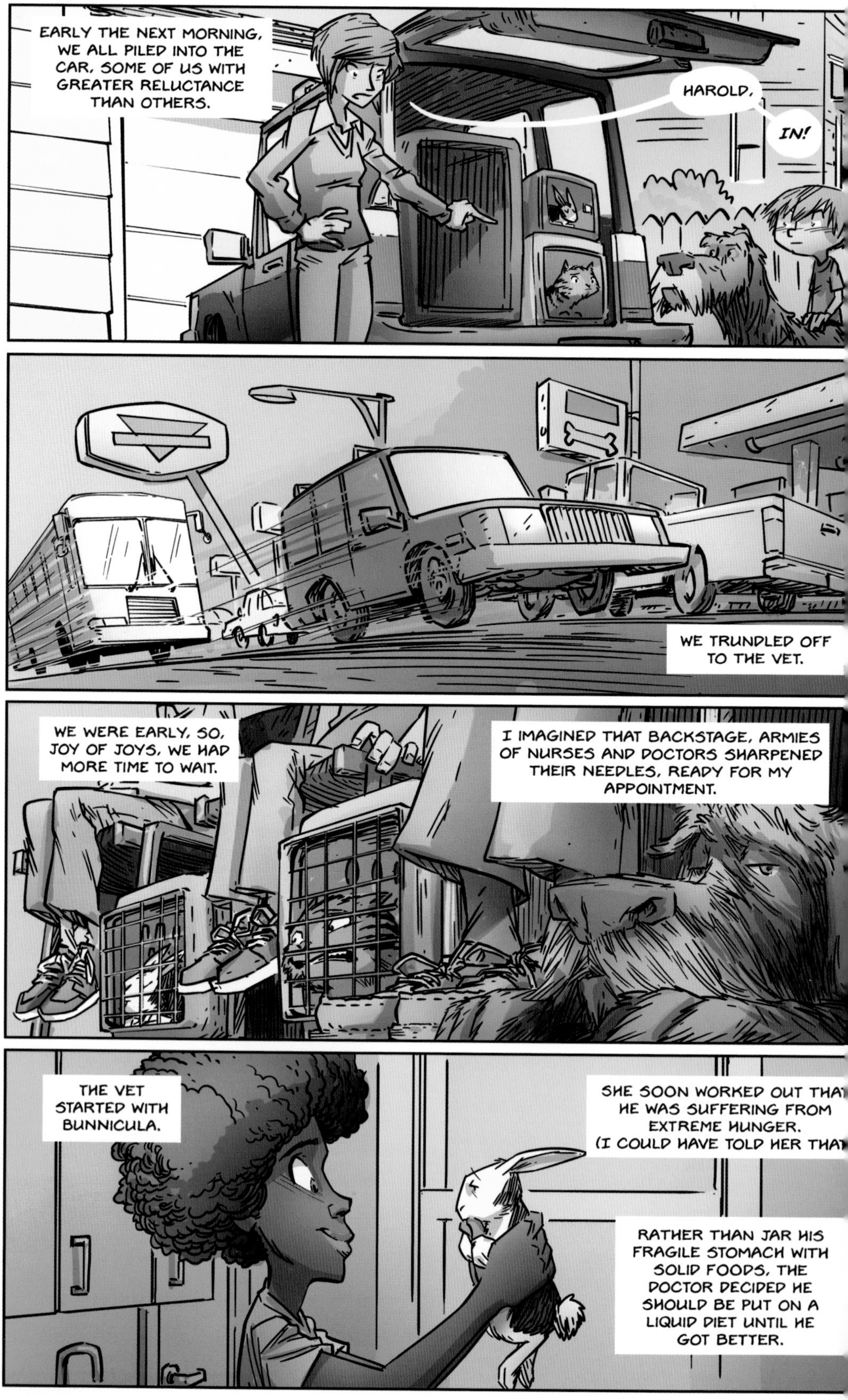
EARLY THE NEXT MORNING, WE ALL PILED INTO THE CAR, SOME OF US WITH GREATER RELUCTANCE THAN OTHERS.
HAROLD,
IN!
WE TRUNDLED OFF TO THE VET.
WE WERE EARLY, SO, JOY OF JOYS, WE HAD MORE TIME TO WAIT.
I IMAGINED THAT BACKSTAGE, ARMIES OF NURSES AND DOCTORS SHARPENED THEIR NEEDLES, READY FOR MY APPOINTMENT.
THE VET STARTED WITH BUNNICULA.
SHE SOON WORKED OUT THA
HE WAS SUFFERING FROM EXTREME HUNGER.
(I COULD HAVE TOLD HER THA
RATHER THAN JAR HIS FRAGILE STOMACH WITH SOLID FOODS, THE DOCTOR DECIDED HE SHOULD BE PUT ON A LIQUID DIET UNTIL HE GOT BETTER.

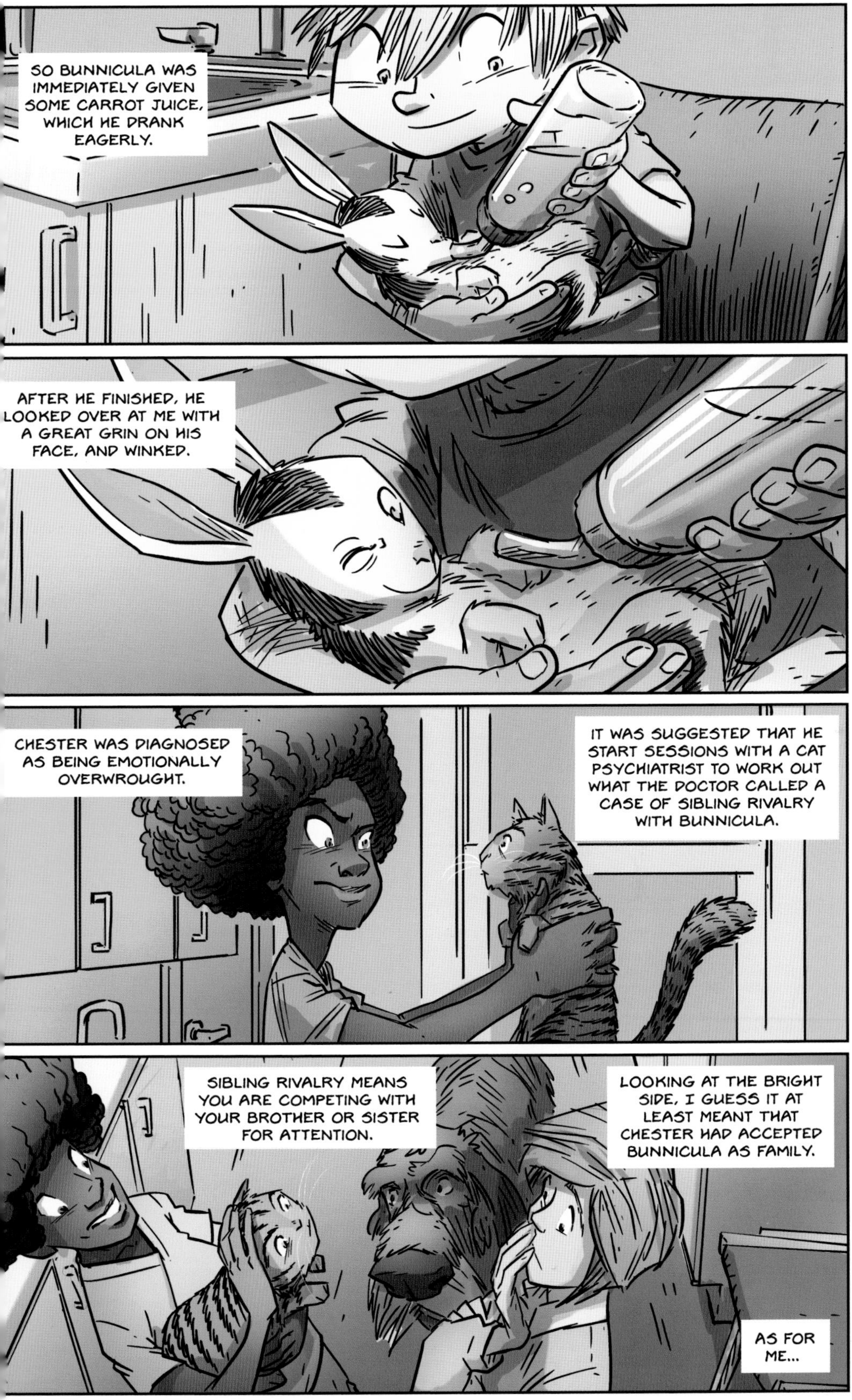
SO BUNNICULA WAS IMMEDIATELY GIVEN SOME CARROT JUICE, WHICH HE DRANK EAGERLY.
AFTER HE FINISHED, HE LOOKED OVER AT ME WITH A GREAT GRIN ON HIS FACE, AND WINKED.
CHESTER WAS DIAGNOSED AS BEING EMOTIONALLY OVERWROUGHT.
IT WAS SUGGESTED THAT HE START SESSIONS WITH A CAT PSYCHIATRIST TO WORK OUT WHAT THE DOCTOR CALLED A CASE OF SIBLING RIVALRY WITH BUNNICULA.
SIBLING RIVALRY MEANS YOU ARE COMPETING WITH YOUR BROTHER OR SISTER FOR ATTENTION.
LOOKING AT THE BRIGHT SIDE, I GUESS IT AT LEAST MEANT THAT CHESTER HAD ACCEPTED BUNNICULA AS FAMILY.
AS FOR ME...

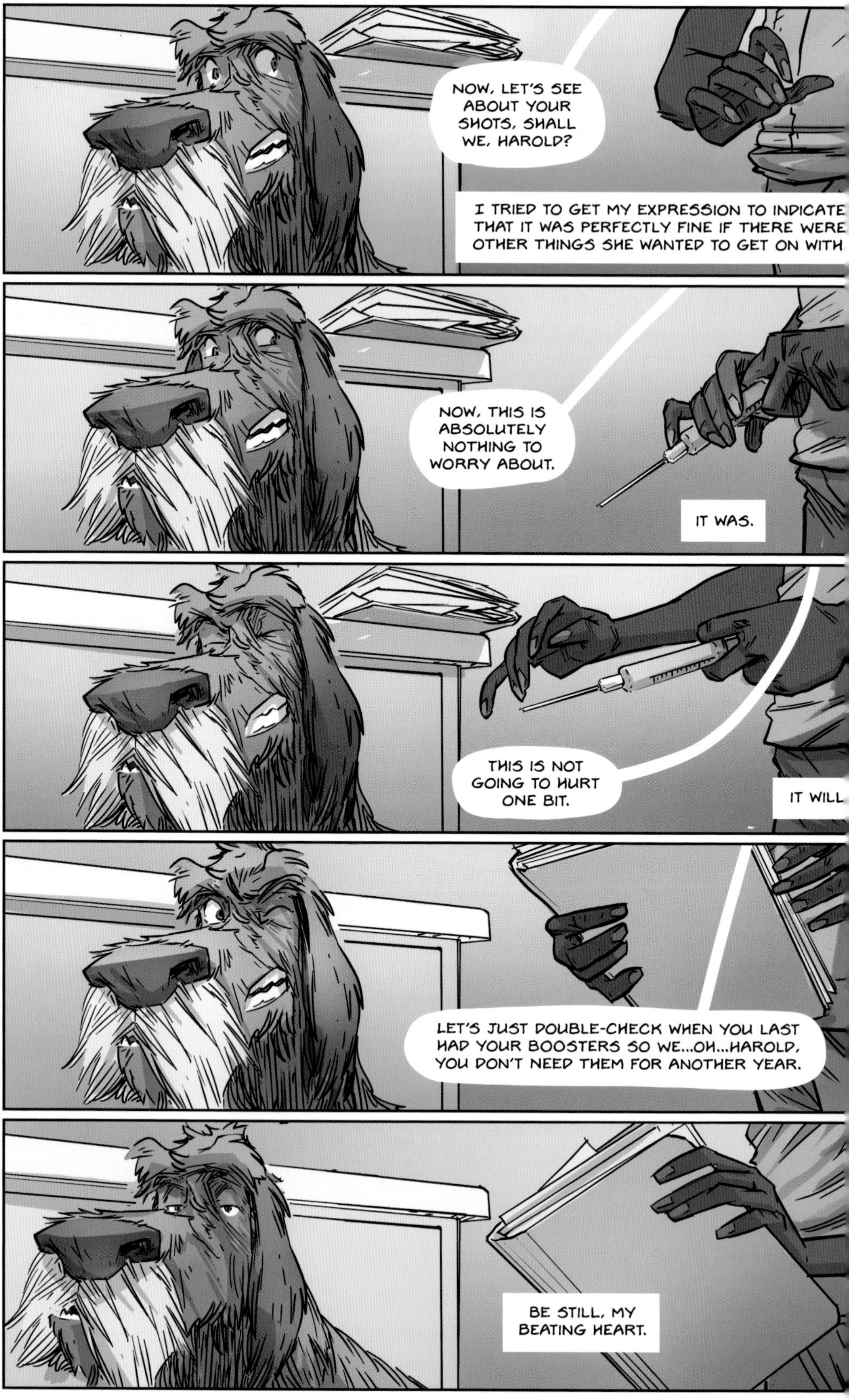
NOW, LET'S SEE ABOUT YOUR SHOTS, SHALL WE, HAROLD?
I TRIED TO GET MY EXPRESSION TO INDICATE THAT IT WAS PERFECTLY FINE IF THERE WERE OTHER THINGS SHE WANTED TO GET ON WITH.
NOW, THIS IS ABSOLUTELY NOTHING TO WORRY ABOUT.
IT WAS.
THIS IS NOT GOING TO HURT ONE BIT.
IT WILL
LET'S JUST DOUBLE-CHECK WHEN YOU LAST HAD YOUR BOOSTERS SO WE...OH...HAROLD, YOU DON'T NEED THEM FOR ANOTHER YEAR.
BE STILL, MY BEATING HEART.

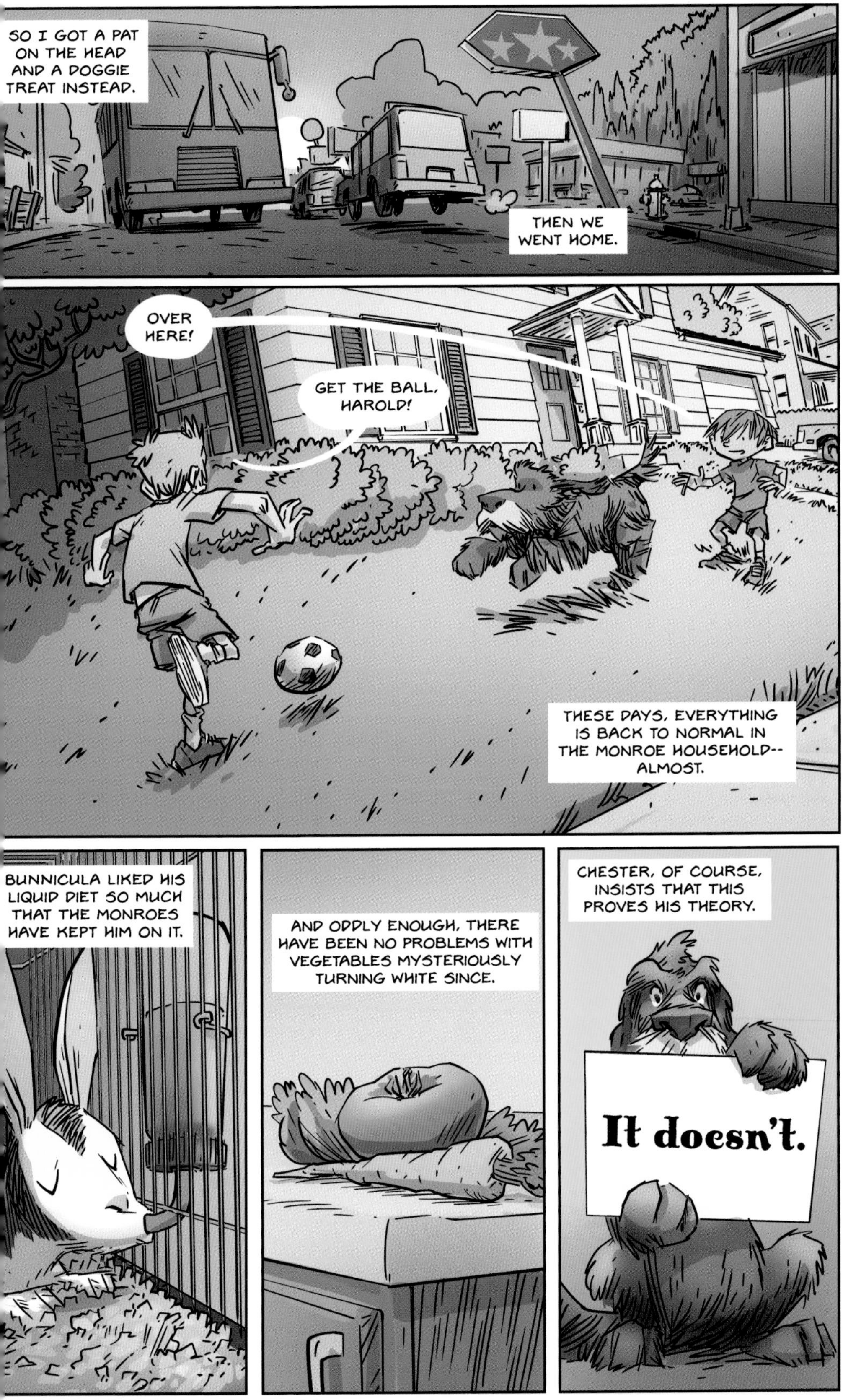
SO I GOT A PAT ON THE HEAD AND A DOGGIE TREAT INSTEAD.
THEN WE WENT HOME.
OVER HERE!
GET THE BALL, HAROLD!
THESE DAYS, EVERYTHING IS BACK TO NORMAL IN THE MONROE HOUSEHOLD--ALMOST.
BUNNICULA LIKED HIS LIQUID DIET SO MUCH THAT THE MONROES HAVE KEPT HIM ON IT.
AND ODDLY ENOUGH, THERE HAVE BEEN NO PROBLEMS WITH VEGETABLES MYSTERIOUSLY TURNING WHITE SINCE.
CHESTER, OF COURSE, INSISTS THAT THIS PROVES HIS THEORY.
It doesn't.

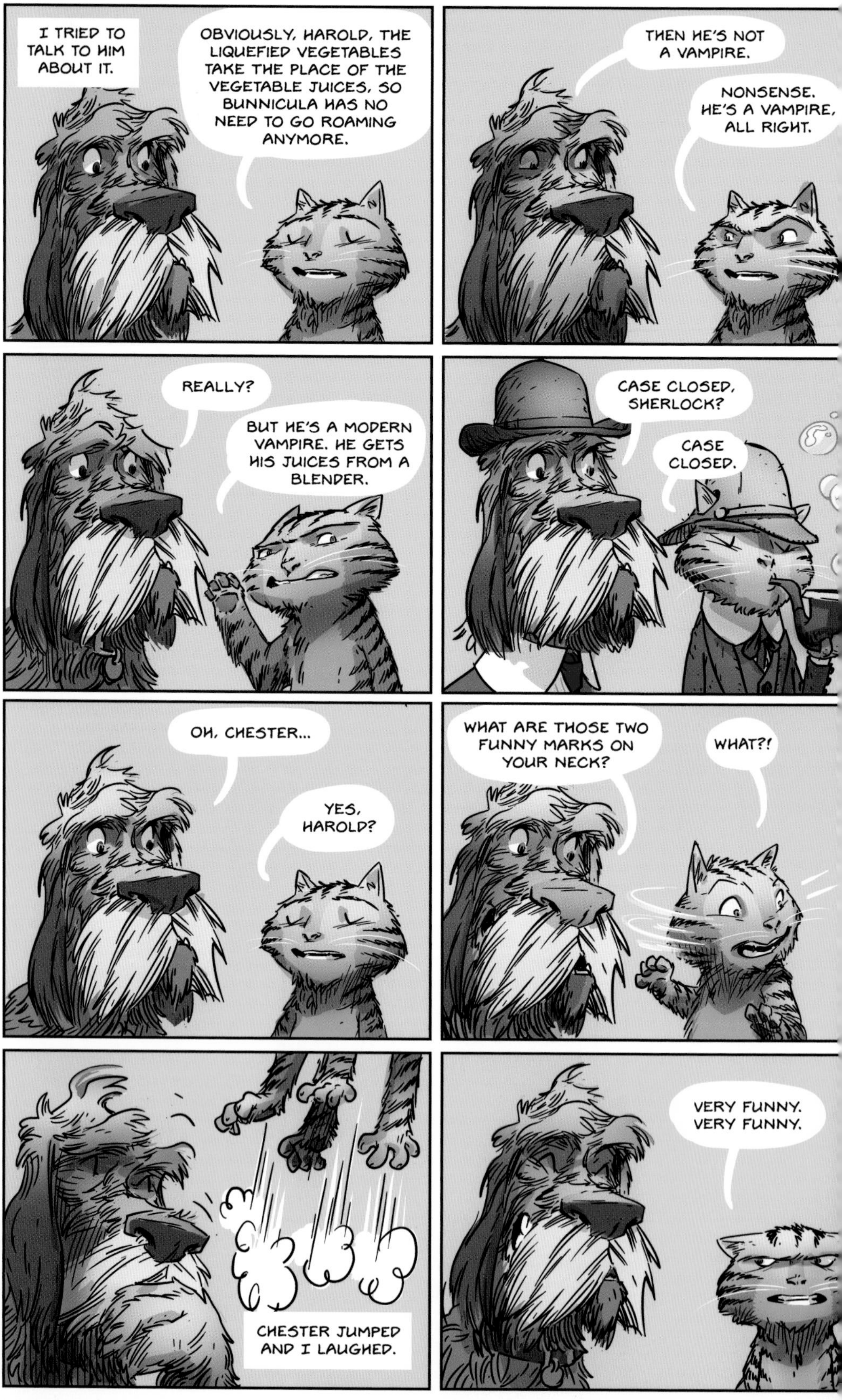
I TRIED TO TALK TO HIM ABOUT IT.
OBVIOUSLY, HAROLD, THE LIQUEFIED VEGETABLES TAKE THE PLACE OF THE VEGETABLE JUICES, SO BUNNICULA HAS NO NEED TO GO ROAMING ANYMORE.
THEN HE'S NOT A VAMPIRE.
NONSENSE. HE'S A VAMPIRE, ALL RIGHT.
REALLY?
BUT HE'S A MODERN VAMPIRE. HE GETS HIS JUICES FROM A BLENDER.
CASE CLOSED, SHERLOCK?
CASE CLOSED.
OH, CHESTER...
YES, HAROLD?
WHAT ARE THOSE TWO FUNNY MARKS ON YOUR NECK?
WHAT?!
CHESTER JUMPED AND I LAUGHED.
VERY FUNNY. VERY FUNNY.

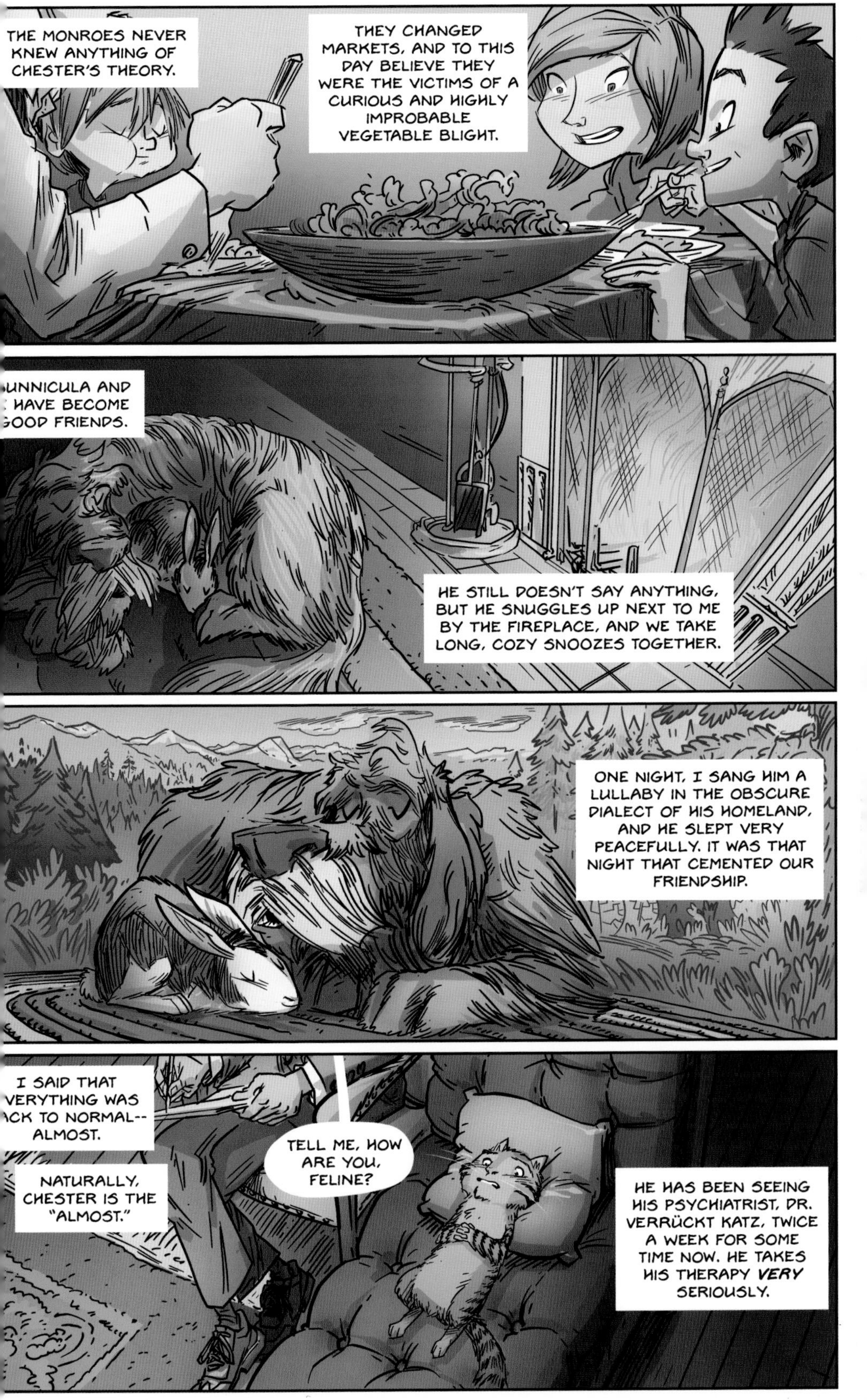
THE MONROES NEVER KNEW ANYTHING OF CHESTER'S THEORY.
THEY CHANGED MARKETS, AND TO THIS DAY BELIEVE THEY WERE THE VICTIMS OF A CURIOUS AND HIGHLY IMPROBABLE VEGETABLE BLIGHT.
UNNICULA AND HAVE BECOME OOD FRIENDS.
HE STILL DOESN'T SAY ANYTHING, BUT HE SNUGGLES UP NEXT TO ME BY THE FIREPLACE, AND WE TAKE LONG, COZY SNOOZES TOGETHER.
ONE NIGHT, I SANG HIM A LULLABY IN THE OBSCURE DIALECT OF HIS HOMELAND, AND HE SLEPT VERY PEACEFULLY. IT WAS THAT NIGHT THAT CEMENTED OUR FRIENDSHIP.
I SAID THAT VERYTHING WAS CK TO NORMAL-- ALMOST.
NATURALLY, CHESTER IS THE "ALMOST."
TELL ME, HOW ARE YOU, FELINE?
HE HAS BEEN SEEING HIS PSYCHIATRIST, DR. VERRÜCKT KATZ, TWICE A WEEK FOR SOME TIME NOW. HE TAKES HIS THERAPY *VERY* SERIOUSLY.

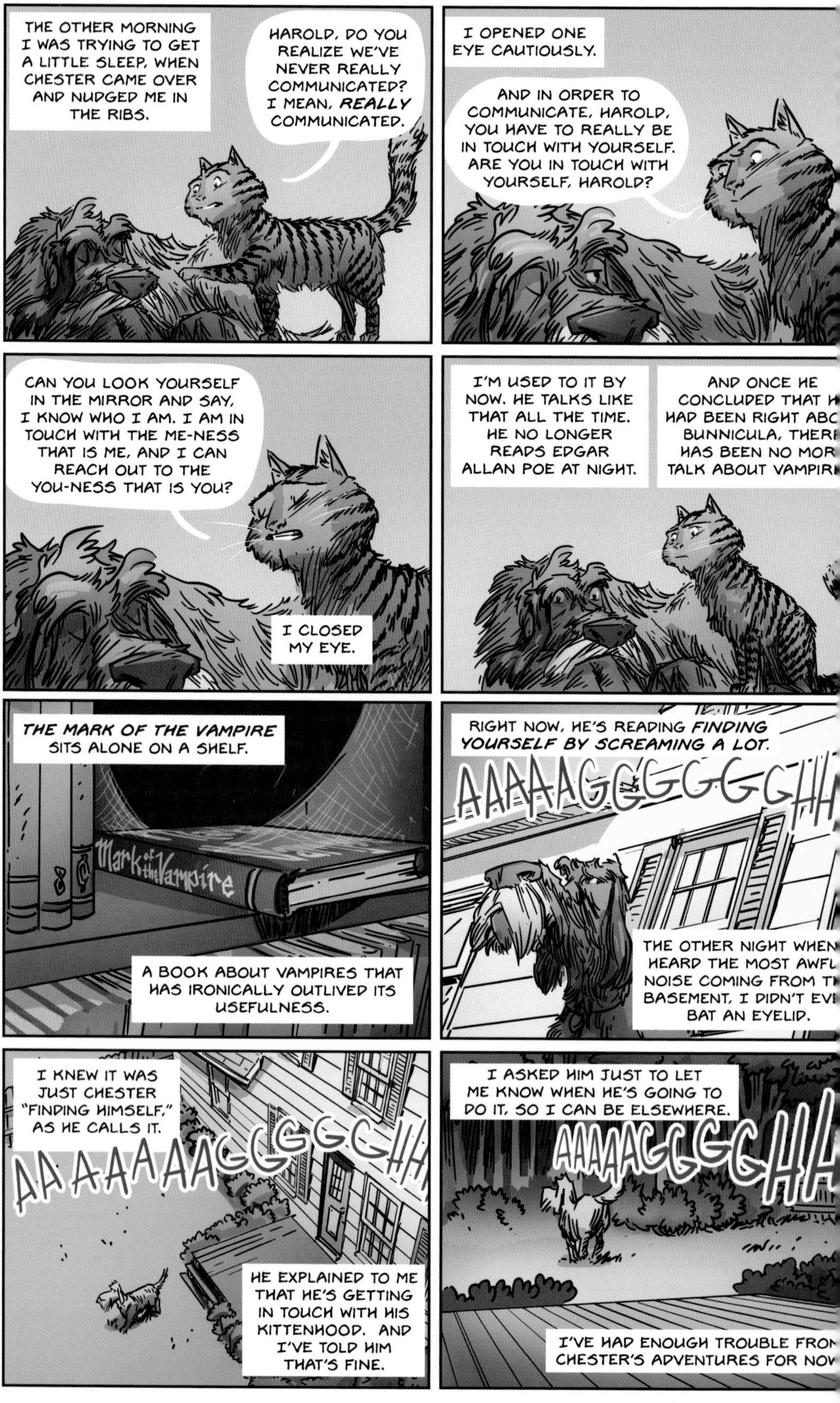

THE OTHER MORNING I WAS TRYING TO GET A LITTLE SLEEP, WHEN CHESTER CAME OVER AND NUDGED ME IN THE RIBS.
HAROLD, DO YOU REALIZE WE'VE NEVER REALLY COMMUNICATED? I MEAN, ***REALLY*** COMMUNICATED.
I OPENED ONE EYE CAUTIOUSLY.
AND IN ORDER TO COMMUNICATE, HAROLD, YOU HAVE TO REALLY BE IN TOUCH WITH YOURSELF. ARE YOU IN TOUCH WITH YOURSELF, HAROLD?
CAN YOU LOOK YOURSELF IN THE MIRROR AND SAY, I KNOW WHO I AM. I AM IN TOUCH WITH THE ME-NESS THAT IS ME, AND I CAN REACH OUT TO THE YOU-NESS THAT IS YOU?
I CLOSED MY EYE.
I'M USED TO IT BY NOW. HE TALKS LIKE THAT ALL THE TIME. HE NO LONGER READS EDGAR ALLAN POE AT NIGHT.
AND ONCE HE CONCLUDED THAT H HAD BEEN RIGHT ABO BUNNICULA, THER HAS BEEN NO MOR TALK ABOUT VAMPIR
THE MARK OF THE VAMPIRE SITS ALONE ON A SHELF.
Mark of the Vampire
A BOOK ABOUT VAMPIRES THAT HAS IRONICALLY OUTLIVED ITS USEFULNESS.
RIGHT NOW, HE'S READING ***FINDING YOURSELF BY SCREAMING A LOT.***
AAAAAGGGGGGHH
THE OTHER NIGHT WHEN HEARD THE MOST AWF NOISE COMING FROM T BASEMENT, I DIDN'T EV BAT AN EYELID.
I KNEW IT WAS JUST CHESTER "FINDING HIMSELF," AS HE CALLS IT.
AAAAAAAGGGGGHH
HE EXPLAINED TO ME THAT HE'S GETTING IN TOUCH WITH HIS KITTENHOOD. AND I'VE TOLD HIM THAT'S FINE.
I ASKED HIM JUST TO LET ME KNOW WHEN HE'S GOING TO DO IT, SO I CAN BE ELSEWHERE.
AAAAAGGGGHH
I'VE HAD ENOUGH TROUBLE FRO CHESTER'S ADVENTURES FOR NO

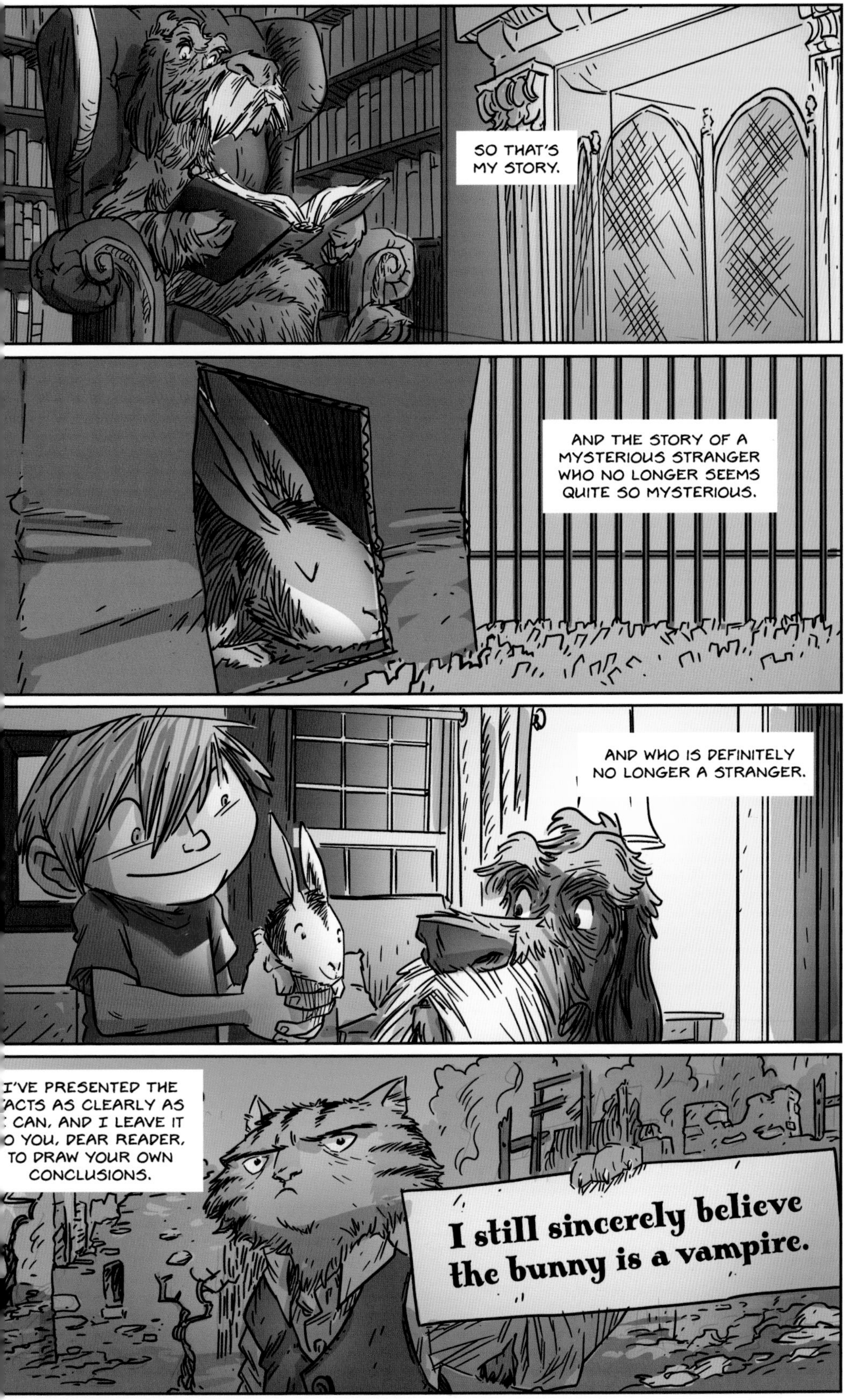
SO THAT'S MY STORY.
AND THE STORY OF A MYSTERIOUS STRANGER WHO NO LONGER SEEMS QUITE SO MYSTERIOUS.
AND WHO IS DEFINITELY NO LONGER A STRANGER.
I'VE PRESENTED THE FACTS AS CLEARLY AS I CAN, AND I LEAVE IT TO YOU, DEAR READER, TO DRAW YOUR OWN CONCLUSIONS.
I still sincerely believe the bunny is a vampire.

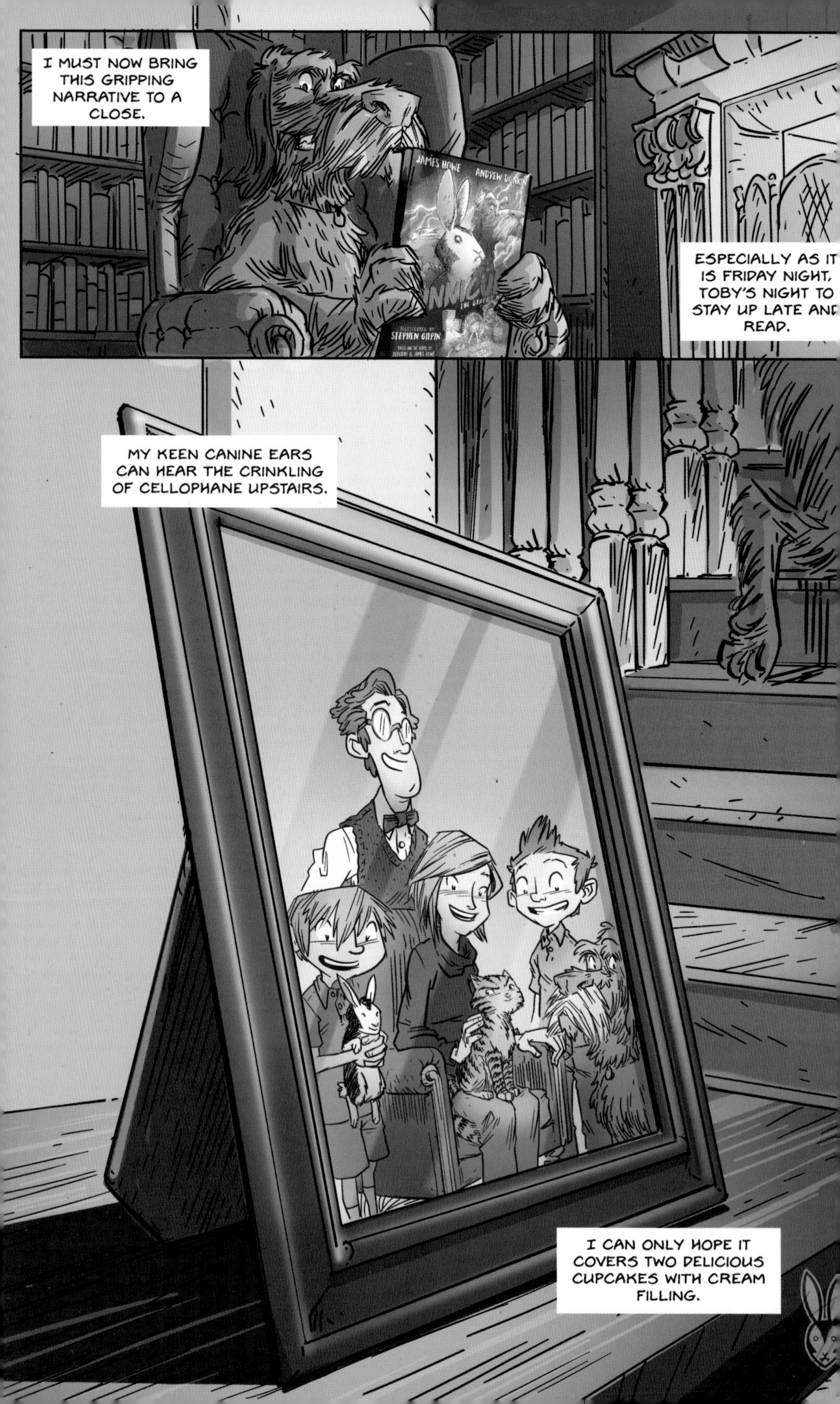
I MUST NOW BRING THIS GRIPPING NARRATIVE TO A CLOSE.
JAMES HOWE
ANDREW DONKIN
STEPHEN GILPIN
ESPECIALLY AS IT IS FRIDAY NIGHT, TOBY'S NIGHT TO STAY UP LATE AND READ.
MY KEEN CANINE EARS CAN HEAR THE CRINKLING OF CELLOPHANE UPSTAIRS.
I CAN ONLY HOPE IT COVERS TWO DELICIOUS CUPCAKES WITH CREAM FILLING.